A MATCH MADE IN HELL

A MATCH MADE IN HELL

CHARLOTTE INGHAM

HOT
KEY
BOOKS

First published in the UK in 2025 by
HOT KEY BOOKS
an imprint of Bonnier Books UK
5th Floor, HYLO, 105 Bunhill Row, London EC1Y 8LZ

A CIP catalogue record for this book is available from the British Library.

ISBN: 978-1-4714-1744-3
Also available as an ebook and in audio

1

This book is typeset using Atomik ePublisher
Printed and bound in Great Britain by Clays Ltd, Elcograf S.p.A.

MIX
Paper | Supporting
responsible forestry
FSC® C018072
www.fsc.org

The authorised representative in the EEA is
Bonnier Books UK (Ireland) Limited.
Registered office address: Floor 3, Block 3,
Miesian Plaza, Dublin 2, D02 Y754, Ireland
compliance@bonnierbooks.ie

bonnierbooks.co.uk/HotKeyBooks

For Kelsey and Charis

There's a five-minute window, in between living and dying, that I can't quite recall.

I remember the beach. I remember so much alcohol running down my throat I snorted some out of my nose. People laughed at me. Noah was furious with my behaviour, so I stormed off and climbed the steep, winding path to the top of the cliff, Sasha's hand in mine. We were giggling, shouting obscenities and feeling completely, utterly invincible. Free. I remember peering over the edge.

I remember Sasha screaming my name.

What I don't recall is falling. Maybe a brief moment, right at the start, where it felt like flying, the wind sharp against my ears as it whistled past my head.

Ending up in this strange limbo, surrounded by nothing but grey mist, doesn't imply a successful landing.

Although my heart still beats a slow, steady rhythm, one that matches the rise and fall of my chest, it doesn't feel the same. It's a habit, purely mechanical, no blood rushing through my veins or air filling my lungs. I hold my breath for practice. It's fun for the first few minutes, but then I kind of miss breathing, so I suck in a mouthful of nothing in case it does enough to kick-start the rest of me back to life.

It doesn't. If anything, I keep getting paler.

That can't be a good sign.

I clutch the ripped ends of my dress, balling the fabric between my fists, wanting to tear it off. It smells like sun cream and vodka and regret. That trip to the beach was supposed to be one last hurrah, my final chance to let Bad Decision Willow make an appearance before I became Responsible Willow forever. The job application destined to change my life was already filled out.

And now it'll never be submitted, all thanks to one crumbling piece of rock.

It's not fair. There has to be a way out of this. I'm not in any pain; that must count for something. Maybe my injuries weren't life-threatening and my body is being worked on by doctors right now. All I need to do is find a way back to it and I'll wake, like a butterfly emerging from a chrysalis, all shiny and new and ready to send that application at last.

Something scuffles up ahead.

My heart – my utterly useless heart – flips in my chest. 'Hello?'

Nobody answers. The scuffling continues.

'Hello?' I risk a step forward, my feet slapping against what feels like damp stone. 'Is someone there?'

Please be someone nice. A medical professional would be ideal.

There's a hiss of a match being struck, and a light shines in the distance, illuminating the domed walls of a dark, rocky tunnel. I move towards that beacon like a ship heading to a lighthouse, if the ship was both confused and slightly stressed about what it might find at the end of the sea.

The match lighter shuffles close enough for me to see its face.

A whimper escapes my throat.

Oh fuck. Oh *fuck*. I stumble back, desperate to get away, I *have* to get away, but I slip, algae sending my feet flying out from under me. My tail bone cracks against stone and – fuck. That hurt. And I felt it.

So the whole not-feeling-pain thing lasted all of five minutes. Well, isn't that wonderful? Isn't that swell? There are now zero upsides to being here, and there's a demon standing in front of me.

I don't know what else to call it. It might pass for human at a quick glance, but a closer look reveals its features are almost fox-like; with bright orange eyes and a nose that's a touch too long. Its nostrils emit little puffs of smoke, causing the candle in its hand to flicker wildly. Aside from a snakeskin loincloth for the sake of its modesty, the rest of its leathery red skin – the same colour as sealing wax on an ancient envelope – is on full display from the top of its bald head to the tips of its four-toed feet.

All it needs is a pair of horns to complete the cliché.

I let out a high-pitched, humourless laugh, because the alternative is to scream *this can't be happening*.

This isn't a waiting room. There isn't a doctor trying to save my life. I'm dead. I'm dead, and I'm in . . .

'I don't understand,' I whisper.

But I do.

Because unless the world has got things very, very backwards, creatures like this don't exist anywhere good.

No. *No.* I press a shaking hand to my mouth. The demon remains silent, like it's waiting for me to catch up with the obvious, but I can fill that silence just fine – or rather, *she* can. Mum. Imagining what she'd say is all too easy.

What did you think would happen, Willow?

Where did you think you'd end up?

That's not the point. I had a plan. I was going to fix everything; become the kind of person who wouldn't end up in *Hell* of all places. I just needed a little more time.

Time I need to get back.

The demon shifts on its feet, and my gaze snaps up. Its eyes glow when they meet mine, a simmering fire threatening to burn a hole all the way to my soul, but I refuse to look away. Showing fear won't get me what I want.

Convincing it there's been a mistake might.

Lying to a demon may not be the smartest thing I've ever done, but excuse me if I'm all out of bright ideas straight after dying. Besides, I do have one useful tool at my disposal – Mum always said I should be more like her, and this is my chance to shine. Mimicking her very best customer-complaint voice, I say, 'I think there's been an administration error. I'm not supposed to be dead.'

No response.

'Are you listening to me?' She's definitely said *that* before. 'I shouldn't be here.'

Nothing.

I try one final line, clicking my fingers for added effect. 'If you can't help, get me a manager. Someone who knows what they're doing.'

This is usually the point an underpaid shop assistant escapes to the back while my face burns with embarrassment, but clearly my imitation skills aren't up to scratch because the demon makes no move to find me any assistance, and somehow my cheeks still end up warm.

I swallow a fresh wave of panic. My ankle is beginning to throb. The back of my head feels like it's been split open. The longer I'm here, the more solid everything seems. Maybe, right at the beginning, that had been my window for escape, but I was too busy recalling my final moments to take the chance while it was there.

'Please.' My voice shakes this time, all traces of Mum gone, leaving me and my fear trembling in her wake. 'I have to go back.'

Finally, the demon acknowledges I've spoken, waving a hand and beckoning me to follow it into the gloom. It hasn't shown any sign it's sympathetic to my plight, so I doubt it plans on leading me anywhere I want to go.

But if this demon won't listen to me, I'll find one who will.

With fresh resolve, I attempt to stand. My legs aren't inclined to agree with my brain on this one, wobbling like jelly as I clamber upright. The demon huffs. Rude. I'm trying my best, despite the algae situation. Would shoes be out of the question? I was wearing an excellent pair of sandals when I died.

I echo the demon's huff, just to let it know that I'm as dissatisfied by this arrangement as it is, before taking several unsteady steps and following it into the depths of Hell.

2

The demon leads me out of the darkness into a cavern lit with sconces that flicker in a phantom wind. The walls are damp, with rivulets of water trickling through cracks in emerald-green stone. Moss sprouts from various orifices. There's enough light for me to take in the large body of water filling three quarters of the cave – around the size of a football pitch – so dark it's almost black, like an oil spill.

On the water is what looks like a Viking ship, with an elongated prow that ends with a snake's head carved into the wood. A figure cloaked in black stands to the side of the sail, a skeletal hand appearing from its sleeve and crooking a finger.

I can't imagine that thing will listen to what I have to say either.

My feet trip over themselves as they try to go backwards and forwards at once. I don't want to go to the oarsman. I don't want to go back to the dark tunnel.

I'm only twenty-one; I don't want to be dead at all.

I wipe my nose with the back of my hand, wishing they had the decency to offer tissues, as the demon forces me across a line shimmering on the ground. Immediately, the cavern brightens, revealing it's not just me heading for that boat. Not by a long shot. There's a cluster of (presumably dead) humans standing on a rocky shore, each with a demon companion of their own.

The demons are dressed in a mixture of loincloths and togas, some made of snakeskin and others of fur, but no matter how much they conceal it's hard to avoid their less-than-human attributes. Several have the same leathery skin as the one by my side, while others glisten with reptilian scales in a myriad of blues and greens. The one nearest to me sports a tail made of bone and shaggy, shoulder-length hair that reminds me of a lion's mane. Ginger curls are scattered over his bare chest.

'Let go of me!' shouts a man in a ripped suit. 'You can't do this. Don't you know who I am?'

I, for one, have no idea who he is, but I admire the sentiment all the same. At least he's doing something. The rest of the dead – ranging from a teenager in a scuffed motorcycle jacket to an old woman in a hospital gown – keep their heads down as they board the ship without argument. If they're trying to avoid attention, it doesn't work. Demons hiss as they pass, their beady eyes tracking the humans' movements like they're lizards sizing up prey. The teenager audibly whimpers as he ascends the gangplank.

At least his presence gives me much-needed evidence in my quest to prove they're capable of an administration oversight, because this boy doesn't even look old enough to *ride* a motorbike. How can he have had the time to do something worthy of belonging here? Ripped-suit guy clearly agrees with me, because when I reach the end of the queue, he's still complaining loudly while trying to tug his jacket from the lion-haired demon's grasp.

'Where am I?' he says. 'What's happening?'

The fact he's wrestling with a demon seems like answer enough, but he looks around anyway, like he won't believe it's real until someone produces a 'Welcome to Hell' sign and shoves it in his face.

Then his sleeve tears off in the demon's hand.

He freezes. The demon freezes. *I* freeze. If he was going to make a break for it, now would be his chance. My breath catches as I wait to see what happens – if he succeeds, I can follow in his footsteps.

The demon turns a fraction, its upper lip curling to reveal pointed teeth stained the same shade of copper as his hair. And still the man doesn't move.

'Run,' I hiss.

He does. He gets all of a metre before the demon springs; silver flashes as claws burst from its knuckles, and then those claws are sinking into the man's shoulders. He screams, trying to shake it off. The demon digs in with a snarl.

Fuck. Okay. In retrospect, encouraging him to run may have been another not-so-smart idea. My belly lurches as I watch them tussle, whereas the spectating demons grin like they've been gifted a free subscription to their favourite sports channel.

The demon tosses the man in the water.

He doesn't make a splash. He just gets sucked under. The demons point and jeer as bubbles pop on the surface, the only sign something's happened at all. I stare at the fluid, waiting for him to reappear, gasping for air he doesn't need.

But the man doesn't emerge.

8

I don't know what that means for him. If breathing isn't a necessity, can you still drown? Is it possible to be more dead than dead? All I know is I'd much prefer to be dead and walking than sink into those depths forever. I look away from the water, ignoring the guilty churning in my gut – the man was in trouble before I urged him to run; his unfortunate end was *not* my fault – and stare at the boat, digging my nails into my palms. I'll need to be extra careful about the next person I plead my case to.

I take a deep breath. Careful. I can do careful. Maybe.

My legs tremble as I climb the gangplank. The boat reeks of decay, floorboards so soft with damp I'm petrified my foot might sink through when I step aboard. Barnacles cling to the mast, but these must be demons too, because they're far too active. They swarm around the wood, scurrying like white spiders newly hatched from their eggs.

Shuddering, I avoid sitting anywhere near them and settle next to a woman who's quietly sobbing. I can't say I blame her. Weirdly, the sound's almost soothing. Her tears are so undeniably human; a reminder not everyone here is a monster.

The vessel rocks as the demons join us – I avoid making eye contact with the lion-haired one – and the cloaked figure dips an oar in the water. We glide smoothly over the liquid towards a pitch-black tunnel.

As we pass under the arch, I fight the urge to hold on to the stranger next to me, curling my fingers around my seat instead, gripping it with such force I'm afraid it might splinter between my hands.

And then there's nothing.

There's the boat, and everyone on it, but around us is just . . . empty.

The darkness presses on me like a weight slamming against my shoulders. Every now and then there's the faint slosh of liquid as the oar spurs us forward, but it's not enough to drown out my thoughts now I've got no distraction from them.

You're throwing your life away.

Those were Mum's last words to me. Words I've replayed over and over since her death, promising myself – promising *her* – I'd be better from now on. My chest tightens. I was so close to making her proud. If only I'd paid attention to the drop below I'd still be at the top of the cliff right now; I wouldn't have –

One choked cry manages to escape my throat before I swallow the rest and stash them away.

My palms are clammy by the time the tunnel opens into another cave. Water tinged with a violet light cascades down the walls, crashing into the rock below. Spray buffets my face as we dock. The lion-haired demon disembarks first, leaping from the side of the boat and bounding up a gloomy corridor in the distance (at this point, I can only assume every corridor is going to be gloomy).

The demons escort us up that same corridor and into another large cavern. Maybe this is the part where someone confirms where we are, as if it wasn't obvious. What language do demons speak anyway? Something guttural like *gurh ragh urgh*.

At the far end of the room, a carving of a snake's head protrudes from the rock, twin fangs dropping from its mouth. A throne is nestled between them, skulls lining its base.

I gulp.

Well, if I want to speak to a manager, I guess that throne's owner is exactly who I need.

Marching over there probably doesn't fit in with the dictionary definition of *careful* though, so I move with the rest of the humans to stand elbow to elbow in the centre of the room. It doesn't make me feel any less alone, not with the noticeable absence at my side. Sasha and I met the first day of high school and have been inseparable ever since; she even applied to the same universities as me so we could move from Guildford to London together.

I'm not used to navigating new surroundings without her, and now I'm in a room full of demons where my only potential allies are a bunch of dead strangers. For the first time in my life, I don't wish I was taller – being five foot five allows me to shrink into the crowd, at least a little. I'd be invisible if it weren't for the way my red hair glows like a distress flare in the dark.

A winged demon standing near the throne clears its throat. It turns out I was right about the way they speak: it *is* low, and rough, and guttural, but I'm able to understand every word when it says, 'Kneel for King Sathanas.'

The demons drop immediately.

My fellow passengers and I follow a little more slowly. We're unsure what – or who – we're kneeling for.

But I have a fairly good idea.

With my head bowed in faux deference, I peer through the curtain of hair draped over my eyes in order to study him when he enters. King Sathanas. The Devil. It must be. I wonder

11

what he'll look like. Bigger than the rest, probably. Scalier. Extra horns. Holding a pitchfork, perhaps. A wooden door to the side of the throne swings open, and my stomach swoops at the sound of footsteps, brisk and sure and growing closer. I steel my shoulders, bracing myself for whatever atrocity those footsteps belong to.

But when the figure walks out, I have to fight to hold back a gasp. Because it's not a demon at all.

It's a man.

3

He gives us a quick glance before settling himself on his throne, planting one leather boot on the ground and crossing his other leg over his knee. A click of his fingers has one of the demons scurrying to his side. I risk raising my head to get a better view, needing to decide if asking for his help is going to get me thrown in the river.

He's not that much older than me. That probably doesn't mean much, not here, but it's the first thing I notice. He's not that scary, either. While the sleeves of his white shirt bunch over his biceps, he's nowhere near as beefy as the demons towering over him. They should be able to rip his head off easily.

But they don't.

There must be something else to him. Some other power he has. And if I can't see it, that makes him all the more dangerous. He's also kind of rude, because we're still kneeling, and it's starting to hurt.

He runs a hand through short jet-black hair. 'How many?' Despite his voice being nowhere near as deep as the demon's, it still feels like the room rumbles when he speaks.

'Five thousand in the last hour, Your Highness,' the demon says.

'She has been busy.' King Sathanas clucks his tongue. 'Does she send anyone to Elysium these days?'

I frown. There were only around fifty on the boat with me. Where are the rest?

'I suppose I should be grateful only one boat has caused trouble today.' He waves the demon away before addressing us directly. 'I don't usually have the pleasure of meeting new arrivals, but I wanted to make sure none of you were inspired by that man fighting back by the river. It's funny, how quickly the fires of rebellion can spread.' He smiles. 'And how easily they can be quashed.'

I clench my jaw. He can try and quash my rebellion all he likes, but I refuse to let myself feel threatened by a man in tight trousers.

'The soul of today's revolutionary will be taken into the Void to think about his actions. He'll float, aware of everything and able to interact with nothing, where his only company will be his worst memories replaying in his head.'

I shiver. Okay, maybe I feel a *little* threatened.

'I would suggest you don't try and find out what other punishments are available here in Asphodel.' Sathanas slumps in his seat, resting his chin on his fist, like speaking to us is a chore he could do without. Well, I, for one, didn't ask him to. All we got was threats and no answers.

Apart from a name. Asphodel. It certainly rhymes with Hell.

'Direct them to their rooms,' Sathanas orders the demons. He waves a hand in our direction. 'You may rise.'

How gracious of him. I resist the urge to roll my eyes as

14

we stand in unison. I exchange a glance with the woman next to me – she's the one who spent the boat trip crying – and although neither of us dares speak, the question on her face is evident. It's the same as mine. *What now?*

I need a plan. At this point, I don't know if escape is an option, or if I'm hoping for a miracle that doesn't exist, but I need to exhaust all possibilities before I'm introduced to one of these unnamed punishments or, worse, this *Void*. I've got far too many memories I'd rather not repeat.

Demons watch us with hungry expressions, tracking our movements, forked tongues flicking out to swipe drool from their lips. Sathanas remains on his throne, looking bored, as a demon murmurs in his ear.

Frustrated by my lack of options, I turn to the woman and whisper, 'Do you know why you're here? Do you think they might've made a mistake?'

If they *have* made a mistake with her, maybe they'll let her go and I can follow them all the way to the exit.

Her eyes glisten with a fresh onslaught of tears. 'I was sick. I don't . . .' She hiccups. 'I don't remember.'

'You don't need to remember how you died,' I press. 'I just need you to tell me if you think you belong here. Because if you don't, maybe there's some exception where –'

She starts to cry again, louder and louder, her high-pitched sobs quickly rising into a crescendo that's hard to ignore. Demons are turning to stare. *Sathanas* is turning to stare.

Oops.

He unfolds himself from the throne in one elegant movement and descends from the podium. His footsteps are feather-light as he prowls towards us with an unnatural grace. The crowd parts to let him through. I shuffle with them, wanting to get as much distance between me and the situation as possible.

It's not far enough. By the time he reaches the woman, he's still too close; I catch the scent of peppermint as he stops directly in front of her. It's easier, now, to imagine why the demons might bow to him. There's a sense of power rippling from his body, one I can't see but I can *feel*, like he's humming with magic. The woman trembles at the sight of him, retreating until she's pressed against the wall. Sathanas cocks his head to one side. 'Is there a problem?'

Well, duh. Of course there's a problem. I doubt she's the first person to work out she's in Hell and start crying. The king's face is a mask, as stony as the serpent guarding his seat, but, just like his magic, his displeasure is palpable.

He strokes a knuckle down her cheek, collecting a tear on his skin. 'Tell me,' he says. 'Tell me what's wrong.'

His voice is soft, gentle, like he's coaxing all her secrets from her. She sways on the spot, lost in his gaze. Maybe hypnotism is his special skill. But then she opens her mouth and vomits on his feet, so maybe not. His facade doesn't break, not even when he shakes yellow lumps from his shoe. A winged demon with brown feathers flies forward to wipe off the rest.

Another demon whispers, '*Tartarus.*'

Sathanas shakes his head. 'Take her to Glacantrum,' he instructs. 'A year or two there, and perhaps she'll be more inclined to accept my hospitality.'

I can't help but raise my eyebrows. I wouldn't call waking in a dark cave, being shoved on a boat and forced to kneel before him *hospitality*.

16

There's more muttering among the demons, as though this punishment will not suffice. Despite this, the winged vomit-cleaner follows the order, grabbing hold of the woman who, of course, begins to scream. Sathanas doesn't so much as blink as she lashes out, trying to scratch him, the demon, anyone she can get her hands on. She kicks and punches and wails as the demon scoops her into its arms, but she may as well be hitting a solid wall for all the good it does. A slight bend of its knee, one swoosh of its wings, and they're flying away.

That's two people punished since my arrival. My gut churns with the idea I might be next.

'Perhaps I should elaborate,' Sathanas says to the crowd. 'Welcome to Asphodel. Your home, should you choose to accept it, and all the pleasantries it has to offer.'

I have no idea what pleasantries he's referring to. As far as I can tell, it doesn't even have central heating.

'Fail to accept and the consequences will be . . . unpleasant. Complaints are not tolerated. Escape attempts even less so.'

My ears prick at this. That implies there *could* be a way to escape, if I can find it.

'Do I make myself clear?' Sathanas continues.

Everyone, including me, nods. As if we'd do anything else.

'Then off you go,' he says. 'Explore. Do what you like. Don't bother me, don't antagonise the demons, and don't go into the Old Tunnels.'

I've never wanted to go in a tunnel more.

Two demons shove open a pair of doors to our rear, and dazzling light bursts from the corridor presumably leading to the rest of Asphodel. I squint, surprised to see that much light here at all. It's like leaving a cinema on a summer's day, when the sunshine is almost blinding in its intensity after being in the dark for so long. The walls of the corridor are painted gold, and the crowd surges towards the glow like a swarm of fireflies.

I'm about to join them when it hits me.

We won't be the only humans inside. Countless boats will have arrived before ours. There's no light at the end of that tunnel, just millennia of dead waiting to say hello.

Which means there's a chance she's here.

Mum.

Shit. Shit. I can't see her. I already have her voice ringing in my ears; I don't need to witness her disappointment first-hand too. If we're ever reunited, it has to be after I've fulfilled all the promises I made after she died.

Sathanas stands close by, watching the crowd straggle through the doors, the demons following in their wake. I bite my lip to avoid making the kind of noise that would have me sent to Glacantrum, wherever that is. As though sensing my stare, he turns his head, and I gasp as I experience the full force of his attention.

Again, it's obvious why he's the one in charge. Because there's something entirely different about him, about how piercingly amber his eyes are. His skin is unblemished, practically glowing, and I'm hyper-aware of every imperfection I have in comparison. I cross my arms and scowl at him. I may be a lowly little human with too many freckles and a poor skincare regime, but I refuse to behave like one. His gaze dips to a rip in my sundress, and for a moment I swear shadows lick up his arm, coiling like snakes over his shirt, but then I blink and they disappear.

'Is there something you need?' he enquires.

Well, let's see, Mr Scary-Devil-Man: to not be dead would be ideal, but I'd settle for a map with a big, glowing arrow marked 'Exit' at a pinch. How much of that can I ask for before you send one of your minions after me?

I take the safer option of shaking my head.

He quirks a brow. It's the first real expression I've seen cross his face, and it makes him look normal, like he's a bog-standard human and not the King of Hell.

I wonder if he did it on purpose, to get me to lower my guard.

'Please,' he says, half goading, half mocking. 'Enlighten me. What is it you want to say?'

Like that woman enlightened him, he means? Although I'm pretty sure I'm not about to chuck up on his shoes, I don't think word vomit is going to endear me to him any more than her physical puke did. Apparently, my mouth isn't listening to my brain though, because I can't stop myself from saying, 'You told us not to complain, so . . .'

'Ah.' He slides his hands into his pockets. 'So you have a complaint?'

Fuck's sake. What is wrong with me? Going through those doors is becoming a lot more appealing; at least a conversation with my mother wouldn't result in me meeting yet another sticky end.

'I'd love to hear it,' he goes on, offering me a wicked smile. 'I'll make you a deal. Whatever you say in the next minute, you won't be punished for.'

'And I'm supposed to believe that?'

19

He shrugs. 'Clock's ticking.'

Bastard isn't even wearing a watch. 'I don't make deals with the Devil.'

'Is that what I am?' His eyes gleam. Maybe it's the light, but they look more golden than before, like living flames are dancing across his pupils.

'You tell me,' I say, willing him to slip up, divulge something. He can call this place Asphodel all he likes; the demons running round are a clear giveaway we're not anywhere pleasant.

He reveals nothing. Instead, he takes a step towards me, one small pace that makes me want to make a big retreat. I force myself to stand my ground. I refuse to let him intimidate me, no matter what powers he possesses, or how many Glacantrums he could send me to.

'I'll tell you what I think about you,' he says. 'You think this is all one giant mistake. That you don't belong here. That you're a good person and you don't deserve what awaits you beyond those doors.'

I ball my fists, wanting to scream that he's got me all wrong. A good person wouldn't have been the reason their father walked out the front door and never came home. A good person wouldn't have driven their boyfriend into ignoring their calls for days. A good person wouldn't have forced their mother to get into –

I inhale sharply. Focus, Willow.

This might be where I belong, but he doesn't need to know that.

'Do you want to know what happened to the last person who asked for my help?'

'Not really.' The cool smile I bestow on him is as much a lie as my words.

'Hm.' He matches my icy expression before looking me up and down again, a hunter assessing the best way to cage his prey. 'Well, don't let me keep you.'

Fuck. My chin trembles as the trap closes. If I pretend he's right about me, maybe I'll get the answers I seek and be sprung free – or maybe he'll twist the key and lock me in for good.

He doesn't give me a chance to figure out which option he's offering. He's walking away now, heading towards the door he first emerged from, taking all of his knowledge and stupid guesses with him, abandoning me to whatever fate lies at the end of that golden corridor.

A fate I can't accept. Not until I've tried everything.

'Wait.'

He turns at the sound of my voice.

We stare at one another from across the chamber. It's just the two of us left in here now, and I'm sure he must be able to hear the way my breaths are too loud, too fast, giving away the nerves my bravado tries to hide. Heat thunders through me. No complaints. No bothering him. Those were the rules. My minute's up, if that deal was even real.

I daren't risk asking anything outright, but maybe I can play into his assumptions about me. I got here somehow; perhaps I can get out the same way.

'How does it get decided?' I ask. 'Who goes where? If somebody did . . . have a complaint. Who would be to blame?'

The corners of his mouth lift. 'Well, that would be down to the Sorter.'

I nod, like his words make any kind of sense. Sathanas jerks his head towards the corridor behind me.

'Third door on the right.' He winks. 'Just for having the nerve to ask.'

4

He vacates the chamber without another word.

Despite the empty space around me, I may as well be stuffed inside a box. My legs won't work. For all I know the third door on the right leads to a very specific torture chamber for those who ask questions. I'll be strapped to a wooden board and my tongue ripped out while a demon shrieks that this is what happens to those who cause trouble.

I used to think having an overactive imagination was a good thing. It allowed me to daydream about all the places I'd never get to see. Now I think that imagination might be the cause of every nightmare I've ever had or will have.

But imagining the worst isn't going to help me find a way home, away from the threat of violent demons or ending up in a Void where I'll undoubtedly be forced to relive a night I've tried very hard to forget.

Finally, I enter the gold-painted corridor, squinting as I adjust to the new-found light. Vines climb the walls. They don't have roots, they're just *there*, and the flowers twining around the stems glow brighter than any bulb.

If I pretend hard enough, I could imagine this is one long

hotel lobby. There'll be a smiling receptionist waiting for me at the other end, ready to hand over a key to my deluxe suite complete with infinity pool. Perhaps this is what the Devil meant by pleasantries.

Is that what I am? Sathanas's words ring in my ears.

Maybe I'm wrong. Perhaps I'm not where I thought and he isn't the Devil after all. But then there's the demons, the boat, the man in the river . . .

I don't get it. I don't get any of it.

The other boat passengers linger in the hall, taking in their surroundings, pointing at the walls like they're in a gallery, but there's only one thing I'm interested in.

I pass one door. A second.

I reach the third.

There's nothing about it to distinguish it from all the others. Mahogany wood. Brass knob. I don't knock. Twisting the handle, I let it swing fully open and step inside. And freeze.

Bodies.

The room is filled with them, all lying on metal slabs that line the far wall, slab after slab, body after body, stretching down the length of the room with no visible end.

I gag. Clasp a hand to my mouth. The sight of all that bare, dead flesh has me swallowing bile, shaking from head to toe as I risk another step inside, not wanting to go any further but equally unwilling to give up on finding answers.

Up ahead, something squeaks.

My pulse skyrockets. In the distance, a cart wielding another corpse comes into view, the wheels whining loudly as they roll over the terrazzo floor. The demon pushing it is small, under five foot, with cropped white hair. Although her features are feminine, she's decidedly not human; her ears are pointed, and there's a tail swishing behind legs that end in cloven hooves.

Bright red eyes lock on mine.

'Are you the Sorter?'

'Might be,' she says. 'Depends who's asking.'

She lifts the body with one arm, like it weighs no more than a feather – which is baffling when her arms are like twigs – and shoves it on to a slab.

'I'm asking,' I say. 'Sathanas, I mean, King Sathanas –' What is the etiquette here? 'Anyway, he said . . .'

'Sath spoke to you?' She wrinkles her nose. Huh. Sath. Sounds like there's no etiquette required at all. Or maybe they're friends and I need to be careful what I say next in case it's deemed to be *complaining*, and she reports back to him. Or decides to punish me herself. The way she handled that body tells me everything I need to know: like Sathanas, with his human form and human expressions, she is something more under the surface.

'Briefly,' I answer. 'He said you . . . make decisions. About who . . .'

'Ends up here?' She folds her arms. 'And let me guess, you're not happy with your lot. Newsflash, darling, no one ever is.'

The Sorter moves to go past me, dismissing me like I'm nothing. To her, I probably am. Just another number among thousands whose life – or death, I suppose – she's ruined.

I block her path. 'I have to go back.'

'Go back?' She chuckles. 'You say that like it's an option.'

'*Is* it?' If I could just get confirmation that it's not, maybe I could find some kind of peace. Or as much peace as it's possible

25

to get in Hell. But I can't give up before I know for sure.

Otherwise I'll never hit 'send' on that job application and become some high-flying businesswoman who complains about budgets until four in the morning. I'll never marry Noah and pop out a bunch of children with hair as red as mine. I'll never visit Mum's grave and say *I did it. I did all the things you wanted me to, and I'm sorry I'm the reason you didn't see me do them.*

'Please,' I say. 'I need to fix this.'

'Oh, there's no fixing you.' She picks up a blank clipboard at the end of a slab and waves it at me. 'I probably have yours somewhere.' She cocks her head. 'Or maybe I remember you. Yes, I think I do. I looked into your soul and saw a river of blood.'

I freeze. 'What are you talking about?'

'You tell me. Could have been your past, could have been your future, who you would have been if you'd lived. Hard to tell sometimes. But all that blood, death, potential for chaos . . .' Her smile turns feral. 'You'll fit right in here.'

'But – that's not –' My mind races. Maybe there *has* been a mistake, because I've no idea what she's talking about. The most blood I've come across was the time I almost sliced off half a finger rushing to make Noah his lunch. 'You're wrong.'

'I'm never wrong.' Her gaze drops to my hands, at the way they're balled into fists, nails digging deep into my palms. 'You seem upset.'

'Of course I'm upset. I'm not supposed to be dead.'

'Your presence here would beg to differ.'

A rush of familiar heat spreads through me, and my whole body trembles. 'I'm here because of an *accident*. I was too close to the edge; I must have lost my footing.'

26

'An accident.' Her smile grows. 'Aw. Poor you.'

'That's why I have to go back, don't you see? I can't be dead because of one misstep; I can't have thrown it all away because I . . . because I . . .'

The Sorter's grin is so wide I think her face might split in two, and I grow hotter still, because she's not listening; no one ever listens and I can't *stand* it.

'Stop laughing at me.' Tears cloud my vision. She laughs harder. 'Stop it.'

She doesn't stop. Her cackles echo and bounce between the metal walls, the sound drilling into my skull until I can't think. I step forward, overwhelmed with an urge to grab her hair, rip it from her head, make her as cold and lifeless as the bodies on the slabs, and see how much she likes being here when she's as miserable as the rest of us.

I hate her, I hate this, I hate –

Something clatters at my feet. I jump, startled, to find a tray full of surgical instruments knocked to the ground. They'd been on a table to my left, out of reach of the Sorter, which means – I glance at my finger to find it's bleeding. A drop of red glimmers on a pair of scissors on the floor.

'Oh dear,' the Sorter says. 'Look at that. Another accident.'

Tantrums will get you nowhere, Willow. I take a deep breath. Another. Anger thrashes inside me but I ignore it, swallowing sharp words until they lie in the pit of my stomach with all the other things I've left unsaid over the years. Arguing my case isn't going to get me anywhere here, either – not when the Sorter is clearly going to mock everything I say.

I steel my expression into one of practised calm, the

transformation into Demure Willow almost perfect apart from the slight shake in my hand when I wipe the wet from my cheeks.

'Don't cry in public,' she tells me. 'The demons don't like it.'

'I know. Sathanas sent someone to . . . Gla . . . something.'

'Glacantrum.' Her face hardens. 'Of course he did.'

Her annoyance piques my interest. 'What's Glacantrum?'

'The Ice Prison.' She taps the nearest corpse's ankle and black ink spreads across the clipboard, looping letters presumably telling their life's tale. The words have barely had time to dry before she yanks a lever at the end of the slab, causing it to tip backwards. The body slides down the chute, thudding as it hits the sides. 'Very cold, very solitary. But there are no demons there, so it's not bad as punishments go.' Her hands curl around the clipboard. 'He has worse options at his disposal.'

A chill creeps down my neck. 'Like the Void?'

'Hm.' Another body gets dumped. This time, black smoke puffs from the chute when it opens, filling the room with the acrid stench of rotten meat mixed with iron. 'I suppose. You can be released from Glacantrum any time, but the Void will keep you trapped for thousands of years, forcing you to relive all your worst moments. By the time it spits you back out there's not a whole lot left of the person you used to be.'

'That sounds worse to me.'

She shrugs. 'Either way, we demons don't get to take part in any of the fun if you go there. The torture chambers in the Old Tunnels, though, *they're* a real treat, when he allows us to use them. And then, of course, there's Tartarus.' She lets

28

out a dreamy sigh, like she's just sipped a cool cocktail on a hot day. 'The lowest level of the afterlife. Probably closer to what you pictured, when you mortals talk about it on Earth. Fire, brimstone, lots of demons scurrying around prodding you with things. People used to be sent there for fucking up here in Asphodel, if they weren't awful enough to be sorted there immediately.'

I suppose I should count myself lucky I wasn't deemed really awful. Lucky old me, falling off a cliff, stuck in a dimension where only *some* of the demons want to prod you with sticks. I hope she's not expecting a thank you.

'And these chutes, do they lead to wherever you . . . sort them?'

'You ask a lot of questions.' Her eyes barely flick over whatever's on her clipboard. Is that all I got too? A momentary glance at a piece of paper, and my whole afterlife decided.

'I'm trying to understand,' I say. 'Once you've made a decision . . .'

'It can't be reversed.'

'But –'

'No buts.' Her trolley squeaks as she rolls it onwards. 'You belong here, Willow White.'

I don't bother to ask how she knew my name. It was probably on her clipboard where she ticked the box 'bad seed' and threw my body away.

'I can't stay here,' I say. '*Please.*'

The Sorter rolls her eyes. 'You're not the first person to say that. You won't be the last. Do you know what you all have in common? A misplaced sense of self-importance. The notion that you're too good to be here. Too proud to admit you have faults –' She breaks off, looking me up and down while making a humming noise at the back of her throat.

I clench my jaw. I'm well aware I have faults, thanks.

The Sorter moves along to the next body. 'Thief. This one's easy.' Down the chute they go. It didn't take her any less time to determine that one as *easy* as it did any of the others. She cocks her head in my direction. 'You said Sath spoke to you?'

'Briefly.'

She hums again, dropping a clipboard into its slot, but this time, she doesn't take another. Her finger taps against the slab. Every beat is a second wasted. A second I'm here when I could be at home, making things right.

'There has to be something you can do,' I say.

'Nope.' She emphasises the word with a sharp pop, but I can tell she's barely listening. Her finger taps, and taps, and taps, her lips twitch, and then she's moving again, wheeling her cart down the room.

I stalk her steps. I didn't come here to leave without answers. 'What if I lay on a slab and you pulled a lever that says *Earth*?'

'Difficult, considering one doesn't exist.'

My heart sinks. I sneak a closer look at one of the levers in the vain hope she's lying, but the only things scratched on to the knob are three arrows: *up*, *right*, *down*. With no further information, my best guess is that *up* is better than here. Maybe if there's no way out I could at least angle for an upgrade, ideally one that comes with fluffy clouds and cherubs playing harps.

'Ugh.' The Sorter lifts a corpse by its foot, grimacing at

whatever she's spotted on the underside of its heel. 'Hand me a scalpel.'

I don't remember signing up to be a surgical assistant, but I comply in an attempt to prove how nice and worthy of help I am. She whips it from my outstretched hand and begins to scrape dead skin from the soles of its feet, her nose inches away from a set of hairy toes.

Gross. 'How do the bodies get here anyway?'

Absorbed in her task, her tone is absent-minded when she answers, 'Not the same way you can get out.'

Aha. I grin. 'So there *is* a way out?'

'I –' The foot is dropped with a loud clang. 'I didn't mean it like that.'

'Of course you didn't,' I console her. If they were less disgusting, I'd kiss those toes for providing such a helpful distraction. 'But let's pretend you did. When you say out . . . do you mean to somewhere nicer? Or out of the afterlife entirely?'

Her gaze is scattered, like she's trying to concoct a lie to cover her tracks, and her tail swishes with agitation. The longer the silence stretches between us, the surer I am.

There's a way out. Like, really *out*.

Hope unfurls in my stomach like a flower blooming in spring. I can leave. I can go home; I can do all the things I promised I'd do.

I can live.

'Tell me how,' I demand. 'Tell me the way.'

She hesitates.

'Think of it like this. You can either tell me now, or after I've worn you down with a million more questions. Because I'm not leaving this room until I know.'

31

Despite the exasperated sigh she emits, it takes her several more tail swishes and a heavy bob of her throat before she relents and says, 'You didn't hear this from me.'

I mime zipping my lips and throwing away the key.

There's another beat of silence. I spend it imagining blood surging through my veins in preparation for my inevitable return to life.

Finally, she utters the answer I've been waiting for. 'There's one way back to the mortal realm. But there's only one person who can help you get there.'

5

Sathanas.

She doesn't have to say his name for me to know I'm right. Knowing that, though, diminishes some of my new-found hope. 'And what's he going to do to me if I ask him for help? He expressly said no complaining or asking to leave.'

'That's the official rule.' She waves her hand. 'But rules were made to be broken. You'd just need to prove yourself worthy.'

I don't like the sound of that. 'Worthy how?'

'It's all very tedious.' She rolls her eyes. 'Sath can explain, if he makes you the offer.'

'Big if,' I grumble.

'So give him a reason to.' Whatever's on her next clipboard is, apparently, far more interesting than my potential escape from Hell. She waves a hand in the direction of the door. 'I've already told you more than I should. Get out and do what you will with it.'

I don't move straight away. More questions ricochet around my brain and they all lead back to one issue: how am I possibly going to pull this off?

The Sorter whistles loudly, drowning out the sound of her

cart's squeaks as she moves on, abandoning me to figure this out on my own.

Well, fine. I've got this far by myself.

If Sathanas needs a reason, I'll give him a reason. I'll give him the best damn reason he's ever heard.

I exit the Sorter's morgue to find my fellow passengers have all gone. I could carry on the way they went, investigate more of Asphodel. Find myself one of these rooms we've been offered, see how bad they are before embarking on Mission Convince the Devil to Help a Girl Out.

But I don't want to explore, or get settled. Not when I have no intention of staying.

Not when an unfortunate reunion with my past could be waiting round every bend.

I return to the entrance chamber. This is stupid, and dangerous, but I can't stop myself. Being dead means I have nothing to lose.

Two demons now guard the doorway I saw Sathanas go through. One is shorter than the other, with longer lashes and lips pressed into a pout, but otherwise they could be twins. Small horns, curved and grey, protrude from foreheads that wrinkle into a frown as I approach. Well, they can wrinkle as much as they like. I haven't broken any rules.

Sathanas told us to explore. I'm exploring.

'May I get past?' I ask, trying to sound polite.

'What for?' It's the taller of the two who answers, although they both narrow their eyes in unison.

'I wanted to look around. Unless . . . That doesn't lead to the Old Tunnels, does it? I wouldn't want to get into trouble.' I smile sweetly.

Tall Demon grunts. 'King Sathanas's quarters are through here. He's not to be disturbed.'

'I won't bother him,' I lie. 'I told you, I'm simply having a look. I'm *very* interested in all Asphodel has to offer.'

The demons blink. I get the impression they're not particularly bright, which suits me just fine. The slower they are, the better chance I have of talking my way through these doors.

I keep smiling until my cheeks hurt, and eventually they step aside.

'Don't go left. Or right. Library only. At the end of the corridor. If you don't return in thirty minutes . . .'

'. . . We'll come and get you,' the second demon finishes the sentence. Her red eyes flash, and she takes a step towards me, like she's already anticipating what she might do when she retrieves me. I swallow.

'Noted,' I squeak, like I have any way to tell the time. My wrist is bare. I hadn't noticed before. Not only is my watch gone, but my bracelet –

Panic flutters in my stomach. Mum gave me that bracelet, a reward for getting accepted into her university of choice. And now I've lost it, the way I lost her, the way I've lost *everything*. I scrunch my hands into my dress to prevent the demons from seeing them tremble, and push my way between them to step through the doorway.

If the corridor leading to the Sorter was like sunshine, this one is night itself. The walls and floor are solid black. The only light comes from toadstools embedded in the stone, shining like the glow-in-the-dark stars I stupidly stuck to my ceiling

35

as a kid, not thinking about how they'd devalue the property, how Mum would have to spend ages tearing them off. They pulsate with my every step, as though I'm as heavy as a dinosaur disturbing a puddle of water.

When I reach a crossroads, I hover, uncertain. It branches into three dark tunnels, giving me the choice of black, off-black, or so-off-black-it's-grey. The demons mentioned the library being straight on, so that's one ruled out, but otherwise I have no idea whether I should be turning left or right if I want to find Sathanas.

Eenie, meenie, miney, mo, which way would the Devil go? My finger lands on the left-hand tunnel and, for lack of better ideas, I follow it. The corridor descends quickly, temperature plummeting, frost crystallising on the walls. Goosebumps erupt over my skin. My breath mists in the air.

Shivering, I debate turning back when, eventually, the path levels out, leading to an open archway. Darkness lies beyond.

'Sathanas?'

The darkness pulses at the sound of my voice. I approach it slowly, not sure if I've chosen correctly and he's hiding beyond that arch, or if I'm about to make another fatal mistake.

I'm given my answer when my feet hit empty air and I'm standing on the edge of nothing.

My stomach swoops. Above me, a thousand eyes stare down from skull sockets in the ceiling. Beneath them, though, is pure black. The faint sound of sloshing water echoes from deep below. I try to back away, but the darkness immediately fills with a thick mist that swirls in the empty space before shooting across the threshold, crawling up my legs like vines made of smoke, latching around my thighs and yanking me forward.

I do not have a great track record with ledges.

The mist tugs again, and I stumble closer to the precipice, hands grappling with the air, searching for something to hold on to before I'm pulled over yet another drop I didn't intend to go near.

My fingers find rock and dig into it like they've discovered driftwood in a violent sea.

Willow, a voice whispers from within the mist. *Come inside.*

No. No, I won't.

What were you thinking? another voice says. One I recognise. My palms are instantly slick with sweat, and my tenuous grasp on the wall slips.

How could you do this to me? The sound crackles. The signal was bad during that phone call – she had to shout to be heard over the rain thundering outside. *Everything we've worked towards, gone, all over some tantrum about –*

It wasn't a tantrum. That's me speaking now. Words I've replayed over and over. *This is what I want.*

You don't know what you want. You're throwing your life away, Willow.

I'm not. I'm not I'm not I'm not –

Give in. The unfamiliar voice returns, and it's closer now, like whoever's speaking has burrowed inside my head; the idea slithers around my skull before taking root like a weed left to fester. *You know what you did. You know you belong with us. Come inside.*

'No,' I say, a little shakily. 'I don't want to.'

The darkness chuckles in response. *The Sorter was right about you. You stink of death and blood. Come inside, before you hurt anyone else.*

My cheeks are wet.

All I've ever wanted is to be proud of you. Why couldn't you let me have that? Mum's voice plays over the chorus of whispers. *You're throwing your life away.* The sentence echoes, other voices joining in, screaming inside my head along with the screech of brakes and a loud, sickening crunch, and I want it to stop, I *need* it to stop, but if they think her words will make me concede, they're wrong.

I am not throwing anything away.

Gasping, I let go of the rock tethering me and force myself backwards. One step. Two. The mist retreats. My head clears. My breaths are coming out too quick, too loud. Nausea swims in my belly.

But it's over. The only voice in my head is mine.

I inhale musty air I don't need, every part of me trembling, remembering what Sathanas said about the Void. How it has the ability to replay our worst memories. It'd be typical of me to walk right into the one place I want to avoid most. I'm always ending up places I shouldn't – after Mum died, I developed a terrible habit of wandering off on nights out, leaving Noah to find me hours later chatting to strangers in a dark corner. He'd pull me away and put me in a taxi, telling me I shouldn't let myself get into situations like that. That I'm only safe when I'm with him. When I'd finished crying, I'd agree it was my fault I made him shout and he only does it because he worries.

He was right about that night on the beach too. If I'd listened

38

to him, I wouldn't be here, stuck in Hell, facing down Voids and listening to my mother on a loop.

If that was a taster of what my afterlife could turn into, it's another sign I have to do everything I can to convince Sathanas to let me out.

I retreat another step, unable to tear my gaze from that black space, that great yawning mouth wanting to swallow me whole. I close my eyes and, immediately, I feel more settled. My body stops trembling. I breathe in, then out. Again. Practised techniques that send signals to my brain to tell it to *calm down*. I'm fine. I'm safe, for now. I didn't get sucked in. I'm *fine*.

Then I bump into something hard. And warm.

A hand clamps on my shoulder. A different voice, one that's much deeper, practically a growl, says, 'And where do you think *you're* going?'

6

Sathanas spins me round.

I nearly smack into him. I'm eye level with his shoulders, and to be honest he needs to invest in better clothing because his shirt is straining to cover the breadth of them – is there a gym in Asphodel, or is he simply built that way? Asking seems inappropriate, given a) I don't know him and b) I'm probably in trouble.

He clears his throat.

Oh. Right. I drag my gaze up, over his shoulders, his mouth, to meet his stare. My throat goes dry. His amber eyes are practically ablaze. I wish I could tell myself that it's some strange reflection from the toadstools, but there's no denying the anger flickering there. I am, very definitely, in trouble.

It's not like I was *trying* to stumble into the Void. The whole experience was deeply unpleasant and counter-productive to what I'm here to do.

'What did I say,' he says in a warning tone, 'about bothering me?'

'How was I supposed to know you were here?' I fold my arms, tucking my hands inside moist armpits. 'Besides, I think *I'm* the one that's bothered. That was . . . I heard . . .'

'What you heard was merely a taste of what the centre of the Void is like.' He cocks his head. 'Pleasant memory, was it?'

I flinch. I've never told Noah the full details of that call and we've been together for three years – there's no chance I'm telling a perfect stranger.

'There was no memory,' I lie. 'Just voices, telling me to come inside. Who were they?'

His gaze drifts over my head, jaw ticking. 'Lost souls. Anyone whose body is destroyed in Asphodel ends up there, alone, unable to see or touch or hear each other. The best they can do is whisper inside your mind in the hope of dragging you in with them.' His focus returns to me. 'And yet you resisted their call. Not everyone does.'

I smile thinly. 'Lucky me.'

'Hm.' A crease forms between his brows for a second or two, and then he shakes his head like he's trying to clear some invading thoughts of his own. 'Come on.'

He turns as though expecting me to trot after him like a loyal dog. I don't move. 'Where are we going?'

'*We* aren't going anywhere,' he calls over his shoulder. 'I'm escorting you out before you end up anywhere else you shouldn't.'

That sets my feet in motion. I don't want to be escorted anywhere, not until we've spoken. I came here for a reason, and the Void made me lose focus. Fear spurs me like a tailwind, and I walk at double speed to catch up.

I still need a reason that'll persuade him to help me. Perhaps a sob story would work, something to gain his sympathy. That

41

should be easy enough. I try to think of something sad. Like the fact I'll never see Noah again, or Sasha, or –

My hand goes to my wrist, the emptiness there, the absence of weight. Not that my bracelet was heavy, but it was always *there*, a solid reminder of Mum; a reminder that sometimes I did do something that made her happy.

But that's one story I can't bring myself to tell. For fuck's sake. There must be something else sad enough to make me cry. I'm dead. That is upsetting in itself. I'm devastated on my own behalf, is that enough?

It'll have to be.

Decidedly, I call out, 'Wait!'

He whirls round. I pretend not to notice the way his hand clenches into a fist.

'I need to talk to you,' I say. My eyes aren't brimming with tears, not yet, but it's only a matter of time. I pinch my leg when he's not looking to speed the process along.

My words earn me an eyebrow raise. 'I see. And I'm at your beck and call, am I? Here to service your every whim?'

It only takes him two paces to stride back down the corridor, stopping a hair's breadth away from me, gripping my chin between his fingers and tilting my head to face his. His breath ghosts my mouth. 'Perhaps I need to remind you how this works.'

My heart stutters. I have no doubt he has more strength in those two fingers than I do in my entire body.

But I also think that if he wanted to hurt me, he would have by now. I shove his hand away and poke him in the chest. He gapes at my finger like it's shocked him. 'Perhaps *you* should have been clearer,' I tell him. 'You didn't mention where the Void was, so how was it my fault I ended up there? Plus, you haven't defined what bothering you means, which –'

I'm silenced by Sathanas wrapping his fingers around the one I'm trying to dig through his shirt. I should have removed it when I had the chance.

'What it means,' he says through gritted teeth, 'is not wasting my time when I could be –'

'What? Sitting on your throne, glowering at people? You're immortal. You haven't got time for a chat?'

He drops my finger. 'You and I have nothing to discuss.'

I flex some feeling back into the digit as I consider how to get him into a more sympathetic mood.

'Please,' I say, trying to convey contrition. The word grates on my tongue. I hate asking for anything, and yet all I've done since I've arrived is beg for help, for answers, for someone to save me. 'Five minutes, that's all I ask.'

He stares at me for a long while, gaze roaming every inch of my face, before turning without another word. I assume it's an invitation to follow, so I can only hope it's to where I want to go, and not into a demon's arms.

I'm in luck.

He leads me into a large sitting room with a bar stretched across the far side. There's a mirror behind it, which, frankly, I could do without. My red hair is tangled beyond belief, and I've got mascara smudged down both cheeks. Dad's eyes stare back at me, a vivid jade green I've grown to hate. They're just a reminder that I hardly ever saw the real thing. As I got older, his business trips became longer and longer, until the day he announced he wasn't returning at all. It was all my fault. *He wouldn't have left us if you'd turned out how we wanted.* I snatch a napkin from the bar, muttering about mascara stains as I wipe my eyes.

Notepaper is scattered across the coffee table alongside an old book. Sathanas gathers it in a bundle, shoving it all in a drawer before gesturing towards the velvet couch – a darker shade of emerald than the walls – and I plop down while he busies himself decanting a bottle of whisky into a glass tumbler. I, apparently, am not going to be offered one.

'Five minutes,' Sathanas says, taking a sip. 'Go on.'

That's four minutes more than last time. He must be warming to me. 'You sent me to the Sorter.'

He sighs, and drains the rest of his drink. 'A mistake.'

He pours himself another. This time, I clear my throat, and he glances at me, eyebrows raised, before snorting and opening a cabinet to retrieve a second glass. He pours a dram and hands it over without a word.

Perhaps he's at my beck and call after all. I hide my smile behind the glass.

'So,' he says, dropping on to the couch beside me. I'm hit with that sensation of power again, that aura of rippling darkness that clings to him like a shroud. Immediately, my smile falls, and I scoot to the far end. I shouldn't let one drink fool me into thinking he's anything other than the Devil. 'What did she say?'

Revealing I know there's an exit probably isn't my best move here. Deflecting, I ask, 'Why was it a mistake to send me to her?'

'It seems to have led you to the unfortunate impression we could be friends.' His arm is draped over the back of the sofa. Another inch and his fingers would be grazing the tip of my shoulder. He's the epitome of relaxed, which makes me all the more tense. 'I had hoped conversing with one of the demons would make you realise asking questions is futile, and yet, here you are, asking more.'

'Aw. And I thought you did it because you're a nice guy.'

'I'm many things, but nice isn't one of them.' His gaze grows hard, and his hand tightens around his glass. 'Is there a reason you're still here?'

'The Sorter didn't tell me anything true,' I complain. 'She said she looked into my soul and saw a river of blood.'

'Then it sounds like you'll fit in nicely.'

'It's not fair.' Shit. Do I sound whiny? I definitely sound whiny. I place my glass on the dark coffee table and fold my hands in my lap in an attempt to appear serious. 'She's punishing me for something that may or may not have been in my future.'

I leave out the part where there's plenty in my past she could have used. That it might not have been my future she was talking about at all.

Sathanas shrugs. 'The Sorter was here a long time before me. I don't question her methods.'

I blink. 'Aren't you the Devil? Shouldn't you have been here since the dawn of time, or whatever?'

His eyes shutter, and I can tell I've overstepped. There's nothing relaxed about him now; he's all tense muscle, sharp edges. That lick of shadow I spied earlier snakes its way around his arm, coiling power ready to be unleashed. The wall lamps flicker. 'Your five minutes are up,' he says, making to get off the sofa.

'Wait!' Panic sparks in my chest. Without thinking, I put a hand on his arm, and immediately flinch. His shirt sleeves are rolled up, and his bare skin is unreasonably warm, almost feverish. His gaze drops to where I'm touching him, like he can't believe I've done it. I should have learned my lesson from the chest-poking incident. Really, I should remove my hand before he removes it for me, but the room is brighter now; shadows retreat from the corners while flames steady in their oil lamps.

'She said there was no way out,' I hedge – this is dangerous, dangerous territory now – 'but that can't be true, can it?'

His gaze locks on mine. 'It's true.'

Liar.

'Please.' This can't be over. I refuse to give up. I have to try one more time to fulfil the vow I made the night Mum died – a night I'll be forced to relive over and over again if I end up in the Void. 'I can't be here. I had plans. And I was putting them off because . . . because . . .' I have no good answer to this. 'I was stupid.'

Sathanas doesn't speak, but he isn't actively trying to kick me out any more, which has to be a good sign. The embarrassing amount of tears dripping down my face must have finally uncovered his sympathetic side.

'I'm not done,' I plead. 'I wasn't done.'

He tenses, going ramrod straight, and his head jerks round. He's looking at me like he's seeing a ghost. 'What did you say?'

'That I was stupid. That I'm not done.' I continue to fling words at him, hoping something sticks and he gives me what

46

I want. 'If you let me leave, I'll be better. I'll do it right next time. I'll be good, I swear.'

That strange expression remains on his face. 'How good?'

What does he want – me to do more for charity or something? I'm always donating my old clothes. It's on the tip of my tongue to say something silly like *how good would you like me to be?* but I catch myself in time.

'The voices in the Void,' he says slowly. 'Was it hard for you to ignore them?'

'What has that got to do with anything?'

'Answer the question.'

'I don't know.' I wish I knew what he wanted. 'I got out of there, didn't I?'

'You did.' His tone is thoughtful as he drums a beat on his thigh. 'Maybe you could do this after all.'

My mouth drops.

'You said you wanted to be good,' he goes on. In the dim light, his eyes had been almost copper, bordering on brown. Now they blaze amber again, mirroring the flames dancing on the wall. 'Would you defy all sin? Denounce all pleasures? Would you refuse to let temptation overwhelm you?'

I'm not entirely sure what he's asking me, but he's very serious about it, so there's only one answer that's going to get me what I want.

'Yes,' I say. It comes out quieter than I expect. I tilt my chin in the air. 'Yes,' I say again, as forcefully as I can muster.

Triumph flickers in those eyes. 'In that case, Willow White, I have a proposition for you.'

7

I did it. I actually got him to offer.

My skin prickles with anticipation, but outwardly I press my lips together and school my face into what I hope conveys innocent confusion. 'A proposition?'

'There is one way out of Asphodel,' he tells me. 'A series of tests to prove your worth. Pass all seven, and you're free to leave.'

If it were that straightforward, surely everyone would be taking the next boat out of here. I narrow my eyes. I want what he's offering me very, very badly, but I'm sure he's only dangling half the carrot, and once I grab on I'm going to find a shark's head on the other end.

Given what I've seen of this place, it might be a literal shark too.

'And you're offering me this out of the goodness of your heart?'

His hand drifts across his chest, as though he's inclined to reach inside and examine how good his heart is. All too casually, he says, 'My interests are my own. Just know, although I'll be forced to tempt you at every turn, I'll be willing you to succeed.'

He's very believable. But he's the *Devil*. I have to keep reminding myself of that. Everything about him is designed to appeal: from the way his dark hair glimmers like it's infused with midnights and stardust, to the perfect angles of his face, to the way that even when he's goading me his voice is laced with warmth, like the embers of a softly glowing fire.

He's temptation made flesh, but it's all a pretty trap, and I won't fall for it. I have to stay focused. 'Tell me about the tests.'

Sathanas sighs. 'The first will force you to face the thing your pride won't let you admit. Complete it, you move on to the next. The remaining six will require you to resist . . . certain temptations. Pass them all, you can return to the mortal plane. Fail, you stay here, just as you were before. You've got nothing to lose.'

He has a point. Say no, I'm stuck here, at risk from the demons and the Void every day. Say yes, I could still end up in the Void.

Or maybe I'll get everything I want.

'I see you're not interested.' He rises to his feet. 'A shame, but perhaps it's for the best. I'll walk you out.'

You're throwing your life away, Willow.

'Wait.' The word shoots from my mouth before I can stop it. I can't lose this opportunity. It's all I have. I need to prove her wrong.

One final cliff edge. One final bad decision to fix all the rest.

He smirks. 'Yes?'

Bastard knows exactly what he's doing. I gulp. 'I accept. I'll do your tests. Please. I have to leave.'

The lamps swell as though they're collectively holding their

49

breaths, and light floods the room. When it subsides, Sathanas's chest is heaving and dark shadows swirl around him before dissipating into the air, leaving a burning smell behind. Once the shadows have cleared, he says, 'Then we have a deal.'

I don't move, waiting for some sign I've made a terrible mistake, but for all the shadow-based theatrics, the aftermath is a little anticlimactic. We stare at each other in heavy silence, like neither one of us can believe I've agreed so readily. I'm still expecting the axe to drop.

Eventually, hesitantly, I ask, 'What happens now?'

'Now we begin. The task of pride first.' He holds out a hand. 'Ready?'

'Oh.' I stare at that hand like it's a nest of vipers. I'm already regretting not asking more questions. Agreeing to do this and actually doing it are two very different things. Plus, there's a slight smile tugging on his lips, and I can't believe anything that makes the Devil happy is going to be enjoyable for me.

'Of course, if you're too scared . . .'

'I'm not scared of anything,' I snap, raising my voice to drown out the lie. I'm scared of plenty, but he doesn't need to know that. Besides, I'm far more scared of failing, of ending up in the Void, than I am of his tasks.

And I've never been one to resist a dare.

I match the challenge in his expression and march over to him, taking his hand before I can second-guess myself. Palm to palm, his calluses scrape against my skin, and then everything heats and I'm engulfed in darkness, a black so pure it's suffocating.

The only thing I'm aware of is Sathanas's hand in mine,

solid and warm and present while everything around me has disappeared. I open my mouth but no sound comes out; there's a pressure in my temple like something's trying to invade my mind, and I squeeze him tighter and tighter, desperate for any connection to reality.

My feet thud on solid ground. He drops my hand. The sting of brine hits my nose.

And I'm home.

I'm *home*.

My head spins. Both from whatever just happened and the fact I'm here – although, I'm not sure where *here* is. I'm on Earth at least, that much I can tell. There's sand everywhere and, despite the circumstances, my eyes widen. What if we're in Hawaii? Or, ooh, *Aruba*. Or Borneo! I wanted to go to Borneo on a gap year before university, but Mum said I shouldn't distract myself from my studies. I'd hoped to convince her otherwise but then she heard from her friends at the country club that *the* Noah Millsbury-Davenport would be attending Royal Holloway with me, and that was that. We were introduced before term started, at some fancy fundraiser at his parents' house in London. He took me to his rooftop garden and told me I was the first person he'd ever brought there, that he recognised I was special the moment he laid eyes on me, and I knew Mum was right. He was everything I needed.

That doesn't stop me looking around this beach for signs I've finally gone further afield, but all I see is a campfire in the distance with a group of figures sat round it.

I tense. If I can get rid of Sathanas, maybe I could convince them to help me. Borrow a phone, call Noah. Or maybe I should just make a run for it – it doesn't matter that I don't have money (or shoes, I still don't have shoes) – if I can get away quickly and flag down a car, I'd be free.

But then one of those figures lets out a familiar laugh, and I realise with a jolt who they are. Where *I* am. There's a bite of chill in the air, too bitter for places with jungles and parrots. This isn't some tropical island I've always dreamed of visiting; it's an extremely untropical beach in Margate. Camping with our three flatmates wasn't the escape I'd hoped for when I begged Noah for a weekend getaway, but I was making the most of it until . . .

Well.

The sunlight is fading, chilling the sand beneath my feet. Grains rise between my toes. The rush of waves crashing against the shore forces me back, spray hitting my face. I usually love that feeling, the cold rush of water like an electric shock to someone who's been sleepwalking, but I don't need any more shocks. Not today. That laugh sounds again, but it's not possible, can't be possible, because that's *my* laugh.

As though in slow motion, I walk towards the campfire until the figures come into clearer view. My heart pounds. It *is* me. Sat on a log by the campfire with my friends, wearing my beloved missing sandals. My head is on Sasha's shoulder, a bottle in my hands. We pass it between us while Danny and Michaela have a contest as to who can stick their tongue the furthest down the other's throat.

I know what night this is.

My stomach twists. I almost wish Sathanas was still holding my hand. I don't want to be here on my own. I don't want to be here at all.

I spin round. Sathanas has been following me without a word this whole time, his light footsteps stalking my path. Not caring whether we're in earshot of the group – or what'll happen if we are – I demand, 'Why are we here?'

'You know why.' He runs a hand through his dark hair. 'You need to admit what happened. What your pride hasn't *let* you admit.' His eyes flick to Sasha, and unease makes goosebumps rise on my skin.

'There's nothing to admit,' I say. 'This whole night was a mistake. I slipped. It was a freak accident.'

'Was it?' he asks quietly. He takes my elbow, drawing me forward, and I regret ever wishing for his presence; I want to be alone now, I don't want to go there, I don't want to see –

'No. No.' I try to wrench my arm from his grasp, and his fingers dig tighter, turning blinding hot for a moment. My eyes sting. I think I might hate him. 'Don't take me. Please, please don't take me to her.'

'They can't see us.'

That's not the issue. The issue is I'm about to watch myself die. I'm about to watch what I *did*.

No. No, fuck this. Fuck all of this. No slim sliver of a chance to go home is worth this; I won't watch it, I won't.

'Willow.' My name on his lips stops my thoughts from scattering any further. 'You're panicking.'

I am not panicking. If I was panicking I'd be, I don't know, running or screaming or something. I haven't got the energy to do either. My knees are shaking, less stable than melted butter, and my fists are clenched so tight I expect my nails will draw blood. I'm vaguely aware my cheeks are wet.

Noah appears in the distance. Without thinking, I grab Sathanas's arm for support. He tenses, but doesn't pull away. Probably because he knows he's the only thing keeping me upright. Sand streams around Noah's feet as he marches down the length of the beach, the town twinkling behind him and chalky-white cliffs at his side. His blonde hair is streaked with pink and gold shadows as the sun sets overhead. My chest constricts.

Noah.

Oh, God. He's got a ring hidden in his underwear drawer – I found it a few days ago and, naturally, panicked – and instead of asking me that question he got to find my dead body instead.

Past Willow straightens when she spots him. Her eyes go wide, pleading. She never knows which Noah she's going to get: the one who sends her message after message about how beautiful and special she is, how he'd be lost without her – words she's craved her whole life and only gets from him – or the other Noah, the one who appeared later on, the one who's cold and detached and threatening to drift away because she can't stop disappointing him.

Sasha smiles as he approaches. 'Here he is,' she says, twirling a lock of golden hair around her finger. They became friends when limited options forced us into living together in our final year of university, but sometimes it's a little jarring seeing the two parts of my life collide, like I can't work out how to slot between them any more. 'What took you so long?'

'Aw, Sash. Did you miss me?' His grin is short-lived as he takes in the sight of Past Willow. 'I was waiting for this one.' He jerks his head at her. 'You told me you'd come back to the tent.'

'No, I –' Past Willow frowns. 'We said we'd meet here.'

He gestures at my current state. 'Do you think you're capable of remembering?'

She shakes her head, but there's a part of her – of *me* – that's sure it's not what they agreed. Biting her tongue might spare her this argument though, and she visibly deflates as she cages the part of her that's dying to fight back.

'Come on. Let's go.' He holds out a hand, but she doesn't take it. The beast she's just imprisoned tries to slide a claw through the bars. She's never been any good at restraining it, no matter how much it ruins everything.

'Willow.' He drops to his knees before her, saying, 'Come on. You can't keep doing this.'

The same shame swims in my stomach now as it did then, except this time it's worse because I know how right he is. Every flash of memory is a body blow, but instead of becoming dazed and concussed my mind becomes clearer.

More sure of what's to come.

Past Willow pushes Noah away, nuzzling closer to Sasha's side. She's still under the delusion she has a plan. It's one she's been putting off, but she *really means it this time*. She just needs one more night to herself.

'I think Willow wants to keep doing this,' Sasha says, pouring more alcohol into Past Willow's cup. 'Maybe we should let her.'

She fills the cup to the brim, despite the fact hers is lying empty at her side.

Past Willow watches on, silently wishing Sasha would stop because she's already had twice as much as everyone else and feels distinctly sick. Sasha's not to blame though. She's learned this is the only way to keep her from crawling back to bed and staying there.

Noah approved of this tactic at first – like Sasha he was pleased they'd discovered a way to stop her moping – but he became less enthused with no end in sight. He couldn't take *this* version of Willow to his family parties. That ring would probably have stayed in his drawer forever.

'Not here, we can't.' He reaches for Past Willow's cup but she snatches it away, lurching to her left and sliding off the log. She gets a mouthful of sand for her trouble. Danny and Michaela, whose mouths have become unglued sometime during this exchange, laugh. Noah swears, hauling her up and murmuring low in her ear, 'You're embarrassing me.'

She doesn't care. For one, wild, blissful moment she doesn't care what Noah thinks. She's not getting Nice Noah tonight; that much is obvious. He's going to take her back to the tent and give her the silent treatment until she begs for his forgiveness because she can't stand the thought of him leaving. Her mother's dead. Her father left. She's all alone, and he's all she has, and she doesn't *care*.

She wrenches from his grasp and whirls on him. Behind them, Sasha's eyes widen.

'If you want to go back to the tent, go back to the tent,' Past Willow says. 'I'm staying here.'

Noah does a double take. Splutters. 'What?'

'You heard me.' The cage unlocks and the beast within roars. Sathanas finally removes his arm from my grasp in order to place his hand on my back instead. He knows what's coming as well as I do.

56

Noah's features soften. He takes a step closer. 'Baby, please. I need you. Come with me.'

No. No. She won't fall into that trap; she knows it won't last. But he said he needed her and she wants him to mean it this time; for *someone* out there to need her. Indecision has her swaying on the spot. Maybe if she acts out a little more, she can scare him into loving her forever.

'Think how your mum would hate seeing you like this.' His voice is gentle now. 'Let me look after you.'

Without mentioning her mum, that line would have worked, but the word is a blade that cuts through the longing for comfort.

'Don't,' she says. 'Don't talk about her.'

'Willow –'

His mouth moves, but she's not listening to him. Not any more. She's glancing around, looking for an escape, looking for a way not to feel all the things she's feeling but doesn't want to feel, because she's a bottle that's been shaken too hard and she's ready to explode and he doesn't understand, doesn't get it, the only way to cope is to numb that feeling until it's gone, to pretend she's fine and perfect like everyone expects her to be, but he won't let her forget, and it's going to be like this forever and ever once he gives her that ring, and she wants to be free, free of his nagging, free from everything –

Her gaze snaps upwards. To the cliff. 'I want to go up there.'

No no no. My throat is hoarse, like I've been yelling silent warnings this whole time and now I've nothing left to give.

Noah's protests are sharp. Panicked. He doesn't know how to deal with a Willow who won't listen. She pulls Sasha to her feet, and they're both giggling, because ignoring the person trying to save your life is apparently hysterical. Sasha grins in his direction right before they go tearing up the path. Noah doesn't follow. If only he had, I might still be here, with *his* hand on my back.

Sathanas pushes me forward. I dig my toes into the sand, knowing what'll happen if I follow, and if I see it then it'll become real, and I desperately, desperately don't want it to be real.

'If we stop now, you'll fail,' he murmurs. 'Your choice.'

That doesn't do anything to ease the jelly in my legs. But if I fail I can't fix this, so I force myself to move, to trail Past Willow up the path. At least the climb doesn't hurt like last time. My calves don't burn. My lungs don't gasp for air. When they finally reach the top, they spin in circles, howling at the moon, Sasha's twirls as graceful as a ballerina's. Past Willow, meanwhile, has just tripped over a rock.

Finally, they come to a halt, gasping. Sasha hesitates before taking Past Willow's hand and squeezing. 'Noah's always upset with you these days. Maybe you two need some time apart.'

'No, we don't,' Past Willow protests. Their – *our* – problems are a blip.

Sasha squeezes harder. 'You could go travelling, like you've always wanted.'

The smile drops from Past Willow's face. 'I can't. I'll be starting that internship –'

'You've not applied yet.' Sasha sighs, looking at me with a pity I don't want and didn't ask for. 'And they won't offer it to you. You don't have the qualifications.'

The same hot rush of anger burns in me now as it did then.

'I'll get them,' Past Willow snaps. She should have gained them already, but she doesn't like being reminded of that. 'It's the only way to fix everything.'

'You can't fix anything.' Sasha's voice might be soft, but her words are weapons, sharp and painful and full of things I don't want to hear. 'You already quit, Willow. It's too late.'

It is *not* too late. It can't be. Past Willow's hands shake to the same rhythm mine do now. I hate Sasha's words, but I hate what they're going to make me do even more.

'You'd love Thailand,' Sasha says. 'Beautiful beaches, boys, parties. The whole time I was there, I thought about how much you'd love it.'

Jealousy and longing twist into an angry knot in my chest. She's been jetting around the world for as long as I've known her. Her parents pay. At first I'd soak up every story like they were my own personal souvenirs, like just being close to her would be the same as me getting on the plane myself. But then she handed in her dissertation early and flounced off to Thailand and I couldn't *stand* it.

When she returned, it was to a Willow whose mother had just died, who couldn't get out of bed. She and Noah would whisper behind my back, partly plotting how to fix me and partly so she could tell *him* her stories. Terrified I was going to miss out again, I let her tug me into the shower and out of the house, and suddenly I wasn't envious of Sasha's life any more because I was living it, living it in a way I never could when Mum was alive.

The freedom was exhilarating at first. Forgetting was easier than remembering. But then it stopped being fun, because deep down I always knew it couldn't last – I'd wake every morning with a pounding head and a nausea in my belly that wasn't just down to the alcohol. I kept saying *this is the last time*, because I had a promise to keep.

Now it's a promise I'm about to break.

'You know I can't drop everything and go on holiday,' Past Willow says.

'You can. All you have to do is *go*.' Sasha moves closer to the precipice and leans over. I wish I could run over there and pull her back, pull her *away*, because it's my last chance to stop all this, stop Past Willow from saying the words that'll ruin everything. Waves slosh beneath us, crashing against the cliff face with a thunderous roar. 'You know, there's a bay where we went cliff-jumping, and the water's gorgeous, so warm and clear –'

'Let's do it now,' Past Willow interjects.

No.

No no no –

Sasha shakes her head. 'It's too far.'

'It's not.' Past Willow gives the water an all-too-quick glance. 'People do it all the time here too. Go on. You first.' Her hand is on Sasha's shoulders.

Tears trail down my face. Every move she makes peels back the veil I've been trying to hide behind, revealing the truth I've been avoiding since I woke up in that tunnel.

'We shouldn't.' Sasha bites her lip.

'You've done it before,' Past Willow says, pulling her closer to the edge. 'This'll just be a little colder. And this is my only chance, before . . .'

60

Before she abandons nights like this for a grey city full of smoke and late nights in an office. The thought of it is a knife through the gut. But she can't change her mind. She just has this one final night, and she needs to make the most of it. Wind howls, blowing her hair round her face. She looks wild, out of control. Dangerous. She advances on Sasha. I close my eyes.

'Watch,' Sathanas commands.

I hate him. I hate him more than I've hated anyone, because I can't do this, I can't *watch* this.

There's no mud for me to slip on or rock to give way beneath me. There's just me, purposefully pushing us closer to the edge because I'm so sick of the way she gets to experience everything and I never do. Just once, I want to feel it too, to have that rush alongside her instead of hearing about it second-hand.

Someone screams. I open my eyes. It's Sasha. Her heels dangle precariously over the drop.

I'm not giving her an inch.

'Let's do it,' I'm saying, over and over, and Sasha is crying, and I'm crying, but Past Willow isn't, because she's –

She takes another step.

Sasha falls.

My knees give way. Sathanas stands behind me, hand on my shoulder, like he's afraid if he moves away I'll do something stupid. There's no need. I'll never do anything more stupid than this.

Because this night wasn't an accident.

Being too mindless to realise what waited below doesn't make this any less my fault. I chose this. Because for all my *this is the last time*, there was always a next time, because I couldn't get it together, couldn't stop looking for an escape, didn't want to lose the freedom I'd found since Mum's death to face reality instead.

Sasha screams on the way down. Past Willow doesn't care, or doesn't notice, because she spreads her arms out wide, and although she's got her back to me, I know she's smiling, because with the wind ripping through her hair, her dress, she's never felt freer, empty of all expectation to be anything but what she is.

Then Past Willow tips forward, and she's gone too.

'No!' I'm crawling to the edge before I realise what I'm doing, needing to know, needing to see – I peer over the ledge, but night has fallen now, the moon a faint glimmer over the sea. I pushed Sasha. I *pushed* her. I can't hide from this reality any more and I can't . . . I don't . . .

'Where is she?' I gasp. 'Is she . . . ? She can't be . . . I didn't mean to . . .'

Panic and nausea claw a path up my throat; my fingers dig into grass and earth as though that can save me, but it's too late, I've already gone over and I took Sasha with me. A whirlpool of guilt churns in my belly. *I did this*. I did this to my best friend.

Someone is shouting – Noah, I think. There's a splash of water. More shouting. I want to call out to him, to tell him it was an accident and I'm sorry, to beg him to tell me he's found her alive, to tell me *anything* that will ease the blade currently carving its way through my heart, but Sathanas's hand is on my arm, hauling me to my feet.

'No.' I struggle. 'No. I need to know what happened. I need to know if Sasha –'

He ignores me. The darkness returns, and I want it to devour me, I want it to never end, because I *did* this, I did this to myself, to Sasha, it's all my fault, I deserve to be exactly where I am – I catch a glimpse of lightning, a car spinning, a tree edging closer and closer until it disappears in a spray of water – and then light gleams, bright and beautiful and shining.

I open my eyes, register we're in Sathanas's sitting room, and immediately topple over.

8

Sathanas catches me before I fall head first into his coffee table.

His fingers dig into my hips as he steadies me, forcing my knees to stop from buckling. My breaths come out in shallow gasps. Although I don't need them, I feel winded anyway, like I've been punched in the chest. *What happened to Sasha?*

'Did she . . . Did I kill . . . ?'

He drops his hands. 'She missed the rocks. Hit the water. She's in hospital.'

My legs give way, and I stumble into the side of the sofa, my fingers clutching the velvet like it's the parachute I didn't have on the cliff. She's *alive*. Well, at least one of us had decent aim. At least I haven't been responsible for another person dying because of one of my stupid, stupid ideas. 'Will she be okay?'

There's a long pause. 'I don't know.'

My fingers dig into the fabric. She *has* to be okay.

I wish he'd never shown me what happened. What kind of person I am.

'I hate you,' I whisper. I hate myself more.

'You asked for this.'

'I didn't ask to –'

'To see the truth?'

Tears stream down my cheeks. 'And what is that?'

'You tell me.'

I know what he wants me to say – that admitting it out loud is the real test – but the words catch on my tongue like flies in honey. The wings of my admission flutter and fail. I always knew I was a disaster; I never realised I was *this*.

But if I don't say it out loud, I'll fail this task too, and I'll be forced to live here with the knowledge of what I've done forever. Another bad memory to add to the pile if I end up in the Void.

Mum was right about me. I'm impulsive. I make split-second decisions without thinking them through. Every bad thing that's ever happened is because of a choice I made – her death, and now *mine*. If I'd followed the path she'd wanted for me, if I'd done as I promised after she'd died, I wouldn't have been on that clifftop. I'd have been safe below, with Noah, the nice, sensible boy she'd chosen for me.

And Sasha wouldn't be fighting for her life in a hospital bed. The thought has me choking and spluttering, drowning in my guilt, and I can't breathe, my chest is too tight, I'm ready to burst open, there's too many tears and I can't get them all out – Sathanas swears and hauls me against him, wrapping his arms around my middle.

I'm so surprised he's helping me that for a moment, I freeze. His warmth and strength seeps into me, solid and unbreakable while I'm fragmenting around him. I feel the rhythm of his breathing against my back, and I use it to try and control mine.

65

In, out. In, out.

I dig my nails into his forearms.

In, out. In, out.

His mouth is against my ear; I think he says my name.

In, out. In, out.

It's enough. Two final gasps and I'm sagging against him, breaths even at last. And I say the words. 'It wasn't an accident,' I whisper. The words burn, scraping the back of my throat like acid. 'It was my idea to jump. I pushed Sasha. I'm the reason I'm dead. I told myself I was doing better because I'd made it out of bed, but it was a lie. I was never fine. I was never coping. I kept saying tomorrow would be the day I'd start over, but tomorrow was never going to come, because it was easier to carry on doing stupid shit than admit I didn't know how to stop.'

I was never going to become Good Decision Willow. Never going to keep my promises to Mum.

Sathanas sighs. 'You've –'

'Everything is always my fault,' I interrupt, louder this time, speaking with more conviction. I know he won't let me pass unless I confess it all. 'That night was no different. I was out of control. Doing all the things I said I wouldn't do. It was my *fault*. I'm an awful person.'

'Willow . . .' He spins me round, keeping his hands on my waist after I make another attempt at falling to the floor. His brow is furrowed. 'You've –'

'That's what you want me to say, isn't it? I'm a monster. I'm the worst person in the whole world. I belong here.' My voice cracks. 'Well, I don't want to belong here. I want to be better.'

The crease in his brow deepens, like this confession still

66

isn't enough to satisfy him, but eventually he says, softer than I expect, 'Willow. You've passed pride.'

Now he's got what he wanted, he lets me go like I'm an emotionally damaged hot potato and stalks towards his bar. He settles on a stool, then pours himself a drink – once again failing to offer me anything – and I'm left glowering at his back while trying to stop my chin from wobbling.

I shift from one foot to the other. I appear to have been dismissed, but I'm not ready to leave yet. Not when I don't know what awaits me in the rest of Asphodel.

'Are all the tasks going to be like this?' I ask, partly in an attempt to make conversation, and partly so I can brace myself for the next one. 'Watching memories?'

His shoulders tense. 'No.'

Phew. I risk a step closer. 'So, what –'

'We'll talk about them soon,' Sathanas says, his mouth paused around the rim of his glass. 'You should get some sleep.'

I don't want to go to sleep. I'm a bottomless well of questions and we've barely touched the surface. His finger taps a drumbeat against the bar. It's a warning. If the finger stops tapping . . . well, I'm not sure what he'll do. I suspect I don't want to find out.

But there's one thing I have to know before I leave. I clear my throat. 'How many people get sorted here exactly?' I say hesitantly. 'Is there a list of names I could check? I need to see if . . .'

'You won't see your mother.' His voice is flat.

'Oh.' I don't bother to ask how he knows who I meant. I deflate, nervous energy dissipating from me like air from a popped balloon. In a small voice, I ask, 'Where is she?'

He turns his head a fraction of an inch, but still won't look at me. 'I'm responsible for a few millennia's worth of souls. You'll have to forgive me for not keeping track of every single one.'

'But would you know if she was in Asphodel?' A fresh wave of panic floods my veins. 'What if she's in Tartarus?'

But Mum wouldn't be there. I hope.

'Tartarus is for the truly irredeemable.' A muscle in his jaw ticks. 'Asphodel is more of a . . . middle ground. Some see it as a new beginning, a chance to live again, free of the constraints of Earth.'

When he puts it like that, it doesn't sound terrible. He is, of course, conveniently leaving out the part about the constant threat of demons and the Void. Besides, I don't want a new beginning. I want to prove myself capable of living the life I was supposed to live all along. I want to go home and tell Sasha how desperately, desperately sorry I am that I put hers in jeopardy.

'With that in mind, you'll find certain areas are locked to you at certain times. The magic here has a way of guiding the dead away from those they had conflict with in the past. If she's here, you won't see her. How can you have a fresh start surrounded by the memories of old mistakes?'

All I've ever wanted is to be proud of you. I shiver. At least this means I won't be having a family reunion any time soon.

'And then, of course, there's Elysium.' Sathanas's voice is the softest I've ever heard it.

'Is that . . . what is that?' I ask, although I can guess.

'It's peace,' he says, sounding a little wistful. I wonder how much peace he gets, here in Asphodel. 'An eternal quiet.'

'So, Tartarus and Elysium are basically Heaven and Hell,' I say. 'Why not call them that?' Elysium is quite the mouthful if you ask me.

He shrugs. 'They were named long before those terms were coined on Earth. Why ruin a tradition?'

'Named by who?'

He blinks as though he's been shaken awake, and then his face turns to stone. He stands, towering over me. 'That's enough questions for today.'

'But –'

He waves a hand and the door sweeps open, handle banging into the wall. 'Go. I'll find you when it's time.'

I stare at him, grinding my teeth and wondering if I dare argue, but black smoke whirls around him, reminding me that he has all the power here. I'm a bug he can squash whenever he likes. He could wake tomorrow and decide he doesn't need me to do these tasks at all, and punish me for even asking.

'Fine.' I drop into a mock bow. 'I await your command, Your Majesty.'

Flames threaten to shoot from his eyes, so I hurry from the room before one hits me. With some trepidation, I head back into the entrance chamber and down the golden corridor, further into the depths of Asphodel than I've gone before.

Rather than light at the end of the tunnel, there's darkness. The corridor opens on to a balcony overlooking a vast underground chasm that reeks of sulphur. I grip the railing, feeling like I'm one misstep from falling into the abyss. The balcony stretches to the side in both directions, encompassing a curved cliff face embedded with lights – no, *windows*. Silhouettes move from one to the other. Laughter and shouts echo through the still air as though there are people out here somewhere, but I can't see anyone close by.

Above me is another balcony. And another. And another. The cliff extends upwards with no end in sight; a skyscraper with no sky to scrape. It disappears into a swirling black mist instead. Dark objects glide up and down the walls like worker ants. Opposite, lava streams down slick black rock.

The low thump of bass music reverberates from somewhere below, and I lean over the railing to peer into the sheer drop. My stomach swoops. The cliff spreads downwards, again too far for me to see the bottom. Perhaps there is no bottom. Just an endless, eternal city of the dead stretching on forever.

Between my palms, the railing rattles. I jerk back, just in time for one of the black objects to swoosh past, not clinging to the building at all, but flying close by in a rush of putrid hot air that blasts my face and blows back my hair, like it's powered by nothing but magic and smoke. I'm shaking when I look over the railing again. It's stopped a few levels below, and several figures jump out on to the balcony, their chatter indecipherable, and then the lift takes flight again, dropping lower. The figures vanish somewhere within before I've worked up the nerve to shout for assistance.

I look around. Maybe I need to call one of these things to take me to one of the rooms Sathanas mentioned. It would be nice if someone left a set of instructions or, better yet, a map. They could at least put a sign on the wall: *Dismemberment Level Four, Demon-Viewing Platform Level Ninety-Nine, A Good Night's Sleep on Three.*

Maybe I'll suggest it to Sathanas. I'm sure there's nothing he'd love more than decoration advice.

For lack of better ideas, I start walking. If I can't go up or down, maybe I need to try and go *in*. A tall iron door sits not too far along the cliff, but before I have a chance to touch the handle it's yanked open from the other side and a girl flies out, nearly barrelling into me. Her bleached-blonde hair is tied into space buns, the ends of which are dyed the same bubblegum pink as her lipstick and fluffy jumper. She studies me, then beams.

'Oh.' She bounces on her feet. 'You must be new.'

I glance at my ruined dress. 'What gave me away?'

'Don't worry, you'll find new clothes in your room. Try down there.' She jerks her head towards the dark tunnel she's just come from. 'One will open for you, when it's ready.'

'Right.' I blink. It makes as much sense as everything else in this place.

'I'm Harper, by the way,' she adds. 'I've been here for a while.' She says it like it's something to be proud of.

'Willow.'

She radiates so much energy I feel like a planet being dragged into a sun's orbit, so I immediately take a step back to lessen her gravitational pull. Making friends is pointless when I plan to get out as soon as possible.

And besides, she's wearing too much pink. It clashes with my hair.

'Once you're settled, you should join us in Dionysus,' she goes on. 'It's like a . . . volcano turned nightclub. Parties every night. Everybody goes.'

71

Her enthusiasm yanks on my stomach. I want to. I want to so badly. To escape, to pretend none of this is happening. But agreeing to party with a bunch of dead people would definitely be on Mum's list of Things Willow Shouldn't Do, and my desperate desire to escape was what got me in this mess to start with. 'Maybe another time.'

'Of course.' Her smile wavers, turning sad, a little sympathetic. She wouldn't feel that way if she knew what happened to Sasha. I'm doing her a favour. A few days with me and I'd probably send her to the Void by accident. 'But being dead doesn't mean you have to stop living.'

Being here must have addled her mind. That is the definition of being dead.

'Right. Well.' I step towards the threshold of a nearby tunnel. 'I should go. Thanks for pointing me the right way.'

'If you change your mind, come back to this ledge and think about visiting floor minus-two-nine-nine. A lift will appear.'

I nod, then head inside so a room can decide it likes me, or whatever. Tunnels have been carved through the cliff, branching off in various directions, but I keep straight. The deeper I go the more the black walls glisten with damp. Flamed sconces light the way, but they're not enough to mask the chill in the air. The same vines growing near the entrance chamber climb the walls here too, but the further I descend into the cliff the more they shrivel and die, leaves turning brown and rotten, their remains breaking from their stems and carpeting the floor.

Doors are constantly opening, closing, slamming, as other

dead go in and out of their rooms. Most travel in packs. A few groups give me friendly glances when they pass, clearly marking me as a newbie, but I avert my eyes. I don't want to know them.

I hate this. I hate the way they're carrying on like this is normal, like they're with their friends on some awful, hellish holiday. How can they accept they're dead like this? I'm about to kick down the nearest door to get away from them, to lock myself away until it's time for my next task, when one clicks open of its own accord.

A tug in my belly tells me this one is mine. I approach it slowly, imagining this is how an inmate must feel before entering their cell for the first time. The room is dark when I step inside. I slide my hand along the wall out of habit, searching for a light switch, if such a thing exists here. I reach around blindly, willing there to be light –

A bulb illuminates on the ceiling. I jolt in surprise, staring around, but there's no switch. The room is little more than a windowless cave with sparse furnishings; there's a single bed with a brown quilt in one corner and a wardrobe in the other, with barely sixty centimetres between them. It's almost as terrible as the room I had in the first year of university, except this one, at least, doesn't have an ominous wet patch on the ceiling.

I sink on to the bed. The mattress dips under my weight. Great. A saggy mattress is exactly what I need to help me sleep in this . . . I was about to call it a hellhole, but it doesn't have the same ring to it when I'm not exaggerating.

The wardrobe is ajar, devoid of the clothing Harper promised, and I wonder . . . If I got that light to turn on by itself, what else can I do? I focus all my energy on the wardrobe and picture soft, comfy pyjamas.

A pair appears. I let out a delighted squeak and grab them. Sunshine yellow, they're almost enough to put me in a good mood, especially if it means peeling this dress off. I change quickly, picturing bed sheets to match, and when I turn round the brown quilt has changed into a duvet with flowers embroidered on the cover.

It's the duvet from my childhood home. Mum chose it. A fist clenches around my heart, and I squeeze my eyes shut. When I open them, the walls are covered in travel posters – beaches, glaciers, mountain ranges. Pictures I collected and kept in a box under my bed. Wedged in between the wardrobe and the wall is a violin. Mum had been a prodigy back in her day. I'd practised until my fingers were sore and blistered, but I'd never been good enough – my music teacher once described me as *enthusiastic but screechy* – and I spent most lessons squashing the urge to throw it on the floor in a fit of frustration.

I hate that thing, but my vision blurs anyway, because it's a piece of home, a place I might never see again.

Just in case, I imagine a door. A key. A tunnel. *Anything*. No magical exit appears, which is disappointing, but unsurprising. Sighing, I climb under the covers, and will the light off.

The room goes black.

Alone, with only the sound of my thoughts rattling round my head, I bite my lip to stop myself from crying. I'm *dead*. I'm dead, and the only way out is to put my trust in the Devil, aka the one person I can't trust at all.

When my eyes finally drift shut, my vision floods red. Blood splatters on a rock. A hand lies broken and twitching.

The image is washed away by a river of crimson. It flows, fast and rushing, through a dark tunnel, like a burst pipe in a rainstorm.

Within the flow of water bobs a skull, the lights in its eyes snuffed out.

9

I spend the next day exploring. Carefully. The last thing I need is another Void experience.

Following Harper's advice, I first head to the balcony and *think* really hard. A lift appears a few moments later. It's nothing more than a semi-translucent black box, big enough to hold around twenty bodies. Generic music plays on repeat. I ignore a group of elderly women who are already inside and retreat to the far corner as it surges upwards in a cloud of smoke.

I pick the number seventy-seven at random, and when I re-enter the cliff I find myself in a greenhouse made of mirrors and filled with carnivorous plants that snap miniature teeth at the dead inside. The chamber is twice the height it should be based on the outside, but who am I to argue with the physics of Hell. Some parts are smaller than they should be: floor minus-four-forty opens out into narrow catacombs that force you to crawl around corners only to find demons with whiskers and pointed tails waiting for you.

I scramble out of there sharpish to find the level above is nothing but open space where pipes pump out a pink noxious gas. Humans sleep, slumped in piles, among the clouds.

I have no idea if they're having a good time or not.

It's like roaming around the world's largest airport or shopping complex. I could travel up and down for eternity and not see it all. Asking to go to the top or bottom does nothing, fuelling my suspicion that the cliff continues forever. My eyes grow wider with every new sight, at the magic of this place, and if I wasn't so determined to get out – Mum would consider everything I've done today as frivolous and time-wasting – I might admit that, if nothing else, Asphodel is . . . *interesting*.

Interesting, and dangerous. Because there are demons everywhere. They loiter at every turn, watching the humans with hungry eyes, like they're waiting for someone to mess up. One snarls at me when I accidentally make eye contact, and I quickly scuttle back to the safety of the balcony.

After hours of exploring, curiosity finally gets the better of me, and I ask the lift to take me to Dionysus on level minus-two-nine-nine, the place Harper mentioned yesterday. This balcony is busier than the rest, and I have to force my way through several groups of raucous humans to enter the cliff and into a long, sloping black tunnel.

It's unreasonably warm inside. Music blares in the distance; loud enough to make the floor beneath my feet vibrate when I draw closer to the large, domed arch that must mark the entrance to Dionysus.

Peeking inside, my jaw drops. It's a cave, easily the size of a stadium, with lava streaming down ash-blackened walls. An array of vibrant cocktails bubble and steam on the bar top, like they've been pulled from a witch's cauldron. At the back of the cavern, rocky stairs lead up to an empty throne – Sathanas's, presumably – that overlooks the packed dance floor, teeming with demons and humans alike. Lights streak red, orange and yellow flares, like a swirling sunset above a band of humans dressed in glittery leotards. They're playing an assortment of instruments, the music part dance, part rock, and loud enough to drown out every other thought in my head.

If the Void is the ailment, Dionysus could well be the cure.

'Going to join them?' a voice says from behind me.

I jump, spinning round to find Sathanas looking over my shoulder, styled much the same as yesterday: hair slicked back, dark trousers, a shirt he can't seem to find the top two buttons for.

'No,' I say, just to be contrary. It's either that or make a sarcastic comment that it's nice he's decided he has the time to talk after throwing me out yesterday. 'Are you?'

'My presence is required on occasion. It helps to keep things in order.'

'Isn't that what your demons are for? They look scarier than you.' I make a show of inspecting him. 'Or do your horns only come out when you're mad?'

His lips twitch. 'I don't have horns. Visible or otherwise.'

A group of humans give us curious glances as they exit the cave, and all emotion dissipates from his face. He nods at me like I'm no more than a stranger he's passed on the street, making to go inside, but –

'Wait,' I say. 'What about the next task? You said we'd talk –'

'Not *here*.' Shadows ripple down his arms. He jerks his head for me to follow him away from the entrance, into a nearby alcove sandwiched between two great columns of rock, one

78

that's too narrow for us both to stand in comfortably without touching.

'We shouldn't speak in public,' he says. 'If word gets out about the tasks they'll be queuing for my attention.'

'You spoke to me first,' I remind him. 'And I wouldn't have to ask questions if you told me what I wanted to know. My next task. When is it?'

'Next month, we'll –'

'Next *month*?' I don't shriek, but it's close. 'I can't wait a month! I have to –'

'There will be one a month until you finish. Or fail.' His tone is flat, and I can't read whether he's annoyed by my outrage or disappointed he's stuck with me for this length of time. 'You have six more in total.'

Six more. That's six *months*. How am I going to survive here for six months? 'Sathanas – Your Majesty –' My fingers curl into the fabric of his shirt.

'Sath will do,' he says, like that's the most important part of the conversation.

'*Sath*.' I yank the material so hard he's forced to brace a hand above my head to prevent from crashing into me. 'I am *not* staying here for six months.'

He pulls my clenched fist away from his shirt, forcing it to drop back to my side. 'It's the way it is.'

'But –' My complaint is cut short by the feeling of Sath going rigid. 'What is it?'

He presses a finger to my lips, and it's blazing hot, like heated metal. 'Stay here.'

I'm left standing alone in the alcove, scowling at the empty space he's left behind. You'd think after all the practice I've had that I'd be good at doing what I'm told, but the part of me I've never been able to tame, the part that always dreamed of more to my existence than textbooks and early nights, has me bouncing on my feet, not wanting to stay anywhere.

Tentatively, I lean out and peek round the column to see what's upset him. The demon with the shaggy hair from yesterday is heading our way, dragging his bony tail along the ground. It ends in a sharp spike that emits sparks as it moves. Show-off.

'Aric,' Sath calls out as the demon approaches. 'You're not going into Dionysus?'

'Not today. A human looked at me funny. Now we're playing hide-and-seek.'

'I see.' Although Sath's tone is clipped, he doesn't add anything to dissuade Aric, which is ridiculous when *of course* this human was looking at him funny. Aric has sharp claws and a spiked tail; who wouldn't do a double take at that? My foot taps a beat. I want to say something. Do something. But bursting into the open is something Bad Decision Willow would do, and I'm only making good decisions from now on.

I dig my nails into my palms.

'I'm going to tear him apart when I find him,' Aric says dreamily.

The scrape of metal on rock makes me wince, sounding the alarm that he's resumed his journey.

'No,' Sath says. 'Bring him to me. I'll do it.'

I freeze. All that talk about how this place was a fresh start, a chance to live again, and his only response to a non-existent infraction is to offer to provide the punishment himself? Some middle ground.

'Aric!' A third voice chimes from the corridor. 'Look who I've found.'

I recognise that voice. It's the Sorter, only she sounds a lot happier than when I last saw her. And I have a horrible feeling I know exactly who she's found. My stomach drops. Surely, *surely*, Sath will put a stop to this now.

All he says is, 'Allow me.'

There's a scuffle of movement, a yelp, and the music inside Dionysus stops, replaced by claps and jeers. A moment later, the drums resume, but it's not the start of a song. It's a countdown.

I creep out from the alcove and into Dionysus as surreptitiously as I can, keeping to the edge of the cave and ducking behind two humans who reek of body odour, peering through the crack between them. The heat in here is overwhelming. Sweat drips down my neck; I'm standing too close to the lava drizzling down the walls.

At least it's a distraction from the way my gut twists around itself, tying into knots I'll never undo. Sath has dragged a man on to the dance floor and forced him to his knees. The man trembles as Sath towers over him, his face devoid of all emotion. Like the man is *nothing* to him; no more than a broken toy ready to be discarded. Sheets of shadows wrap around Sath's arms. Demons stand around them, forked tongues flicking out like they can taste the man's fear. Maybe they can. Aric is to Sath's right, grinning so wide he displays a pearly-white set of fangs.

Then he rushes forward, pouncing on the man, biting into his neck, and the chanting of the demons gets louder and louder, the beat of the drums gets faster; blood sprays over the floor as another demon joins in, and the man's screaming, and *I* want to scream because they're going to rip him apart and no one's doing anything to stop it, and if they keep going his body will be destroyed, his soul lost to the Void for thousands of years, to hear those voices and his worst memories over and over again. And he's not done anything *wrong*.

'Enough.' Sath's voice is louder than the drums, the demons' jeering. For a split second I think Aric might disobey, but then he rises to his feet, red staining his jaw as he resumes his place at Sath's side. The man's curled himself into a ball, trembling arms wrapped around his knees. He rocks back and forth, whimpering, reminding me that no matter how *interesting* a day I've had, this place is nothing more than a nightmare waiting to invade your dreams.

A hush falls throughout the room. 'What is his crime?' Sath asks in a soft voice. This isn't the gentle softness from yesterday, when he spoke of Elysium, but the quiet lull that comes before a storm, where the clouds are gathering and the air feels charged.

'I told you.' Aric folds his arms, resembling a petulant child. 'He looked at me. Like he was thinking of hurting me.'

Please. I've never heard such a blatant lie.

'Is that true?' Sath asks the man.

The man shakes his head.

'He was found by the river, trying to escape,' the Sorter chimes in. Her eyes glitter with malice.

There's a sharp intake of breath from the humans. They're like an audience who've been to every show and have memorised every twist, and they're not excited about what's coming.

82

'Ah,' Sath says. 'Did I not make the rules on escape attempts clear?'

The demons press closer, forming a tighter semicircle around them.

'I wasn't . . . I didn't . . .'

'Was my hospitality not good enough for you?' Sath readjusts his collar, before glancing over at the humans, all clustered together like our numbers will be enough to save us. 'And what about the rest of you? Are you enjoying what Asphodel has to offer?'

Nobody speaks.

'Would anybody else like to go in the river?' he asks. Carefully, deliberately, he undoes the buttons of his shirt cuffs, rolling the sleeves up to his elbows and tucking them in just as slowly. The room stays silent. 'As I thought.'

The man whimpers. 'I want to go home.'

Quick as a flash, Sath pulls him into the air, holding him by the throat while his feet dangle somewhere around Sath's knees. 'This is your home,' Sath says, voice like ice. 'A pity you didn't accept that. Now, what am I to do with you?'

Immediately, the demons chant, '*Tartarus! Tartarus!*'

Sath's jaw is locked, his shoulders tight. More black shadows ripple down his arms, and then they set alight, because they're not shadows at all, but dark flames that burn down his newly exposed forearms, his hands, leaping on to the man who immediately goes quiet as the flames form a cloak around him, shielding him from view. Some of the demons clap.

The Sorter, I notice, doesn't. She's scowling. So is Aric.

The flames subside once the man's fully disintegrated into

ash, smouldering flakes floating into the air like errant dust particles. I stare at those fragments of a person, of a life, as they drift from the room. Gone. Lost to the Void. Sath brushes his hands on his trousers. He's unscathed, like he hasn't just set himself on fire and burned someone. Not a single strand of hair is out of place.

I should have asked more questions before agreeing to work with him.

A split-second decision is a bad decision. I've done it again, haven't I? Fuck. *Fuck.* Even when my intentions are good I get everything wrong.

I promised myself I wouldn't be fooled by the way he looks, the way he appears more human than the others. But he's not, and I fell for it. I made a deal with the Devil – a cold, unfeeling murderer – and I have no idea what the consequences are going to be.

I need to find out. The music resumes, and the demons immediately return to gyrating, tails swaying in time to the beat, not caring that they're trampling over someone's remains.

Sath leaves them to it, stepping from the dance floor and leaving Dionysus without giving them a backwards glance. Without giving *me* a backwards glance. I'm storming after him before I can stop myself – swerving a demon with antlers that's approaching like it intends to drag me on to the dance floor – determined to discover who, exactly, I've aligned with.

By the time I've weaved my way out, he's halfway down the corridor, shrouded in smoke.

'Wait!'

I expect him to outright ignore me, but to my surprise, he

halts and turns around. His eyes are more ablaze than ever, shining so brightly I could be basking in the sun. Instead, I'm frozen. My heart pounds faster than the drums in Dionysus. Confronting a murderer doesn't scream sensible, but if he's planning on sending me to the Void at some point, we may as well get it over with. And if he *doesn't* burn me to ash for yelling at him about what he's just done, I'll know he really does need me to stick around and complete these tasks.

Which means I'll have some leverage over him.

'What were you thinking?' I ask.

He looks away, clenching and unclenching his fists. When he meets my stare again, his gaze has dimmed from molten gold to honey brown. 'Not now.'

'Yes, now.' I fold my arms. There's something liberating about picking a fight with someone you don't care about. He can hate me all he likes after this and I won't wake up desperate to plead my case, to beg him to return, to admonish myself for saying all the wrong things. It makes me bold. 'How can you justify what you did? Do you really think that man deserved to be sent to the Void?'

'Would it make a difference if I said no?'

'No. If anything, that'd make it worse. Because you did it anyway.' I can't believe I was foolish enough to make a deal with him.

Sath runs a hand through his hair. 'He was caught. There are rules here, ones I have to follow. The demons will accept nothing else. He had to be punished.'

'Why are you bowing to the whims of the demons? Aren't you the one in charge?'

'Pardoning him would set a precedent.' His jaw clenches. 'I did the best I could with the situation at hand.'

How can he say that? How can he *possibly* say that?

'You didn't have to set him on fire! You should've –'

'I should've *what*?' Sath closes in on me, forcing me against the wall. My back thuds against stone as hard as his expression. 'They wanted to send him to Tartarus. He'd have been tortured, torn apart and stitched together until the end of time. I spared him that pain. Those flames were a quick end, where I ensured he felt nothing.'

Oh. My shoulders sink. That's better than what I was imagining, I suppose, but – 'You still should've let him go. He'd done nothing wrong, and now he's spending eons in the Void with his worst memories because of *you*.'

His throat bobs as fresh wisps of flame loop down his arm. 'I did what I had to.'

'Then you're as bad as any demon,' I say, ignoring the way he flinches. I'm the one with the power now. By trying to rationalise his actions, he's played his hand – if he wants me to forgive him, it means he needs me. So, I take a deep breath and say, 'Which means I quit.'

'You *what*?'

'You heard me.' I shrug. 'I don't trust you. So, I quit. I won't do the tasks.'

He can't mask the flare of panic on his face in time. I press my lips together to hide my smile. When I agreed to his deal I was backed into a corner, unable to think about what I was agreeing to. From his expression, the taste of his own medicine is *quite* the bitter experience.

'You can't quit.' There's an edge of desperation in his voice. 'You want to go home, don't you?'

'Not if it means working with you,' I say. Then, idly, I add, 'Of course, I could be persuaded to reconsider.'

'Really,' he says flatly. I can't tell if he wants to laugh or strangle me. Maybe he wants to laugh *while* strangling me. 'Let me guess. You want something.'

'I want to know what you're getting out of this. Why do you want me to complete these tasks so badly?'

Chatter rings out in the distance – a group of humans who've left Dionysus are staggering down the corridor we're occupying.

Sath huffs, closing the gap between us and angling his body so all they'll see is the back of his head. I stiffen. He's too close like this. 'I can tell you this much,' he murmurs, breath fanning my face, 'if you were to succeed, a certain concession would be granted to me. Something I want very much.'

'But you won't tell me what it is.' For all I know, his concession could be *let's close that loophole where a girl gets to go home if she completes a series of stupid tasks.* 'If it's that important, why wait till now to offer the tasks to someone?'

'You assume you're the first.' His hand snakes around my waist, drawing me flush against him as the humans pass. I wriggle as he dips his head, placing his mouth to my ear and whispering, 'You're not.'

'And what happened to the last one?' The humans disappear round the corner, and I shove him away. 'Let me guess. You won't tell me that either. Because I won't like the answer, will I?'

He sighs. 'If you must know, they're in the Void. But –' he holds up a hand to stop me interrupting – 'only because they tried other means of escaping after they failed. I couldn't save them any more than I could save that man tonight. But if you fail, that doesn't have to be your ending. Not if you behave afterwards.'

Oh, good. Behaving. The one skill I don't have. Plus – 'How do I know you're not lying?'

'If I wanted to harm you, Willow, there are far easier ways for me to do it.'

He makes a good point. I look away from him, thinking. Aric's tail has marked a path where he scraped his spike on the floor, the line like chalk on a playground, only this game is far more dangerous.

I can't stay here. I can't trust Sath. I'm floundering in the dark, searching for a solution that doesn't exist, unable to make a good choice because there's none to be found.

'Come on,' he coaxes. 'We both know you don't want to quit. This is your only way home. You need me as much as I need you.' His tone is all charm now, laced with seduction and sin.

'In that case, don't do that. Don't be all . . . devily around me. If you need me so badly, you don't get to treat me as some subject you can manipulate and threaten.'

His brow quirks. 'Devily?'

'What? It could be a word.'

He snorts, shaking his head. 'Fine. Agree to continue with the tasks, and I promise, in private, I'll try and be less . . . devily, as you put it.'

'And in public?'

The humour dissipates from his face. 'I won't lie. If you're seen challenging me, I'll be forced to do to you what I did to that man.'

I swallow.

'What do you say?' His eyes gleam. 'Truce?'

The only thing stronger than my uncertainty is my desperation to leave.

'If I say yes, it doesn't mean I agree with what you did.'

'I don't blame you.'

'I think it makes this place just as bad as Tartarus.'

'The demons will be delighted to hear it.'

'And if I discover this concession of yours will hurt me, I'll find a way to put you in the Void instead.'

He inhales. 'Noted.'

Since he's being agreeable, I try, 'And if you wanted to do the next task right away and get me out sooner, I'd be okay with that.'

'I'm sure you would be.' He grins. The expression is so transformative I have to blink several times. 'I'll see you next month. Try not to get in trouble in the meantime.'

10

Trouble has a habit of finding me whether I go looking for it or not.

The first week, I keep to my room, scratching off the days on my wardrobe. It's safer that way. I stare at the four walls with nothing better to do than dwell on all the things I miss about home. The days where Noah's in a good mood and he brings me pastries in the morning. Where we spend hours lying in the park, hands entwined, and evenings in crowded bars filled with laughter – Sasha's loudest of all.

On day eight, I risk going to Dionysus again. Being driven mad by boredom and longing is just as dangerous as entering that dance floor. If a distraction's what I need to get through this, I don't see how that can be a crime. Hands caress my waist, my hips – at one point I'm pretty sure a cold pair of lips skim my neck. At first, I cringe away. Noah and his ring are waiting for me back home.

I hope he's missing me.

I hope he's missing me so much that, when I get home, the relief of seeing me is enough for him to never want to lose me again, and all our days turn into good days.

But that only makes me realise that missing me is not the same as waiting for me. He thinks I'm dead and gone for good. What if, by the time I return, he's moved on? The idea of arriving on his doorstep to find I've been replaced has me letting the next pair of hands stay where they are. Demon, human, I don't care. Something about the music makes me too delirious to worry who they belong to.

This repeats, night after night after night, time stretching in immeasurable amounts, like the sun has risen and set above us and we're still going in a blur of motion. I never see the same group of humans twice – apart from one. Harper. She always smiles and waves me over, and I always respond with a shake of my head, ignoring the yearning in my belly that wants to tug me towards her. Friendships in the afterlife have the potential to be permanent – for everyone but me.

Time moves so strangely in Dionysus that when I do stumble back to my room, it's hard to know whether I should be adding one scratch or two to my makeshift calendar. I get confirmation I've miscounted when I open my door on what should have been day twenty-five to find Sath waiting for me, leaning against the opposite wall. He's dressed more casually than usual; instead of a shirt he wears a cream jumper that's softened with age, paired with dark jeans and canvas shoes. I guess he's taking Not Being Devily seriously.

'Good morning,' he says.

'It's been a month already?'

'It has.' He glances around, checking for witnesses before holding out a hand. 'Ready?'

As if he needs to ask. Not caring what I might be in for, I grab his outstretched hand. Immediately, his grip tightens, and he tugs me towards him with such force I slam into his chest. I let out a startled gasp, trying to push him away. 'What are you –'

He flashes a wicked smile. 'Hold on tight.'

Everything goes black, similar to when he took me into my memory, only this time we're spinning, my feet lifting from the ground while air rushes past my ears, and we drop into a tunnel with a pop. I stumble from the force of the landing, careering straight into a wall and scraping my palms on rough stone.

'You could've warned me.' I whirl on him. 'I get carsick.'

'Good job we weren't in a car,' Sath says lazily. He looks immaculate, not a hair out of place or wrinkle on his clothing to be seen. 'Come on. There's still a way to go; I can't portal us directly into where we're going.'

We're in a darker, danker part of Asphodel than I've discovered on my explorations so far. As I follow him, I get the sense we're further underground than ever. Water drips from the ceiling, plopping a steady beat into an ever-growing puddle beneath my feet, and the stench of damp and mould lingers in the air.

Torches are staked into the ground, but they're dim and don't give off any heat. I shiver, wishing Sath had thought to tell me he'd chosen a jumper for good reason. My plain white tee is not up to the task of keeping me warm.

'Where are we?'

He doesn't answer until we reach the end of the tunnel. A rounded door stained red with rust is inset into the wall, a set of thick bolts sealing it shut. 'The Vaults of Asphodel,' he finally replies.

'Right.' My throat is dry. 'And what's inside?'

'Centuries worth of treasure. Some items the demons have pillaged, some the Sorter stole from dead bodies.'

Instinctively, my hand goes to my wrist. Sath's gaze follows the movement, locking on my fingers as they skim the empty space where my bracelet used to be. Anger flares at the thought the Sorter might have taken it from me while I was lying there all . . . I shudder.

'Are you all right?' he asks.

'Fine.' I crack my neck. I can't think about my bracelet right now. The task. Focus on the task. 'What do I have to do?'

Sath merely smirks, and blows the door off its hinges.

I gasp, stumbling as the blast buffets me backwards. The door falls at a ninety-degree angle, first with a groan and then with an almighty thud as it crashes to the ground. The whole cave reverberates with the impact. I gape at him. 'You couldn't have used a key? What if someone heard?'

'Demons don't come down here any more, and I've made sure the Sorter's occupied.' Sath shrugs. 'The door's easily repaired.'

I'm not convinced the theatrics were necessary, although I'm intrigued by *how* he did it. First fire, then portals, then door ripping. With his mind. My stomach knots, but it's not fear. It's . . . want. Life would be easy if I had that kind of power. Nobody would judge me or tell me what I can or can't do, too blinded by my abilities to notice all the shortcomings hidden behind the smokescreen.

The interior of the vault hums, and there's a sense of magic in the air, so powerful it feels like I'm walking into a room with excess gravity, the pressure slamming into me, making me dizzy. The ground is streaked with sand as golden as the bullion stacked from floor to ceiling. Glass cabinets hold a collection of sparkling diamond necklaces, jewelled rings, bracelets and earrings.

My focus is on the tiara.

Silver, studded with rubies, it sits on a plump purple cushion in the middle of the vault. My mouth salivates. How powerful would I feel if I had *that*? For a fleeting second, I picture myself wearing it on the snake throne Sath occupied the day I arrived. The image sends a thrill through me I can't explain, but I push it aside. I don't want to sit on a random throne in Asphodel. I want to go home.

With that tiara. The tiara is important.

Why do you never bring me anything, Willow? That's Mum's voice. *The prize money would have been yours if you'd tried harder.*

I swallow. I'd come second in a science competition and she'd been furious when I'd returned empty-handed. Never mind the bags under my eyes because I'd been working on my project until midnight for weeks, or that the winner had the advantage of being the son of an actual physicist. All I heard at dinner was that I'd failed, and failure wasn't an option, not in this household. I'd shrunk into my seat as the mantra played on repeat, my clenched fists shaking and teeth biting my tongue to stop myself rising to my own defence, knowing my defences weren't defences at all, but excuses. If I'd tried harder, I could have won.

Dad left soon after that.

Now look what you've done.

The next award I lost out on, I reached into the winner's bag when they weren't looking and fished out the trophy along with the envelope of prize money. You'd think I'd have brought home this tiara, the way she reacted, calling her friends, blowing up Dad's phone telling him there was finally something worth coming home for. He never responded. Then I got found out, and the screaming started anew.

Well, you can make it up to me now, can't you? It's still her voice, but it's been twisted somehow, turning deeper and more guttural, like something demonic has corrupted the sound.

Take the crown. Bring it home. You'll be sensational.

I would be. I picture it now. Mum always said working hard was meaningless if you had nothing to show for it, nothing tangible to prove your success, but nobody would question how hard I worked if I returned home drowning in gems. They'd take one look at me and assume I was capable of anything. I'd be Willow the Failure no more.

The thought has me salivating harder.

I'd surpass Mum, even. That tiara is better than all her possessions combined. I could plant it pride of place in her collection of things, outshining every crystal ornament until it succumbed to dust like the rest of them.

'Beautiful, isn't it?' Sath murmurs.

It is. The force of magic in the air intensifies and I can't move away, not from him, nor the tiara. It's mesmerising, the way it glitters. It looks bigger, now. Heavier. The gems are like fat teardrops. My arm outstretches. I want to touch it. Hold it. Place it on my head. Maybe I'll take some coins too, and build my own throne of gold. Nobody can judge me if I own *everything*. Sath's hand is on my back, nudging me forward, urging me on, on, on.

I don't need his assistance. This is exactly where I want to be. Here, with my shinys. I sway a little. Then swallow. I'm definitely drooling.

'It would be lovely on you, don't you think?' His voice is like a lullaby.

He's right. It would.

Sath trails a finger down my arm. 'Why don't you put it on?' His finger stops on my wrist, right over my fluttering pulse point, and I frown.

The skin he's touching shouldn't be bare. I used to have a bracelet there. The memory is vague. It's hard to imagine the shape of it. The way it weighed on my wrist. But it meant something. It was given to me on the one day I'd done something to make Mum pleased.

If I take the tiara now, I won't get that chance again.

Why do you never bring me anything, Willow?

'No,' I whisper. Stealing that prize money didn't work. Stealing the tiara won't work either.

The tiara shines brighter, reminding me what I'm declining. The vision of me on the snake throne floods my mind again, but this time there are familiar faces kneeling at my feet: my parents, Sath, Noah, Sasha, all gazing at me reverently, whispering their approval. Only someone brilliant and wonderful would wear that tiara. My fingers twitch.

I'd give anything to be considered brilliant and wonderful.

But first I have to earn it.

'No,' I say again, with more conviction.

'No?' I can practically *hear* the eyebrow raise in his voice. His lips press against the shell of my ear. 'Think how ravishing you'd look in a crown, Willow.'

'I don't want a crown,' I say firmly. 'I want to go home and make amends. Owning something shiny doesn't make me a better person.'

'Are you sure?' He's playing with me, like a cat toying with a mouse it wants to eat for dinner.

I spin round to face him. 'I'm sure.'

'Last chance.' Sath hooks a necklace on to his index finger. He pulls my hair to one side, and I arch my neck instinctively, giving him room to lay it across my collarbone, shuddering beneath its cold weight. Sath studies it, then me, his gaze so molten I could sink into it. 'Wouldn't you like to keep this? It makes your eyes shine. Your face glow. It really is fit for a –'

'I said –' I force the word out – 'no.'

'Well, all right. You win. You've passed the second task.' He smiles, but the moment feels kind of anticlimactic. At least, it does until he jerks his head at the necklace. 'You should keep that. A gift, for doing well today.'

'Really?' I brighten, tracing a finger over the thick chain. It's no tiara, but it's *something*. A sign I can do this. I'm about to fasten it, to show off my accomplishment for all the world to see, when something about Sath's posture makes me pause. Despite the casual way he leans against a cabinet, hands tucked into his pockets, there's a tension in his shoulders that wasn't there before. I cock my head, studying him. 'You didn't give me a gift for passing the first test.'

'A mistake I need to rectify.' The smile fixed on his face doesn't meet his eyes. 'You should always have a present for doing well. Take the necklace. You've earned it.'

I don't feel like I've earned it. The same way I never felt like I earned my bracelet either, because Mum pulled strings to get me on that course. I'd been so greedy for the approval it offered that I'd slapped it around my wrist anyway.

'Go on,' Sath says. 'You deserve this. Have it.'

I want to believe him. I want this necklace as proof I've done something right. But it feels more like a choker now, tightening into a noose that strangles my every breath, reminding me that doing well comes with expectations to do even better next time.

This necklace, just like the bracelet, is a trap. A carefully constructed fake floor concealing a pit beneath, and once I've tumbled in the only way out is to build a ladder of meaningless things, always seeking the next rung in the hope that it'll raise me to the surface.

For once, just once, I'd prefer my one deed to be enough.

For me alone, unadorned by trinkets of victory, to be *enough*.

I pull the necklace from my chest and dangle it in front of Sath's face. 'I don't need a present,' I say. 'I just need to get out of here.'

He studies me, smile growing wider. I glower in return. There's a silver trident hanging on the wall behind him, and I fill the silence picturing it falling on his head.

Finally, he nods. '*Now* you've passed greed.'

The magical energy pressing on my head lifts and it becomes easier to breathe, like I've entered a room with air-conditioning after running a marathon in suffocating heat.

Perfect. Wonderful. I can't bring myself to be relieved as he takes the necklace from me and returns it to its case.

'You didn't have to lie to me.' I stomp towards the exit,

wanting nothing more to do with this vault full of things I can't have. He reaches out a hand as I pass, fingers encircling my wrist.

'For what it's worth,' he says, 'the necklace might have been a lie, but you did do well.'

His words suffuse me with a warmth no necklace could imbue.

'Oh.' I tuck a strand of hair behind my ear. 'Thanks.'

We leave the vault side by side. The tunnel is brighter now, torches burning with more strength, revealing all the things I missed before, including doors, row upon row of them, all covered in white marks, like someone – or something – has drawn their claws across the wood.

'What is this place?' I ask.

Sath's footsteps falter. 'We're in the Old Tunnels.'

Goosebumps erupt on my arm. 'You mean the place you ordered us to avoid?' The place the Sorter told me they'd used as torture chambers.

Without waiting for permission, I shove open the nearest door. Inside, a lone iron maiden stands well over six foot tall, with a screaming head sat atop the chamber. It's wide open, a copper taint covering spikes which protrude, sharp and gleaming, from both sides.

'We don't use this area any more. I managed to put a stop to that, at least.' Sath sounds bitter, self-deprecating.

I almost retort, *now you set humans on fire instead*, but when I glance at him, the barb sticks in my throat. His fists are clenched so tight his knuckles are deathly white, and he can't bring himself to meet my gaze. I think he might be shaking.

And I don't think it's an act.

Maybe I'm a fool. Maybe this is all part of an illusion and

I'm yet to witness the big reveal. For now though, I believe it. 'We should go,' I say softly. 'I've seen enough.'

Sath does look at me now, surprise in his eyes, like he was expecting a blow that never came.

Further down the corridor, a door slams.

His head snaps in the direction of the noise.

'I thought you said nobody came down here?' My pulse kicks up a notch, fluttering with panic.

Sath blocks the doorway as he scans the corridor, while I bounce up and down, trying to peer over his shoulder. I'd be less afraid if I knew what was going on.

Another door slams.

And another. And another. Every single door in this whole damn tunnel is opening, shutting, opening, shutting, and something is wailing, high-pitched and shrill. I clamp my hands over my ears to try and deafen it before it deafens me. An icy wind sweeps into the room, the gust blowing me backwards, back towards the *maiden* –

'Sath!'

He either doesn't hear me or doesn't care, because it's not affecting *him*, he's a great oak weathering a storm while little Willow over here gets blown about. I dig my feet into the floor to stop myself moving any further towards that contraption, and am considering tugging on his arm for some attention, when everything stops.

I gasp. 'What's –'

'Shh.' Sath spins round. His eyes glow, and even in those human clothes he is painfully inhuman. 'We're not alone.'

11

'What –'

'What part of *shh* –' Sath closes the gap between us – 'did you not understand?'

I purse my lips. He seems quite distressed by the idea of one of his demons running around. If he's the one in charge, can't he tell them to go away? I would ask, but I am extremely busy being quiet. I fix him with a glare so he knows how much I'm enjoying being given orders.

'I suppose asking you to stay hidden while I deal with them is too much to ask?' Sath says.

I smile sweetly. 'Thought you told me not to speak?'

Sath looks torn between rolling his eyes and throttling me. Black flames swirl down his arms, sending a blaze of heat over my face, but I don't recoil. Despite everything, I'm confident these flames aren't designed to hurt me.

In fact, they're not designed to burn at all, but create. The flames twist and turn around one another, forming into metal. A dagger. Sath passes it to me without a word. It's heavier than I expected, with an intricate floral pattern carved into the handle. The blade is curved and deadly sharp.

Seriously, is there nothing he can't do? 'How –'

'Not now, Willow.' His flames are already forging something else, something bigger. A sword this time, made of black metal that flickers blue when he waves it in the air. A sapphire gleams from a pommel inset into the hilt, with a rainbow of six smaller gems encircling it.

I'm suddenly less touched by the fact he gave me a knife.

'Why don't I get a sword?' I grumble.

I'm not provided with an answer, so I can only assume he's doing it to be difficult. Leaving the iron maiden behind, we head into the corridor, Sath in front. He stops when we reach a fork, head cocked to one side, before taking the right-hand turn decisively.

Something in the furthest room is screeching.

'Stay behind me at all times,' he orders. 'Or, better yet, don't come in at all.'

Unfortunately for Sath, my disposition has always leaned towards disobedience. Plus, there's no way my curiosity is going to allow me to stay behind. It's a shame we don't have phones here; I'd be an internet sensation if I got footage of whatever's in this room.

Sath kicks the door in, despite a perfectly good handle being right there, waiting for it to crash to the ground before stepping over the splintered wood. My curiosity is immediately washed away by a wave of fear.

Because it's not one demon. It's five. And unlike the demons I've seen here so far, there are no human-like qualities to them at all.

They're shaped like bats, if anything. They shriek and extend their wings at the sight of us, membranous tissue stretching out wide. They'd be kind of cute, if they were smaller. And didn't have fangs.

And weren't flying towards me.

One shoots through the doorway and dive-bombs into my chest. I go down. Hard. My teeth rattle as it leaps atop me, jaw opening wide, stretching longer than its whole head. Oh shit. I kick and scream and writhe beneath it, hopelessly unequipped for this. I've never taken a self-defence class in my life.

Perhaps I should have listened to Sath when he suggested I hide.

Sath. The knife he gave me is still in my slick grip. I twist, trying to shove it upwards at something, anything, that might hurt it. The thing shrieks again, and then it's leaning towards me, mouth descending towards my neck, pincer-sharp fangs inches from me now; my heart beats a frantic rhythm in my chest, slamming against my ribcage as teeth graze my skin, and I refuse, I simply *refuse*, to let it bite a chunk out of me.

Using abdominal muscles I'm shocked to discover I possess, I sit up and headbutt its muzzle. The bat flies backwards in a gust of wind, hurtling into the room towards Sath. He shoots a bolt of fire, but it dives out of the way before reversing and coming for me again.

I jump to my feet, lashing out, trying to shove it; it swerves my hand and sinks its teeth straight into my forearm. *Fuck*.

The knife drops from my hand. My scream echoes through the corridor. Tears leak from the corners of my eyes. Sath calls out a warning, but what good is that to me; I need him *here*, now, fighting it off.

A quick glimpse into the room, now flooding with smoke

as he sidesteps a two-pronged attack, tells me he won't be coming any time soon.

Well, fine. I growl, both at the bat and the situation, and yank its ear. Its mouth loosens and I drag my arm free, diving to the floor and scrambling for my knife. My vision blurs as a fresh spike of pain shoots through me, but I don't stop moving. I find the hilt of the blade.

The shadow of the bat looms overhead, and I whirl round, shoving the weapon straight into its belly. It meets resistance and I slam it harder, my teeth grinding together with the effort. Black blood spurts out the edges of the wound. I twist the knife, dragging it up and round its insides; it squeaks and squeaks and I don't care, I have to kill it – tears run down my cheeks, but I can't stop, not until it's *shut up*.

Finally, it slumps forward. I pull the knife out and scuttle away, trembling. The blood on my hands is almost like tar, so sticky I can't shake it off no matter how hard I try. I stare at the body, panting.

Something crashes inside the room. My knees threaten to buckle as I hobble over to check if I can assist in any way. Running would be the safer option, but, apparently, I hate myself.

The room is a replica of the previous: an empty cave, save for the iron maiden in the centre. Sath is battling the final bat, his arms aflame, shooting arrows of fire at its head. But it's too quick. It ducks and dodges each attack, wings flapping furiously. Sweat gleams on Sath's face.

He's killed the other three, at least. Their heads are rolling around near the doorway, while their bodies twitch in the far corner. I avert my gaze in time to find the bat hurtling straight for me. I raise my knife – I shouldn't have come back for Sath, *why* did I come back for Sath? – but before the bat can reach me, Sath's there, back to my chest, pressing me into the wall and shielding me from the oncoming attack.

The bat crashes into him instead, the tip of its wings slicing into his stomach. He shudders against me, and his flames go out. I check his hands: empty. His sword has disappeared.

But I still have my knife.

The bat rears, gearing up for another charge.

'Sath, *duck*,' I whisper.

He drops, rolling underneath the bat as it lunges, allowing me to plunge the knife into its eye. No hesitation this time. I don't care. Not about the blood, or its scream, or the fact I've taken another life. It's a demon. A monster. It deserves to hurt. I picture Aric's face when he watched that man burn, and I want to stab the bat again. I want to stab it over and over and over – I'm breathing hard by the time I realise I've driven the knife so deep the bat is spasming around the weapon, like I've embedded it into its nervous system.

I gasp, squashing that lingering urge for *more*, and pull the knife out. The bat falls to the ground. Blood oozes around its body like an oil spill. I look away, feeling distinctly nauseous, my rage dimmed by the sudden silence in the room. The initial sting in my arm has subsided to a dull ache, and I flex it to check everything's still working before looking over at Sath.

He's coated in more blood than me – I guess from all the beheading he was doing while I was busy getting bitten – and it leaves streaks over his face, his neck, his hands. His cream jumper is ruined.

There's also red pooling across his stomach.

'You're hurt,' I say, fighting the entirely inappropriate instinct to reach out and inspect the wound. He does not need me to care for him. He probably doesn't *want* me to care for him. But he did get that injury defending me, which is making me feel all kinds of inconvenient things like gratitude and guilt. I lock my arms to my sides, just to be safe.

Sath lifts his jumper to reveal a sliver of tanned skin with a deep cut sliced through the muscle. 'It's nothing.'

'That is not nothing.' My hands are pressed against his flesh before I can stop them. I pause. Look up at him. Touching the Devil is probably a massive no-no. But the wound is deep, and he isn't doing anything to stem the bleeding. Instead, he's staring at me, a muscle in his cheek ticking. 'Will you heal, like, magically? Or I could try and . . . I don't know, stitch it, or something.'

I say that like I have any idea *how* to stitch a wound. Blood, fresh and red, coats my hands as it leaks over my fingers. It's so . . . human. So different to what came out of those bats.

'I'll heal.' He frowns, noticing my arm for the first time. 'You're hurt too.'

I wince as he lifts my arm, examining the twin puncture marks the bat left behind. His fingers prod my skin, his touch deft and light as he brushes blood away using his thumb. I step closer, like he's a magnet, drawing me in. Beneath my hand, I can feel his stomach rise and fall with his every breath.

And I feel it stop moving when his breath hitches.

I peer at him, and something in the air shifts. I seem to have taken another step without knowing it. He's dangerously close now, our chests almost brushing, and although he's staring at my arm I don't think that's where his attention is. His eyes flare.

'Why do they do that?' I ask. 'Your eyes. Sometimes they're brown, and sometimes they're like . . . molten gold.'

Sath inhales. When he finally meets my gaze, his eyes are brown again, but I'm sure something flickers beneath the surface, like a candle behind a curtain threatening to burn the whole building down.

'My powers come from Tartarus,' he tells me. 'The flames of Hell itself, to be used at whim. You only see it when it comes to the surface. Sometimes it happens when I want it to. Sometimes it's when I lose control of . . . certain emotions.'

'And what happens when you lose control?'

His grip on my arm tightens. I return the favour by pressing harder on his stomach. We've just fought side by side – don't I deserve the truth? There's a beat, two, three, before he finally speaks.

'It can be overwhelming, sometimes,' he says in a hoarse voice. 'It's hard to know what's real and what's my power, whispering dark things in my head, encouraging me to do worse. The feeling of . . .' He breaks off, shaking his head. 'I should clean your wound.'

I narrow my eyes, debating whether or not to let him get away with that half answer, but am immediately distracted by his nail digging into one of my puncture wounds.

'Ow!' I'm about to push him off when he stops me with a look.

'Sorry,' he says, still probing the bite mark. 'They have toxins in their saliva. Their poison can't kill you, but –'

His nail presses harder into the wound, and I nearly bite my tongue to stop from screaming, clutching a handful of his jumper. My vision blurs, and I go hot and cold all at once. The next thing I know, Sath's hand is off my arm and on my hip instead, palm splayed over the waistband of my jeans to stop me falling.

'Ouch,' I say.

When he's sure I'm not about to keel over, Sath holds up a finger. At first, I think he's trying to show me my own blood, and I'm about to tell him I have no interest in beholding such a thing, when I spot a speck of acid green glistening amid the crimson. Sath offers me a satisfied smile. 'All gone.'

I take my hand off his stomach. He can bleed out for all I care. 'You couldn't have tried being gentle?'

His smile is positively feline. 'That *was* me being gentle.'

When I leave this place, I'm buying him a dictionary. Huffing, I stare at the corpses littering the floor. 'You said no demons come down here. And why do they look so . . . different?'

'All demons used to look like humans, once. The more time spent in Tartarus giving in to their basest urges, the more beastly they became.' He bends to inspect one. 'I've not seen these before. They've arrived recently.'

'From Tartarus? But . . . how . . . ?'

'It's a good question.' Sath straightens, brushing dust from his trousers – as though that's the problem with how he looks, and not the bloodstains. He glances at me. 'There's something I want to show you. First, though, I need to burn the bodies.

Help me pile them up, would you?'

It's unclear why we can't leave them here to rot, but I retrieve the one I killed in the corridor with only a small amount of whinging, while Sath manages the other four.

'Demons can't die in Asphodel,' he tells me as he sets the bodies alight. 'Their wounds will stitch together and return them to life. Only the flames of Tartarus can truly destroy a demon and send it back whence it came.'

I watch as those flames get bigger and bigger, engulfing the bats. Grey smoke fills the room, its stench acrid and decaying, and I retch, retreating to the doorway. 'Gross.'

It does make me wonder though. Sath claimed he had to punish the man in Dionysus to keep the demons happy, despite the fact he's clearly capable of punishing the demons instead. 'Why don't you –'

'I can't.' The flames have died now, but Sath remains motionless, staring at the mound of ash left behind.

I fold my arms. 'You don't know what I was going to say.'

'You were going to ask why I haven't killed them all, weren't you?' he murmurs, sounding almost like he's in a trance. 'There's too many. Using that much power would destroy me, and then there'd be no one to stop them from –' He sighs. 'This is the part where it's easier if I show you.'

He leads me out of the cave and to the spot we originally portalled in to.

'I'll give you fair warning this time,' Sath says, a smile tugging at the corner of his mouth. 'Try not to get travel-sick.'

I'm so pleased he finds my legitimate problem amusing. I glare at him, which only makes the dimple in his cheek grow, but there's something about that dimple that has me reaching for his hand, almost on instinct. This time, we're not just palm to palm. Our fingers interlace, locking together as he tugs me closer than before. I wrap my other hand around his waist and squeeze.

I do feel sick when we land, but not because of the motion.

My feet are planted directly in front of a large set of gates. They're bronze, and tall, three times Sath's height, and the iron is wrought into figures of demons, snakes, dragons . . . and screaming human faces. Heat blazes from the metal. I half expect Sath to open the doors and reveal the sun itself.

I take a step back, shielding my face, sweat dripping down my forehead. The sweat is nothing in comparison to what my heart is doing. My whole chest feels tight, constricted, and it can't beat fast enough, hard enough, reminding me that I'm here, I'm here, and I may not be alive, but I'm still something, because I have every confidence if those doors are opened I won't be anything any more.

I don't need Sath to tell me what they are. Where they lead. I already know.

These are the real gates of Hell. The way into Tartarus.

12

The doors thud, like something's headbutted them. Hard. Despite how thick the metal appears, it rattles vigorously, and smoke bursts from the cracks around the hinges.

These doors do not, in any way, look stable.

'Why have you brought me here?'

Sath is unaffected by the heat. His shoulders are rigid as he runs a hand over the gates before bending to examine a slight gap at the bottom, barely big enough to slip a piece of paper through.

The gates rattle again, with enough force I half expect them to blow open. I picture a demon with a ram's head launching itself at them, its horns leaving indents in the metal, and then more demons join in, a collective effort to break them down.

Sath turns to me, brows furrowed, an expression on his face I've never seen before. I think it might be concern. And if the Devil himself is concerned, I guess I should be too.

'The enchantments binding these gates are weakening,' Sath says. 'Demons have been . . . slipping through . . . for a while now.'

My insides flip. 'And what's the difference between the ones slipping through and the ones that live here?'

Another puff of smoke blasts from the doors, like steam from an engine about to blow.

'Nothing. All the demons here originated from Tartarus. They were allowed through for disciplinary purposes, to keep the humans under control.' Storm clouds gather across his face. 'They've never forgotten the way they lived in Tartarus. There's nothing they'd love more than for these gates to open and for their brethren to spill into these halls.'

The image this conjures ties a knot in my stomach. Swathes of demons in all shapes and sizes pushing through the doors like a violent sea crashing over rock, bearing down on all the humans here, tearing them apart, slicing through flesh – but always, always careful enough to keep them from entering the Void.

I see now why Sath thought it was a mercy to send that man there. I'd take Mum's voice over that any day.

'Why are the gates weakening?'

Sath sets off down the corridor, black smoke trailing in his wake like a cloak made of shadow. I hurry after him. I'm not sure where we are exactly, although the walls are the same as the ones near his sitting room – glittering obsidian rock that darkens as he passes, like his presence snuffs out the light. I guess it makes sense the gates to Tartarus would be near where he dwells, so he can keep them in order.

Or not, as the case may be.

'Do you know how to fix them?' I continue my interrogation. '*Can* you fix them?'

'I can't.'

'Why not?' He's the ruler of Asphodel, it should be his job

to fix them. I might be heading for escape, but everyone else here will suffer if those gates open.

He runs a blood-streaked hand through his hair. 'You ask a lot of questions.'

'You can hardly blame me.' I trot alongside him, trying to keep pace with his strides. He seems to think he can escape my questions by outwalking me, but if there's anything that gives me a tailwind, it's curiosity. 'Besides, you didn't have to show me those gates. But you did. Do you want to know what I think?'

'I'm sure you're going to tell me.'

'I think you don't have anyone else to talk to.'

He chokes back a laugh, finally stopping and turning round with a look of incredulity on his face. 'I have plenty of people I can talk to.'

Now it's my turn to snort. 'Really? Who? The dead people who are scared of you? The demons who supposedly serve you, who'd secretly love those gates open? Tell me, Sath, how many friends do you have to confide in about your broken-gates woes? Poor King Sathanas, all alone –'

The whole corridor trembles, making the candles on the walls – they're inset in skulls, of course, because if there's one thing this place needs, it's more skulls – flicker so violently some go out. Sath's fists clench. 'You're wrong.'

'Then why are you angry?'

His only answer is a new whorl of flame twisting around his arm as he leads me into his rooms. At least, I think he's leading me. He's gone, and I've followed, which is the same thing. If he wanted rid of me he should have been more specific.

Once we're inside, I plop on to his sofa with a weary sigh. It's only when I sink into the comfort of soft velvet cushions that I fully comprehend how exhausted I am. My muscles are tight and aching; my head pounds to the same beat as the lingering throb in my arm. And I'm *cold*. I fold my arms, shivering.

'You'll recover from the blood loss faster than you would at . . .' I think he's searching for a word that won't send me into a spiral. He settles for *home*, which is not ideal, given it's my fault I'm not already there.

As though he's sensed he's made an error but doesn't feel inclined to deal with it, Sath waves a hand in my general direction and tells me to *wait there* before removing his bloodstained jumper, which is an instant distraction from any maudlin thoughts of home. I blink at his bare back as he retreats into the next room, catching a glimpse of what looks like a large bed with silk sheets – I blink harder at the images *that* conjures – before he slams the door behind him.

Well. Rude.

Without him, the room is vast and empty. Soundless. No traffic outside. No clock ticking in the corner. I wonder if he ever listens to music. I peer around for something that resembles a phone, or a laptop – a record player would do – and then I realise I'm missing an opportunity.

I'm alone. I'm in the Devil's rooms, and I'm *alone*.

There is no amount of exhaustion my nosiness cannot cure. I haul myself to my feet and head towards a set of cabinets. There could be a clue here that'll help me pass the next task, or tell me what the concession he's getting at the end of this will be.

114

Perhaps I'll find Devil-related things, torture items like whips and chains. Except he wouldn't use those for torture, instead he'd – my gaze slides to the closed bedroom door and heat floods my cheeks. Focus, Willow. Any scenario in which Sath is wielding a whip is not one I wish to be a part of. Obviously.

I yank a cabinet open to distract myself, but when I bend to inspect the goodies inside I find . . . nothing. It's empty.

What the fuck. How can you be immortal and not own any *stuff*?

I open the next one. It's empty too. Even the book he was reading the day I arrived has gone. I can't believe –

'What are you doing?'

I lift my head out from inside a cupboard, aiming for an air of innocence. He's changed into a pair of sweatpants that hang low on his hips and a plain black T-shirt. The difference in appearance is alarming. In that garb, he doesn't look like the ruler of Asphodel, or someone with the power to inflict all kinds of misery on troublemakers. He looks like . . . a person. One who I'm starting to find kind of interesting.

On a professional level.

And then he goes and hands me a hoodie. I gape at the garment being waved in my face. 'Why are you giving me your clothes?'

He flicks a glance at my threadbare T-shirt. 'You were shivering.'

'Oh.' I didn't expect him to pay me that much attention. I take it from him, and I'm briefly enveloped in darkness along with the scent of peppermint and rain, before emerging into the light feeling distinctly warmer. It's a pity I can't appreciate how gorgeously soft it is, because Sath is smirking at me. I scowl, fully ready to tell him I wouldn't need his hoodie if I wasn't suffering from the aftershocks of being attacked by the demons he's lost control of, but all words disappear from my vocabulary when Sath reaches out and strokes the top of my head.

'Static,' he says by way of explanation, although that doesn't excuse the way his fingers linger, tangling themselves in strands of red before finally dropping to his side.

This hoodie is too thick. I am suddenly far, far too hot in it.

He gestures at the open cupboards. 'Why are you going through my things?'

'What things?' I ask. His lack of possessions is truly baffling. 'It was too quiet when you left. I was trying to find . . . Do you have any music?'

I omit my whips-and-chains theory for both our sakes. Or maybe just mine. Either way, I must be a better liar than I thought, because Sath clicks his fingers and classical music begins to play. The high-pitched whine of violins swells, filling the room with a plaintive melody. I stare around in amazement. I can't tell where the sound's coming from. There are no speakers that I can see.

'How does it work?' I ask. 'Your magic?'

Sath shrugs. 'It just does.'

'It just does,' I echo. 'That's your answer?'

'The underworld has been here since the dawn of time, and the magic came with it.' Sath heads to the bar and pours two drinks. 'It's no easier to comprehend than anything else in existence. But I didn't bring you here to talk about how magic works.'

'Then what did you bring me here for?'

'You wanted to know about the gates.' He gestures to the stool at his side. 'Let me enlighten you.'

I settle next to him. His arm brushes mine as he slides a bottle towards me. It's unlabelled, and the liquid inside is a bright acid green, much like the bat venom Sath pulled from my wound. I sniff it. Apples.

This doesn't rule out bat venom. I was in too much of a panic to sniff them at the time. I'd like to hope he didn't save me from those bats only to make me drink their insides though, so I take a tentative sip, and the taste of sour apple, melon and something else citrusy floods my mouth. It burns my throat on the way down.

Whatever it is, I like it. I take another sip, waiting for Sath to speak.

'Only Asphodel's ruler should be able to open or close the gates,' Sath tells me. 'But as you can see, my control over them is fading.'

'Why?'

He stares at his glass, his thumb running concentric circles around the rim, before lifting it to his mouth and draining the contents in one. 'The why isn't what's important.'

Of course it isn't. That would be too much like giving me a real answer.

'If the gates can't be kept shut . . . nobody deserves that kind of carnage,' he says. 'It would be unimaginable. The demons, of course, would love nothing more. I deal out the fastest punishments I can to appease them. If I refused to act, the demons would revolt, and the only way to kill them all would be to allow my powers to overwhelm me. That loss of control would result in the gates opening anyway. I was slower than I should have been against those bats today because of it.'

I swallow. 'Do the demons know how close they are to getting everything they want?'

'They know something is happening. Asphodel is changing. Walls that used to be beige have turned black. Lava spews from cracks that shouldn't be there. Plants that used to grow in abundance have died. I spread a rumour it's all down to Asphodel stretching to make room for more souls, and in the meantime I visit different areas each night, making public demonstrations of what I can do so they won't consider challenging me. They have no idea I can't stop them.'

'It's a shame there isn't a set of gates leading to Elysium to balance it out.' I narrow my eyes. 'Unless there is, and you've hidden them from me.'

Sath huffs. 'Believe me, I've looked. There's no easy route into Elysium. I imagine they didn't want us disturbing their peace and found a way to stay hidden. A pity we didn't do the same before Tartarus came calling.'

'And now they're at the door, your only solution is to pretend to be awful for eternity?' That isn't fair. Sadness drifts off him in waves. Instinctively, I put my hand over his and squeeze. It twitches beneath mine, but he doesn't pull away.

He stares at our hands for a minute, and then looks across at me. 'We're all pretending to be something.'

I flinch, a little too visibly to be casual. I've pretended to be multiple people over the years: dutiful daughter, model student, perfect girlfriend. Three things that should belong together but I've never been able to get the patchwork to stitch. Pretending is probably the problem. I need to find a way to *become*.

Maybe he needs to become something else too.

'You said you were losing control of the gates,' I say. 'Can't you get it back?'

'No.'

'But –'

'It's gone, Willow. I'm done.' He swigs another drink like it's water. 'It's done.'

His words are a vice around my chest. Not only because of the fear of what's to come for him, for me, for all of us, but because of his sorrow too. I don't understand how he can be so defeated. He clearly doesn't want the gates to open, so how can he give up when he's the only person with the power to stop it from happening?

Sath clears his throat. 'I don't think I need to say you can't tell anyone this.'

'I figured.' I shift closer, nudging his knee with mine. 'Why *are* you telling me?'

A smile tugs on his lips. 'Maybe you're right. Maybe I don't have anyone else to talk to.'

'Hm.' I tap my glass. I don't know what I expected when I asked him to *be less devily*, but it certainly wasn't for him to offload all his issues on to me. He must be desperate, because I'd make a terrible therapist. I can't even solve my own problems.

Being alone can't be good for him. He's completely disassociated from the humans, meaning he has no idea what it's like to be one. If he cared more about them, maybe it'd remind him they're worth fighting for. And I need him to fight – just because I'm leaving soon, doesn't mean I won't be back eventually, and I'd like to return to somewhere that isn't overrun with bats that want to eat me. 'What do you do when you're not ruling?'

The question seems to throw him. 'Well, there was the year I attempted to memorise the dictionary.'

'The year you . . . Oh, *Sath*.' I have got to find this man a hobby.

He looks at me like I'm the one who needs to be pitied in this scenario, like I'm a fool for even suggesting he take some time for himself. 'I don't have time when I'm not ruling, not really. If there's trouble on the boats, I get to threaten the newcomers. Otherwise, I'm in Dionysus reminding everyone how scary I am.'

He says it flippantly, a wry smile on his features, but I wonder what cracks those jokes are papering over. He said this place was supposed to be a new beginning, but he doesn't act like he's living at all, hiding away in his room reading the *dictionary* for fun.

He turns to face me, and a lock of dark hair falls over his forehead. The sight of it does things to me it shouldn't.

'Do you have a beanie?' I blurt out.

'Excuse me?'

'A beanie. Like a hat.'

'I know what a beanie is, Willow.'

'Perfect.' I beam at him. 'Put one on and meet me in the projection cave.'

Sath sighs. 'I can't be seen –'

I put a finger to his lips. They're softer than I expected. He sucks in a breath, sending a rush of cold air over my skin, but he doesn't move.

'No arguments,' I say. 'Make yourself unrecognisable, and we'll hide at the back. If Asphodel is supposed to be a middle ground, you shouldn't be treating it like your own personal Hell.'

He blinks at me. I take a moment to congratulate myself on shocking the Devil, before slipping from the room. It'll be dark enough in the cave that he can sit undetected, but I don't think we should be seen arriving together.

I scurry through the entrance chamber and am back on the balcony in record speed, calling for a lift. It's strange, given the size of this place, how quickly I've learned my way around the various floors, along with which ones are best to avoid (for example, I have no idea why anybody would choose to spend a single moment of their afterlife in a fish market. The smell is unbearable).

I found the projection cave on day three of my explorations, down a rabbit warren of corridors on the entertainment level. It's a small room, soundproofed to drown out the sound of arcade games and pinball machines next door. I don't know where the power supply comes from, but I do know it's usually demon-free, unlike the endless corridors I have to walk through to find it again.

Aric's loitering in one, arms folded and snarling at humans that pass by. I keep my head down, but I feel his eyes watching me as I enter the cave. Humans lounge on beanbags littered sporadically over a carpet made of grass, faces dimly lit by the images flickering from the screen.

The film's already started – it's *Twilight*, of all things – and I drag a beanbag into a dark corner, far away from the rest of them, although they're not paying me or the film much attention as they giggle and whisper in each other's ears, passing popcorn back and forth.

We used to have film nights like this at the flat, before Mum died. When everything was right and normal. Sasha and I would hide under the duvet while Noah forced us to watch some awful horror movie, but he'd keep us entertained with a running commentary that had us both shaking with laughter.

I wonder if Sasha's out of hospital now. If they're watching those films without me. If someone else is holding her hand when she gets scared.

A yearning sets root in my stomach. I have to go back before they replace me. But more than that, I want something like that here. Now. I miss *company*, and I'll take it in any form.

Even if that form is the Devil.

I recognise the broad outline of Sath's shoulders when he steps inside the cave, the way he walks with a confidence that says he's the most powerful person in the room. I sincerely hope nobody *else* recognises that. They may not react well to sharing film night with the Devil. For me, though, I press my lips together to hide my smile. He came. And I should not be this excited about it, but I've been coming to this cave for a month, and it's going to be the first time I have someone sitting next to me.

Also, the beanie really suits him.

He spots my (subtle) waving and weaves through the humans

before dropping next to me on the beanbag. It sinks with his weight, dipping in the middle and making me slide into him.

Although I adjust so we're not touching, I'm still hyperaware of his proximity when I whisper, 'Hi.'

'This is a terrible idea,' he mutters.

I'm starting to think he has a point, but for very different reasons.

He's the Devil, I remind myself.

But darkness is a mask. It gives us anonymity, the ability to be something other than what we are and start over. When our arms brush, I don't shrink away, and neither does he. Eventually, we end up leaning against one another, his thigh against mine, his hand dangling lazily over my knee.

He's the Devil.

I can't concentrate on the film. My pulse sounds too loud in my ears. My skin prickles all over. Because when we glance at one another to confirm we're laughing at the same thing, he doesn't feel like the Devil at all.

He feels like he could be a friend.

13

Sat beneath a coconut tree in a tropical-themed dining hall for – according to my not-entirely-accurate wardrobe calendar – the fifty-seventh day in a row, I stare glumly at some humans on the next bench over and poke fried pineapple around my plate. Eating is a habit more than a necessity. Sometimes I come here to smell the sand dusted along the floor and pretend I'm staying in a hotel by the sea, but my imagination is failing me today. The scrape of cutlery and buzz of chatter is like white noise I want to drown out but can't. Every day, I'm the new kid in school with no one to sit with.

I haven't seen Sath since our trip to the cinema. Not properly, anyway. When he's in Dionysus he stays on his throne, refusing to engage with anyone apart from the demons whispering whatever monstrosities demons like to whisper into his ears. Sometimes, his gaze catches mine, and he offers me a small smile, like we're sharing a secret. The feeling of warmth it suffuses in me is brief, a match sparking before being snuffed out, leaving me colder than before.

Clearly my attempts to get him to feel more human have backfired, because I'm the one left with a hollow ache in my chest, a gnawing in my stomach, a weight in my legs that makes it hard to rise in the morning.

Every day, home feels a little further away. I can't visualise what it looks like any more. Noah may as well be on Pluto at this point. I don't want to do another task; I want to lie under my covers and never come out again.

You're throwing your life away, Willow.

I shove my turtle-shell tray across the table. I'm one self-pitying thought away from turning into Sath, sticking my head in the sand, with no motivation to solve my problems because I've become so distant from the world I've forgotten what I'm fighting for.

A splash of bright colour draws my attention across the room – it's Harper, the girl I met on my first night, the one who was nice to me for no reason. Her hair is blue today, and her skirt resembles an artist's palette, covered in splotches of red, green and yellow. She's laughing with two others, a boy and a girl who are like faded watercolour in comparison to her.

I jump to my feet, staring at her retreating form, a plan manifesting. Days felt like weeks when I lay in bed moping after Mum died. I'd listen to Noah come and go, not knowing how much time had passed because he never checked on me, thinking I'd emerge when I was ready. I was never ready. It was only when Sasha returned and forced me outside that time sped up again, those nights of distraction moving my life forward like a bullet train I couldn't stop.

I need time to move faster here too.

Sasha may not be an option, but Harper is. Her giggles, bright and infectious, echo in my ear. This wouldn't be like last time. I'd make sure of it. I know the cost of getting too distracted now, of spiralling out of control. This would simply be a conversation or two to help me make it through the day.

Thus, my fruit salad is abandoned in favour of Mission Find Willow a Friend, and I leave the cave with a spring in my step. This'll work. I'll have something to perk me up between each task and I'll be home before I know it.

I increase my pace as Harper and her friends board a lift. Shit. It's moving upwards before I can jump in, so I settle for hopping on the next one, wedging myself between a boy who smells inexplicably like petrol and a girl who I suspect may be new if the tear tracks on her cheeks are anything to go by.

I think *follow Harper*, and hope this contraption will understand where I need to go. Something tugs on my stomach when we reach the entertainment floor, so I rush off, poking my head into rooms filled with pool tables built out of bones and balls that look like enlarged eyes. Personally I do not think a ball staring at me would help me take my best shot, but the dead in here are not to be deterred, cheering when a particularly bloodshot-looking ball drops into the corner pocket.

No Harper though. I keep moving, past a bowling alley (the skittles are, once again, made of bone, but the balls are sensible at least) along with the arcade room and projection caves. Each room blazes with colour, like every open doorway is a television screen blaring brightly in a place where all the other lights have been switched off. They're the antithesis of the corridors themselves, where the cliff is crumbling in places, rock peeling like old paint to reveal darker stone beneath.

Further down the corridor, there's a yell. A bang. Someone screams, '*Stop!*'

Something growls in response. Something distinctly inhuman. The floor beneath my feet shakes.

My heart stalls for a second, and then I'm running towards the noise.

I skid to a stop outside one of the smaller rooms, used for private games and tournaments. Harper's inside with her two friends and, of all people, Aric. The sharp spike of his tail repeatedly bashes the sides of the pool table so hard I think the legs may splinter.

Shit. When I said I'd be what I needed to be to make a friend, heroic saviour wasn't on my list of options. I'm neither heroic nor a saviour. Getting involved with Aric will get me killed; I saw that much my first night here. If I manage to stop him doing whatever he clearly wants to, he'll go complaining to Sath and I don't know if Sath would be able to protect me from punishment. Not if it'll risk inciting the riot he fears.

Harper's face pales when she catches sight of me. Shakes her head and mouths something that looks suspiciously like *go*. My feet are rooted to the spot.

I'm on another cliff edge: run and save myself, or stay and deal with the consequences later.

There's only one smart choice.

And yet I don't move.

Aric's tail collides with the pool table once more, and the leg snaps. The table buckles, crashing to the floor on one side; Harper and her friends dart out of the way as balls pelt towards their feet. Aric grabs the top end of his tail, caressing it before twisting it round his palm like he's preparing to use it as a whip. Nausea churns my stomach.

Nausea, tinged with rage. Once again, I'm reminded of how the demons are ruining this place. If this is supposed to be a middle ground, maybe the demons should start acting like it, instead of milling around instilling fear into everyone. Forget setting them on fire with Tartarus's flames, if the gates weren't broken, I'd go to Sath right now and demand he shove every last one through. Let them torture each other for eternity instead.

'Little humans,' Aric says. 'You have been naughty, haven't you?'

Please. They weren't that far ahead of me; they can barely have been in this room more than a minute. As someone who's been called *naughty* more times than she can count, I can say with confidence you need at least two minutes.

'I'm going to cut you into pieces.' Aric drags the spiked end of his tail across the boy's cheek, slicing into his skin. Blood wells in the thin cut. Aric smacks his lips, and sighs. 'Oh, I will enjoy eating you.'

Ew.

This is definitely the part where I should leave.

Absolutely. Definitely.

And yet for some reason, my hand finds itself grabbing a pool cue. Harper's eyes go wide. She shakes her head a little more vehemently. But the three of them clearly aren't going to do anything, and someone has to. Why should Aric get to do what he likes because he's bigger than them, because the rules allow him to – because *Sath* allows him to? He's a demon with a bad haircut, why should he get to decide who does or doesn't get chopped to pieces today?

Fuck it.

'Hey!' I call out.

Aric spins round.

'Leave them alone.'

At the sight of me, Aric's lips curl, revealing a set of long fangs protruding from his gums. Gross. He sniffs the air – sniffs *me*, my scent, most likely, to see if he deems me tasty – the gesture reminiscent of an animal waking from a nap because their owner waved a treat in front of their nose.

But the way he looks isn't the worst part of him. No, it's the way I can sense his malice leaking from his pores, like the evil is a stench he can't wash off; he's a rotten apple, rancid and reeking, only growing worse with age.

His yellow eyes glow red, as though, like Sath, he holds a part of Tartarus within himself.

Unlike Sath, though, he has no desire to keep it under control.

His tail whips back and forth. Harper and her friends hold hands, cowering away from its movements. If they wanted to return the favour and come to my rescue, now would be the time, because I regret both my life and death choices right now.

I should have kept my nose out.

Aric springs into the air. I dodge him, barely, and the spectators, such as they are, gasp and scream. His claws tear through my shirt; scattered pieces of yellow fabric drift to the floor around me. I bare my teeth. Aric swipes at me, catching my chin this time, the pain a sharp sting along my jaw. I brandish the pool cue, trying to act threatening. I'm not sure what my

129

plan is here. Aric is all muscle and I'm, well . . . I'm five foot five and have never set foot in a gym.

He lunges again. This time, I'm ready for him, sidestepping the attack and ramming the cue towards his stomach. He moves so fast I think he impales *himself*; the cue punctures flesh with such force I can't take any of the credit. He doesn't stop coming though, allowing the cue to go deeper while leaning towards me. Blood leaks out the side of his wound, coating my hands.

I gag, trying to pull away, but instead he drags me closer, arms locking around mine, and I can't escape, can't get away from his hot, putrid breath as his face draws near. My arms tremble.

He burrows his nose in my hair and all but moans, 'You smell . . . *divine.*'

Ugh. Fuck this creep. I twist the cue with all my might, and eventually I must hit something that hurts because he whimpers, spasms, and drops to the floor. He rolls from side to side – acting like a bit of a baby, honestly, I'd have thought a demon would have a higher pain threshold given how much they enjoy dealing it out – while his hands grapple to pull out the cue.

Standing over his writhing form, staring into eyes which burn with hate, hate for *me*, hate for what I've done, I can't deny the small thrill I get from having this much power over him. I've never had power over anything before.

And with that power, I can stop him hurting anyone in this room.

I march over to the wall and retrieve another pool cue hanging from a rack. I stare at Aric again, cue poised to strike. The humans whimper, but they don't speak. Don't try and stop me. They want this too.

Maybe we really are all bad people.

I ram the cue into Aric's eye. His legs jerk out, like I've jolted his nervous system with electricity. His arms flail around. He's desperate to get up. I can sense how badly he wants to hurt me; every snarl is a promise of retribution.

He can't do a thing. Not now, not when he's at my mercy.

Finally, he goes still, and I exhale a shaky breath. A smile threatens to bloom on my face as a jolt of victory shoots through me. I *saved* Harper and her friends. I did something good, for once.

The next thing I know, I'm engulfed in bubblegum and fluff as Harper throws her arms around me. 'You saved us.'

A tentative smile spreads on my lips. I pat her on the back, awkward at first because she's unfamiliar in my arms, softer than Sasha and smaller than Noah, but soon my body relaxes, relishing in the first human contact I've had in weeks. It feels a little like peace.

And then she pulls away, lashes stained with tears, and anything resembling gratitude on her face fades into worry as she looks at Aric's prone form.

Oh shit.

Only the flames of Tartarus can truly destroy a demon.

What have I done?

All the adrenaline in my veins drains away, leaving me shivering in its absence. Panic gnaws at me, chipping at my victory until it seems like more of a loss.

Tantrums will get you nowhere, Willow.

This is exactly the kind of situation a calm, responsible person would not be getting themselves into. I toss the cue

131

on the floor as though it's a red-hot poker. Sath might not pardon me for this.

Maybe Aric won't remember what happened. There's a pool cue in his eye, that's got to leave some lasting damage. His brain will be so scrambled he won't ever be able to accuse me. No one will find out I screwed up yet again.

A girl can dream.

'We have to leave,' I tell the others. 'Don't tell anyone you saw me here. Don't tell anyone *you* were here.'

They nod. Like they'd dare do anything else. Harper's friends are staring at me like I'm a demon myself. Maybe I am.

But then a voice sounds from the doorway, and any hope of covering this up drains away.

'Well, well, well,' the familiar tone says, 'haven't you all been busy?'

14

Sath leans against the doorway with his arms folded over his chest, one leg crossed in front of the other. He isn't slapping me in handcuffs – or whatever the Asphodel equivalent may be – which I have to take as an encouraging sign.

Maybe he hasn't spotted Aric yet. The humans trembling in fear are probably distracting, along with the dismantled pool table. I sidestep to try and hide the body, and his eyes are immediately on me. I avert my gaze, which I'm sure screams innocence.

'I'm waiting for an explanation.' He points at Harper, who's crying less than the other two. 'Speak.'

I'm reminded of the one and only time I got detention in school. Sasha had taken it upon herself to spray-paint our English teacher's car, shoving the can into my hand at the end so I could perform the final touch. We were caught running away. Pinned down by the headteacher the way Sath pins us now, demanding an explanation.

Harper's voice is no more than a whisper. 'We were –'

'Louder.' This isn't the Sath who cleaned my arm or confided in me about some gates that are falling apart. This is King

Sathanas, ruler of Asphodel. He prowls towards her, those flames of his licking up his arms, and I'm half afraid he's going to burn her alive right here, right now. I take one tiny step in her direction, but a quick shake of Sath's head has me pausing. His words from before haunt me.

If you're seen challenging me, I'll be forced to do to you what I did to that man. I suspect coming to their defence falls under the category of challenging him. Pfft. I shut my mouth and scowl, just in case he had any doubts about my opinions on the matter.

'We said . . . we said we wanted to . . .'

'Yes?'

'To see the sun,' Harper finishes. 'One more time. It . . . He . . . overheard, and she . . .' Her eyes flick to me, just like Sasha's had on that day. The can was in my hand. There was no reason she should take any of the blame.

'Ah.' Sath clucks his tongue. 'How very, very calamitous for you all.' His voice is soft, the words somehow both a caress and a curse. My stomach knots. I really want to believe he won't hurt me.

I may not have given him a choice.

Sath comes to stand beside me. I tense at his proximity, but all he does is nudge Aric's prone form with his shoe. His gaze drifts to my hands, and the blood encrusted there. I suppose it's too late to shove them behind me.

Sath inclines his head towards the others. 'I'm going to do the rest of you a favour and assume this girl is responsible for what happened here today.' His eyes lock on mine, although his words are directed at them. 'Leave.'

To my surprise, Harper's feet remain planted on the spot. 'It wasn't her fault,' she says. 'We were the ones who upset him; she was only trying to help –'

'Are you questioning my judgement?'

I shake my head furiously in her direction. I have no idea what she thinks she's doing. The blood on my hands is far more damning than any can of paint.

'N-no,' she says. Her friends are already edging towards the door. 'I . . .'

'Get out.'

She flinches at the raw power in his voice, but doesn't move, her gaze flicking between me and him.

'It's fine,' I say. 'Go. I'll be fine.'

She has no reason to believe me – *I'm* not sure I believe me – but, finally, after a staring contest which I manage to win, she nods and backs away, giving me one last panicked glance and mouthing *I'm sorry*, before disappearing.

And we're alone.

I hold my breath. I'm not sure how much of this is part of his act. Sath is what I would call *glowering*, simmering flames in his eyes, smoke uncurling from his arms. He inhales deeply before clicking the door shut, and when he faces me again he's a little more Sath-like and a little less Devil-like.

Doesn't stop him sounding utterly exasperated when he says, 'What were you thinking?'

I bristle. 'I was *thinking* that your demon here was about to attack three people for no reason. What was I supposed to do, let him hurt them?'

'Yes!' He closes the gap between us, but I don't cower away, standing toe to toe with him. Heat emanates from his body, searing into mine. 'That is exactly what you should have done!'

'Unlike you, I'm not prepared to sit around and do nothing while innocent people get hurt.'

A muscle in his jaw twitches. 'That's not fair.'

'What's not fair is putting me in this position.' I fold my arms. 'This shouldn't have been a decision I had to make. If you would stand up to the demons . . .'

If he'd stand up to the demons, I wouldn't be given the opportunity to do exactly the kind of dumb shit that got me here in the first place. It's his fault I messed up; *his* fault I've failed at yet another chance to prove I can walk away from bad situations.

The least he can do is get me out of it. 'Could you do your thing already, and set him on fire? How long do we have until he wakes?'

Sath sighs. 'I can't set him on fire. Not this time.'

I do a double-take. I can't have heard him correctly. If he doesn't get rid of him, Aric will tell the other demons what I've done, and then they'll be out for my blood, which –

Every inch of me goes as rigid and cold as a popsicle when I realise what this means. Sath has no intention of helping me. Of getting me out of this.

'Nobody knew of those bats' existence,' Sath explains. 'It was safe for me to return them to Tartarus. Aric, on the other hand . . . if he were to go missing, all kinds of questions would be asked. Ones that neither of us would like to answer.'

I'm going to the Void.

I'll hear Mum's voice on repeat, reminding me all I had to

136

do was listen to her and I'd have been safe, free of this place, and I can't do it, I won't go there, *I won't*.

'Sath,' I say. I'm reaching for him before I can stop myself, my hands making a fist in his shirt. 'The tasks. Your . . . Think, Sath, if you send me to the Void, you won't get your concession, whatever it is. You can't . . .' I'm babbling. I'm definitely babbling. 'You can't do this. You need me, remember?'

'When did I say anything about the Void?' He sounds completely calm, like he hasn't signed my second death sentence by deciding Aric is more important than me.

'If you keep Aric alive, won't he make you? Otherwise, he'll come after me himself.' I bite my lower lip to stop it wobbling. 'Maybe you could . . . torture me a little?' I cringe at my own words. I think my self-respect is as dead as I am.

Sath blinks. 'Torture you?'

'Punish me?' That sounds less painful. 'You can punish me.'

He quirks a brow. 'Do you *want* me to punish you?'

'Obviously not,' I retort, forgetting I'm supposed to be begging for rescue. 'But if you won't set fire to Aric –'

'Leave Aric to me.' Sath stares at the body, darkness gathering in his expression, like clouds rolling in before a storm. 'There is one thing I can use as leverage. I'll make sure he doesn't bother you.' His gaze shifts to meet mine. 'I promise. He won't touch you.'

The dread coiling round my chest loosens, and my next breath comes a little easier. 'Are you sure?'

'I'm sure.' He clicks his fingers, and Aric's body disappears. 'I sent him to my chambers; he won't wake for a few hours. I'll deal with him then.'

'And what about me?' I can't help asking. 'How are you going to deal with me?'

Sometimes I wish I knew how to keep my mouth shut.

'Careful.' Sath smirks. 'All these questions, I'm starting to think you *want* to be punished. Tell me, Willow, how would you like to be dealt with?'

My mind, ever helpful, conjures up images of the whips and chains I'd convinced myself I'd find in his cupboards. My cheeks grow warm, which only makes his smirk grow, as though he can see every single outrageous thought in my head.

'I don't,' I snap, furious with myself. 'I just assumed you'd yell more. Aren't you angry?'

'Oh, believe me, I'm angry,' he says, sounding perfectly cordial. If this is anger, I've never seen it like this. 'However well-intentioned, what you did was reckless. If Aric had got the upper hand, you *would* have ended up in the Void.' His gaze drops to my torn T-shirt. 'Did he hurt you?'

'I'm fine.'

He slides a finger across the freshly exposed skin, just beneath my collarbone, before snatching his hand back into a clenched fist.

'Nothing about this is fine,' he says, eyes flashing gold. 'He hurt you. And instead of punishing him, I have to play damage control.' He shakes his head. 'I'm not angry with you. I'm angry with this place.'

Now doesn't seem like a good time to suggest, once again, that he does something about it.

'Come on.' His hand finds my elbow. 'I'm only here because I was searching for you.'

'You were?' I have a horrible feeling I sound far too happy about that.

'Yes.' Sath, however, does not sound happy. His face is grim when he says, 'It's time for your next task.'

One of these days, it would be nice to get some advance warning about a task. Sath is gracious enough to let me change first, telling me the task of sloth is next and that I should *wear something warm*, which isn't much of a clue as to what it might entail. After examining the faint scratches on my chin and chest – they're sore, although Aric didn't draw blood – I settle for a thick black jumper.

Sath leads me to, of all places, the Sorter's morgue.

'My task's in here?' I witnessed enough dead bodies on my first day to satisfy a lifetime's curiosity. 'Will the Sorter be there?'

She may have appeared less violent than some of the other demons I've come across, but she's still a *demon*, and therefore, by definition, dangerous.

'Don't worry about her,' Sath says, gesturing for me to enter first. 'Unlike Aric, her bark is worse than her bite.'

This doesn't fill me with confidence. The morgue is colder than I remember, and there's a strong smell of bleach that burns the insides of my nostrils. The slabs are empty. Something in my gut clenches; what if one of those slabs is for *me*? What if I'm going to be forced to lie there, while the Sorter cuts me open and shows Sath all my sins, all my deepest, darkest thoughts, what if –

Sath's hand wraps around my elbow. 'Are you okay? You're breathing heavily.'

'Fine.' I shudder. 'What am I doing, exactly?'

'She'll explain.' Sath jerks his head down the row of slabs. The squeak of her trolley indicates she's close by. 'I'll be back later.'

'You're *leaving*?' The last thing I want is to be left alone with a bunch of corpses and a demon with a scalpel collection.

'I'll return when the time's right.' He bends to murmur in my ear, 'Don't worry. It's only me who gets to tempt you.'

I go to jab him in the stomach, but he dodges my elbow with ease. Bastard. He winks before sauntering from the room, hands in his pockets. I resist the urge to throw something at the door, if only because I know he has Aric to deal with.

My pulse kicks up a notch. What if this supposed leverage isn't enough?

'Are you going to stand there all day?' the Sorter's voice calls from down the room. 'There's work to be done.'

Her trolley squeaks closer. Hopefully my work will involve oiling those wheels, because if I have to listen to them much longer my ears will bleed. She's finally visible, her white hair bobbing behind her cart, like the moon peeking over the top of a mountain.

Every inch of me is on high alert. She stood right by Aric's side the night that man in Dionysus died, and she acted like she enjoyed every second. She's probably on team open gates. Also, I've just stabbed her friend with a pool cue. I suspect this will not endear me to her if she finds out.

141

'What work, exactly?' I fold my arms. I hope I don't have to cut anyone up – the one time I tried to dice a raw chicken breast there was a lot of squealing involved. Shouldn't sloth be relaxing? I suppose a nap is out of the question.

'Sorting.' She clicks her fingers, and the slabs are immediately full of naked bodies, their modesty preserved by thin paper towels. My heart sinks. 'Clipboards are on the end of the bed. Read 'em, make a decision. Lever goes up for Elysium, to the right for Asphodel, and down for Tartarus. Get to the end of the row, and you're done.'

Sounds easy, apart from I can't see where said row ends. I could be here all night. I could be here *forever*.

I stare at the nearest clipboard. More to the point, why should *I* decide someone's afterlife? I couldn't get my own life right. I shouldn't have that kind of power over judging someone else's. My fingers hover near the paper, afraid to touch it.

The Sorter clucks her tongue. 'Don't dally; there's more where this lot came from.' She grabs the clipboard I'm dithering over and touches the body until the page is full of words. 'Look. No crimes, but a predisposition for selfish behaviour. Ooh, and they got their sibling cut out of their parents' will. Naughty, naughty.'

'Maybe the sibling deserved it.'

'Maybe.' She shrugs and tilts the lever to the right. 'Anyway. Asphodel it is.' The slab tilts, and the body is thrown down the chute.

'That's it? That's all he gets? And what about me? You said you saw –'

'A river of blood,' she finishes my sentence. 'I remember. I stand by it. It was on your chart.'

142

'Well, how do you know these charts aren't fiction?'

She ignores my perfectly legitimate question and taps the next clipboard. 'You're supposed to be working.'

My hands tremble as I reach for it. The body I'm assessing is a girl, barely older than me. A rose is tattooed on the inside of her forearm, but the red is tinged blue now, like the rest of her skin. The paper is blank. Nausea rises in my throat when I realise what I'm going to have to do, every instinct I have trying to stop me from placing a finger to her skin – as soon as I do, a rush of something hot and powerful flows through me. I get a brief glimpse of a life that's not mine: a hand strumming a guitar, feet pounding a racetrack, a test paper being plucked from a filing cabinet in the dead of night.

It lasts barely more than a few seconds, but when I glance at the clipboard, the paper's full. It doesn't tell me how she died though. Whether it was a mistake. How many things she's going to miss out on now she's here.

I don't want to subject her to this.

Studying the sheet of paper intently, I try to find words such as *good* and *perfect* and *deserving of peace*. They're notably absent. Should I send her to Elysium anyway? The Sorter's not watching. My hand hovers over the lever.

Push it up. All I have to do is push it up, and I won't feel any guilt.

Unless this is part of the task. Maybe if I sort somebody wrong, I won't make it to the end. I can't fuck this up. The text in front of me may as well be written in neon lights: *liar . . . fraud . . . cheat.*

Fuck's sake. I close my eyes, turn the lever to the right, and hope she doesn't hate this place as much as I do. Everything sounds too loud: my breathing, my feet scuffing the floor, the sound of the chute opening. The way her body thuds as it drops. I bite my lip, refusing to cry in front of the Sorter.

The next one is marginally easier. And the next. On and on I go, hating myself every second, but I turn that lever to the right time and time again. Nobody here is good. Maybe Elysium is a myth. Perfection is impossible; the very nature of humanity is to do what we want and screw the consequences.

For me, that consequence was death. I ram the next lever so hard it rattles.

Ahead of me, the Sorter is practically chipper as she condemns people to this place, whistling a jaunty tune and flicking her tail.

'How did you get this job, anyway?' I ask, desperate to take my mind off the task at hand. 'Did you appear at the dawn of time and start sorting?'

'Not exactly.' She grins at her clipboard, revealing a set of pointed incisors, and shoves the lever down. My blood runs cold despite the heat blasting from the chute when it opens, black smoke pluming within. The body sizzles as it descends.

I can't stop my eyes welling with tears this time. Wiping them away in violent strokes, I mutter, 'I cannot wait to get out of this place.'

'Hm,' the Sorter hums. Sending someone to Tartarus has given her a bounce in her step, making the clop of her hooves sound like a vigorous tap-dance. 'You're welcome, by the way.'

'For what, you letting it slip about the tasks?'

'Maybe I didn't let it slip. Maybe it was my good deed for the century.'

I roll my eyes. 'Yeah, you're all heart.'

'Well, now, *that* would be difficult,' she muses. 'We demons don't have hearts.'

'You don't?' I blink. My next question follows almost immediately, like I'd snatch the answer from her mouth if I could. 'Does Sath?'

What if he's as heartless as the rest of them? The thought stings, and I'm not sure why.

The Sorter smiles. 'You sound worried. Afraid those sad eyes of his are just for show?'

I shove the lever on my next corpse with barely a glance at the paperwork. 'Of course I'm not worried.' I add a shrug for good measure. 'He seems almost human compared to the rest of you, but he has to be in charge for a reason, right? I was curious, that's all.'

'If I were you, I'd spend a little less time being curious about Sath and a little more time focusing on passing these tasks.'

'Because you care so much about me getting to leave this place.'

'I care as much as he does,' she says sweetly.

My fists clench. Riddles upon riddles upon lies. Sath doesn't care about me leaving, not really, he just wants his concession when I pass – whatever it is. I can't see any way their visions could be aligned – Sath says he wants Asphodel to be safe, whereas the Sorter is friends with Aric who wants to tear this place apart.

My stomach twists. Unless Sath is lying to me. Unless he is a demon, soulless and empty inside, and he's only pretending to worry about the humans here because he knows I want him to. I thought it the day I met him: he's temptation itself. What if he's moulded himself into someone good and decent

145

because he's realised that's what will tempt *me*?

We work the next few hours in silence. I have more questions, about a million of them, but I can't trust the answers she'll give. Besides, as time passes, I'm struggling to remember what they were. My eyelids droop. My wrist aches from the endless shoving of levers. I want to stop.

I don't. The lights dim for hours before flickering back to life, like day has turned to night and back again. I have no idea. I move on autopilot, ignoring the way my feet burn. I go on and on until my legs buckle, struggling to hold my weight a moment longer, sending me flying towards the next slab. My knee knocks the edge, sending a blinding pain into my already throbbing head. I shove the lever to the right without reading the clipboard. It's always the same.

And the row doesn't end.

I sag. 'I can't . . . I need a rest.'

Nobody responds. The Sorter's disappeared. I have no idea when it happened. I just know I'm alone and there's nobody to hold me up, and I can't do this.

Why did I think I'd be capable of completing these tasks? I've always fallen short at everything I've tried to do, no matter how much I wanted it, no matter how much effort I put in. And this, out of all the things I've wanted, is the most impossible thing of all. The row of slabs stretches further and further ahead into an invisible horizon. Slumped against the nearest one, my eyes drift shut.

I jerk.

Inhale deeply. I can't fall asleep.

Then again –

If I'm going to fail, there's no harm in having a lie-down first. The Sorter's gone. No one will find out. It's not quitting if nobody knows.

'Getting tired?' Sath's voice is like a defibrillator to the chest.

Jolting upright, I find him standing less than a metre away, arms folded. Skin fresh and dewy like he's had a refreshing night's sleep. Well, good for him. I hope he swallowed a spider when he was snoring away.

My tongue is heavy and thick; I can't remember when I last had a sip of water. I have to unstick it from the roof of my mouth to ask, 'When did you get here?'

'You can stop, if you like.' He ignores the question. 'Do you want to stop?'

I'm about to say *yes, obviously*, but I've enough awareness to realise this is part of the test. Clipboard. Where's the next clipboard?

'No, thank you.' The words on the paper blur. I imagine one of them says *liar*; the rest of them certainly have. We're all lying about something. No rivers of blood though – I'm a special case in that regard. I glower at the lever as I send them to Asphodel. 'I'm having a lovely time.'

The slab before me turns into a bed. Plush pillows, a sumptuous mattress, a duvet that's thick enough to wrap around me three times over. My knees go weak.

'You don't need to complete these duties.' A warm hand settles on my back, nudging me forward. 'You can rest now. You can finish tomorrow.'

Tomorrow. That would be good. I'd sleep, then wake re-energised. I'd complete it faster then.

I said the same thing about that job application. I'll send it after my weekend away. One final read through, like it hadn't been proofread ten times before. Like I hadn't said *tomorrow* or *there'll be other jobs, I'll apply for the next one* for all the other emails I never sent.

And then I died.

'I'd rather finish now,' I say.

'Do you think you can?' he asks. The syllables may be different, but all I hear is *you're not good enough. You're a failure.* That warped version of Mum's voice is in my head again. *Give up now, Willow. You can't do this. Quitting is all you know.*

It's too late.

She's wrong. They all are. I'll show them. I know the consequences of quitting now, of giving up, and I'm not going through them again. 'I can do this.'

'You don't have to,' Sath says. 'Get into bed, Willow.'

I grit my teeth. 'No.'

'It's never-ending, this room. Carry on for miles and there'll still be another body. More work to do. More responsibility. Wouldn't it be easier to not do the work at all?'

It would. My eyelids threaten to close again. His hand shifts higher, and a thumb digs into my shoulder blade. The rush of pain-pleasure shooting down my spine spurs me onwards, and I sort another five bodies in rapid succession.

'It's impossible.' Sath dogs my every step. 'Being in charge of all this. All these afterlives in your hands. Why should you have that responsibility? Why should any of us?'

'Someone's got to do it.' The next chart says: *murderer*.

148

I freeze. What do I do? My hand wraps around the lever. It's a man. His knuckles are bloody. Who did he kill? How many?

He must deserve what I'm about to do to him. He must.

'You don't want to sort him, do you?' Sath continues. 'You know where he needs to go. What they'll do to him there.' There's a strain in his voice now. This wasn't part of the plan.

He's scared I'll fail.

People always are.

I tug the lever down and watch the body sink into black flames.

'I'll sort whoever I have to,' I say, resolute. 'I am not failing this task.'

Why not? You've failed everything else.

'Give up now.' He cuts across my path before I can take the next board. 'Where there's one, there's another. And another. Until the end of time. There is no end of the row.'

My shoulders sag. 'There has to be. You're lying. I won't quit.' My voice is scratchy. 'I won't. Not this time.'

I push him aside. Push the next lever. Tears stream down my face. I push the next. *There is no end of the row. You can't do this. You're not good enough.* I keep going. And going. And going. Sath needles me the whole time.

'You can try all you want; it won't work,' he says, barely more than a whisper, like this is as draining for him as it is for me. 'It'll never be enough. I'll never –'

I ram another lever, take a step forward, and hit a wall.

I blink at it. It's metal, just like the slabs, stretching from floor to ceiling. A dead end.

An end.

My face erupts into a smile. This is the nicest, prettiest wall

I've ever seen. If I thought it'd respond, I'd wrap my arms around it and give it a hug, but I settle for patting it instead, my touch almost reverent, like I'm caressing a long-sought-after relic. 'Is this . . .'

'Congratulations.' Sath's smile doesn't meet his eyes. 'You passed sloth.'

I sag against the wall, aka my new best friend. 'I did it.'

I actually did it. I didn't quit, and I *did* it. In this moment, I feel invincible, like I could jump off any cliff and survive because I'm that strong.

Smoke plumes from Sath's jacket, tiny wisps indicating a displeasure he can't hide. What's he got to be upset about? I'm a champion. A victor. There is no task I can't win.

He holds out a hand. 'Let's go.'

I allow him to portal us out of the room so I don't have to retrace my many, many steps. It also means we don't have to say goodbye to the Sorter, wherever she may be. Probably lazing on a hammock somewhere and laughing while I do her job.

Outside the morgue, we lean against opposite walls of the corridor. Some of the vines growing here have died since I last saw them, leaves curling and shrivelling around Sath's head. Red glows through a small crack behind them.

Sath assesses me. 'Are you all right?'

'Peachy,' I lie.

The past few – hours? Days? – are a blur of repetition, of one corpse after the other until they no longer resemble people at all. Despite that, the conversation I had with the Sorter remains vivid.

I can't help staring at Sath's chest, wondering if there's

anything inside at all. Can I ask? *Should* I ask? Sath's always cagey whenever I question what, exactly, he is, and I have plenty of other questions he might be more willing to answer. Starting with, 'Is Aric . . .'

'Dealt with.' It's not a snap, but almost. Guess I'm not as forgiven as I thought.

'Thanks.' I scuff my feet on the floor. 'I'm sorry if I . . . caused you a problem.'

'Caused me a –' Sath huffs a mocking laugh, shaking his head. A moment later, he's stone-cold sober. 'Did you find this task easy?'

'Not especially.'

'Well, they're only going to get worse,' he says. 'Everyone faces them in a different order, depending on their particular vice, and after your performance with Aric I don't know if you can control yours.'

Well. My sense of victory didn't last long. Now I'm a superhero that's just been shrunk by a ray gun. 'Why? What do you think my vice is?'

'You're impulsive. Hot-headed. Angry.'

Everything we've worked towards, gone, all over some tantrum about –

'I am none of those things,' I say loudly, over the memory.

'Really?' He arches a brow. 'The demon with a cue in his eye would beg to differ.'

'That was different.'

'Always an excuse. If you can't stop yourself lashing out, what's the point in doing any of this?' His eyes simmer, and maybe it's my imagination, but I swear I catch the smell of burning.

151

'Maybe *you* should get yourself under control first,' I throw back at him. 'Aric was a lapse of judgement. If a task was involved, I wouldn't have . . .' I break off.

I've no idea what I would have done.

But I've just proven I can do impossible things, and this is not the motivational pep talk I was hoping for. Would it kill him to say *well done, Willow, good job today*?

Sath sighs, and the fire in his gaze goes out. 'Let's hope you're right.'

'I *am* right,' I inform him. 'Maybe if you weren't determined to be grumpy, you'd see that.'

'I'm not grumpy.' He rakes a hand through his hair, suddenly looking as exhausted as I feel. 'Sloth is . . . difficult for me. Having to tempt you, it sets me on edge.'

I peer at him. 'The idea of being lazy sets you on edge?'

'Sloth isn't about laziness. It's . . . dereliction of duty, neglecting to take care of what one should.' He laughs bitterly. 'Something I know all about.'

The floor beneath us rumbles.

'What's happening?'

'Nothing,' he mutters, shoving shaking hands into his pockets. 'I should go. I'll see you next month.'

My chest constricts. I don't want to wait another month to see him. I'm not sure what that says about me as a person. He's possibly a demon and definitely a murderer. The Sath before me now could all be an act – and I don't care. He's the most interesting person here.

I should want to curl into a ball and sleep after the task, but standing near him has me wide-awake again, alert to every shift of his body as he tries to abandon me. Which can't be good for him either, honestly, if he's going to spend the whole time brooding.

Really, I'm doing him a favour.

'Sath,' I call after him. 'Wait. Do you want to . . . Are you busy?'

He opens his mouth, then closes it again. This happens several times. Finally, he says, 'Willow . . . that day in the cinema . . . I got caught up in the idea of being someone I'm not. I can't make that mistake again.'

'I'm not asking you to be someone you're not. I'm asking to hang out with you, just as you are. Is that such a crime? We can go to your rooms if you're worried about anyone seeing.'

Sath licks his lips. 'It's a bad idea. For many reasons.'

'You're talking to a girl who jumped off a cliff for fun.' I check no one's around before stepping into his space, forcing *him* to press against the wall for a change. Flames spark along his skin. 'What's one more bad idea?'

He makes a show of studying me, as though deciding how bad an idea I am. Despite the fact that every inch of me is covered in thick clothing, he makes it feel like all of me is on show. My stomach tightens. Other parts of me tighten. The more he looks, the more I'm free-falling towards something I shouldn't be, only this landing will split me open even more than the last.

'Fine,' he says, eyes gleaming. 'We can . . . hang out, as you like to put it.'

His expression turns wicked, mouth curving into a dangerous smile, although not for the reasons I expect.

'Tell me,' he says. 'How do you feel about Scrabble?'

16

I do not feel good about Scrabble. I am terrible at Scrabble. And yet somehow, we end up playing it all night. Sath wasn't joking about spending a year learning the dictionary, because he trounces me every time with ridiculous words like *callipygian*. I don't know what it means, but he laughs every time I ask, so I can only assume he's cheating. By the time I've persuaded him to magic over some other options from the games room, I'm too tired to play, my eyes closing and my elbow slipping from the arm of the sofa.

'You should get some rest.' Sath scoops up his tiles and deposits them in the drawstring pouch.

I stretch. I *should* sleep, he's right, but I can't bring myself to leave. My room is cold and far away, whereas this sofa is right here, along with Sath, who's – as always – emitting as much heat as a small furnace. Besides, this is the first night since I arrived where I've been able to forget where, exactly, I am. It's easy to pretend there are no demons lurking outside when I'm not caught up in my own thoughts, staring at the ceiling of my room, terrified to fall asleep in case I have another nightmare. Time is finally moving at a sensible pace, and I want to keep that momentum until the next task.

'Okay,' I say eventually, hoping my disappointment isn't evident. I eye the pile of games we haven't played. 'Maybe tomorrow . . .'

'Tomorrow I'll need to make an appearance in Dionysus,' Sath cuts me off like a sucker punch to the gut. I must not hide the pathetic way my face falls in time because he plants a hand on my shoulder before I can exit in a huff, and adds softly, 'Perhaps the night after?'

His words stoke the embers of a fire in my belly, warmth blooming within me in a rush. Maybe my Find Willow a Friend mission hasn't been a total failure after all. Outwardly I shrug, gifting him with the smallest of smiles. 'Sure.'

I half walk, half skip to my room, and not even the stares of two demons loitering in the entrance chamber can bring me down. It's only when I'm inside that I worry those stares may have been something other than curiosity at seeing me leave Sath's chambers.

What if Aric's been talking?

Despite how shattered I am, I don't sleep well. Semiconscious, I toss and turn, feeling sweat pool in my armpits, down the back of my neck, unable to open my eyes and do anything about it. I dream of the tunnel again, of blood crashing over me in one great wave, only now there's a shape within that fluid, a shape with a spiked tail and sharp claws.

I wake with my heart pounding and my hair in a matted knot.

Knowing sleep is lost to me now, I drag myself out of bed and head to the showers on level three hundred. The cliff opens into a cavern hosting a communal swimming pool, a waterfall tumbling down one side of the rock face, the splash of water so thunderous it nearly drowns out the shrieks of humans playing with a colourful beach ball or jumping off the sides into the shallow end.

My feet slap against damp stone as I make my way past the pool. One section is unoccupied, and it's only when I draw closer I spy something green deep beneath the surface – a demon lying in wait for anyone who draws too close.

I shiver, hurrying towards an archway that leads to the showers housed in hundreds upon hundreds of alcoves carved into the grey stone. Our privacy is maintained by a black veil that shutters over every entrance as soon as you step inside. I walk down the corridor – I've never reached the end – searching for a free cubicle. Humans clutching towels pass me with chattering lips and gooseflesh skin. The showers here are fairly pathetic, the spray of water barely more than a trickle and tepid in temperature. Maybe that's part of our punishment: we're staying in a budget hotel that didn't pay for decent boiler pressure.

The corridor splits in two halfway down, and a familiar voice makes me pause. The other tunnel leads to various hot springs, and I peer through the mist and steam in the first of many small caves to find Harper and her friends sitting in the pool. A pang of longing pulsates in my chest, like the reverb from a string that's just been plucked.

Even if Sath holds to his promise of a rematch tomorrow, I still have tonight to deal with, plus all the others he declares himself unavailable.

I'm tired of being alone.

Watching them interact, I deliberate whether or not they'll accept me after what they witnessed yesterday.

I step soundlessly through the mist, so they don't notice me spying on them. Glowing crystals are inset in the walls of the cave, bathing them in an ethereal green light, and the smell of salt stings the air.

The boy is in the water, dark curls plastered to his face. Harper and the girl sit with their legs dangling into its depths, Harper's arm around her shoulders, her fingers playing absent-mindedly with strands of black hair. They speak in low murmurs, and then the boy grins and jumps up, splashing the pair of them. They shriek, leaping into the water after him, ducking his head under before allowing him to resurface with a gasp. Their laughter bounces around the walls of the cave as the three of them swim to the edge of the springs.

The way Harper looks at them makes my chest ache harder. Noah used to look at me like that, at least in the early days. I can barely remember it now. His whole face is a fading dream, his features turning vague, pictures of a puzzle I can't piece together. Guilt is a stone in my stomach. I spent last night playing Scrabble with the Devil, and I didn't think of my boyfriend once.

As though sensing my presence, Harper turns her head. Her eyes go wide when she spots me. 'Willow!'

'Hello again.' I wave, a gesture I hope says *I am not a violent person and you would not be at risk if you let me join you.* 'I can't stop bumping into you.'

'Asphodel has a way of leading you to where you need to be,' the boy says.

Please. If that were true, it would have led me to the exit by now.

Harper lifts herself out of the springs, a puddle forming at her feet, before wrapping a towel around her waist. Her hair is streaked pumpkin orange today, contrasting with the blue in her eyes.

'This is Amelia and Henry.' She gestures at her companions. 'We weren't sure . . . We thought King Sathanas might have . . .'

'Set me on fire?' It's weird hearing his name on someone else's lips. To me, he's Sath, and to her, he's a stranger. Someone to be revered, feared. All I want to do is beat him at Scrabble. 'He did something else instead.'

I let her infer what she wants from that. Besides, it's not like the tasks aren't punishment, in a way.

'Why don't you sit with us?' Harper says. 'And tonight, we're going to Dionysus, if you want to join. You're always there alone.'

I bristle. She makes it sound like a flaw, rather than a choice. But admitting why I've been avoiding people would be a can of worms I'd rather not open, so I settle for saying, 'That'd be nice.'

It's not a lie, but it's not the truth either. Nice would be getting out of here. This is merely a way for me to keep my sanity before I do.

I shuck off my sandals before sitting on the edge of the springs and dipping my feet into the water. The temperature here is much hotter than the showers; the steam mists over my face, a little too warm to be comfortable.

'So, let's start with the obvious,' Harper says. 'How did you die?'

I freeze.

'*Harper*.' Amelia nudges her in the side. 'You can't keep asking people that.'

She pouts. 'Why not? It's an icebreaker.'

'You need to find better icebreakers.' Henry rolls his eyes and hoists himself out of the water. 'Don't tell her anything you don't want to, Willow. She's a frightful gossip.'

'I don't *gossip*, I listen. There's a difference.' Harper loops her arm through mine as though it's the most natural thing in the world. 'But fine. I'll tell you about me instead. When I was alive, I'd attend all these balls and high-society parties, and I loved them, don't get me wrong, but after a while all the people were so . . . similar. Every person Mama introduced me to wanted to talk about the weather. And now I'm here, meeting new people every day and collecting all these stories I never would have heard before. I wouldn't call that gossiping, would you?' She shoots Henry a glare that's got as much force as a feather. 'It's . . . good fun.'

I glance at Henry and Amelia in turn, waiting for them to tell her she's clearly lost her mind. Instead, they stare at her with an unfathomable fondness.

'You realise there are demons here, right? Nothing about this is fun.'

'You learn how to avoid them eventually. Besides, they're a small price to pay for everything else. I couldn't look like *this* when I was alive.' She gestures at her hair.

This, at least, earns me some solidarity from Henry, who exchanges an incredulous glance with me before saying, 'I'm not sure magic hair dye is going to win her over, Harp.'

'Well, it's not *just* the magic. Or the people. Have you found the art gallery yet? The library? Or what about Asphodel's garden? It's so beautiful. I can take you if you like.'

I'm hit with a familiar sense of longing, of desire for new things. I chew my lip. There's no harm in a tour, I suppose. I can't get out any sooner – the tasks will happen when they happen. I'm not wasting time, I'm merely filling it.

'Okay,' I say. 'I'd like that.'

Harper beams, her smile warmer than the sun, but then she catches sight of something over my shoulder and her smile falls. Henry angles his body as though he can shield Amelia. A crawling sensation creeps up my back, the feeling of eyes on me, eyes that burn with loathing. I swallow before turning to face . . . Aric. Of course.

He lopes into the room, fully recovered after our confrontation, settling on a bench embedded into the rock that people usually use to store towels. He doesn't speak, merely watches, red eyes fixated on me.

'We should go,' I murmur.

Harper nods, not moving. I don't blame her. I'm rooted to the spot in the same way, not knowing what Aric will do when we climb out of the pool. Despite the heat of the cave, I'm cold all over. What if Sath failed to protect me, and Aric's here for revenge?

Sath. I think his name over and over, as though he's a magic lift.

'You reek of him,' Aric finally speaks. He cocks his head to one side. 'One day, I will reek of you both.' He eyes the other three. 'Of all of you. Your blood will bathe my tongue, delicious and sweet.'

Nausea coils in my gut. 'You're a real charmer, you know that?'

Harper gasps. I wince, regretting the words the second they leave my lips. Aric's here because of me, and if I don't keep my mouth shut they could well be the ones to suffer the consequences. I fold my hands together in what I hope demonstrates contrition. I need to get everyone out of here before I do something inherently stupid.

The room trembles before I get the chance.

Dust shakes free from the ceiling. Henry lurches from the far wall right as a jet of lava punches a hole through it, spewing thick orange liquid into the springs. I pull my legs from the water, scrambling back as the lava bubbles and spits heat at my face. Stone grinds all around us. Rocks drop from above and are immediately swallowed whole, melting beneath the surface.

It stops almost as soon as it started, the room rumbling to a halt, like the world was spinning on its axis too quickly before righting itself. Mouth ajar, I pant for breath, but it's only me acting surprised by this turn of events. Harper and the others merely look perturbed, whereas a quick glance at Aric tells me that, whatever just happened, he's delighted about it.

Asphodel is changing.

This is the kind of thing Sath warned me about, a sign Asphodel is cracking at the seams.

Aric's upper lip curls, revealing a glimmer of white fangs. 'Not long now,' he whispers. Directly to me, he adds, 'When I tear them apart, I will let you watch.'

My fists clench. Sath must have the patience of a saint. Five minutes in Aric's presence and I want to do more than set him on fire. My anger radiates off me hotter than the steam from the surface of the springs, and I'm on my feet before I can stop myself.

Aric tuts, waving a finger at me. 'Not today. But soon.'

He disappears before I can tell him what I think of him. Whirls of mist coil around my feet like ghosts of snakes, and I kick them away before turning to face the others. The springs glow red behind them, but they barely give the lava a second glance, like it's as mundane as traffic on a Monday morning.

'Does this happen a lot?' I ask. What I mean is *join me in alarm, why don't you?*

'I suppose,' Harper replies. 'Lava gets everywhere in this place. We used to have a lovely ballroom – *so* fancy compared to Dionysus – but it got flooded a few years ago. I heard Asphodel has to stretch to make room for more people.'

Another of Sath's lies. Maybe I can press her into working it out on her own. 'Flooding kind of defeats the purpose of stretching.'

She contemplates this for all of a second before shrugging. 'Maybe it stretches because of the flooding.'

I press my lips together, wishing I wasn't bound to secrecy. Wishing Aric hadn't seemed so damn happy about what just happened – like he knows full well what it means.

'Come, sit.' She taps the ground beside her. 'It should be settled for the day now.'

The word *settled* is doing some heavy lifting there, but I comply, sitting cross-legged at her side and finding myself agreeing when she asks me again to join them in Dionysus tonight. My attention is on the lava blackening before my eyes, layering the springs like charred pond scum.

This is supposed to be for eternity, Asphodel an hourglass that will never tip the other way, but now it feels like the glass has been turned, the sand already falling.

And if I can't complete the next four tasks, I'll sink with it.

17

Despite my lingering foreboding, Asphodel stays still for the next few weeks, and I settle into a routine. I spend half my nights with Sath, learning he is a terribly sore loser when it comes to games that aren't Scrabble, which fills me with no end of joy. The rest of the time I'm with Harper. She takes me around Asphodel during the day, and it appears she has a habit of collecting strays because every floor we visit I'm told *I simply must introduce you to Fatima* and *oh, look! There's Percy. I love Percy.*

I've come to the conclusion Harper loves pretty much everyone she meets, which would explain why she's putting up with me. Still, it's nice, having her attention. When we're in Dionysus she tends to attract crowds of admirers, like the dead are moths to her flame, but she sticks to me, Amelia and Henry the most.

Despite Dionysus being twice the size of any club I went to on Earth, she is impossible to lose, her hand constantly entwined with mine. It doesn't stop me looking over my shoulder every five seconds like I'm expecting her to disappear. Sasha disappeared all the time. I'd go to the bar for us both and find her missing on my return, leaving me to spend the rest of the night alone, wandering around like a stray puppy. By the time I'd found a group to adopt me, she'd have called Noah to say I was lost and needing claiming.

As far as this new routine goes, I don't hate it. When I wake, I feel lighter, somehow. Every day is filled with a new possibility now they aren't planned out for me. I don't have to worry about disappointing Noah and then having to worry about saying the right thing to make him stay. I can just . . . *be*.

It's only when I come across Aric lurking round corners that the smile drops from my face, and I remember I do not, under any circumstances, want to stay here. Not when at least one demon actively hates me, or when the gates could burst open at any moment. When I'm constantly at risk of ending up in the Void listening to that all-too-familiar voice telling me I failed at becoming all the things I promised I'd be. I have to get home and prove that voice wrong instead.

My counting is more out of whack than ever, and there are only eighty scratches on my wardrobe when a dress appears inside. There's a note pinned to it, written in elegant cursive, that says *wear me tonight*. I swallow. It's jet black, with thin straps and a plunging, heart-shaped neckline. Tiny sequins are stitched into the bodice, glistening like fallen snow under a moonlit sky. The skirt is floor-length and sheer, a thigh-high slit on one side and intricately beaded flowers trailing up the other.

My skin prickles, nerves twisting my insides into knots as I try to work out what kind of task requires an outfit like this. Noah's bought me several dresses over the years, a new one every time he took me to some fundraiser or gala hosted by

165

his family – tedious things, honestly, but Noah saw them as networking opportunities, schmoozing his way through the crowd and picking up future business contacts while I smiled prettily at his side – but those dresses never looked like this. For one, they had a lot more . . . fabric. He didn't like me having too much on show, saying he already knew I was beautiful, and if I cared for him at all, I shouldn't want to catch anyone's attention but his.

This dress, though, makes me feel beautiful without the need for his validation. The material is cool against my skin, fitting me like a glove, gliding over my body like water rippling over rock and clinging to curves I didn't know I had. I run my hands over it, barely recognising the person in the mirror as I admire it from every angle. I have to force myself to turn away in order to apply make-up: smoky-brown eyeshadow, a quick flash of eyeliner, a smidge of dark red lipstick which hasn't quite dried by the time there's a rap at the door.

My stomach falls to the floor.

I allow myself one final glance in the mirror, smoothing non-existent creases in my dress and patting tangles in my hair I didn't try to tame. Another, more insistent, knock has me frowning. Maybe I'd be ready if I'd had some warning, did he ever consider that?

My palms are sweaty as they go for the handle. I don't feel an iota of surprise when I find Sath standing there, two glasses in his hand, one containing the green liquid he's given me before, the other fizzing with something bright pink. I do, however, feel plenty of iotas about the way a lock of dark hair falls over his forehead.

I miss the way it was when I first met him. Short, cropped too close to his head to be this distracting. Now it makes me want to reach out and –

I ball my hands into fists at my sides. Sath, meanwhile, is running his gaze up and down my dress, drinking in every inch of me, giving no indication whether it's to his satisfaction or not.

It seems safer not to look at him at all, so I jerk my head at the two glasses instead. 'One of those for me?'

'Your next task. Gluttony.' He hands the pink drink over to me. 'One drink, and no more.'

I take it, sniffing cautiously. 'What is it?'

'Wine, containing snake venom,' he says. 'It can be . . . addictive. Among other things.'

That sounds wholly unappealing. 'What other things? And how addictive?'

'It'll make you thirst.' His tone stays bland, but I do not like that word choice. *Thirst*, not thirsty.

Knowing he won't elaborate, I take a deep breath, and bring the glass to my lips. Indecision keeps it hovered there, the rim chilling my lower lip. I have no idea what this is going to do to me.

'You'll need to resist another drink for three hours,' Sath adds.

Three hours. It sounds manageable, if it weren't for the lingering threat of what a *thirsting* Willow might do.

If I want out of here, I haven't got a choice. I drink it in one.

It tastes like sugar and strawberries, and it's thick, almost like cough medicine. Despite that, it goes down easily and, immediately, I'm tingling. My fingers buzz like they're connected to some sort of electric-shock machine, and my legs are weightless, like I could simply float and float forever. I swish the skirt of my dress around. It's lovely and breezy. Sath should give it a go; he must be hot walking around in tight pants all the time. What if he's got a tail like Aric's hidden down there, and it gets crushed? I burst out laughing, beaming at him, because he's really very pretty, but Sath merely raises an eyebrow and holds his own drink to his mouth.

I want it. I take a step towards him. His eyes flare gold, halting my tracks. 'This doesn't have the venom, I'm afraid. You don't want this one.'

How does he know what I want?

If it tastes the same, I want it. I'm parched already. My throat is empty, my stomach a cavern. Why can't I have it?

Sath drinks before I can snatch the glass from him. I pout. His gaze flicks to my lower lip, to the way it juts out in protest, before taking my arm and portalling us to the balcony on Dionysus's level.

He keeps his distance as we head towards the entrance and the area grows busier, which is a pity, because walking is proving difficult. My head spins. The cavern's fuller than usual, packed with bodies, the music barely louder than the buzz of chatter.

'I'll find you later,' he murmurs, fingers brushing my lower back so quickly I might have imagined it. Then he melts into the crowd as though we're perfect strangers, as though entering at the same time was by chance and not design.

I bite down a smile. I like the idea of him being my secret, the King of Hell who talks to no one but his demons, whose only interaction with the humans is when they need punishing. Not me. I'm special. Unable to contain it any longer, I grin at a nearby demon. It flutters its wings in response. They're like cobwebs, made of fine silvery strands, and I want to touch them, to strum them like a harp, they're beautiful –

The moth flies away. Rude. Where did it go? I want it. I want to touch the moth, its wings, they're pretty, and I'm special, why won't it let me touch it when I'm Sath's friend? Maybe that moth should be bowing to me and not him.

I stumble into a pillar.

Fuck.

That drink did a lot more than make me thirsty. I clutch the pillar, dizzy now, the lights in the cavern too bright. My pulse is erratic, and my tongue feels fuzzy. I want another drink. That would be best. I'd feel better after that. One more drink, then another, and another, and then I can touch the moth and – *ooh*. Another demon prowls past me. Maybe I'll touch that instead. I can yank on its tail; that would be good fun. It roams out of reach. Everything's out of reach.

The music is too loud.

I try to focus. Sath watches proceedings from his throne, situated on a dais high above the dance floor. A waterfall of lava streams behind the seat, bathing him in an orange glow. He's unfairly beautiful. Why have I never noticed before? It's not like I was unaware he was attractive, but now it's as though I've been seeing him through a misted lens and the drink has stripped away the fog.

It'll make you thirst.

I knew there was a threat there I didn't like. I can't stop staring at him: at the angles of his cheekbones, the fullness of his mouth, at the way he's neglected to button his shirt properly, revealing an expanse of skin I didn't need to witness. I swallow. Wanting a second drink suddenly seems the least of my problems. I try to picture him like he is on our game nights: sweatpants, T-shirt. An infuriating smirk on his face because he's beating me at Scrabble, again.

It doesn't help. In a room full of people, he's all I see.

A demon with pale scales approaches him, carrying a tray with more green drinks, and Sath takes two glasses. My eyes widen. One is for me. I know it is. He won't give me the pink wine so he'll give me this instead; a lovely treat for lovely Willow. I beam, shoving through the crowd, needing to get to him, get to that drink, my throat is dry, every part of me empty and bare, I need it to be filled, I need –

Sath drinks them both in two gulps.

Bastard.

I can't work out what's louder: the drums or my own raging breaths. He took my drink. I'm so thirsty.

And hungry.

Do they have chicken nuggets? I want chicken nuggets. Suddenly nothing is more important, not even ogling Sath. The room is as scattered as my thoughts, a blur of movement bathed in the streaky lights the strobes cast overhead. I need to find a chicken demon. I can cut it apart. Then I can have my chicken. Cluck, cluck, cluck. I raise my hands in the air and spin, round and round like the other humans. We're all spinning, spinning together, isn't that lovely –

Except they're laughing.

They're loud. Too loud; I don't like it. I press my hands to my ears. I need them to stop. I need –

'Willow!' A hand grabs my wrist. I jerk back. It's hard to focus. Harper stands in front of me. Her hair is tied into space buns again; I want to poke my finger through the middle of one, but I'm dimly aware that would be inappropriate. I settle for staring at her brand-new nose ring instead. She waves a hand in front of my face. 'Are you okay?'

I am more than okay. I am delightful. I open my mouth to tell her, and fail. My throat feels like I've swallowed sandpaper. It hurts. I still don't have my nuggets. The room tilts on its axis. 'Have you seen any chicken?'

'No . . .' She peers at me. 'Are you sure you're all right?'

'Perfect,' I say, wrapping an arm around her shoulders and leading her to the dance floor. Amelia and Henry are there too, and Henry is wearing the most spectacular pair of flared trousers I've ever seen. Silver and glittering, like a disco ball exploded near him. I press a kiss to his cheek, leaving an imprint of dark red on the corner of his mouth. In return, he hands me a glass full of pink wine. 'I was told to give you this.'

I can't grab it fast enough.

The glass is cool against my fingers. I swirl the liquid round and round. I want it. I want it badly. Maybe just one sip. Sath won't find out. Except –

I turn to find his eyes are on me. One leg crossed over his knee, his elbow leaning against the arm of the throne, the picture of relaxed. But I know him better than that. I know what it means when his eyes turn golden, like honey: that the flames are only a moment behind, and it's me making him angry, because he thinks I'm going to do something stupid, to fail –

I spill the contents on the floor. 'I don't want it.'

171

It's a lie. I'm trapped in a desert, sinking into the sand, and I've thrown away my only oasis. But it's fine. Everything's fine. I. Am. Delightful. We dance in a circle, and through the throng of people around us, I catch a glimpse of red eyes, a spiked tail, a feeling of burning loathing spearing in my direction. I ignore it. Aric can't touch me tonight, not when I'm floating like this. Henry performs flamboyant dance moves and I laugh and laugh and laugh, Amelia's arm linked through mine, Harper's grin almost enough to pour warmth into that empty space in my stomach. Almost, but not enough.

I'm so very, very thirsty.

Despite it all, my gaze keeps drifting to Sath. He sits alone. Nobody, not even the demon handing him drink after drink, talks to him. He must be sad, spending an eternity by himself.

The pounding in my head propels me towards him. He has what I want. A whole tray of drinks sits next to him now. He can spare me one. He can.

I just have to make him want to.

I leave my friends behind – the only thing I need right now is Sath and his delicious tray of alcohol – and mosey over to the throne. The charcoaled steps leading to the dais are awfully steep up close. Sath's lips twitch as I clamber up in a manner which cannot, in any way, be described as graceful.

I think I may be sweating. I'm certainly warm. I don't let that deter me as I plop on to the arm of his throne and smile benevolently at him. I'm doing a good deed. I'm keeping him company.

My mouth waters.

'Come for another drink?' Sath takes a sip of his own. I follow the movement of the glass to his lips, of the way his throat bobs as he swallows. I want to rip the glass from his hands. I want to open his mouth and take the fluid right out of him. I want, I want, I want . . . I toss my hair over my shoulder. My neck is damp. Sath puts the glass down and gestures at my current position on his throne. 'I could send you to Glacantrum for insubordination.'

'You could,' I say. 'But you won't. I'm the only one who talks to you.'

'Is that so?' The corners of his mouth turn up. A little thrill shoots through me; I did this, *I* made him smile, because I'm his favourite. I've never been anyone's favourite before.

Then I realise he's not smiling *at* me, he's smiling *because* of me.

I appear to be falling into his lap.

I straighten. 'I'm dizzy.'

'It's the drink.'

'*You* don't seem dizzy.' All the drinks next to him are green. Will wine without the venom be enough to soothe me? It'll have to be. I lean forward, towards the tray on the other side of him, my arm reaching out –

'Unlike you,' Sath says, lightly pinching my elbow, 'I can hold my liquor.'

The sting on my skin is enough to snap me out of my blatant attempt at thievery. Huffing, I readjust, trying to get comfy. The slit up the side of my dress spreads apart, revealing bare skin and too much thigh. Sath stares at the exposed flesh for a second before taking another drink and observing the crowd.

I survey them with him, like we're holding court together.

173

From up here, on a night like this with no violence, and the tingling, floating feeling singing in my veins, it's almost pleasant. I catch a glimpse of the Sorter on the dance floor, her head thrown back, grinning at a demon with antlers protruding from its forehead.

A touch on my calf jerks my focus. It's nothing, light as a feather, one stroke then another to get my attention, but something about it sends a fresh rush of need racing through me, one that's more all-consuming than my desire for a drink.

'It's not safe for you to stay too long,' Sath says. 'The demons will ask questions. You should get back down there.'

I stare at him, pulse racing. Willow should do this, Willow should do that. What about what Willow wants?

I want him to touch me.

My hand clamps over his, keeping it pressed against my leg. The warmth of his palm is a lightning strike to my every nerve ending, a welcome distraction from the burning in my throat. I try and shuffle closer without falling on him again. 'But I like it here.'

He tries to pull his hand from mine, but I don't let him.

'Willow.' His eyes darken. 'What are you doing?'

'I don't know,' I whisper, dragging his hand higher, until it reaches my knee. I just know this is a different kind of desperation to the one that had me climbing up here, and I don't want it to end. 'Is this so terrible?'

His thumb skims, just once, over my knee, a temporary indulgence before he tugs his hand from mine, more forcibly this time, and settles it safely in his lap. 'You don't know what you're doing.'

'Yes, I do.' I pout.

'Hm.' His gaze drops lower, landing on the slit along my thigh, and then he clenches his fists. 'You really should leave.'

That lock of hair has fallen over his eyes again. Before I can second-guess myself, I smooth it back, my touch lingering on the curve of his cheek. He gapes at me, shadows drifting off him in waves as I lean closer and murmur, 'What if I don't want to leave?'

'Then I'll offer you another drink.' Despite his earlier protestations, his fingers dance around my ankle, teasing the idea he might touch me again. 'And that would be bad.'

'What if I want to be bad?' My voice is raspy and hoarse. It sounds nothing like me. I don't know what I'm *saying*. I only know the pounding in my head has returned, and my throat is parched, and I need something to cure all the aching parts of me.

'In that case . . .' Sath holds out a glass. 'Drink.'

I stare at it. It's everything I want. To quench the thirst, to lose control, to go down there and dance with everyone I can find, to dance with *Sath*, if he's willing, to see what happens when those fingers stop teasing and start doing; I spread my legs a little wider, and I have no idea if this is a good idea or not, but I'm not allowed to drink, I'm not, I'm not, and this seems like a suitable distraction, and –

Was that a chicken?

I saw feathers. A white tuft of fur atop someone's head. Sath's hand stills. 'Willow?'

I swear it was a chicken.

'I want nuggets,' I mumble.

175

Sath pulls back. My skin feels cold.

'Go,' Sath says. 'It'll be over soon.'

I whip round to face him. 'Can't it be over now?'

I'm already gagging for another drink, for those nuggets, for Sath – I blink, and cross my legs. I am not gagging for anything where Sath is concerned. My breaths come out too fast and too uneven to be normal as I will him to declare the task completed.

He doesn't.

'You have two more hours.' He jerks his head at the dance floor. 'Go.'

And I'm dismissed, sent stumbling into the waiting crowd, my skin burning in every place he touched me and my thirst nowhere near abated.

A thirst I don't think a dozen goblets of venom-laced wine could quench.

18

Time passes in bursts and fragments. The more I sweat, the thirstier I get, and the more I need to do to distract myself. I can barely see through the blinding lights, the stinging in my eyes, the crush of people surrounding me. There are hands everywhere. On me. Next to me. I can't bring myself to care.

It was like this whenever I lost Sasha in a club and I had to find new friends for the night. They'd talk and I'd pretend to listen, feeling like the whole world was spinning round me while I stayed completely, utterly still, not knowing what direction to take.

All I ever wanted was for Noah to come and find me. To take me home and press a kiss to my forehead and tell me everything was going to be okay.

I want someone to tell me that now.

My stomach tightens. I stop dancing. I sway, lost and lonely, on the floor, bodies bumping into me and making me trip. Tears prick my eyes. The dancing isn't enough, being touched isn't enough, I want . . .

I want, I want, I want.

You want another drink, Willow. What harm could it do?

It could do plenty. *One more drink* is how I ended up on that cliff top. How I ended up *here*, with demon voices in my head I need to ignore at all costs.

Despite all that, my gaze drifts to the throne.

It's empty.

My eyes widen. I whirl round, furious he'd leave without saying goodbye, without *giving me another drink*; thirst claws at my throat, and where has he gone, I need him, I need him to help me, because without the distraction of dancing all I can think is I'm alone, and I'm thirsty, and he's the only one who can fix this.

Several turns around the dance floor and I finally find him, standing with a group of girls on the edge of the room. They're young, and beautiful, and don't have the usual panic in their eyes at being near him. His head is bent low to allow one of them to whisper in his ear. What is she saying? Why is he –

'There you are!' Harper clamps her hand around my arm. 'I was worried.'

'Sorry,' I mumble. I can't bring myself to look at her. Sath's laughing. He's laughing in a way he's never laughed with me, not that I can remember, and I don't know why I care, why it matters; he's my ticket out of here, I'm going to get him his concession and he can laugh with whomever he wants.

I'm going home to Noah and forehead kisses and the ring that's waiting for me.

That doesn't make me feel any better. I don't want Sath laughing like that with them; I want him to laugh like that with me. I'm the one he shares secrets with, the one who's been in his quarters, who he has game nights with, I'm the *only* one.

Unless I'm not.

The thought hits me like a freight train. A cold chill sweeps down my neck at the idea I'm not special at all. *Taking care of business*, that's what he says when I ask where he goes the nights I don't see him. What if he's with one of them? What if he's with *all* of them? Maybe he has hundreds of us trying to fulfil his tasks; maybe I'm not special after all, because why would I be, I'm just a girl who died after doing something idiotic, who ignored her boyfriend's perfectly sensible advice because she couldn't cope with what happened to –

Copper fills my mouth. I've bitten my tongue, but I barely feel the sting of pain.

'Willow,' Harper tries again. 'Are you okay? Do you want me to take you to your room?'

Yes. No. My head pounds. I try to pull her into the throng of dancers, but she slips from my grasp like an unspooling rope, leaving me unmoored and drifting in a sea of demons. Claws scrape my dress. Fangs graze my neck. My heartbeat thrums to the beat of drums. I don't like it here any more, but I don't know how to escape. Something tugs at me. Hard. I want it to stop.

My mouth is dry. I can't scream.

I'm pulled, back and forth, side to side, like a boat caught in a storm, and they're going to tear me apart, and there's nothing I can do to stop it; maybe that would be better than staying here, doing Sath's tasks, feeling important when I'm not important at all, the bastard –

'Enough.'

The floor rumbles beneath my feet at the sound of that voice.

Immediately, I'm released. Demons scatter; the pressure on my body dissipates. Without anyone holding me, I topple, but then hands catch me and spin me round, pulling me against something firm. I breathe in the scent of rain and peppermint, and I hate the relief that smell instils.

I glower at Sath. I refuse to be grateful he's come to my rescue, because it's his fault I needed rescuing in the first place. 'Protecting your investment?'

He raises a brow. 'Do you not want me to?'

'I'm not sure you need me.' I scowl as we begin to sway on the spot. 'I saw you just now. How many others have signed up for your tasks?'

'You sound jealous.' Sath smirks. 'Well, that bodes well for envy.'

My scowl deepens. 'Answer the question.'

'Some recent arrivals who have yet to see my capabilities stopped to talk to me,' he replies. 'Sometimes I can't help but indulge in the fantasy I'm not something to be feared. They'll learn otherwise soon enough. As for the tasks . . .' His head dips lower. 'You're the only one, Willow.'

I shudder, wanting to believe him but not knowing if I can. If he's that desperate for someone to succeed, he'd want the best odds possible. I should have thought of it sooner. But I *am* the only person he's danced with tonight. That must mean something. Much to my dismay, the music's slowed, and it's less distracting this way. I'm all too aware of how close we are, of the way his hand presses lightly but deliberately against my hip. I don't remember putting my hands around his shoulders, and yet there they are. Everyone around us is too distracted to notice the Devil's in the middle of the dance floor, and it feels as though we've been sealed inside a bubble no amount of laughing girls can pop.

I'm warm, and I'm not sure why.

'You're sweating,' Sath murmurs.

His other hand is on my back; he must be able to feel the moisture through my dress. I can't bring myself to be embarrassed. The thirst is returning. Maybe that's why he's here, dancing with me, touching me, maybe this is all part of his temptation, because I've never wanted to ask for another drink more. I have to have it. The longer we stay like this, the more I'm gasping for air, my fingers tightening around his shoulders, digging into his shirt, curling themselves around the silken fabric.

'Talk to me,' I pant.

'About what?'

'Something. Anything.' My brain scrambles to form a coherent sentence. I need more wine. 'The other tasks. What's left. You said something about anger, and . . .'

'Wrath will be last. First you'll have envy, then lust.'

'Lust?' I echo. My voice sounds high-pitched.

A ghost of a smile flickers over his lips. 'A personal favourite.'

My throat feels more parched than ever. What will I have to resist for *that*? Maybe he'll bring me Noah. I'll have to prepare an apology for before we get down to the tempting. I'll tell him I'm sorry for being so exhausting, for all the times my moping dragged him down, for being dumb enough to die, and then I'll show him how sin-free I am by passing the test with flying colours.

It'll be easy. And then I'll pass wrath just as easy-peasy because despite what people say I *do not have anger issues*, and then I'll go home, having proven myself perfect and ready to live my perfect life.

My cheeks hurt from smiling. I have no idea why Sath is frowning at me.

'What?' I ask.

'I've . . . never seen you this happy,' he says. 'I wasn't aware the idea of spending the night with me was so appealing.'

I freeze. Humans and demons gyrate around us like glitter in a shaken snow globe, while we're the miniature figurines glued to the bottom. I gape up at him. 'What do you mean, spend the night with *you*?'

He cocks his head. 'Who did you think would be tempting you?'

Noah. My perfectly safe boyfriend, who Mum chose for me for that very reason.

With Sath, the only safe option is to run in the opposite direction.

'Well, that should be easy,' I lie. 'Because I have no interest in being tempted by you.'

'Really?' His hand slides down my back, settling on my waist and pushing me closer. The material of my dress is far too thin; I can detect every inch of his muscled body lined up against me. He leans down to murmur in my ear, 'Then why aren't you breathing?'

'I'm dead,' I remind him. Not that that's stopped me from breathing before.

I hope he can't feel how fast my heart is racing.

A knuckle skims up my ribcage. 'That's not why.'

'Fuck you.'

'That's precisely what we're trying to avoid.'

I really think I might hate him. He sounds endlessly amused, completely unaffected by everything; his mouth is still against my ear and I can tell his lips are curled, like I'm some silly human getting flustered over nothing.

Which I am. It's nothing. His wine is making me hot and bothered, and thirst for that is making me thirsty for *everything*, and as soon as this night is over I won't have any interest in the way he feels warm and solid against me, his knuckle resting just below my breast, his other hand holding me against him like he's the only thing between me staying upright or falling to the floor and never getting up again.

Okay, so that last part might be true. My knees are *very* shaky.

He spins me round, my back flush against his chest, and his hands – those damn hands – are moving lower, down my waist to the top of my legs, the material of my dress bunching in his fists as he drags it upwards. Instinctively, I arch against him, reaching round and threading my hand through his hair.

Sath's fingers find the slit in my dress, sliding beneath the fabric and over bare skin, and I don't understand how lust can be any worse than this, because I'm burning and aching; something hard presses into me and I grind against it, making Sath hiss in my ear and move his hand further along the inside of my thigh, and I should be asking him what he thinks he's doing, where he thinks that hand is *going*, but his mouth is against my ear, his breath warm on the side of my face. And then he says, 'Have another drink, Willow.'

Bastard. I tread on his toe.

'Absolutely *not*,' I say, wrenching from his grasp and spinning to face him, despite the voice in my head that's saying *yes . . . whatever he offers you . . . yes*. 'Is all this –' I gesture between us – 'what you're doing, just to distract me into failing this task?'

He steps back into my space. Before I can stop him, his hands are on my waist, tugging me against him once more, and I am forced to ignore the obvious indication this wasn't all for show pressing against my stomach. I shiver, looking over his shoulder, desperate for a distraction. Those dancing nearby still aren't watching us, too lost in their own daze, spurred on by a combination of the music and the potency of the drinks, and I can only hope they've been like that the whole time.

'As much as I'd like you to pass,' Sath says, answering my question, 'I have a job to do. I have to offer.'

'And hope I say no.'

'And hope you say no.'

We stare at one another. I don't want to say no. I don't want to say no to any of it. And that scares me. I sink against him, letting the music take over, dancing for the sake of dancing and allowing his hands to roam up and down my spine. All those nights back on Earth, I danced with plenty of people. Never like this though. The thought should be a cold bucket of water on my head, telling me to stop, that this isn't acceptable, I shouldn't be letting him touch me like this. I have a boyfriend. Who doesn't know I have a way to get back to him, but . . . semantics.

Sath's trying to get me flustered. He's admitted as much. But there's something almost gentle in the way he touches me now, and it makes me ache for something I haven't had in a long time. His fingers find a new path, up my arm this time, tracing along my collarbone and towards my neck.

They settle against my pulse. My stupid, traitorous, racing pulse.

It shouldn't even *be* there. And yet it beats anyway, telling him how close I am to losing control, to demanding –

I don't let my mind go there. There isn't anything else I want.

Nothing apart from going home and becoming Willow 2.0, a person who doesn't attack demons or get confused when she dances with the Devil.

Even the need for wine is fading. The fog clouding my brain lifts as a fresh band takes over from the musicians in the corner, their set complete. I'm no longer floating and dizzy, but grounded against Sath. Sath, whose chin is resting against my temple. He turns his head a fraction, burrowing his nose into my hair, and I swear he *inhales*.

I pull away. He stares down at me, eyes dark but not aflame, looking at me like I'm the only person around, the only one who matters. He might not have said any of the honeyed words Noah used to make me fall under his spell, but I'm entranced anyway.

His grip on my waist tightens. Trapped under the weight of his gaze, I am suddenly sure of two things: 1) I would not be opposed to him kissing me right now, and 2) I have got to get out of here, because I do not know where point one has come from.

This is a problem. This is a big problem. My chest constricts; my heart scrambles for escape. Alarms are screeching in my head, but my body is ignoring them all. I'm rising on tiptoe, wanting to close the gap between us once and for all, and Sath is leaning down, fingers leaving my waist to cup my chin, tilting my head up to meet his, but it's the wine, this whole thing is down to the wine –

A pair of particularly energetic dancers bump my shoulder. It jolts me into reality, and I gasp, jerking back. What am I doing? *What am I doing what am I doing what am I doing?*

Sath blinks, dropping his hands to his sides and staring at me like he's never seen me before. Like he wasn't just about to . . . Blood thunders in my ears. How dare *he* act like the one who was about to make some misguided mistake when he instigated this in the first place? Every confused feeling I'm having is his fault, for blurring the lines between reality and the game we're playing.

Blind fury crushes every other emotion.

'It must have been three hours by now.' I fight to stop my voice trembling. 'I don't want your drink, okay? I don't want anything from you. Let me go.'

A cloud of black smoke curls around his shoulders.

'Then congratulations.' He sounds cold now, detached. 'You've passed gluttony.'

'Perfect.' It comes out as more of a screech, and I shove past him to get off the dance floor, get away from this place. I want to rip this dress off my body and scrunch it into a ball and pretend it never existed, pretend he never touched me in it. I think he calls my name, but I could easily have been imagining it, because I'm still, despite everything, so thirsty, so desperate for him to haul me towards him and do all the things to me I want him to.

I feel marginally better when I step outside Dionysus and the cool air hits my flushed skin, although it's not enough to quell my parched throat or fill my barren stomach. Clutching the wall for support, I half walk, half drag myself to my room, where I promptly crash into my wardrobe before draining a glass of water and tumbling into bed.

For once, I don't have nightmares. Instead, I dream of hands on bare skin, lips against my neck, and when my hand slips between my legs, it's not Noah's face I'm picturing.

19

Harper ruins my plans to mope in bed by dragging me to Asphodel's valiant attempt at replicating a garden. Almost. We're in a cave (of course), and the grass is peacock blue, but there *are* a lot of plants. Credit where credit's due, it's definitely garden-adjacent. Although the dim light is good for my headache, the scent of lilies is nauseating to my already nauseated stomach. They grow from nothing, bright pink petals the size of my head, swaying in a breeze that only touches them. To me, the air is stifling and still; the heat plasters my hair to my neck. Groups of humans play Frisbee and tennis on a large lawn, but I've no idea how they manage it in this climate.

I groan for what must be the fiftieth time since we arrived. 'I think I'm dying.'

'You're –'

'Don't say it.' I roll over. 'I'll rephrase. If I wasn't already dead, this hangover would finish me off.'

'You were pretty out of it.' Harper is on her back, arms extended, index finger tracing patterns in the air. The roof of the cave is partially obscured by the tree canopy, and through the gaps in the fronds, candles blink down at us, shaped like constellations. A good imitation of the outside world, but not good enough. 'Still, you were enjoying yourself by the end. You even found yourself a dance partner.'

I cringe.

'Willow.'

Ugh. I crack an eyelid. 'What?'

Her brows are raised so high I think they might leave her forehead and drift into the false twilight. I know exactly what. But talking about what she may or may not have witnessed on that dance floor would mean admitting it happened at all, which I would prefer not to do.

Sath would be Mum's definition of a Bad Choice. The epitome of what I should be avoiding if I want to make her proud. If I could scrub last night's events from my brain, I would.

'I'm not judging you.' Harper sits up and dips her toe in the bubbling brook we're lying beside. It hisses, puffs of aqua-blue steam billowing upwards like a geyser. 'We all have a type. I just didn't expect yours to be someone who's cruel and distant and threatens to –'

'He's not like that,' I snap. 'You don't know him.'

Harper grins, like I'm a hapless mouse and she's the cat who's got me cornered. 'You like him.'

'What is this, high school?' I prod my finger into the grass. Maybe if I prod hard enough, I can dig a hole to crawl into. 'I have no opinion of him whatsoever. I just think underneath that persona, there's . . . more,' I finish lamely.

'Yes, that sounds like someone who has no opinion.' Harper kicks her feet, and I'm hit with a splash of warm water. 'Look, if you say he's different, I believe you.'

I frown. If Sasha was here, believing me would be the last thing on her mind. When Noah and I first got together she wouldn't listen to a word I said in his favour, telling me I'd be better off single, like her. He ended up changing her opinion all on his own, once we lived together and she was able to see the sides of him I'd always seen – I caught her once smiling softly at one of the notes he left on the fridge for me, a quote from some romantic poet that, honestly, I'd never heard of, but it was the thought that counted.

Sath has never quoted poetry at me. I'm not sure the man knows what a compliment looks like.

'Last night was a mistake,' I say adamantly. 'It was the wine.'

'Mm-hmm.'

'It *was*,' I repeat. She doesn't understand the consequences of what this could mean. I refuse to *let* it mean what she's implying. The venom allowed Bad Decision Willow out of her cage and now she's safely locked away again. I could go to Sath right now and not feel a thing. Maybe. Probably.

Perhaps I should test the theory.

The fact I'm so keen to find out is not a good sign. I pull out a lump of grass, crushing it between my fingers, mulling over my options. If I can prove to myself it was the wine, perhaps this sick, guilty feeling will dissipate.

I sit up. 'I need to go and – see something.'

'Willow, wait.' Harper's hand finds mine. 'Before you go, I wanted to ask you about . . . Sometimes you seem . . . I don't know. Sad.'

'Well, I am in Hell.' The response is automatic, flippant.

The lily blooming like a halo behind Harper's head splays its petals wider, as if to ask *are you sure?*

There was a point last night I may as well have been.

But Harper's still holding my hand, her face a portrait of patience, like she'll happily give up some of her eternity to sit here and wait for me to confess the truth. This isn't like Sasha or Noah, asking if I'm okay in one breath and suggesting I get off the sofa in the next – this is someone who has all the time in the world to listen.

I bite my lip, then admit, 'Maybe I am a little sad.'

She tilts her head, waiting for the rest. When it doesn't come, she says, 'You don't have to tell me. Henry always says I'm too nosy. But I wouldn't ask if I didn't want to know. And I can keep a secret.'

The words want to spill out of me, like water building behind a dam, but still I hesitate. Talking about feelings isn't something I'm used to. When you grow up getting told the way you feel is wrong you quickly learn to shut up. I wasn't sick, just pretending. I wasn't sad, I was overreacting. I wasn't lonely, I was needy.

But the fact that Harper is waiting for an answer is a marked improvement on anything I've had before. Maybe her reaction will be an improvement too. I take a deep breath. 'Before I died, I was . . . not in the best place. I'd just lost my mum and I kept finding myself in crowded rooms feeling totally alone, trying to keep all the broken parts together while everyone around me was solid and whole. There was a moment last night that felt exactly like that and I . . .' I shudder. 'I don't want to feel like that any more.' *That* kind of isolation is more like Hell than Asphodel could ever hope to be. 'I'm sorry. I'm being silly.'

She squeezes my fingers. 'No, you're not. But the good thing is you don't have to feel like that any more. Not in Asphodel.' She gestures around the park and elicits several waves in response. 'With this many people, you don't have to be alone unless you choose to be. I can introduce you to –'

'You've introduced me to plenty,' I say, all too quickly. They'll just be names I'll have to forget when I leave. Not wanting her to think me ungrateful, I add, 'Besides, I have you and . . .'

Her pesky, all-knowing eyebrow rises higher. 'And?'

'No one. Nothing.'

'Hm. Well, I'm glad you know you have me. And no one, whoever *they* may be.' She nudges me with her toe as my cheeks heat once more. 'Didn't you say you needed to go somewhere?'

I fire a glare in her direction, but there's no intensity behind it. I have no idea if my prove-it-was-the-wine plan will work – or what I'll do if it doesn't, but sitting here trying not to think about last night clearly isn't working.

At least if I see him I'll know how much trouble I'm in.

'I'll come find you later.' I give Harper's hand one final squeeze before exiting the park, rushing through a patch of trees with trunks as thick as elephant legs and out into the corridor. After the humidity of the garden, the blast of cold outside is welcome. I lean against the wall for a moment, ignoring the rattle of small pebbles falling from the ceiling when my back hits the rock and the whole cliff *shudders*.

Once I've gathered myself, I head to the entrance chamber. There are no demons waiting outside to sneer at me today, which is a welcome change from the usual stares I get during

Scrabble nights. It's strange, though, for this section to be unguarded, with both the gates and the Void waiting to be stumbled upon by an unsuspecting human.

Maybe that's what they're hoping for.

I increase my pace. This section is quieter than usual too, an unnatural stillness in the air. Far in the distance, there's a high-pitched whine, one that sends a tremor rippling through my body as though ice-tipped talons have scraped down my chest.

'Sath?' I call out, not expecting an answer.

The noise doesn't sound again, but the atmosphere remains uneasy, like the whole corridor is a drawn bow waiting to be released. Before sense can stop me, I take the right-hand path leading to Sath's sitting room.

At the sight of me, he jumps from the sofa, slamming shut the book in his hand. I can't believe he's been lounging around reading while I've been having a crisis. Also, he clearly didn't get the memo there's a weird noise outside.

And my insides haven't got the memo that last night didn't mean anything. There's all kinds of fluttering going on in my belly, my skin prickling as it remembers every place he touched. I want to peel it off and shred the memories with it. Bad Decision Willow hasn't been put back in her cage at all; she's the one who tricked me into coming here in the first place. She really is infuriating.

Sath tucks the book – I don't get a glimpse of the title, only that it's old and almost falling apart – inside a drawer before approaching me.

'I think we need to . . .' He blinks. 'Why are you wet?'

My jaw drops. 'How dare y—I am no such thing. And for your information –'

'Willow.' He tugs at a damp curl. 'Your hair. It's wet.' His gaze flicks lower. 'As are your clothes.'

I slap his hand away. I feel like a live wire ready to spark. 'Harper was splashing . . .' Mentioning her name reminds me of the teasing I've just run away from. 'Never mind. I don't know why I'm here.'

Liar. Liar. Liar. I'm a yo-yo, swinging from place to place, unable to settle because everything is awkward and uncomfortable. I curse the treacherous part of me that led me here in the first place. Curse the equally treacherous parts that want me to stay.

'Wait.'

Despite my cursing, those same treacherous parts halt at the sound of his voice.

'About last night . . .' He trails off, running a hand through his hair. 'You don't have to worry. It was nothing. We'd both had a drink. You don't have to run away.'

'I'm not running. Why would I be running? Nothing happened.'

Apart from the point where his nose grazed mine. When I felt his breath on my lips. When his fingers curled around my waist. When I'd forgotten every single reason I might want to go home because all I could see and feel was him.

It might have been the wine for him, but standing in this room makes it ten times harder to claim it was for me. It's like the toxin woke me from a slumber and now I can't doze off again. I'm consumed with awareness, flinching every time his body shifts, half in fear he might come closer and half desperately hoping he will. I can't blame Bad Decision Willow for this. This is all me.

This is a mess. It's not part of the plan. It's everything I shouldn't be doing.

I don't know how to stop.

In an attempt to sound more convincing, I add, 'I wasn't running. I remembered . . . I made plans. With Harper. So, I need to go. Right now.'

Sath arches a brow. I suspect I may be rambling. But rambling doesn't necessarily mean *lying*. Except, of course, I am.

'I'm sure Harper can wait for your charming company, given you were just with her,' Sath says. 'Stay. Can I make you a cup of tea?'

A cup of tea. A cup of *tea*. The man who had his hand dangerously close to my underwear wants to pretend nothing happened over a *cup of tea*.

How dare he. Every confused thought I'm having is all his fault, and he has the audacity to offer me hot beverages.

'No, I don't want tea,' I retort. 'I told you, I'm meeting Harper. My friend. My *human* friend. You can drink tea and play Scrabble with your fellow demons for a change.'

If my words hit the way I intend, he doesn't show it. Which is fine. I don't care. I don't know why I'm trying to get a rise out of him. Really, I want some indicator last night affected him as much as it affected me. But it didn't, of course it didn't. Why would it? It was a game in an endless string of games. He probably did the same thing with the last person he put through his tasks. The whole situation must be amusing to him, watching all these humans falling at his feet because we're planets orbiting his sun, and he gets to choose when he shines his light.

Maybe the Sorter *was* trying to tell me something in the morgue that day. Maybe Sath doesn't have a heart, and doesn't care one jot for how I'm feeling. Or, worse, what if everything about last night repulsed him – *I* repulsed him? It would explain why he's not bothering to ask me what's wrong.

Not that I want him to ask. I'd probably cry uncontrollably. But him not asking is also very annoying and frankly inconsiderate. I would like some acknowledgement and then to be left alone, is that so much to ask?

'If that's what you want,' he says, eyes narrowing. He regards me for a moment before adding, 'I'm glad you made some friends here.'

'Why? Because you think I'll fail the tasks and end up staying here forever?'

'Did I say that?'

'It was implied.'

We've ended up standing toe to toe in the middle of the room, like opposite ends of a magnet drawn together. I have no idea when it happened.

Sath frowns. 'Are you going to tell me why we're arguing, or do I have to guess?'

Oh, good. He's noticed. Took him long enough. For a however-many-years-old Devil he's as stupid as all the boys I've ever known. I open my mouth in the hope a witty comeback will fall from my lips, but before I can dazzle him with my repartee, everything shakes.

The floor rumbles, like there's something – something *big* – rolling underneath it, while dust and rock fall from the ceiling, coating Sath's dark hair with grey flecks that look like ash shaken from an urn.

I probably should've mentioned that noise.

Sath braces his legs wide, and I clutch his arm for support, waiting out the tremors, my pulse skyrocketing as the trembling gets worse, building to a crescendo, glasses smashing behind us as they're thrown from cabinets to the floor. Sath's arm is tense beneath my hand, his skin as burning hot as the fire building in his eyes.

When the vibrations have come to a complete stop, I stare at him, wide-eyed, before letting go of his arm. The less interaction I have with any part of him the better. 'Was that Asphodel falling apart again?'

There was no deluge of lava like that day in the hot springs, but it sure felt similar.

A muscle in his jaw ticks. 'Did you see my guards on your way here?'

'No . . .' I swallow. 'And there was this sound. Like a whining, in the distance. Why?'

Flames erupt down his arms and I jump back.

'Someone tried to open the gates.'

20

I go cold.

'Tried to, or did?' I ask. 'How do you know the difference?'
I really hope he knows the difference.

Sath doesn't answer, which isn't encouraging. Even less
encouraging is the sword that bursts from his hand.

'Sath?' My voice sounds small. 'Did something get out?'

He strides outside without bothering to look at me, instead
calling over his shoulder, 'Go to your room.'

'No.'

Sath stops, shoulders tense. 'Willow. This isn't a discussion.
Go to your room. Lock yourself in.'

Fuck that. 'No,' I say again. 'If something's happened, I want
to help. I'm not going to hide –'

'Will you listen to me, for once?' Sath prowls towards me.

I dodge out of the way before he can press me against
something. I'm not sure what he's getting so antsy about. I'm
always doing what I'm told.

Until now, that is. Because if Asphodel is falling apart right
this second, there's no point cowering under my covers and
hoping Sath will save the day.

'Why don't *you* try listening to *me*?' I say, prodding his chest as hard as I can. He's like granite, but it makes me feel better to pretend it might hurt. 'As long as I'm stuck here, whatever happens to Asphodel happens to me. I can't finish these tasks if I'm captured by a demon in the meantime. If I can help, I will. And if I can't, then . . . well. At least it'll be over quickly.'

His stare bores into mine, like he expects to discover my pupils dilated, still under the effects of the wine. He won't. My head is clear; my thoughts and terrible decisions all my own. And I am not leaving him to face this alone.

'We're wasting time,' I remind him. 'If they're open, don't you want to get them shut again?'

Sath rolls his eyes and mutters something which I presume is a curse. I offer him a bland smile in return. He stalks away without another word, but I take his silence to mean *it's your funeral*. I refrain from reminding him I must've already had one.

I'd quite like another one of Sath's magic-flame knives, but he's either forgotten to make one for me, or thinks me following is so stupid he's refusing to give me one out of pettiness. I'm going to assume the latter. For the Devil, he is *such* a child sometimes.

I stick close to him as we turn down the corridor that leads to the gates. It's darker than usual, or maybe that's my imagination seeing shadows in every corner. Candles on the walls flicker as we pass.

When the gates finally come into view, Sath's shoulders sink, and we both release a relieved sigh in unison. They're shut. But the shaking continues, rhythmic and pounding. Every bash of the door sends steam gusting out from between the hinges, buffeting my hair like a strong wind. A green substance leaks through the crevice where the two doors meet.

'Sath?' I say tentatively. 'Can it . . . Will it . . . Will anything get out? What's happening? Why are they . . . ?'

'Something's called to them,' Sath replies in a low voice. The gates rattle again. In an even lower voice, one that promises death, he adds, 'Or *someone*.'

A shiver ripples down my spine. We're at a dead end, the doors nestled between a great chunk of rock. There's nowhere to go but back the way we came, which means if someone was here, they're not here now.

Sath closes his eyes. Black tendrils ripple from him, not quite flames, not quite shadows. They spear out across the ground, the walls, like an ink spill, and – *there*. Those tendrils latch on to a shape, sketching an outline around it, and two pairs of yellow eyes meet mine. Demons. Devoid of horns or scales, they'd be fairly human-looking if it weren't for the way their skin changes colour like a chameleon's. Caught in the act, they step forward, abandoning all pretence and turning a garish shade of red.

'Kora. Ash. What is the meaning of this?' Sath asks. They remain silent, and his knuckles tighten around the sword. 'Get on the floor.'

They kneel without argument, trembling from their heads to their feet. Good. If they'd succeeded in what they'd come here to do . . . Now it's my turn to tremble, because the thought of what would happen to me, to everyone here, has my legs turning to butter. Being dead is bad enough. Being dead and tortured would be, well, worse. Obviously.

'Speak,' Sath says. 'What were you doing? Whose orders were you enacting?'

They exchange glances before answering.

'No orders, my king,' the taller of the two – Ash – says. I make a conscious effort not to scoff. *My king*, my ass. If they were loyal to Sath they wouldn't have done this. 'You were –' his gaze slides to me – 'occupied. We thought we'd take the opportunity to turn Asphodel into what it should be.'

'Asphodel *is* what it should be.' Sath's arm sets alight, the flames burning brighter than the heat emanating from the doors. 'Perhaps I should remind you of my feelings on the matter.'

Flames coat his sword, flames that will send them to Tartarus the moment he unleashes the weapon. They bow their heads, ready to lose them, but Sath's words have me thinking. Maybe they *do* need a reminder. Maybe they all do.

'Wait!'

Sath's arm freezes mid-swing. He glances at me, looking slightly incredulous. 'Don't tell me you want to spare them.'

'Absolutely not.' I place a hand on his arm, wincing at how hot he is to the touch, and jerk my head, indicating he should follow me out of earshot. The demons remain where they are, knees in the dirt. They're afraid of what Sath can do, but not afraid enough, in my opinion.

'You can't kill them yet,' I say. 'If it was a human mis-behaving, the demons would want you to make an example of them. Why not do the same to a demon, if it's threatening the rules you've put in place? Why should they be treated any differently?'

Sath's eyes glitter. 'You want me to kill them in public?'

'Yes.' I fire the word like a bullet. 'You're their king. They defied you. The other demons need to experience what that means. They need to see you look them in the eye as you spill their traitors' blood. You're so scared of losing control; you've let them forget who you are. What you can do. You need to remind them of that. You need to show them who's in charge here.' I step towards him. 'And you need to make it hurt.'

His throat bobs. An expression I can't decipher crosses his face, but then his jaw goes hard, his gaze unyielding. 'Well, all right, then.' There's a deadly undercurrent beneath the softness of his tone, one that has my flesh erupting in goosebumps.

He grabs both demons by the scruffs of their necks – he makes it look effortless – and hauls them upright before dragging them down the corridor.

I trot behind them, keeping a careful distance. They're going to suffer because of me. They must know it. Sath was about to offer them a clean, merciful death and this tiny, pathetic human has made their fate ten times worse. But I shouldn't feel bad about that. They wanted this tiny, pathetic human ripped to shreds by whatever was behind those gates. They *deserve* to suffer.

The chamber is full when we emerge. At first, I assume a boat has arrived, before realising there are no humans present. Just demons, snarling and snapping, like Sath has magically summoned them here and they're furious as to the reason why. Winged demons swoop overhead. They drop to the ground when they spot Sath, while I hover in the doorway, unsure of my place.

The demons need to think this was all Sath's idea, if he

wants to ensure they stay compliant. We can't risk another attempt to open the gates, not when they're close to breaking apart. Not when I can still feel slight tremors beneath my feet.

As Sath settles on his throne, I duck behind the door, pushing it halfway shut while leaving a big enough gap for me to peer round. Hopefully they'll all be too distracted to spot my curious eyes peeking out.

Kora and Ash haven't moved. Good of them not to resist their eventual execution. I just hope nobody *else* tries to resist. Suddenly, my plan doesn't seem as ideal. Sath's right; the amount of power he'd have to use to stop an uprising would be immense.

'These two were caught trying to open the gates to Tartarus,' Sath says. He hasn't raised his voice, but the sound carries around the cavernous room. 'I shouldn't need to remind you that crime is punishable by death.'

Low murmurs break out through the crowd. Aric slips to the front. My heart races. What's he going to do? Fuck. Surely, if this was a stupid plan, Sath would have told me. Aric stops at the front of the dais, staring at the two demons, nose twitching.

'Silence,' Sath says.

The room rumbles, not dissimilar in feeling to when the gates were in jeopardy. Now, though, that rumbling is a source of comfort. Sath's power is threaded through it, and knowing it comes from him makes me feel like I'm listening to a storm outside while I'm tucked up in bed, safe behind bricks and unbreakable glass while he hammers hail at the demons who've wronged us. So long as the demons sense that power too, hopefully they'll stay sedate.

Sath rises from the throne, face impassive. 'The gates are mine to control. I decide when they open. I decide who goes to Tartarus. I decide what gets out of Tartarus. And let me also remind you, Asphodel is *not* Tartarus. We are an in-between. We are the middle. We punish those who disrespect our rules, but we do not harm those who behave. And anyone in this room who seeks to destroy that balance will face the full force of my powers.'

Flames ripple down his arms and shoot out, black strands like whips of fire that curl around the two demons' torsos. They howl, writhing as their skin hisses with steam. Yellow pus-filled boils erupt on the flesh closest to the ropes. They don't die though. Sath is toying with them.

Good.

The remaining demons take a step back, Aric included. I don't look away. I watch as those boils bubble and pop, the same way the demons watched when Sath burned that man on my second night here. This is for him. For every other innocent they've forced Sath to punish.

And these demons are getting a far worse punishment. Because it's clear from their screams how much Sath held back before, how he really was telling the truth when he told me he made it quick and painless for the humans.

All too soon, though, the flames disappear. Sath cocks his head to one side. 'Who told you to open the gates?'

They don't reply. Sath grabs Kora and tugs her to her feet. 'Do you expect me to believe,' he says, voice like a caress, 'you came up with this plan all on your own?'

I glance at Aric, but his face gives nothing away. Kora lets out a small sob. The sound doesn't do anything to thaw the ice in my chest. I don't care how much they squeal or plead, they brought this on themselves.

Sath relinquishes his grip, allowing the demon to tumble to a heap on the floor. I grind my teeth. He'd better not be going soft on them now, not this quickly. They won't have learned their lesson yet.

Thankfully, Sath hasn't finished. He grabs Ash by his throat, crushing his windpipe with enough force it visibly indents. The demon gasps, kicking his feet, scrabbling for air, but Sath squeezes and squeezes until his eyes nearly pop out of their sockets. My own breath halts. Ash's claws scratch Sath's arms, trying to push him off, but he's not strong enough; he may as well be a doll in Sath's clutches for all the power he has to escape.

'You don't want to tell me?' Sath croons. 'What a pity.'

He releases him, and, in a blur of movement, punches through his chest. Black sprays over the floor. I recoil on instinct, although it's not me in the line of splatter: it's Aric, along with a few others, who have that pleasure. Blood coats the bottom of his legs and the metal spike on his tail. He tries to shake it off, lips curling.

Ash's body flops forward, a river of blood streaming from the hole left in his chest. Sath merely flexes his hand.

'What shall I do with him next?' he asks the watching congregation. 'Send him to Tartarus? Or wait for him to heal, and kill him all over again?' He prowls in a circle around Kora, who's trembling, head bowed. 'What about you? What would you like me to do to you? Should I make it quick, or . . .'

A sudden burst of flames has her howling. Sath smirks as she writhes on the floor. The congregation finally have the sense to look unnerved; even Aric backs away as Sath steps towards them. *Yes*. Power rolls off him now, a trail of shadowy fire following in his wake, a reminder they shouldn't dare get too close to him.

It's enough to make me reconsider whether Sath *could* stop a revolt, if he put his mind to it. I can almost picture it: Sath, a blur of black clothes and black smoke, moving like lightning between them. A slice here, a cut there, puncturing flesh, bone, muscle, the occasional tail or two. A litter of bodies at his feet in a flaming heap. The thought has me swallowing a sudden onslaught of saliva and curling my fists so tightly my nails pierce the skin.

Out of the corner of my eye, a figure leaving the chamber catches my attention. The Sorter, the white of her hair stark against the dark walls, leaving like she's seen enough. Aric, meanwhile, is enjoying his front-row seat. Sath gives him a pleasant smile as he strolls past, moving through the crowd, stopping every now and then to brush his fingers over certain demons' necks, to send strands of fire curling through the air and trailing over their bodies, making them wince and twitch and cry out. The cavern stinks of fried skin and scales.

'I want to make it clear,' Sath says, 'if any of you disobey me again, I'll make it hurt in ways you couldn't fathom.'

Then he's standing in front of Kora. He's facing my direction now, allowing me to witness the way his face is set in stone, no remorse or mercy on his features, his eyes golden and brimming with lethal power. This time, he doesn't go for the chest, for that empty space where her heart should be, but takes her chin between his hands. He twists her head to the left, more, more, until there's a sickening crack.

The room falls silent as the body drops to the floor. I expect him to turn, to show the spectators what he's done, the power and strength he has, but instead he staggers back, shoulders heaving. Strands of hair fall over his forehead. He reaches up to smooth them away, before closing his eyes and rubbing his face, smearing the blood on his hands over his cheeks, his lips.

My chest rises and falls in time with his, a little too quick, breaths a little too shallow.

The demons shuffle on their feet, wondering, I think, if the show is over. Sath's eyes snap open, but he doesn't turn to face them.

Instead, he looks at me.

Is this what you wanted? he seems to ask. I stare at him. Stare at the blood glistening on his hands, the streaks of it he's left all over his face, black droplets staining his lips like a deathly kiss. The smell of copper taints the air, and with it comes the faint tang of fear from everyone else in the room.

Not me.

These demons have been causing trouble for too long, and I want them brought in line here. Now. I want them to know they can't get away with this any longer, and if suffering is the only thing they understand, then suffering's what they'll get.

Is this what I wanted?

Yes. I lift my chin in answer to his silent question. *Yes.*

21

Sath sets fire to the dead demons a moment later. Ashes pile high in the pool of blood, like dead ants congealing in poison. He orders two others to clean up the mess and dismisses the rest with a growl before storming towards his quarters, throwing open the door with no heed to my hiding place and sweeping past me without a word.

I slam it shut before anyone spots me and watch Sath's retreating form. My pulse races as I consider my options. His ignoring me wasn't much of an invite, but I can't not talk to him after what just happened, even if he is in one of his shove-Willow-against-a-wall-and-look-angry moods.

Weirdly, the thought doesn't upset me as much as it should.

I follow him into his study, twisting the doorknob slowly so as to give him time to tell me to stop. The main lights are off, the neon glow from behind the bar the only thing illuminating Sath's form, sat on the sofa. He's utterly still.

I think *on*, and the sconces lining the walls come to life. Sath remains a statue. I edge towards him, carefully, cautiously, like I'm approaching a wounded animal. His eyes are fixed on a spot on the wall, a vacant expression on his face, tears running down his cheeks. Something in my chest twists.

I've never seen him like this before. I don't know what to do.

I hover near the sofa, debating whether or not to leave him to whatever breakdown he's having, knowing I am wholly unequipped to deal with it.

'Sath?' I risk another step. 'I . . . Are you . . . What are you doing?'

The question is unnecessary. I can see what he's doing. He is moping. Dark hair sticks to his forehead, while his skin shines with sweat. My feet move of their own accord, bridging the gap between us until I'm sinking into the seat next to him. I take his trembling hands in mine.

When he finally speaks, his voice is hoarse, like he's been screaming for hours and nobody heard. 'Are you happy now?' He tugs away from my grasp. 'Did you enjoy it? Seeing them in pain? Watching them die?'

'Yes,' I answer without hesitation. 'I don't understand why you're freaking out. They wanted to *open the gates*. Humans would've been hurt. They deserved everything you gave them, and more.'

He shakes his head. 'Revenge isn't always the answer.'

'That wasn't about revenge. That was reminding the demons what happens when they cross the Devil. That was about showing them who you *are*.'

He shudders. 'And what if who I was out there isn't who I want to be?'

I don't have an answer. It's his job. Last I checked, Asphodel doesn't have an HR department he can walk into and hand over

209

a resignation letter. And I can't sympathise with this, because I can't fathom why he wouldn't want that kind of power. He can walk into a room and make anyone tremble. Can make up all the rules and have no one tell him no. No decision is a bad decision, because he's the one who decides what's good and what's bad.

He's oblivious to how lucky he is, having no voices in his head calling him a disappointment for always picking wrong. For me, that kind of freedom would be a dream.

For him, it's a nightmare. Dried blood on his face strips free, like old paint peeling from a wall, as more tears slide down his cheeks. I wipe one away with my thumb, leaving the digit resting against the side of his face. He's warm, feverish almost, and I'm not sure if it's because he's upset or hot is . . . normal for him. In every sense of the word. Even dirty and distressed, he's hopelessly attractive, and after last night it's all I can notice.

He really has no business being this good-looking. It would be enough to make the saintliest girl alive flustered, and I am, by way of being here, no saint.

Fuck's sake. I pull my hand away. 'You weren't this troubled over the human you killed,' I say. 'Is it only the demons you don't like hurting?'

'Who said I wasn't troubled?' Sath sags into the sofa. 'You should go.'

'Why, so you can brood in peace? How's that working out for you?'

His gaze flicks to me, then away. 'You shouldn't see me like this.'

'Because you think it makes you weak?'

'Doesn't it?'

I don't answer. In some ways, it does. He's the King of Hell – Asphodel, whatever – he shouldn't be crying and regretting every punishment he doles out. But at least he has the guts to admit he hates it rather than carry on pretending to be something he's not.

'You're upset.' His voice startles me. My hand is on my wrist, tracing the space where my bracelet used to be.

I force myself to let go, dropping my fingers to my side.

'No, *you're* upset.' My knees click (surely I'm both too young and too dead for this) as I get back on my feet. 'Let me help you.'

Scanning the room for something I can use to mop him up, I'm struck by how messy it is. When I first arrived, everything was pristine, not a cushion out of place and no clutter in sight. Now there's a stack of board games in the corner, a book of mine on the coffee table, one of my jumpers strewn over a chair. I'd taken it off in a huff during a rousing game of Monopoly (I won). It's like my presence has infected everything, a virus spreading, slowly seeping into every corner of his life.

I wonder if he minds.

At the bar, I locate a towel along with a small bowl which I fill with water before sitting beside Sath once again. He watches in silence as I soak the towel, the only sound the water sloshing in the bowl and dripping from the rag when I drain the excess. And my heart. My heart which sounds impossibly loud, like a cannonball ricocheting in my chest. I'm convinced Sath must be able to hear it.

This is ridiculous. I am ridiculous. The man is covered in blood and crying, and I'm having a meltdown over the fact I'm about to touch his face.

There's something . . . intimate about it. The lights are dim in here at the best of times, but Sath's distress is casting extra shadows round the room – the only thing I can make out clearly is the amber in his eyes and the paleness of his face. He's a star in a dark sky; the only thing worth seeing.

I don't remember a time all I saw was Noah. The world was a distracting place. There's no TV or social media to divert me here, nothing I can turn to stare at instead. I'm hyperaware of every point our bodies touch: his thigh is lined up alongside mine, our knees knocking together, my arm brushing his. Now it's my hands that are shaking when I place one on his shoulder to steady myself. If he notices, he says nothing.

I am a mess. I am a mess with a stupid crush on someone I should not have a crush on. It would be easier if he was evil. Then I'd spend the tasks hating him, and not grinding against his – oh, God. I have got to stop thinking. Why did I never learn to meditate? The ability to empty my brain would be super useful right now.

When I leave, I'm taking up yoga.

'This'll be cold,' I tell him, the towel hovering in mid-air, dripping wet down my hands. The water does nothing to cool any part of me.

'I can take it.' His lips twitch, and I'm so relieved to see a sign of the old Sath, of *my* Sath, that I sigh, audible and shaky. Sath's gaze drops to my mouth. Oh shit. Now he's going to think I'm panting all over him. Focus, Willow. For lack of better ideas, I slap the sodden material to his cheek. Sath winces, which makes me feel better. A distracted Sath means he won't notice a distracted Willow.

212

My next wipe is a little more gentle though. I smear away blood and tears from his cheeks, his nose, his forehead, stripping away the stains and revealing the man beneath. After a moment's hesitation, I wipe the towel over his lips, my thumb following the rag's path and tracing a line of its own as it clears away the remnants of blood specks. His mouth parts beneath my touch.

Well, he won't notice me panting and gasping and breathing hysterically any more. I'm not sure I'm breathing at all. Looking at his mouth is doing strange things to me, so I peer into his eyes instead, which is a terrible idea, because his stare is burning and intense, locking me in place. It locks my hand in place too, because I can't bring myself to stop touching him. His breath ghosts over my thumb, and it's quick and uneven, the same pace as my pulse.

I swallow.

I have to get out of this room. But that seems discourteous, given the circumstances. All I've done is clean Sath's face, and not actually solved the problem that the Devil doesn't want to be the Devil. I toss the towel on to the coffee table and sit back. Away from him. No thigh touching, not today.

'Can't you get out of it?' I ask. 'You said you weren't always the Devil. Can't you . . . not be? How did you become him in the first place?'

Sath rubs his face. Rude. I did an excellent job. 'I can't tell you that.'

'Can't, or don't want to?'

'Can it be both?' The question is punctuated by a huff. 'Let's just say, if I'd known . . .' He trails off. The glasses behind the bar clink as the ground beneath us trembles.

'Was that the gates?' I grip the arm of the sofa as tightly as panic grips my chest. 'Sath? Have the demons –'

'It's not the demons,' he says glumly. 'Not this time. That was me.'

'Why –'

'To keep the divide between Asphodel and Tartarus, you need to be –' he glances at me, and swallows – 'good. Otherwise, the realms will bleed together. But how can I be good when I'm constantly required to do bad things? How am I supposed to control the gates when I can't control –' The shaking gets worse, lights wavering on the walls so violently they threaten to snuff out, my book bouncing to the edge of the coffee table and falling off. And something down the corridor rumbles, roars, *clanks*, like gears are churning, like the gates are opening –

'Sath!' I shake his shoulder. He doesn't respond; his eyes are amber bright and smoke curls off him. '*Sath*.' I grip his chin and force him to look at me. 'Sath.'

This time, he blinks. The shaking stops. I exhale.

'You can't go on like this,' I say. 'If the gates open . . . There has to be something you can do to control it.'

His eyes flicker. Not with his flames, not this time, but with actual, human emotion, like he's warring with himself; every movement they make is like his brain processing a new thought and putting it to one side, trying to decide which to settle on. His gaze lands on me, properly, and it's like he's had a sunrise snatched from him too soon. He immediately looks away.

'No,' he says. 'There's nothing.'

I tilt my head. 'Nothing at all?' The gates have been here

214

since, what, the dawn of time, and now they're falling apart and he can't do *anything*?

'Nothing,' he repeats. And then he looks at me again, and it's filled with such an unexpected longing that my lungs stop working.

I mean. They weren't working anyway. Now they can't bring themselves to pretend.

I've seen that look before. The memory's hazy, but it's there. Last night, with the wine, when his hands were on me, and I was leaning towards him, wanting him, and – I grit my teeth. I have got to stop thinking like this. I can't let a fleeting attraction turn into something more, not when I'll be leaving. If I thought I could go home and forget him, I'd be tempted to suggest we start something fun, with a clear time limit and no strings on either side.

Only Sath is made of nothing but strings, and I'm tied to every one. There's no forgetting that.

'Well,' I say. My throat feels scratchy. 'You seem . . . calm now. I should go.'

His throat bobs. 'That's probably best.'

Oh. I thought he might at least try and offer me tea again. Well. Fine. That's good he didn't.

I leave with a nod, lingering in the corridor outside with my back pressed to the wall, trying to use the coolness of the stone to slow my breathing.

I have got to get myself under control. I shouldn't be having thoughts like this at all. There's a ring waiting for me back home. The ultimate accessory, one that declares I'm a grown-up with an idealistic future headed her way. Everything Mum wanted for me.

Think of Noah. Think of Noah. Think of Noah. It's more difficult than it should be. His memory has faded; I can't get his image into focus. *He'll keep you safe*. Honestly, I think Mum was more concerned with the bank balance he'd have once he was a hotshot lawyer. Money is safety. Happiness is irrelevant. Look at her and Dad.

I squeeze my eyes shut, trying to remember the last time Noah made me happy. It's difficult. Everything about him is far away, and I want to chase after him – I'm *supposed* to chase after him – but he's out of my grasp, my mind latching onto nothing, and as the vision of his face fades entirely, I realise I'm not scared about losing Noah.

I'm scared that I'm not scared at all.

22

The solution to my current predicament is clearly avoidance.

If I can stay out of Sath's way until the next task, maybe I'll have gotten over . . . whatever this is. It may not be the most mature solution, but it's the only one I have. I see, now, why he made me wait a month between tasks. All of this would have been easy in the beginning, with Noah fresh in my mind and Sath nothing more than a stranger.

I spend the next week suffering more of Harper's raised eyebrows and constant questions. Today we're in a large, domed cave filled with oil paintings, statues made out of clay, and crude figures scratched on the walls. I guess all the real artists have taken up residence in a part of Asphodel I've not found yet, because every piece on this floor is the definition of *well, it's nice you have a hobby*.

Abandoning Harper while she inspects a statue of – honestly, I'm not sure, but I think it's a slug with a basket on its head – I retreat to a far corner of the cave. Mushrooms growing from the walls glow with a dim blue light, as though the piece in this section is sensitive to anything brighter.

Clusters of humans talk in low voices as they admire the

art. Everything here changes daily to keep things interesting, but there's one painting that remains fixed. It's fairly abstract, a grey arch on a black canvas, a jagged line sliced through the middle. From within that line bursts a large blue spiral, like a child has spray-painted what they think a tornado looks like atop the whole thing, with a scowling sketch of a screaming, snake-like head at its centre.

'That's his favourite.' Harper sidles up to me. Earrings shaped like fairies rattle as she moves. 'He's been obsessed for the last year, coming in here to stare for hours on end.'

I don't bother asking who she means. 'Then he has terrible taste. It's hideous.'

Looping my arm through her elbow, I drag her away from the ugly picture before she can use it to turn the conversation to Sath once more. She's been like a dog with a bone ever since that day in the park, like me giving her a sliver of truth about my life gave her a taste for more. But confessing why I'm evading him would mean confessing I'm not staying here at all, and that opens up a whole heap of questions I'd rather avoid.

She beams at various humans as we weave through another section of statues – these are all moulded into misshapen clay flowers – calling out invites to Dionysus to everyone we pass. Sometimes I think of her as the Pied Piper, only she offers smiles instead of music and the dead come running.

'How do you do that?' I ask. 'You've been here centuries and people still . . .'

'Still what?'

It sounds pathetic, saying it out loud. 'They still *like* you.'

'Are they not supposed to?' Her tone is a combination of

218

genuine confusion and gentle mockery as we settle on a granite bench near a painting of a lake covered in swans.

'Of course they're supposed to,' I say. 'I just don't know how you do it. How you . . . make people stay.'

Dad left. Noah went from wanting to be around me all the time, blowing up my phone with endless *you're so perfect*s and *I want you all to myself*s, to me having to beg for the tiniest crumb of attention because I'd lost his and didn't know how to survive without it any more. When Mum introduced us, I suppose he thought he'd been presented with a diamond, someone who knew how to behave in his social circles and he could show off at family parties, but then he polished that diamond too much and found nothing but disappointing rock underneath. No matter how hard I tried to shine, the sparkle always wore off. I didn't know how to behave at all.

'Don't be silly.' She knocks her knee against mine. 'Not everyone here likes me; that would be statistically impossible. But Asphodel has a way of . . . leading you back to the same people. Or sometimes *away* from people. I was once good friends with a man named Gustav and then I beat him in a paintball fight and I've never seen him since.' She sighs. 'I miss Gustav. Even if he was a sore loser.'

I suck in a breath. One day she's going to find *me* missing. 'Well,' I say, throat tight, 'if you never see me again, it won't be because of that. I fully accept your paintball superiority.'

'*We* have never played paintball.' She grins and jumps to her feet. 'Not yet, anyway.'

Her laughter is infectious as I let her drag me out of the gallery, although to my ears mine sounds slightly hysterical, over the top, a desperate attempt at shoving away my lingering guilt at leaving her behind.

But it's not like she needs me. We collect a troop of humans on the way to a cavern turned arena a few hundred floors down. Wooden outposts shaped like castles fill the space, and by the time I've clambered up a tower to find a better vantage point, I'm almost distracted enough to not think about how this might be the one and only time I play this with her. Almost.

I stay in my tower for the duration of the game, getting splattered with neon powder every time I risk poking my head over the top – I am now fully convinced Harper was a sniper not a socialite in her past life – but I do manage one hit of my own, when I spy a demon tail poking out from behind a barrel. I duck low before it can ever find out it was me.

When we're finished, Harper is the only person not covered in multicoloured specks. She flicks my nose, sending a spray of yellow and pink puffs into the air. '*You* need a shower before Dionysus tonight.'

'Only if *you* teach me how to aim.' We crush into a lift with the rest of the group, all slightly sweaty and out of breath. I catch a glimpse of my reflection in the black glass – it's murky and distorted, but there's a visible shine in my eyes to match the sheen on my forehead, and a smile lifting the corners of my mouth.

It feels like a lifetime since I last saw that smile.

There's a glow in my chest for the rest of the afternoon. We split up so I can shower and change before Dionysus, as though this is one big holiday, and after a day at the beach I need to wash sand from my feet before we go out for the evening dinner, if the evening dinner took place inside a volcano and half the wait staff wanted to eat or torture me. I'm applying the last flecks of mascara to my lashes when there's a knock on my door.

Despite there being no clocks in Asphodel, Harper, I have discovered, has a sixth sense for when I'm running late. I fluff my hair and smack my lips together, then swing the door open, only to find it's not Harper outside at all. It's Sath.

Oh no. My stomach falls to the floor.

'Evening,' he says.

Instantly, my mouth feels like it's been stuffed with marshmallows, too clogged to form coherent words. He's leaning against the frame, wearing a pair of dark jeans and a thick green jumper that wouldn't be amiss at a festive gathering. I can easily imagine him sitting in a cabin drinking mulled wine by a log fire, with me snuggled against the side of that jumper, which looks very huggable and – how long has he been standing there? Oh, God. I think it's been a while, and I'm gaping at him like a fish on land.

Words. I need to find words.

Any words will do. A complete sentence would be lovely.

Except the only thing I can think to say is *you look very snuggable today, Sath*, and I can't say *that*.

I am losing my mind. I am actually losing my mind. I stare at him, horror-struck, my eyes wide and mouth open. I swear I used to be good at flirting. Every time Noah went distant I'd reel him back in with a flutter of my eyelashes and some filthy promise whispered into his ear. The problem is I don't want to flirt with Sath. I mean, I do. But I *shouldn't*.

Right now I can't remember why.

'What are you doing here?' I force the words out.

'You're avoiding me.' Sath takes it upon himself to enter my room, ignoring my protests (which involve me screeching *hey* and *privacy* in increasingly incoherent pitches) and perching on the end of my bed.

This room is not big enough for two.

'Are there space constraints in Asphodel?' I ask. There's no chair, and standing leaves me with nothing to do with my hands other than think about alternative things I could be doing with them, so I settle on the far side of the bed, near the pillow where there's no danger of accidentally coming into contact with Sath. 'You couldn't have sprung for a –' Fuck. I can't talk to him about double beds. 'I mean –'

'Willow.' Sath's voice is coaxing, like he's shaking a box of treats in front of a cat that's gone into hiding. 'Why are you avoiding me?'

'I'm not.'

He raises an eyebrow.

'I'm not.' If I say it enough, maybe one of us will believe it. 'I assumed you'd come and get me when you were ready for the next task.'

'That hasn't stopped you coming to bother me before.'

'Oh, what, did you miss me?' I scoff.

Sath is silent. He stares at a groove in the wardrobe where the wood has chipped – probably when it came into contact with my head after gluttony – with a furrow in his brow. My pulse kicks up a notch.

'Did you?' A smile creeps over my face. 'Did you miss me?'

He doesn't answer, but the corners of his lips have upturned ever so slightly.

He *did*. The thought delights me more than it should. I crawl towards him.

'Sathanas, King of Hell,' I half sing. 'Did you miss the lowly human beating you at board games?'

Sath faces me, mouth curling upwards even more. 'You have never beaten me at Scrabble.'

'No, but I kicked your ass at Monopoly.' Realising I'm still on all fours after my less-than-sultry crawl, I drop into a position that doesn't make my butt stick in the air, sitting cross-legged next to him. My knee brushes his thigh, and neither of us makes any attempt to shift apart. 'Which we haven't played since, by the way. Don't think I haven't noticed.'

'Ah, but we could have,' Sath muses, 'if only you weren't avoiding me.' His expression turns sombre. 'I'm sorry you had to see me like that.'

'Like what?' I've never been sorry to see him. That is precisely the problem.

'You're right,' he goes on, which would be delightful if I had any clue what it was I was right about. 'I had to make a stand. I shouldn't have let it get to me like that. I shouldn't have –'

'Wait,' I interrupt. 'Do you think I'm avoiding you because you were crying?'

'At least you're admitting to avoiding me.' He frowns. 'If not that, then why?'

I wince. Maybe I should have lied. Avoiding someone's tears is a lot less embarrassing than admitting you keep picturing them naked. But I can't let him think I spent the last week refusing

223

to speak to him because I think less of him. 'You're allowed to admit when you're upset. Pretending you're not feeling certain feelings is just going to make things –' I gulp – 'worse.'

Ugh. Okay. I need a new plan. Because I'm right, and I'm also guilty of the exact same thing. What am I supposed to do instead – think of nothing but Sath naked and hope I get bored by the idea?

I'm not sure that'll be possible. I have an extremely vivid imagination, and there are simply so many things I could do with him. I'm growing warm, causing me to blurt out the only solution I can think of. 'We should speed up the tasks. I don't want to wait another three weeks. I want out. Now.'

I expect him to argue, but he merely looks resigned. 'I came to say the same thing.' His hands twist in his lap. 'You've been here long enough; the remaining sins will be a sufficient challenge. And you're right. We both need this to be over.'

Something about the word *over* hits me like a missile coated in poison, the blow sharp and unexpected and painful. When I made the deal with him all I wanted was to return to what I'd left behind. To be the person I was supposed to be and fix everything I messed up. Now I'm leaving something *else* behind, a whole world full of infinite possibilities and paintball tournaments, and that comes with regrets of its own.

But I can't stay dead. I'm twenty-one. I *refuse*.

I'm going home, and I'm not going to miss him, or Harper, or anyone. Not one little bit.

I ignore the twinge in my chest telling me I'm lying, and say, bright and breezy and with zero cares in the world, 'Perfect. So, we can do one right now?'

His throat bobs. 'We can.'

He sounds almost hesitant. A small, foolish part of me hopes it's because he's had a taste of missing me and doesn't want to watch me go – but then, with a resolute nod of his head, he gets to his feet and flashes me a smile. Despite the fact it doesn't meet his eyes, the sight of it – along with a dimple in his cheek – causes a twinge in my chest, like he's reached in and squeezed my heart with his bare hands. I wish I could tell him to put his goddamn dimple away, but instead I'm taking the hand he's offered me, greedy for contact, for any piece of him I can get before I leave.

Sath pulls me to my feet, and winks. 'Try not to get sick.'

Blackness envelops us.

It takes longer this time, that squeezing sensation worse than ever, Sath's hand the only link to anything solid and real, and when we finally land it takes me a while to settle. I blink, dizzy, taking in the sights in front of me.

We're in a side alley, litter and broken bottles at my feet and the smell of piss stinging my nostrils. Outside, though, on the main street . . . there's *life*. People chatter and sing as they stroll down the road. Not a demon in sight. Twinkly red and green lights are strung between lampposts, and I move towards them, hypnotised, ignoring the biting cold nipping my ears. I wish Sath had told me to bring a jacket.

I wish he'd warned me we were coming *here*.

Home. I'm home. My mouth waters as we near a stall selling hot doughnuts and spiced wine. I don't think this is a memory or an illusion; those are Christmas lights above me, because December's here – it would have been my first Christmas

225

without Mum – and those are people, actual alive people, milling around me. It's the reminder I needed why I'm doing this. So I can be one of them once more. So I can walk with them, laugh like them, live with no daily threat of demons or Voids.

'This is where the task of envy will take place,' Sath says, but I'm barely listening, staring around open-mouthed at all the things I thought I'd never see again. He places a hand on my back and tries to push me forward.

'We're not invisible here,' he murmurs. 'Act natural.'

I spin to face him. 'Are we really here? But . . . how . . . ?'

What if I can slip away?

'My magic allows me to portal here,' Sath is saying. 'Only for forty-eight hours. Any longer – Willow, are you listening?'

Of course I'm not listening. I'm *home*.

The next thing I know, Sath has my chin gripped between his fingers. 'Focus,' he says. 'The magic that allows us to leave Asphodel is limited. Only I can access it. Try and run from me . . .' He grimaces. 'It wouldn't be pleasant for you.'

I scowl, slapping his hand away from my face. Of course he knew what I was thinking. Shivering, I wrap my arms around themselves, and he makes no move to offer any assistance. I'm stuck in a strapless dress (yes, fine, I don't usually wear one and yes, fine, I only put it on in case I bumped into him), goosebumps erupting over my skin as I bounce on my toes. 'Can we get this over with?'

Sath nods. 'Remember what I said. We can be seen here.'

Plenty of people have seen us already. The street teems with festive merrymakers as we walk past shops long closed for the night and head towards the nearest pub. If he was worried about us being spotted, maybe he shouldn't have taken me to one of my old drinking grounds. There's a strong chance not everyone here will be a stranger.

If this task is supposed to represent envy, I have a horrible feeling that might be the point.

Inside, the carpet is as awful as I remember: burnt orange with gold swirls and saturated with stains. People cram around the bar, waving notes and cards at harassed staff.

Sath steers me towards the rear of the pub, positioning me behind a pillar and instructing me to peer round.

When I do, my heart drops.

Sasha is sat at a table with Danny and Michaela, four empty glasses in front of them. My knees nearly buckle. She's alive. Seeing the proof with my own eyes is different to hearing Sath tell me. I want to run and hug her, to feel how warm she is in my arms, to tell her I'm sorry I ever put her in jeopardy at all. Her laugh is tinkling, melodic.

'Don't you think it's unfair,' Sath says, 'that she lived, when you didn't?'

'What?' I blink. 'Of course not. She's Sasha.'

'And why does Sasha deserve good things, and not you? She got to go on all the holidays you never did. She got to see the world. She even got better grades than you while she did it. She's never struggled for anything, has she? And now she's living the life that could have been yours.'

'This won't work,' I tell him. 'I'm glad she didn't pay for my mistake. I'm glad she's –'

She's *okay*. The realisation sinks in further. My chest swells.

She's not in a hospital attached to wires or curled up in bed crying because she lost her best friend. And, okay, fine, I won't deny I'd be flattered if she was, but I'm too relieved not to have killed her to be chastising her for not grieving appropriately.

At least I know if I mess something up and fail a task, or get sent to the Void for some minor infraction, she'll be fine. I haven't ruined anything. I haven't ruined *her*.

'I see. I suppose, in that case, you'll be fine with this too.'

I follow the direction of his pointed finger to see a figure moving through the crowd, and my stomach tumbles to the floor. Noah. He sets a tray of drinks on the table before dropping into the seat beside Sasha.

And then he takes her hand in his.

She twirls a lock of hair around her finger as she smiles at him, puckering her perfectly pink lips in his direction until he relents and presses a kiss to her mouth. Danny hoots. My insides squirm, like the pair of them have sliced my stomach open and allowed the wriggling contents to spill out.

'Jealous, Willow?' Sath murmurs beside me. 'She took everything from you. And so quickly. So easily. Don't you wish you were in her seat instead? Why don't you walk over there and claim it?'

I don't listen. I can't look away. My breaths are too quick, too uneven, like she stole some of my oxygen when she stole my boyfriend.

'When.' My voice is low and cold, the complete opposite of the way I feel, a rumble of thunder before the downpour begins. 'When did it start.'

Did they even wait for me to die? My mind races over my final month: the way she disappeared on a night out and I couldn't find her no matter how hard I searched. How she'd call Noah to collect me once I was in a state, but *she* never seemed to be, coming home sober after he'd deposited me in bed. They'd stay up watching a film and he'd wake me hours later, smelling of her perfume. Then there was that final night on the cliff, where she encouraged me to leave him behind and go travelling. She was probably waiting to swoop in the moment I'd gone.

'Why don't you go and ask?' Sath suggests. 'Tell them exactly what you think of them. You'd feel better for it, wouldn't you?'

You know why this happened, Mum's voice needles. *Why would he want you when he could have her? She's perfect in a way you could never be. I always thought she'd make the better daughter.*

Her voice deepens. *Doesn't that make you furious?*

I shake my head. 'No.'

'She graduated with honours,' Sath says. 'Has an internship with a firm in London. The one you never applied for.' His lips brush my ears. 'She has everything you ever wanted, and it was effortless.'

If only you'd listened to me about how to behave.

If only you'd tried harder to keep him.

But I did. I *did* try. I was attentive, and sexy, and loving, even when it wasn't being reciprocated, like I could be enough for us both if I only did everything right, but when Mum died, the one time I needed him – the first moment he'd ever seen me fall apart – he *abandoned* me. He spent three years pretending to be my life raft only to set me adrift when my ship went down, and Sasha watched it happen.

And then she capitalised on it.

I'm not jealous. I'm not even angry.

There's no rage to tamper down, no harsh words to swallow. Just the same level of indifference they showed to me in my final months.

To quote my mother, they are simply an *extreme disappointment*, and quite frankly it's nice not to have that phrase directed at me for a change. I guess Sasha isn't so perfect after all. All that time I spent wishing I was her and, in reality, she was jealous of *me*, to the point she was actively trying to destroy my relationship. She spent the first few years Noah and I were together listing all his faults to me, and when that didn't turn me against him, she turned *him* against *me*, encouraging me to become everything he hated so she could steal him for herself.

The group chortle about something that's probably not funny, and the pang of longing doesn't come. The smile on my face after paintballing today was far realer than any I would have made here. I get my fill of jokes from Harper and the others now, from Sath even, when he's in the right mood to make them. I lean against him, and he slides a hand around my waist.

'Do you envy them? How happy they are?' Sath asks.

Truth be told, I don't feel much of anything. I could be looking at a group of strangers, or having that awkward moment when you meet someone you used to know in the street and have no idea what to say because your lives have moved so far apart. And their life feels too small for me now – I think in some ways, it always did, like I was always aware there was *more* but I didn't know how to find it – constrained by the four walls of the same pub they visit every Friday. Of course they ended up together. They have no idea what else is out there.

The answer to his question falls from my lips as easily as melted butter from a spoon. 'No. No, I don't envy them.'

He stares down at me, frowning, looking for the lie that's not there. 'This should have been one of your hardest tasks.'

'Then give me something worth being jealous about,' I say. I've been dead under four months and they've forgotten I've existed. Why should I give them a second thought? 'This isn't what I want any more.'

The hand on my waist tenses. 'You don't want to go home?'

'Here?' I take in the stale, faded wallpaper, listening to the idle chatter of people who haven't battled demons or lived in a magical cliff that has *everything*. 'Maybe I don't.' Then, because he's still frowning, I add brightly, 'Maybe I'll move to Aruba.'

Sath huffs a laugh. 'Why Aruba?'

'Why not Aruba? I could live in one of those beach hut thingies.'

I'm joking, obviously, although the idea is not unappealing. There's nothing to say I can't be successful with my toes in the sand. Sasha can spend her days making tea and shuffling papers around a desk, while I work remotely from the beach. Not *all* my daydreams are frivolous.

Sath's laughter dies. 'You've passed envy. We should return to Asphodel.'

Oh. Daydreaming will be harder in the dark. I drink in my surroundings one final time, imprinting the splashes of garish colour into my memory before I lose them again, and follow Sath on to the street. He doesn't speak, staring at the moon

231

while wind rifles through strands of his black hair, a look of such yearning on his face that it makes me yearn for him.

'Sath . . .' I say cautiously. 'This forty-eight-hour thing. Do you ever use it? Do you ever . . . go anywhere?'

He glances at me, brow pinched. 'No. I've never thought about it.'

'You can portal anywhere in a matter of seconds, and you've never thought about it?' Sometimes I have to question his intelligence. It's on the tip of my tongue to invite him to come and visit me in Aruba, but that seems like a dangerous invitation. Sath in swimming trunks would not be good for the health of my freshly restarted heart. Still, it makes me wonder what else he hasn't done in a while.

'You know what you need?' I say. 'A night off.'

Sath sighs. 'That's not a good idea.'

'It's an excellent idea.' I fold my arms. 'You spend all your time worrying about ruling Hell.'

'Not true,' he says, the corners of his mouth turning up. 'Sometimes I'm worrying about you.'

'Well, now I'm worrying about you. You have the whole world at your disposal, and you're not using it. We don't have to go yet. We can . . . pretend we're alive, for a night.' I jerk my head over his shoulder. There's a little bar nestled on the street corner, one I wouldn't usually go in because it's way too overpriced for a venue where the toilets stink and all the surfaces are sticky, but I also know we won't be spotted by anyone who expects me to be dead. 'Please, Sath. Let's go *out*. Have some fun. What's the harm?'

He presses his lips together, rocking on his heels. He's

232

wavering, a domino poised to fall, and I just need to give him a push.

'You're forgetting drinks need to be paid for,' he says. 'And neither of us have any money.'

'If you can summon swords out of thin air, surely you can magic up some cash.'

His eyes flare gold. 'Perhaps I can only do that in Asphodel.'

I glance around to find wisps of black smoke drifting down the street. Then I spy something else, and grin.

'Well,' I say, sidling closer, 'unless this lump in your pocket is because you're happy to see me . . .' Holding his gaze, I slide my hand into his jeans, ignoring the sharp intake of breath he makes when my palm skims his thigh, and grab on to something made of leather and distinctly wallet-shaped. 'I'd say you're lying.'

I yank it out and pull it open. Several twenties peek out at me. I beam, tapping it lightly against Sath's chest – he's biting the inside of his cheek which tells me he's as pleased by my discovery as I am – and say, 'Come on. You're buying.'

23

We're greeted by the delightful stench of sweat mixed with soured alcohol, both of which are days old if the lack of patronage is anything to go by. My shoes stick to the floor. Sath makes a less-than-pleased noise behind me, which forces the bartender to glance up from her phone and pay us attention. She looks as shocked to have customers as Sath is to be here.

Her mouth tilts upwards as she takes Sath in. I scowl at her. He's obviously here with me – his hand is on my waist as he mutters we should leave for somewhere nicer – but I lean closer to him anyway, to prevent any further confusion.

'Pick a booth,' I tell him. 'I'll get the drinks.'

'Willow . . .'

'Trust me.' I nudge him towards the back of the room. 'If you don't want anyone to spot us, this place is where we need to be.'

With a frown, Sath does what he's told. But that's okay; I have a plan to remove that frown. It involves tequila. Whatever he's drinking in Asphodel isn't doing anything to loosen him up, and if there's one thing Sath needs, it's *loosening*. He's like a rusty old bolt stuck in the same position for years, and he needs me to prise him free. I've never thought of myself as a spanner before, but there we are. I am declaring myself the spanner to Sath's bolt, and he should be thankful for it.

While we're here, maybe I can loosen him into spilling some of the secrets he insists on keeping from me. I'm nothing if not a multitasker.

I sidle over to the bar, where the girl can barely hide her disappointment that it's me and not Sath before her, and purchase a whole bottle of tequila. It's presented to me alongside two shot glasses with fingerprint stains on the sides and dust coating the bottom.

Sath raises a brow when I deposit them on the table in front of him. 'I wasn't aware we were in Tijuana.'

'Like you've ever been on spring break.' The idea of Sath doing shooters off someone's stomach is laughable. The image of it, though, is not unappealing. I shake my head to clear away the thought of Sath's head moving down my body, his lips – I shake my head harder, as the first attempt hasn't worked. My brain is unstoppable.

The problem, I think, isn't that Sath's good-looking. I've met plenty of good-looking people. The problem is I *know* Sath. I like Sath. Worse, despite seeing parts of me most people would deem disappointing, he acts like they don't matter. I've never felt judged in his presence, which makes him all the more dangerous. I don't have to pretend to be something else, which leaves my mind free to picture things it shouldn't.

Mum always said my imagination would get me in trouble.

After a moment's deliberation, I choose the more perilous option of sitting on Sath's side of the booth, to stop him escaping my interrogation.

'Let's play a game,' I say, twisting the lid off the bottle. 'Truth or shot.'

Sath leans closer, his knee nudging mine. 'Are you trying to learn my secrets, Willow White?'

Something about the way he says my name has my toes curling in my boots.

'Nope.' I shrug. 'You're free to take as many shots as you want.'

'Ah, so you're trying to get me drunk.' He shifts again, the arm draped over my seat moving closer to my shoulders, before a finger lands on my neck and trails a slow, deliberate path down towards the nape. His voice is low, husky, when he asks, 'What were you planning on doing with me?'

I shiver, flinching away before he can notice the goosebumps erupting all over my flesh. Can't he let me suggest a perfectly pleasant game without trying to wind me up over it? I clench both my teeth and my legs before hissing, 'Nothing worse than what you did to me during gluttony.'

I fling the words as effectively as a bucket of cold water. Sath tenses before sitting back and removing his arm from my shoulder. Instantly, I regret saying anything, because this bar is cold and my dress is too thin. A Sath-shaped furnace is definitely required.

An indecipherable emotion flickers in his eyes. 'I hadn't realised it was so terrible,' he says lightly, 'dancing with me.'

'I didn't . . .' I bite my lip. 'I didn't mean it like that. I meant . . . not being in control.'

'And what if you had been in control?' He takes the bottle from my hands and does what I've been too distracted to do: pour two shots. 'Would you have danced with me then?'

Are we playing? This seems like he's accepting the conditions of the game. Truth or shot, Willow? My mouth is dry, but I don't drink. 'Yes,' I whisper.

The air around us stills. He holds my gaze, and swallows. I can't quite catch my breath.

'My turn,' I say. My voice comes out squeaky, and I fake a cough in an attempt to hide it. 'How did you become the Devil?'

Without hesitation, he takes a shot. My eyes narrow. 'It's no fun if you don't tell me anything.'

'It's no fun if you ask questions I can't answer,' he shoots back. 'If you're not planning to return to Noah, do you still intend to do the final tasks?'

'My life doesn't revolve around Noah.'

'I'll take that as a yes.' His smile is taut. 'Are you as motivated now as you were the day we made the deal?'

'That's another question. Wait your turn. How old are you?'

'Twenty-six.'

Is he really gonna make me do the whole *Twilight* thing? 'And how long have you *been* twenty-six?'

His lips twitch. 'A while.'

I regret ever dragging him to the cinema.

'So,' Sath says, '*do* you remain committed to the tasks?'

I open my mouth to say yes, and nothing comes out. Fuck. I run my finger round the rim of my shot glass. Of course I'm committed. I *promised*. And I'm close now, close to proving I can do this, that I can be more than the Willow Who Always Screws Up.

Changing my mind would be running away, and I've done too much of that already. The back of my throat feels scratchy when I finally answer, 'There's nothing I want more.'

'Why do you do that?' He nods his head towards my wrist. My fingers have found the bare patch again, tracing the space where my bracelet used to be. 'Whenever you touch that wrist you always get this far-off look in your eye.'

I'm tempted to drink, but resist. 'I used to have a bracelet there. It was . . . important to me.'

His face tightens. 'A gift from Noah?'

'Noah never got around to giving me the one piece of jewellery he bought for me.' He'll probably recycle that ring and give it to Sasha. 'No, the bracelet was from my mum. She . . . had a lot of expectations for me. High expectations. I was never very good at meeting them. If I came second, I should have come first. If I came first, it wasn't to a high enough standard. But the more I tried, the more exhausted I became, and the more I failed. I could never get it right. And then one day I did.

'She was desperate for me to get into her old university. When the acceptance letter came, I'd never seen her so happy. She said I'd finally done something worthwhile, and went out and bought me the bracelet. And I loved it. I loved it so much, because it was proof I wasn't a total failure, that I *could* be all the things she wanted me to be. But it didn't last. I messed up. And then I died and it was gone, because I *was* a failure, and I didn't deserve it after all.'

'Whatever mistakes you think you've made, I wouldn't say they make you less deserving of anything,' Sath says, his thumb sweeping over my wrist. Frowning, he adds, 'Were you wearing it when you died?'

238

I nod, wiping my face. I can't believe he's managed to turn this into a cross-examination of me. This is *not* the fun time I had planned. 'That's three questions you've had now. My turn. What's your concession?'

He takes a shot. Maybe I need to warm up to the big stuff, so I choose something innocent next, biding my time, luring him into a trap. 'What's your all-time favourite meal?'

The answer is, inexplicably, lasagne. Sath accepts my change in direction and we continue like this all night, watching the bottle of tequila slowly deplete. Sometimes we drink for silly questions – like when Sath refuses to tell me his favourite colour for the sake of taking another shot – although I do establish he has a thing for musicals (*Phantom of the Opera* is his favourite) and that Sathanas isn't his real name, but one he chose when he became . . . this. When I press him to tell me his real one, he drinks. I can only assume it's something old-fashioned like . . . Alfred. Or Barnabas. Oh, God, please don't let him be an Edgar.

On second thought, let him be Edgar. Maybe it would stop me thinking about how his smile is a little lopsided, and how much his hair has grown out since we first met. It falls in dark waves over his eyes, constantly tempting me to touch it. I settle for wrapping my hands around the bottle instead, and taking a sip. Sath asks me another question, but I barely hear it, not over the roaring in my head. Danger alarms are flashing. I pretend I can't see them.

At some point, his arm ends up back over the top of the booth. And then my shoulders. And then I'm tucked against his side, and it doesn't feel like either one of us is dead, rather that this is the first time we've come alive. Sath is grinning. I don't even know why. I just know everything is warm and fuzzy, and my skin is tingling because his hand is rubbing the top of my arm. He asks me some other ridiculous question and I laugh so hard tequila squirts out my nose. It must be frighteningly unsightly, and I should be embarrassed – Noah would be rolling his eyes and huffing my name right about now – but Sath hands me a tissue with a shake of his head. I guess he's used to me behaving like an idiot.

'Hm.' I'm running out of things to ask. I should return to my original attempt at interrogation now his guard is dropped, but it's nice to pretend Asphodel doesn't exist. I'm on the surface, feeling pleasantly buzzed, pressed against my not-unattractive friend in a very unattractive establishment. The previous occupants of this booth left a large portion of their drinks smeared on the surface, and Sath winces as his jumper unsticks from the table like Velcro as he takes the bottle from me.

I sense this is some kind of measure to get me to slow down, although he's still smiling when he wraps his mouth around the open bottle to take a swig. I try not to think about the fact my lips had been there, a few moments ago. I am not successful. I watch the way his Adam's apple bobs as he swallows, which is weirdly mesmerising, and –

I blink and look away.

Sath puts the bottle down. 'I should thank you,' he says. 'For tonight.'

This gets my attention. 'You should?'

'It's been a long time since I did anything like this.' He

offers me a soft, sad smile. It finally makes my overactive heart slow, the organ twisting in my chest instead, like that smile has wrenched it out of place. 'You help me forget everything that goes on . . . down there.'

'Well,' I tell him, very seriously, 'that's because I'm your spanner.'

Sath's mouth drops open. 'Pardon?'

'I'm your spanner,' I say again. Then, leaning forward, I whisper, 'I'm going to tighten your bolt.'

This time, he splutters. '*Pardon?*'

'No. Wait.' I frown. 'I'm *loosening* your bolt.'

He stares at me, and then his whole face blooms into the most beautiful smile I've ever seen while his shoulders wobble with laughter. I beam at him. Like I said, I'm his bolt. Screwdriver. DIY item I've never used. Whatever. I'm growing hungry. I'm pretty sure there's a takeaway down the road, and they sell the most delicious chicken nuggets.

I think I may have drunk more than I thought. And I don't think Sath has drunk enough – he's still got the reflexes to swipe my shot glass out of the way when I'm an inch from knocking it off the table. Through my dizziness and desire for nuggets, panic flares. This was my chance to get answers, and I got distracted.

I need to do something. Get the conversation back on track. One last *truth or shot*. I should try again to learn about his concession. Find out, for real, what he's getting out of helping me. But Sath's laughing, and I want to touch him very badly, so instead of asking anything sensible, I lean forward and press my hand to his chest. 'What's in here?'

241

Sath goes still. Uh-oh. Possibly this was stupid. But I have to *know*. He's so human sitting here next to me, like we're a normal couple on a date that's going very, very well. I need some kind of confirmation he's capable of feeling the same.

Not that it matters. Obviously.

All the warmth is lost from his voice when he says, 'What did you say?'

Now would be the time to move away and pretend I was making some dumb joke, but his gaze has me frozen. 'You heard me,' I say, keeping my hand where it is, splayed across his jumper, feeling his warmth seep through the wool.

And it's there.

Thud. Thud. Thud.

'You're human,' I whisper. 'You're not a demon. You're not one of them.'

He gapes at me. 'You were checking if I was a *demon*?'

'What else would I be checking for?' I frown. 'The Sorter mentioned they didn't have hearts, and . . . you're their ruler. You have all these powers. I thought, maybe, you might be one too. But not really. Because you're nicer than they are. I was pretty sure you were human. And you are. Which is great.' I'm definitely babbling now. Anything to avoid admitting the full truth which is: if my heart is doing somersaults, I want to check yours is too.

I'm pleased to confirm it is.

'Great is a stretch,' Sath mutters, rubbing his chest. Then he freezes. 'Why do you care what I am?'

'I don't,' I lie, breaking the rules of my own game. It shouldn't matter one jot what he is. What he can feel.

242

But it does.

It *does*.

His eyes flare the moment he recognises my lie.

'Willow . . .' His other hand lands on my knee, skimming the bare skin beneath the hem of my dress. I shuffle towards him – even like this, we're not close enough. His breath is warm against my face; it quickens as his hand trails upwards, pushing the skirt dangerously high. My fingers find his jumper again, fisting the material and tugging him closer.

And then he audibly inhales, releasing my leg and sitting back. He nudges the tequila bottle to the other side of the table as though it's solely responsible for our current situation. 'We should go.'

I don't understand. This isn't what I expected. It's not what I *wanted*. 'But –'

'I have responsibilities.' His tone is as cold as I am, now his arm has left my shoulder.

I also don't think my takeaway idea is going to go down well, which is equally disappointing. I may never see a chicken nugget again.

'Fine,' I say, aiming for nonchalant. 'Let's go home.'

I slide from the booth, stumbling on a step I swear wasn't there on the way in, and am halfway down the length of the room when I realise Sath isn't following. Instead, I find him staring at me, mouth ajar. It's the same look he's given me before, the one I can't read but desperately want to. Like I'm a sun rising behind a town bathed in darkness for too long.

Which makes what just happened all the more confusing.

I fold my arms. 'What?'

'Nothing.' Sath shakes his head and finally squeezes out of the booth to join me, holding out his hand. 'Let's go.'

Our fingers entwine. He gives me another smile – I've lost count of how many I've been gifted with tonight, and this one seems different again, more hopeful, a rose divesting itself of its thorns – and the idea I'll never see it again has me wanting to crack in two.

Has me wanting to say *to hell with the tasks*. My chest constricts. Just having the thought sends a stab of guilt sliding between my ribs. I promised. I *promised*. No more Bad Decision Willow. Someone always gets hurt in the crossfire of what she wants.

What she wants is him.

The bartender waves as we depart, but Sath doesn't look at her. Not once.

He can't take his eyes off me.

24

There are butterflies in my stomach.

I didn't need or ask for them, but they've been there all morning, a festering nest of wings that flutter sporadically. Mostly when I let my mind wander to places it shouldn't. Currently, my legs are doing some wandering of their own, guiding me to Sath's rooms for no real reason other than I can't stay away.

Not even the sight of Aric stops me. He's standing in the open doorway to the Sorter's morgue, tail swishing like an agitated cat.

From inside, an equally agitated voice says, 'I'm serious, Aric, you can't, not when we're this close to –' The Sorter breaks off when she spies me trying to scuttle past. 'Willow. Wait.'

I wince. Aric looks especially feral today; his hair needs a trim and his claws are extended, dragging a screeching path along the wall.

'Get lost.' One of the Sorter's hooves meets his shin. 'I want to talk to Willow.'

Aric snarls, but, to my surprise, flounces off without argument. Staring at his retreating form, I ask, 'Does he always follow orders like that?'

'Unfortunately not.' Her response is as sour as a lemon. 'Come on. Come inside.'

She assumes *I'm* going to follow orders. I am curious, though, what she wants from me, so I follow her in, relieved to find the morgue empty of death for once. The slabs are gleaming, scrubbed free of residue and splatter, and the temperature has been raised a notch with no smells to mask.

'I bumped into Sath earlier,' she says with no preamble. Her nose screws up. 'He was all . . . gooey.'

'Gooey?' Honestly, in this place, I have no idea if she means it literally.

'Happy.' She says it like it's a dirty word, choking on the syllables as though her tongue's grown too big for her mouth.

'Right.' My butterflies return in full force. 'Is that bad?'

'Oh hells, you're gooey too.' Rolling her eyes, she hoists herself on to a slab, hooves dangling a foot from the ground. With a sly smile, she adds, 'You should know, I found your chart.'

Clipped of their wings, the butterflies tumble to the pit of my belly and disintegrate. 'And?'

'And I thought you'd like to read it,' she says. 'Here you go.'

It materialises at her side, and she's shoving it into my hands before I can stop her.

I want nothing to do with it, but the ink is a magnet to my gaze. *Disappointment. Failure. River of blood? Too selfish. Impulsive. Responsible for her mother's death. More blood? Quits. Threw a tantrum and* –

If the handwriting wasn't different, I'd assume Mum wrote this herself. I read the words over and over; they burn my eyes

246

the way her voice burns my memories, and I need them to stop, to go away, because I don't want them to be true. I tear the paper from the board and crumple it into a ball that's not small enough – I want it gone; I want it shredded into pieces – and toss it to the floor. A lump forms in my throat. 'Why are you showing me this?'

'I found it.' She blinks rapidly. 'I was being nice.'

'If this is your version of nice, I'd hate to see you be awful,' I retort. 'I am more than the person on that page.'

'Whatever you say.' She jumps off the slab with a loud clop. 'How long have you been here now – three, four months? How long does it normally take for someone to notice?'

'Notice what?'

'What you're really like.' The paper is retrieved from the floor like an evil boomerang I can't escape. She smooths out the wrinkles and hums as she reads the sheet. 'I suppose you'd better finish the final tasks before anyone *here* notices. Which would you say is worse? *Murderer, selfish, impulsive* – that one might be an issue for Harper, given what you did to your last friend. Do you think you'll shove her in the Void yourself, or goad Aric into doing it for you?'

Roaring fills my ears. 'Shut up.'

'Let's see, what about Sath?' She taps her lips. 'What parts of you will he end up hating?'

I snatch the paper before she can draw a conclusion. More words jump out at me, emphasised with sound this time, like I'm standing next to the Void all over again. *All I ever wanted was to be proud of you. How could you let me down again? If you're not careful, Noah will leave you, and then what will you do? Such a disappointment, a failure, a fraud. How could you how could you how could you?*

Crumpling the paper once more, I yank the nearest lever down. To Tartarus. The chute opens, expecting a body, and I toss the paper into that great, yawning mouth instead. It's incinerated immediately, a belch of black smoke filling the room before the chute snaps shut again.

'You seem angry,' the Sorter says gleefully. 'What's wrong?'

'Why are you doing this?' I whirl on her. 'Do you get a kick out of making people miserable?'

I'd woken up in such a good mood, but now I'm as deflated as a popped balloon and the Sorter's stolen all my helium.

'I'm a demon.' She clicks her fingers, and a fresh pile of bodies pop on to the slabs. 'Of course I do. I don't know why you're so upset though. You're leaving, aren't you? Complete the tasks fast enough and they'll never discover the truth. You'll never see the sad look on Sath's face when he learns how disappointing you are.'

I think of the way Sath stared at me last night, full of hope and promise, like I was the answer to a question he'd never asked. Mum had hope for me once too. Then I made the wrong choice at every turn, abandoning my promises and stamping on every dream she had for me.

I don't ever want Sath to look at me the way she did.

'Unless . . . You weren't thinking of giving up, were you?' the Sorter goes on. 'You do have form for that, I suppose.'

'Of course I wasn't.' My voice is too loud, too high-pitched, trying to drown out the lie. 'I'm not quitting. You saw me in sloth. I can pass anything. I *will* pass everything. I'm going home to prove everything on that paper wrong. You'll see.'

'That's the spirit.' She pats my shoulder. 'Told you I was being nice.'

Her version of nice is to sprinkle sugar over poison. She enjoys seeing me suffer, that much is clear from the bounce in her step. But no matter how vindictive showing me that clipboard was, it's the jolt I needed to carry on.

A tissue is shoved in front of my nose.

'I'm allergic to tears,' the Sorter says. 'And my generous nature only goes so far.'

I pluck the tissue from her hand with an exaggerated sniff before wiping the wet brewing in the corner of my eyes. 'Was there anything else, or do you consider my day sufficiently ruined?'

'I think your day is just the way it needs to be.' Her cheeks dimple with satisfaction as she gestures to the door. 'I'm sure we'll be seeing each other again soon.'

Not if I have anything to do with it, we won't.

I lean against the wall outside, dying vines drooping over my shoulder like they're attempting to give me a hug. They can fuck off. I don't want sympathy; I want this to be *over*.

Two tasks.

That's all I need to get through.

Then I remember the conversation Sath and I had that night I drank the wine, and I recall what task is next. What I'm going to have to say no to. *Who* I'm going to have to say no to.

Lust.

Him.

25

Although we agreed to speed up the tasks, we seem to have come to a mutual understanding that I am not stable enough to deal with lust straight away. As much as I want this done, I need to be in a position where I'm not salivating over him the second we're together. Unfortunately, despite a lack of bell-ringing, I am basically one of Pavlov's dogs whenever he's around.

I also don't have the self-control to stay away.

We spend the next few weeks in an awkward stasis, where I try to remain a metre's distance at all times while keeping my drool in check. Or maybe he's keeping a metre away from me. Either way, we're spending most evenings attempting to play board games sat halfway across the room from each other, and it's not going well.

It's almost a relief when a note is slipped under my door. *Tonight.*

Oh, God. My breaths can't come fast enough. My whole body is on fire at the thought of what he's going to ask me to do, and the fact I badly want to do it. I don't know what to wear. Do I go sultry and keep in theme, or do I wear a sack in the hope it kills the mood? Maybe several sacks. So many sacks it takes him all night to remove them.

Although, with his magic, he can probably click his fingers and remove everything at once. Or maybe he'll grow talons and shred my underwear himself, or –

Oh, God. I have got to stop thinking like this. I have got to stop thinking at all.

It's one night. I just have to say no. I can do this.

I settle for a dress. Similar to the one I wore during gluttony, pure black with spaghetti straps and a slit up the side, only this one is shorter, finishing mid-thigh. Probably a mistake, but . . . I want him to *want* to tempt me. I don't want tonight to be just about a task.

I want him to suffer as much as I will.

I match it with a pair of heels and totter out of my room, wishing he'd had the courtesy to offer me a portal. Humans gawp at me in the lift, like they've never seen a girl dressed to resist the Devil before.

I should have gone with the sack.

The remaining journey is a blur, my feet moving on autopilot towards his quarters. I suck in a deep breath outside his door, but my hand still trembles when I knock.

Sath swings it open and scans me up and down, his gaze trailing over my bare legs, my hips, the swell of my breasts. His hand curls around the door frame, and when our eyes meet, he visibly swallows. 'Hi.'

'Hi.' My heart is in my throat. There is a strong possibility I may collapse. Maybe I'll win the challenge by fainting before it begins.

Sath steps aside. 'You didn't have to knock.'

I brush past him, my steps slow and unsteady. Of course I knocked. I was trying to delay the inevitable. Besides, what was I supposed to do, breeze on in and say *I'm ready to be seduced now.*

God. I have got to get a grip. I completed the last five tasks; I can't let a teeny-tiny crush ruin everything now. He might be temptation itself, but at this point, I am the epitome of resistance. The saint to his sinner.

I *will* do this.

'So.' I fold my arms, attempting to seem unbothered. 'How does this work, exactly? Are you going to stand there and throw your best lines at me?'

'Not quite.' He gestures towards the bedroom door. Although his expression is stoic, the tightness in his jaw suggests he's about as unbothered as I am. 'After you.'

I lead him wordlessly into the bedroom. The walls are cream, contrasting with the black silk sheets adorning a large bed that occupies the majority of the space. Mahogany nightstands flank its sides, both covered in burning candles that fill the room with the scent of jasmine.

Sath closes the door behind us, and it's like time stops. We're in a vacuum, empty of sound except for our own breaths – both a little too loud, a little too quick – and every movement he makes sets me on edge. I prickle with anticipation. An ornate mirror covers the left-hand wall, and a quick glance into it tells me my cheeks are flushed, my eyes wide, like a deer in headlights.

I have to kill this mood.

'Lust must be easy for a lot of people,' I say, moving to his dresser and examining a display of seven clocks. None are working. 'You can't be everyone's type.'

'Some are taken to the surface,' Sath says. 'But not you.'

I emit what I hope is a mocking laugh. I suspect it sounds slightly hysterical. 'Because you think you're my type?'

'Because your breath hitches when I enter a room.' He prowls towards me. A lion circling prey. 'Because your legs clench when I get too close.'

I can't bring myself to be irritated he's noticed, because I'm too busy doing just that. Liquid heat curls in my stomach. Lower. Sath cocks his head, appraising me. Now we're in here, he's taken on his other persona, the Sath everyone expects him to be.

The Devil.

I can see the real him underneath. His hand shakes when he slides it into his pocket. There's a gentleness behind the gold flare in his eyes. His smirk isn't wide enough to be genuine. I should know – fake smiles are a speciality of mine.

All these pretences make up pieces of who he is, and it only makes me like him more.

I try again to defuse the tension. 'And how many have come before me?' I ask, knowing there's a strong chance I'll loathe the answer. 'How many failed this task?'

'Some passed. Some failed.'

My stomach twists. Some failed. I knew they would have, but the thought of someone being in this space, of being on that bed before me . . . I can't look at him. I've no right to be jealous; I've no claim to him, then or now. He's not mine. I'm not his.

We're friends. Comrades in task-taking. But my back is against the dresser now, one of the drawer knobs pressing into my spine, and I barely notice the discomfort. I *like* the discomfort. Anything to distract me from the other things I'm feeling. Like the desire to gouge out the eyes of anyone who's ever touched him. *Not mine, not mine, not mine.* I repeat the mantra as he comes closer, within touching distance now, bracing both arms on either side of me, caging me in.

I refuse to be one in a long line. I *will* pass this.

'We should establish the rules for tonight,' he says.

Right. The rules. Because this is a task. A game. It doesn't mean anything. I'm doing this to leave; he's doing this for his precious concession. But when our eyes meet, my breath hitches. There's something burning in his gaze that's hotter than the usual flames, and it makes me think this temptation isn't all for show.

Which makes it all the more dangerous for us both.

He's closer than ever, his scent of mint and rain overpowering me, hard muscle on his chest pressing against mine, and then he's leaning down, fingers on my chin as his breath ghosts my mouth. I fist his shirt. His top lip grazes mine. My stomach jolts, and I gasp, because it's happening, it's finally happening; my heart is thundering and he's soft and warm and everything I want and –

Sath stops, and sighs. 'I haven't yet told you the rules.'

If kissing is against them, I don't care. Can't he see I don't care? Bad Decision Willow has taken over me the same way his powers sometimes take over him.

I grip his shirt tighter, wishing I had the strength to tear through it. 'Who needs rules? I thought you were supposed to be making me fail.' Clearly, I should've worn something more low-cut. Maybe then he wouldn't be neglecting to kiss me.

He offers me a rueful smile. 'I'm allowed some restraint.'

Retreating, he unbuttons his shirt sleeves and rolls them to his elbows. This only makes my chest heave more. I had no idea I was into forearms. Apparently, when it comes to Sath, I'm into everything. I cannot fathom why he's decided to cross the room.

'The rules,' he says, voice taking on a tone of command. 'The task will last one hour. There will be . . . touching.'

I'm going to need him to stop talking, because this is conjuring up all kinds of images. Every part of me is liquid. My fingers grip the edge of the dresser in a desperate attempt to remain upright. At least now he's on the other side of the room, it's marginally easier to think. Maybe I can do this after all. At least it sounds like some touching might be involved without failure.

I really want there to be touching.

'If you ask me to fuck you, I will,' he goes on, because apparently he hasn't noticed I'm about to combust, 'and the moment I do, you'll fail.'

'Right,' I squeak. 'Well, that sounds easy enough. No asking for . . . that. Super. Fine.'

It's only an hour. An hour's nothing. That's less than a Scrabble session, and I've survived plenty of those without jumping his bones.

Shadows of flame coil down his arms. 'I won't be able to stay on this side of the room all night.'

255

The threat has my toes curling.

Well, if we're going to play, let's play. It's a dangerous game, knowing how easy it would be to fail, but if he's going to torture me the least I can do is return the favour. I toss my hair over my shoulder, exposing my neck, my bare collarbone. I slide one strap down my shoulder, Sath's eyes following the movement.

'Come here, then,' I say.

I've lost the moment he's in front of me again. In one swift movement, he lifts me on to the dresser, my legs spreading apart to allow him to step between them. His left hand wraps around my waist, his right coming to rest on my shoulder, one finger tangling in the strap I'd just been playing with. He bends his head to press kisses beneath my ear, down my neck, the fingers on my waist digging tighter and tighter into my skin with every kiss.

'Sath . . .' I'm not supposed to be begging, but his name sounds like a plea in itself. 'Can I touch you? Is that allowed?'

I'm already reaching for him, wanting to strip him bare, to smooth my palm over the planes of his chest, when his hand snaps up to ensnare mine. 'Best you don't, love.'

'But –'

'Willow.' His voice is raspy. 'Please. My self-control is hanging by a thread.'

I can't help but be a little gleeful about that. 'Really?' I tighten my thighs around his hips, and he closes his eyes, grinding his teeth. 'Who's tempting who here?' To annoy him, I add, 'If anything, I'd say you're going easy on me.'

His eyes flash open. They're pure molten now, ablaze with power and heat and want, and I've almost certainly made a mistake. He smirks. 'Challenge accepted.'

I'm picked up and thrown on the bed. My dress rides up my thighs, far too high to be decent, but Sath is already kissing a path up my legs, his mouth on my calves, the backs of my knees, my lower thigh, higher and higher, until his head disappears beneath my dress. I gasp as his teeth graze the sides of my underwear – I can't remember what I put on, I was busy worrying about my dress, and oh my God, please tell me I had the sense to choose something lacy – but then his head re-emerges, which is simultaneously upsetting and wonderful, because as much as I liked where it was heading, he's . . . adorable. His hair is mussed up, sticking out at all angles, and his cheeks are flushed pink.

As if on autopilot, I sit up, leaning towards him, towards that mouth, because I have to kiss him, I *have* to –

He dodges me, pushing me down and settling on top of me. I writhe beneath him, almost out of my mind with want and need and *emptiness*; I say his name as he moves his mouth over my neck, sucking and kissing and dragging his tongue over my skin. It's not enough. This is never going to be enough. He cups my breasts through the fabric of my dress, and I gasp, arching towards him.

The ache is too much to bear. Ignoring his orders from earlier, I set to work undoing the buttons on his shirt. He doesn't stop me this time, shifting position to help a little, allowing me to slide it free from his shoulders. I run my hands over his chest, the ridges on his abdomen, the line of dark hair below his navel, before tucking a finger under the top of his waistband. He hisses, pressing against me, allowing me to feel what this is doing to him.

My mouth goes dry. 'Sath . . .' I remove my hand and curl it behind his neck instead, dragging his face to mine. 'I want –' I break off, frustrated, desperate to say the words. I was wrong before – I'm not the saint to his sinner, I'm simply the damned.

He stares at me, panting heavily. His gaze is unfocused and his hair is plastered to his forehead. The sheen of sweat gleams on both our chests. I've no idea how we got like this, grinding like teenagers, but the sheer force of restraining from this never-ending want is an exercise in itself. We'll be Olympic medallists in not having sex at this rate.

Except, having sex is all I want to do, and I'm not bothered about winning gold.

His head lowers. My pulse rockets – apparently there are no limits to how fast it can get down here; I can only presume in the real world I'd be having a coronary at this point – because he's finally going to do it, I'm going to have him, I am I am I am, but then he drops his head on to my shoulder and practically growls, 'Fuck.'

I want to scream with frustration. How important is this concession of his that he's willing to forgo *this*? 'I've basically failed already. You might as well make it official.'

'I told you.' He nips at my shoulder. 'You haven't failed unless I fuck you.'

The thought makes me grip the sheets tighter. 'So, we *could* kiss –'

'What do you think would happen if we kissed? Would you be able to stop?'

He has a point there. I squirm. I need *something*. I'm aching and empty, and he's right here, and I can't remember a single one of the reasons why I'm trying to succeed in these tasks.

I roll over, balancing my head on my elbow and drinking in my fill of Sath, shirtless by my side. I cannot comprehend how I'm not naked at this point. It says more about his restraint than mine. I trail one finger down his chest. 'If we didn't stop,' I say, 'what would you do to me?'

Shadows flicker in every corner of the room. Sath has turned predatory, a cobra poised to strike, every inch of him taut. 'Think very carefully about whether you want me to answer that question.'

I shuffle closer, close enough for our noses to graze, our mouths inches apart. His breathing is steady now, no longer out of control. Probably because he knows I've lost it. He could do whatever he wanted to me and I wouldn't stop him. We wrap our arms around one another, one of my legs tucking between his, but this isn't a frenzied grope-fest, not any more. It's sweet. Tender.

'Tell me,' I say.

His smile informs me it won't stay sweet and tender for long. He draws a slow, lazy path up my arm. 'First, I'd kiss you until you couldn't remember your own name.' He rolls on top of me. 'Then I'd remove this ridiculous dress.'

I frown, affronted. It's a perfectly nice dress.

'I can't think straight with you in it.' He presses another kiss to my neck. 'Then I'd . . .'

He shifts, tilting to one side to allow his hands access to the hem of my dress, to what's underneath. One finger tucks inside my underwear, and I want to flinch away, knowing he's going to recognise how badly I want him – as if he didn't already – but when that finger pulls my underwear to one side and strokes up the core of me, he swears. Profusely.

'Then you'd what?' I ask, trying to sound casual. It would help if I wasn't panting heavily.

Sath takes a moment, as though he too is struggling to form coherent sentences – personally, all I can think is *more more more* – and then he dips that finger inside me. It takes every ounce of willpower I have not to cry out. I bite my lip, fingers clutching the bed sheets, my entire focus going to the feeling of that finger filling me finally, finally, but it's not enough, not *nearly* enough, not when I can feel him hot and hard against me and I know how much better that would feel instead.

'Then I'd do this,' he answers. The finger slides out. In again.

It's slow, and it's torturous, and I take back everything I've said before. *Now* is the point I combust.

'Then I'd go down on you,' he murmurs, his finger still moving at a snail's pace – I move on him, urging him faster faster faster, and at this point I can only assume he's ignoring me on purpose, the bastard. 'Taste you with my tongue. How do you think you'd taste?'

Attempts at propriety lost, I mutter both obscenities and his name repeatedly; I'm going to break apart, splinter in two, explode into a million little pieces that he'll have to put together again. I'm on the edge of a cliff, but this time when I go over I'm not going to fall to my death, I'm going to fly, and he's going to give it to me –

He withdraws. I gasp. 'What are you –'

What the fuck is he thinking. He can't stop *now*.

'Did you want to ask me something, Willow?'

Yes. A thousand times, yes. For once, it's my voice urging me on. I don't need any encouragement from disembodied voices in this situation.

'Willow?' Sath's finger teases me once more.

I bite my lips before forcing one word through them. 'No.'

'Hm.' He presses down on a point that makes me see stars. 'Looks like I'm not trying hard enough.'

'How –' Forming sentences is proving difficult. 'How much longer do we – ah – have left –'

Tracing lazy circles around that same spot, he says, 'Thirty minutes.'

I groan, although I suspect the meaning behind the sound is murky. 'Thirty minutes, Sath, I can't –'

'You can.' His mouth finds my neck, sucking and nibbling the flesh there while I clench around him, arching off the bed. 'Ask me,' he whispers. 'Just ask me.'

His lips move upwards, brushing my jaw, my cheeks, my mouth. Feather-light. I chase after them, needing more of him, and he darts out of the way, forever unobtainable. 'Ask me.'

I want to.

I want to so badly it hurts. But –

What about Sath? What parts of you will he end up hating?

As loath as I am to admit it, the Sorter's right. I always disappoint in the end. I don't want to stick around and watch him make that discovery.

'I can't,' I tell him. 'We can't.'

A second finger joins the first. 'Are you sure?'

No. Yes. I whimper. 'Sath, please –'

'What was that?' He's moving far, far too slowly. 'Did you need something?'

What I need is for him to stop this torture. Pressure builds again as he finally increases the pace; the bed sheets tear in my hand as I twist them too hard, my breaths quickening with every move he makes. I throw my head back, mouth parted, grinding against him, I can't get enough and –

He pulls away.

I could scream.

'Well? Did you need something?'

'No.' I throw an arm over my face. 'Go away.'

He chuckles. 'Look at me.'

I acquiesce. Reluctantly. While pouting. As soon as our eyes meet, his fingers slide into place. Holding my gaze, he moves in and out once more; our chests rising in time like we're puppets held on each other's strings. I'm lost in his stare, sinking into its golden depths as my body matches his rhythm. I touch his face, trailing a path down skin as hot as coals, my thumb resting on his lower lip.

It builds faster this time, the threads tying us together tugging me onwards, upwards; I'm floating, reaching for release –

He stops again. Starts. Stops. He doesn't protest when my eyes flutter shut. It happens over and over, bringing me closer every time but never close enough. I wriggle and writhe. Curse him under my breath. Curse him loudly when I'm denied what I want. I suspect nothing is coherent. He whispers that I should ask him, and I cling to him just as hard as I do the thought that I *mustn't*. I wish it wasn't so hard to remember why.

His face hovers over mine, lips dangerously close, as I tighten once more, the inferno trapped inside me threatening to rage at last; I cry out, clenching around him and –

He stops. Of course he does. I kick the sheets with frustration.

'Sath.' It hurts to speak. My throat is raw; my eyes are filled with the threat of tears. 'You have to . . . I can't . . .'

'You can have everything you want.' He unsticks my hair from where it's plastered to my neck and tucks it behind my ear. 'All you have to do is ask.'

No wonder I always put off doing the right thing if it feels like this. Like my ribcage has cracked open and bone shards are digging into my organs, burrowing inside until there's nothing left but pain and longing for all the things I want but can't have and don't deserve.

'No,' I whisper. 'No, I won't.'

On the dresser, one of the broken clocks ticks, the hands moving into a new position before going still.

Sath exhales and drops his head, burrowing it into the crook of my neck. His heart pounds against my skin, and for a moment it's not enough to feel it there; I want to reach inside his chest and fuse it with mine.

I let out a shaky sigh of my own, although I'm not sure mine is out of relief. I'm trying not to be too offended by his – he's still pressing insistently against me, so he can't have been *too* desperate for me to say no – and assume it was out of delight that I've passed another task.

But.

Wait.

'Have I passed?' My mouth is so dry the words crack on my tongue. 'Is that it?'

'Mm.'

'Could we –'

'Willow . . .' He says my name like a groan, and not in the pleasurable sense. Not at all. He lifts his head. There's no playful smirk on his face now, or fire burning in his gaze. No Devil left in him. His eyes have returned to chocolate brown, and they brim with sympathy when our stares meet. I don't like the look of it. 'We shouldn't.'

'Oh,' I say in a small voice. 'Okay.'

Once again, I was so caught up in him that I forgot tempting me was his sole purpose in this. The Sath in front of me clearly doesn't feel the same as the Sath with the Devil's cloak wrapped around his throat. And I almost let him trick me into *failing*. My cheeks burn with embarrassment. Now the haze has passed I can see where his one finger glistens with moisture, with *me* and – oh, God – the noises I'd been making –

Fresh tears well in my eyes. I can't let him see. I scramble to rearrange the straps of my dress; I don't know why I *wore* a dress, why why why did I wear a dress when it didn't matter, when he had to do this anyway, when it's literally his job, and he's done it with tens or hundreds or thousands of people before me?

'Look at me.' Sath reaches for me, but I slap his hand away. 'Please. You have to know I –'

He grabs my wrist before I can jump off the bed, because I can't look at him, I won't; not when I'd just been splayed out and vulnerable before him and now I'm not sure if he even liked it.

'*Willow*,' he says, and this time I do turn my head. His voice has taken that tone again, the commanding Devil voice that sends his demons to their knees. My own legs tremble. 'I want you. Believe me. But if you knew . . . There are things I . . . We just can't.'

I hate how plaintive I sound when I ask, 'Why not?'

He opens his mouth. I wait with bated breath, convinced he's going to answer, but then he clamps it shut, a muscle in his jaw ticking, and it's obvious he's not going to tell me anything.

Fine.

Fine.

I've passed. I've got one task left, and then I never have to see him again. Which is good. Perfect. All I've ever wanted since I got here.

This time, when I make an ungraceful exit from the bed, he doesn't make a move to stop me. He doesn't say a single word.

26

I spend the next day stewing in one of the hot springs, watching other humans come and go as though they have no care in the world. Good for them. My fingertips are beyond pruny from being in the water so long, but whenever I contemplate leaving, I get another flashback from last night and I start to shake. The memories are mortifying. Me, begging Sath for something he didn't want to give. Me, reaching for him like a starving woman seeing a fresh baguette. Me, considering failing the task because I thought there might be something for me here. Like maybe going home wasn't my only option.

Of course it is.

It would be great if my wobbly lips and tear-filled eyes would catch up. There is nothing to be upset about. I am one task away from everything I've wanted since arriving here. My life will be returned, never to be thrown away again, and I'll bask in the knowledge that I did it, I proved myself, and the sunshine that knowledge provides will chase away the lingering shadows making me feel like I'm about to lose something I never had.

God. I have to get a hold of myself. I force myself out of the pool and dress quickly, with the intent of finding my friends. Anything to take my mind off –

No. I refuse to say his name. He can go back to being the king who got his shoes vomited on the day we met. The recollection cheers me a bit – I haven't seen those shoes since; hopefully they're ruined and he's sad about it – so I leave the springs with a skip in my step, picturing all of Sath's clothes covered in projectile.

By the time I find Harper and Amelia in one of the recreation rooms, I'm practically beaming.

Then I see the way their hands are entwined and my heart clenches. I want it. I want it so badly it hurts.

The clack of pool balls jerks my focus. It's busy in here today, groups of humans laughing and whooping when they make a decent shot. A pinball machine dings in the corner. Someone's made popcorn and the scent of butter and salt wafts in the air.

Being dead doesn't mean you have to stop living. I hadn't understood what Harper meant the day we met, but I get it now. Being in Asphodel gives you a thousand chances to make a thousand mistakes and get a do-over every time.

I plop into a chair beside her. She narrows her eyes at me and I brace for an interrogation about what I was doing last night, but I'm spared having to conjure a lie by the sight of Henry hurrying towards us.

We leap from our seats in unison. His right eye is puffy, and there's a bruise purpling on his cheek. A chunk has been torn from his shirt.

'What happened?' asks Harper, grabbing his arm before he can topple over and steering him into the chair she's just vacated. 'Are you okay?'

He's obviously not okay. I curl my hands into fists and kneel beside him. A few humans are looking over at us, a mixture of curiosity and alarm playing on their faces, while others leave the room entirely as though they think we're a magnet for trouble they'd rather avoid. In a low voice, I say, 'Was it Aric?'

'What do you think?' Henry pulls at his ripped shirt with trembling fingers. 'It doesn't matter. It was my fault.'

'*Your* fault? How can it be your fault?'

'I got lost in the catacombs,' he replies. 'I heard a rumour they'd placed an orb at the centre, one that would let you see Earth. I only wanted a glimpse. Just to remember. But I kept going round and round, and then I hit a dead end. When I turned around, he was waiting. Said the usual spiel about how I'm a *naughty little human*.' He snorts. 'Naive, maybe. There is no orb. The demons made it up to get us there. They killed a few –'

'How many?'

'I was a little busy running away to keep count.'

He can be as glib as he likes, but I can tell from the way his voice catches he doesn't mean it. If this orb had existed, what would be the harm in looking? Nobody would have been hurt.

I hate this. I hate that the humans are punished for dreaming, for wanting to cling to all the pieces of themselves that make them human. I hate that they're punished for every innocent thing that makes them happy because some demon decided what *they* want, what *they* think is right, is more important.

And the one person capable of changing how this place works refuses. Is too scared. Suddenly, I'm not just angry at Sath for rejecting me, but for rejecting *all* of them, for not doing more to stop the demons. He's never bothered to try. All he does is sit around whining about the gates, about how he doesn't like to be mean, boo-fucking-hoo, about how he can't possibly kiss someone despite making them ache for him, because he's a soulless, lying bastard who plays with people's feelings and makes them confused and desperate and he probably enjoyed toying with me and –

I inhale. I'm thinking again. Thinking is bad.

I can't change how Sath may or may not feel about me. But I can try and change the way he rules Asphodel before I go.

And if it gives me an excuse to yell at him about other stuff too, well, fine. I'll multitask.

'I'm going to fix this,' I tell the others. 'Leave it with me.'

Harper's eyes go wide. 'You can't start another fight with Aric, you'll –'

'I'm not going to start one with Aric.' My tone is almost serene. 'I'm going to start one with the Devil.'

This doesn't do much to persuade them I've not lost my mind. Amelia and Harper gasp, while Henry's one good eye widens.

It's Amelia who speaks first, whimpering my name before saying, 'He'll kill you.'

Not if I kill him first. The mood I'm in, the thought is not unappealing.

'He won't hurt me,' I tell them.

Except he already has. Just not in the way they'd expect.

'Amelia's right,' Harper says. 'Just because you and he – well, I'm not entirely sure, but that doesn't mean it's safe to start an argument with him.'

'Trust me, okay? Sath and I have an understanding. If I can

make him listen . . . Think about it. You wouldn't wake up in fear any more. You could go anywhere in Asphodel without peering over your shoulder. You'd be happy here. An endless supply of entertainment, food and drink, an eternity together with no worry one of you is going to be torn apart by a demon with a temper problem.'

Saying it out loud, it sounds almost pleasant. If Sath got the demons and the gates under control, would I want that for myself?

All I ever wanted was to be proud of you. I'm not sure my becoming a revolutionary was part of Mum's plan.

But as usual, I can't keep my mouth shut.

'Asphodel shouldn't belong to the demons,' I go on. 'That's not what it was built for. They've corrupted everything good about this place for too long. Let me try and help you before –'

The words stick in my throat. I'm about to leave them before I ever got to know them. For all my complaints that Sath made me wait between each task, I want to beg him to drag out this final one. Time has slipped away from me like granules of sand running between my fingers, and now my palms are empty. Just like in my life, I wasted what I had, delayed the things I should be doing.

The least I can do is help them before I go.

'Wait here.' Ignoring their cries of protest, I storm away. Sath's not in his rooms – probably avoiding me, the coward – but I find him easily enough, hiding in a far corner of the library. He's sprawled on a large armchair, supposedly reading another one of his dusty books, although it appears to be upside down. Notes are scattered all over the floor, some sort of diagram etched on the closest piece of paper, but it's hard to make out what it depicts. It would be pitch-black in here if it weren't for the way the shelves glow blue, like tanks in an aquarium that contain books rather than fish, and the way that light bathes Sath's face makes him look otherworldly. Beautiful. I hate him for it.

The topmost shelf is easily twenty feet above me, and there are no ladders to be seen. I stare at a particularly thick tome and think *down*.

To my immense satisfaction, the book flies from the shelf and drops on his head.

Sath swears at the impact, jerking upright and – his gaze locks on mine. I go hot and cold all at once.

He rejected me. He *rejected* me.

'Willow . . .' He tucks the book down the side of his chair. 'I'm glad you came.'

I have just enough self-control to refrain from pointing out that, as far as last night goes, I categorically did not come. 'If you wanted to see me, you could have found me yourself.'

He piles up the notes and tucks them into his jacket pocket before answering. Given his lack of immediate apology, I'm going to assume they don't contain a love letter. 'I wasn't sure you'd want me to.'

'I don't,' I retort. 'I'm only here because I want you to make me a promise.'

He approaches me carefully, like a hunter closing in on a wounded animal that can still bite. 'If it's within my power, I'll give you anything.'

A dangerous offer. There are plenty of things he has the

power to give me that he's already refused to give. 'When I'm gone, I want you to do something about the demons. Once and for all. No more hiding, or excuses. Aric attacked Henry again today, and I can't leave knowing they're in danger. I can't live the rest of my life wondering what's happening to them. Promise me they'll be safe.'

His throat bobs. 'I promise . . . once your final task is complete, I'll do what needs to be done. They'll have the best chance I can give them.'

I narrow my eyes. He's being awfully accommodating. Maybe he's feeling guilty. 'Well. Good. Glad that's settled. I'll leave you to your book.'

'Willow, wait.' His hand snakes around my wrist, and my pulse jumps at the contact. Traitor.

I snatch my arm away. 'We have nothing else to discuss.'

'I got you something.'

This makes me pause. I love presents. 'Is it something nice?'

'I hope so.' The corner of his mouth tugs up. 'I went to the vaults earlier today, and I found –'

He pulls something small and silver from his pocket.

Something I recognise.

Mesmerised, I stare at it, the metal band making me forget every reason I had to leave this room. 'That's . . .'

'You said it was important to you.'

I take the bracelet with shaking hands. It's exactly as I remember, with a heart dangling from the band. It's chipped. The engraving *to Willow, from Mum* is still there, but there are scratches on it from – I've no clue, honestly. I treated this bracelet about as well as I did my whole life.

'She died,' I whisper.

Sath hesitates. 'I know.'

Tears fill the corners of my eyes. I don't wipe them away. I spent weeks pretending they weren't there, all to spare Sasha and Noah the hassle of dealing with them, and they still gave up on me. My mum died. She *died*.

I let out a shuddering breath as I put the bracelet on, wincing as I force it over the part of my wrist that's a tad too wide. Although the weight's familiar, it's also a shackle, chaining me to the person Mum wanted me to be. The person I'm supposed to be becoming.

Everything about it is uncomfortable.

I twist it round and round, trying to make it fit. 'I told you why she gave it to me. I didn't tell you what happened afterwards.'

Sath stays quiet, waiting. There's no tequila on the table, no stupid game I've made up to force this confession from me. But I want to tell him. I feel *safe* telling him.

'Once the novelty of pleasing her had worn off, I hated every second of that course. I would sit there in lectures and stare at this bracelet, trying to remind myself it would all be worth it at the end. I was a few months from graduating when I realised it wasn't going to be just those three years. It was going to be my whole life. Everything mapped out for me in some boring career I never cared about, everything dull and grey and dreary when all I wanted was colour. Sasha couldn't stop talking about her trip to Thailand, and it was eating me up inside that I'd never get to go. Noah had no interest in travelling, and Mum kept reminding me over and over again that I had to stay with Noah, but the more she said it the more it felt like I was suffocating. The day Sasha left, I snapped. I quit. One of my lecturers was this stuffy guy wearing tweed who told me I needed to *apply myself better* if I wanted to pass my final exams, so I told him to apply a stick up his arse instead, and walked out.'

My voice turns shaky.

'Mum was driving to see me,' I say. 'Screaming over loudspeaker about what a mistake I'd made. How I'd disappointed her, that I'd let my temper get the best of me and thrown my whole life away. It was dark, and foggy, and . . . the car went off the road. Crashed into a tree. I heard the whole thing.' Tears flow into my mouth, fat and hot and wet, flooding my tongue with salt. I choke, and Sath's arm is around my shoulders, pulling me into him.

I shrug him off. I can't stand him touching me after what's happened, and, besides, I don't deserve his pity. I did this to myself. If I'd endured that class, she'd still be alive right now. *I'd* still be alive right now.

'Do you know what the worst part was? There was a little piece of me that was relieved,' I whisper. 'For the briefest of moments, I felt . . . free. Like I started breathing the moment she stopped.'

'Willow . . .'

'I'm a monster. You don't have to tell me that.' I swallow. 'I knew it was wrong as soon as I had the thought. So, I made a promise. A vow to be a better person, to live my life the way she wanted as penance for all the terrible things I've ever thought or done. A way to keep her memory alive, to prove everything she did for me wasn't for nothing. But I kept breaking that promise at every turn. Kept delaying re-enrolling on to the course, putting off applying for jobs. First by refusing to get out of bed, and then finding every possible distraction I could. She saw me as a failure, and what if she was right? What if I was never going to be good enough? I was too scared to find out.'

'You've proven you can do anything you put your mind to,' Sath says. 'Maybe not in the way she expected, or wanted, but that was on her, not you.'

'No, it's on me.' I shake my head. 'Every choice I've ever made has been the wrong one, and it got her killed. Now, after the tasks, I know I can do better. I can say no to all the things I want, and I won't hurt anyone else.'

'You didn't make her get in the car,' Sath says gently. 'She could have accepted your decision or waited for the weather to clear. Sometimes bad things just happen.'

His words loosen one of the many cords that have been choking me since her death, but it's not enough. There are too many tangled threads for him to undo them all, especially not with platitudes we both know aren't true.

'What about my own death, did that just happen? You saw me that night. You were the one who forced me to admit how awful I was.'

'If you'd let me get a word in edgeways, you'd have known you passed the moment you admitted it wasn't a freak accident. That was all the task required – for you to own up to what you couldn't accept at the time. That you weren't coping. You were making mistakes, yes, but they don't define you. They don't make you an awful person.'

'Yes, they do! A better person would have coped. A *better person* wouldn't continuously make bad decisions the way I do.'

Sath falls silent.

'No rebuttal?' I should be pleased, but this is one argument I don't want to win. I want him to tell me I am good and perfect and all the voices in my head are wrong. I want him to keep talking until all my ties are cut and I never hear Mum again.

'The only one I have is selfish.' He pulls me closer, holding my hand to his chest. 'I was going to say, how wrong can your decisions be, if they led you to me?'

Butterflies I thought I'd squashed smash free of their chrysalis to do all kinds of acrobatics in my stomach.

'You don't mean that,' I tell him. 'Not when you didn't want –'

No. No, I am not finishing that sentence. I should have left the library straight after he gave me that promise, before he thawed my icy exterior and left me melting under his touch all over again.

He lifts my hand to his lips and presses a feather-light kiss to my knuckles. His eyes glisten. 'I'm sorry, Willow.'

'Sorry for what, exactly?'

'I'm just . . . sorry. For a lot of things.' He drops my hand. 'Just know, everything I've done has been for a good reason. I hope you remember that, at the end.'

27

The end comes sooner than I'd like.

I'd eaten breakfast alone – Harper and the others not in their usual spot, probably too scared to leave their rooms after Henry's run-in with Aric yesterday – to find Sath waiting outside the dining cave. Vines hang at his back like rotten ropes. Humans side-eye him as they scuttle past but he ignores them all, gaze locked on me.

'It's time,' he says, voice clipped. 'We'll do the final task today.'

'Oh.' I wait for a rush of adrenaline that doesn't come. My stomach flips, and I regret eating that second dragon fruit. Unease makes my skin prickle. I'm plummeting towards a finish line that's sprung up out of nowhere and I don't know how to stop.

'Are you coming?' Sath's hand is outstretched, waiting for me to take it.

'I'm scared,' I whisper. What will I do when I go back?

Sath narrows his eyes. 'Have you changed your mind?'

'No,' I say quickly. I haven't removed the bracelet since he gave it to me, and I spin it round my wrist, reminding me why

I have to finish this. Its weight feels heavier than ever. The last time I changed my mind about something, my mother climbed into a car and got herself killed. If I told him I was having doubts, who knows what awful chain of events I'd set off this time.

She could have accepted your decision. Sath's words are a more pleasant memory than the ones that usually loiter in my mind, but they're not enough to stop me taking his hand. Maybe for the last time. I grip it tighter than ever, and I think he's gripping me too, like if we both hold on hard enough this won't be happening, I won't be leaving, I won't be forced to work out what to do with the rest of my life.

We portal to a floor of Asphodel I don't recognise, landing outside a large set of metal doors not dissimilar to the gates. The only difference is that these are lacking the carvings of monstrous faces, and there's no blazing heat or steam being emitted from the iron.

'Where are we?'

'The Pits.' Sath's thumb brushes my knuckles. 'The demons host regular fighting tournaments here. Helps to suppress some of their urges. This is where the task of wrath will take place.'

My gut twists into knots. 'What am I doing here? Am I expected to fight?'

Beating Aric that one time was blind luck more than anything. Or, if this is a test, maybe I'm supposed to *not* fight, and just stand there while one of them uses me as a punching bag.

The knots loop tighter. What if this has always been the plan? My final punishment for wanting to leave is to push me into a pit and watch me get pummelled, until I'm nothing but bloody parts that float into the Void.

278

'No fighting,' Sath says, turning me to face him. His face is grave, worry filling in his eyes, which doesn't do much for my nerves.

He thinks I'm going to fail.

'Don't react.' He grips my upper arms. 'To anything. No matter what he says, or does, you have to let it happen –'

'Wait. He? Who's he?' The answer hits me straight away. It'll be Aric. Of course it'll be Aric. My voice shakes when I ask, 'What's he going to do?'

Sath swallows, leaning down to rest his forehead against mine. I breathe in his familiar smell and imagine we're alone in a misty forest somewhere. My eyes are welling up again.

Whatever happens in that arena, I'm going to get hurt, one way or another.

'What'll happen if I pass?' I whisper. 'Will I go back straight away, or would we have some time to –' To what, Willow? We're never going to be together. But he's holding me now, arms snaking around me, drawing me into his chest. He's wearing another jumper, and I was right, he is *very* snugglable in one.

I clutch at him like I've already gone over the cliff and he's the last bit of rock I can grab on to to survive. Something brushes my forehead, so quick and light I might have imagined it.

'What if I can't pass?' I say, almost to myself. 'If Aric attacks me, how am I supposed to –'

'He won't attack you,' Sath says. 'Not unless you attack him first.'

This is not encouraging. I've already proven I don't have much self-control when it comes to that. And didn't he deserve it?

No. No, I mustn't think that.

Even if it's true.

Fuck. Sath's shoulder is wet with my tears, and I pull a face when I lean back to look at him, patting the damp like that's going to help in some way. 'Sorry.'

'It's fine.' Sath gives me one final squeeze before releasing me. 'You should go.'

'But –' He hasn't answered my question. If I pass, is this goodbye? Is this *it*? Thoughts flurry around my brain like a snow globe that's been shaken too hard, and I can't catch my breath; Sath is reaching for the handle, and all I can think is *too soon, too soon*.

The doors open with a whine.

Inside, everything is black. Every part of me is churning and panicking, but my legs move as though on autopilot. As I get closer to the entrance, I catch a whiff of stale air and sweat, tinged with copper.

Once I'm over the threshold, I realise Sath hasn't moved. 'You're not coming?' I ask. 'Don't you need to tempt me?'

Sath falters. 'I think you'll be tempted enough.'

His faith in me is astounding. I wish I could be angry, but a) I'm practising not being wrathful and b) he's probably right.

As I go deeper into the Pits, the door slams shut behind me, plunging me into darkness. With a loud clack, floodlights switch on, one by one, each sending my nerves jolting. They illuminate an arena dug into the ground, a set of steep stairs leading to the rocky floor that's streaked with sand, dirt and dark red stains.

Aric stands in the middle. And he's not alone.

His hands are wrapped around Harper's throat, his tail curled

280

around her leg. I freeze. Did Sath know he had her? He wouldn't. Surely, he wouldn't. He must know I can't let this happen, can't stand by and do nothing as Aric chokes her. This is *Harper*. Harper who took me under her wing, who introduced me to the fun side of Asphodel, who senses when I'm upset and cares enough to want to fix it. I've always compared her smile to the sun, but now her face is eclipsed with blue, her fingers scratching and scrabbling to rip Aric's hand away from her throat.

What do I do? What do I do what do I do what do I do?

'Willow White, come to play,' Aric says. 'The king was right. It was worth waiting to kill you, if only to see the look on your face now. So sad. So confused. So angry.'

All the air leaves my lungs. What does he mean, *the king was right*? Right about what?

It was worth waiting to kill you.

I take a step back.

Aric grins as he watches whatever emotion is splayed across my face. *The king was right*. My pulse thunders in my ears.

Then it hits me. Sath's leverage.

He promised Aric this, to stop him punishing me after the cue incident. Maybe he could've set fire to him all along. Instead, he let him live, let him carry on antagonising me and my friends, all to get us to this moment. My fists clench. Maybe that whole fight in the games room was staged to create an enemy for me.

I swallow. If Sath lied about that, what else has he lied about?

'Poor Willow,' Aric goes on. 'Killed her mother. Alienated everyone she knew. Even if you win this task, you don't get a happy ending.'

I close my eyes. Perhaps they only want me to *think* Harper is in danger. That would make more sense, would be more in line with my Sath. This is a trick, and I need to be calm. Serene. Picture fluffy clouds and kittens and become the living embodiment of that *Sound of Music* song. It's difficult.

If I'm wrong, Harper will end up in the Void.

I remember the way it felt watching Sasha fall off the cliff. The panic. The fear. The desperation to know she was okay. And Harper wouldn't get lucky the way Sasha did, she'd just be gone.

I can't let it happen. I can't let another person get hurt because of me.

My bracelet is shrinking, gripping my wrist tighter, a reminder of what'll happen if I fail this task. Who I'll disappoint. I can't stand it. It's too heavy, too tight, making it hard to think through the pain.

'Don't you want to play?' Aric says. 'Why won't you look? Should I cut her open, would you look then? Shall I show you her pretty insides?'

God, I hate him. I force my eyes open and descend the stairs, scanning for something I can use as a weapon. Just in case. Harper whimpers, which only fuels my search, anger simmering in my veins like someone's turned up the heat on a gas stove.

'Let her go, Aric. It's me you hate.' The floor is empty. There's nothing on the rocky walls encircling the pit. Aric has donned a loincloth for the occasion, but I don't think he's got a knife hiding up there.

There has to be *something* here I can use to get him off her.

A flash of silver catches my eye. Lying in the dirt is a dagger I swear wasn't there before. I rush towards it, grabbing it like it's my salvation. It's a good, solid weight in my hand.

Aric smiles.

I smile back.

He drops Harper to the floor, where she gasps before passing out. I don't glance her way. I can't. Saving her shouldn't be my priority, but it's all I can think about.

All I ever wanted was to be proud of you.

My palm clenches and unclenches around the knife.

Sometimes bad things just happen.

Letting Aric hurt Harper would be bad. Breaking my promise to Mum would be bad.

Indecision takes root.

'Should I kill you now,' Aric muses, 'or let you watch what I do to her? Maybe I'll pin you up and let you see the gates get unleashed.'

'Those gates are not opening.'

'Oh, but they will.' Aric's tail scratches a deep cut down Harper's leg. 'There are things in motion you couldn't begin to understand. The gates open tonight.'

No.

I have to warn Sath. Whatever the demons are planning, Aric seems confident it'll work, his shoulders stretched back and his head cocked to one side. The thought of what'll happen to everyone here has that anger simmering inside me bubbling into something more, something that has me baring my teeth at him. My skin is slick with sweat, which only makes me grip the dagger tighter.

Why do the demons get to decide our future, just because it's what *they* want? Why should anyone get to dictate someone else's life? It's not fair.

Cracks splinter across the metal cuffing my wrist. Aric growls.

But isn't that exactly what she did to me? Mum. She tried to pour me into a mould that didn't fit and blamed me when she got burned by the spill. And I let her. For so long, I let her.

I'm not sure that was fair either.

Perfection is impossible. I saw that during sloth. I could have done everything she asked and I still would have ended up here. Going back won't change that.

So, what am I going back for?

Aric bares his teeth while my bracelet squeezes and squeezes, as if to say *you're being ridiculous, Willow.*

It's not ridiculous to say I've been happier in Asphodel than I ever was on Earth. It's the truth. And I've been too afraid to admit it out of fear for what could happen, fear I'll screw everything up here the way I screwed up there.

The bracelet pinches tighter, but the warning doesn't work. One of the reasons I've been happier here is because I've been *me* here. Maybe my constant screw-ups were because I wasn't being true to myself; because I was never going to fit in to the life Mum wanted, the same way this damn bracelet is always going to be the wrong size. Because it's not *right*.

'Are you thinking about how beautiful it will be?' Aric says. 'A sea of blood. I will drink for days, while the humans watch from cages made of their brethren's bones.' He runs a tongue over his canines. 'And then I will taste them too.'

I won't let him do this. I refuse. I don't want to go home and punch numbers into a computer because of a promise I made in the depths of despair. I want to save Harper and the humans. People who've accepted me, welcomed me, who put a smile I barely recognised on my face because it had been so long since I'd seen it. They're worth saving, and I want to be the kind of person who saves them.

And I want to kill Aric.

Not because I'm snapping, or throwing a tantrum, choosing to throw anything away. I could walk out right now. I know I could. I just don't want to. The only thing I'm discarding is the pressure to be something I'm not – and if Mum can't be proud of me for that, maybe Sath had a point. That's on *her*. I quit that course to make myself happy. Sometimes bad decisions lead to good things, and we have a lifetime to balance them out.

My bracelet digs in more than ever, like it wants to burrow into my skin and hold me hostage in its grasp, tightening and tightening until I can't see where the metal ends and my skin begins – I grit my teeth, hissing through the pain, trying to claw it off, to thrust my fingers beneath the cuff and prise it from my flesh, but it doesn't stop, won't stop; tears leak from my eyes and a cry escapes my throat as I finally push my index finger beneath the band, wrenching it upwards, pulling it *off*, I want it gone along with everything it represents –

And then it snaps in two.

The pieces clatter to the ground, shattering in a spray of silver and abandoned promises. I stumble back. Aric shifts in my peripheral vision – I guess Sath wasn't lying when he said Aric can't attack first, because he's rooted to the spot, shifting from one foot to the other, snapping and snarling.

Not for much longer.

Free of my shackles, I straighten, twirling the knife in my

hand while a phantom wind drifts through the pit, lifting the ashes of my bracelet and stealing them away. There's a spring in my step as I circle him now, my whole body lighter without the expectation that one tiny piece of jewellery wrought. I can have a life of my own. Instead of seeing the world, I'll get to explore each and every floor of Asphodel with Harper. I'll spend every night with Sath without caring that Mum would have hated him. The fact she chose Noah, someone who toyed with me for years and then discarded me like a broken doll, shows how little she knew me.

I'm giddy with the possibilities of *next* in a way I never have been before.

And all I have to do is kill him.

'Look at you, thinking you've won,' Aric says. 'How I would love to rip that smile from your face and eat it. Perhaps tonight I shall.'

'I already told you, those gates aren't opening.'

'Yes, Willow White, they will. And you will stand there powerless when it happens.'

'No.' This isn't the usual, burning, hot-headed rage I feel when I'm out of control and don't know what to do – the kind that leads to a bad decision. This anger is made of ice and steel, as cold as the weapon I'm going to kill him with. He doesn't get to decide my future.

I do.

And then I'm running, launching myself at him; I don't think he expected me to do it because his eyes widen in surprise when I reach him, my shoulder shoving into his chest and sending him tumbling to the floor. I follow, going down with him, raising the dagger in the air before slamming it into his stomach.

The blade punctures skin. Something pounds in the distance; Sath shouts my name. I tune him out. I will whatever magic that allowed this knife to appear to keep the doors locked. There's just me, and Aric, and a weapon. My hands are drenched in black ooze. I drive the dagger deeper, twisting it around, tugging it out only to slam it in again.

The humans have been hurt too many times; *I've* been hurt too many times. Years of poking and prodding and torment, years of being told our feelings were invalid, and it's enough. Today it ends. I will *not* let those gates open.

The pounding on the doors grows more frantic, but anger is a seed taken root, erupting in my insides, the stem blazing and burning as it shoots through my veins. I can't stop. The flames are all I see. Aric's a monster. He deserves this. Sweat drips down my back. He *deserves* this.

I plunge the knife into his chest next, into that hole where his heart should be, and he finally stops writhing beneath me. Panting, I stare at his prone form, at the mess I've made, and lean forward. 'I guess you were the powerless one after all.'

The dagger clatters to my side. Blood leaks from his wounds. All I want to do is *laugh*.

For once, there's no anger left to suppress, nothing to lock away and pretend I don't notice the way it's clawing to get out. I'm free. I'm finally free. I crawl to Harper, patting her face, listening to her shallow breaths in the silence.

'It's going to be okay,' I whisper. 'Aric can't hurt you now.'

And no one can hurt *me*. I'm unbound, unchained, my future my own to decide.

As if they know who, exactly, I want in that future, the doors blast open. My smile widens. I'm *staying*. I'll have the chance to tell him how I feel. Properly. Not the way I begged for him during lust, because it's not just his body I want – as appealing as it is. I want the man who listened to me, who never judged me, who accepted me the way I am.

And I don't believe he doesn't want me too. Maybe he was afraid to say something because he thought I was leaving, but now we have a whole eternity to figure this out. A chance we didn't have before.

Happiness warms my chest, glowing so bright I want to burst. I'm *staying*.

I rise to my feet on shaky legs, waiting for him to see, for him to realise I'm not going anywhere. That I had the chance to choose who I wanted to be, once and for all, and instead of Good Decision Willow or Bad Decision Willow, I chose *Willow*. I chose the people here. I chose him.

Then I catch the look on his face. My smile wavers.

'What the hell did you do?' Sath's voice is barely more than a hiss, but it hits me like a roar.

'It's okay,' I reassure him. 'I chose to fail. I wanted this.'

'You wanted this,' he echoes. He isn't catching on that this is a *good thing*. Wet slaps sound as he marches through Aric's blood to stand inches from me, heat radiating from him. He gestures at the black glistening on his shoes. 'You wanted *this?*'

I fold my arms as though they'll be enough to shield me from the burn. 'Aric was threatening to open the gates. He needed to be stopped.'

'He's *always* threatening to open the gates.' He can't hide the bite of frustration in his tone. 'It didn't mean you had to go and believe him. Do you have any idea what you've done?'

As the adrenaline wears off, my lip wobbles. Instead of being the tiniest bit pleased I'm staying, he's treating me like a small child needing a scolding for a misdemeanour – although I suppose stabbing a guy is somewhat worse than stealing a lollipop.

I jut out my chin. 'I did what *I* wanted to. That's not a crime.'

Why should I be denied what I want a moment more? Maybe my sin is I care too much. I am greedy and selfish and want things I shouldn't, but I will also fight for those I care about. Asphodel was at risk and I was prepared to do something about it, which is more than I could ever say for him.

He grinds his jaw so hard I think his teeth might crack. Finally, he looks away from me, raking his fingers through his hair and saying, 'Let's not do this here.'

He douses Aric's body in black flames, turning him to smoke and ash. Another wave of his hand and Harper disappears.

'Is she –'

'She'll wake in her room, none the worse for wear.' He draws closer and takes my hand. The movement is gentle, at odds with the way he's spoken to me so far, the slow slide of our palms connecting sending a shiver down my spine as our fingers interlace.

My heart swells. Harper's okay, and Sath's touching me, and everything is alive with possibility again, but then his grip tightens, too tight to be comfortable, and fire blazes in his eyes. 'I wish I could say the same for you.'

28

He portals us into his sitting room.

I avoid looking at the bedroom door and drop on to the couch, suddenly boneless. I failed. I really failed. I'm not going home. It feels like a weight has been lifted only for another to be dropped straight on me, because Sath still hasn't said one thing to suggest he's pleased about the development.

A drink is placed on the table. I don't touch it. Sath downs his in one and sits beside me, keeping a careful distance. We're like two bookends with no tomes between us, just empty space and unsaid words. I have so many things to ask him but, for once, can't bring myself to speak.

Sath breaks the silence. 'What were you thinking?'

'I was thinking . . .' I muster the energy to shoot him a glare. His lack of enthusiasm is starting to grate. 'That Aric's a bastard who deserved to be stabbed. He was threatening everyone here.'

'Aric's always been a bastard,' Sath retorts. 'All you had to do was control yourself for once and you –'

'What did you think would happen?' I throw the words at him like weapons. 'He's been torturing us for months. Following us around, making his sly threats, sharpening his teeth. He attacked Henry yesterday. What did you *think* I'd do when I was presented with a knife and locked in a room with him?'

'I thought, after everything you've overcome, you'd pass.'

'Well, I *chose* not to.' We glower at each other. 'Sorry all your effort went to waste. Aric told me what you did. How you promised he could kill me if he kept quiet about that day in the games room. Did you promise him Harper too?'

'Of course not,' Sath says, sounding weary. 'After your fight, I saw an opportunity. I told him if he let what happened go then he'd get his chance for revenge. I lied to him, not you. He was supposed to antagonise you during wrath, yes, but he couldn't attack first and I assumed you'd have the sense not to attack him. And I never gave permission for him to hurt Harper.'

'Then you're an idiot. Of course he hurt Harper. He's a monster.' My hands shake. 'And if I'm a monster for hurting him back, so be it. Guess I always belonged here.'

Sath looks away. The dismissive gesture is like a knife to my own gut. 'You say that like it's a good thing.'

'Isn't it?' My voice is small as I ask the question that's been on my mind since I saw his face in the pit. 'Is it that terrible, that I'm staying?'

I'm *staying*. The realisation seeps in further, a trickle of water pushing through a dam until the knowledge bursts. I'm dead. I'm dead, and I'm staying that way.

And Sath doesn't care.

'Is this about your concession? Was it really more important than –' I already know the answer; it's written all over his face. It was. Every moment we had together was all designed to help me pass, to get him whatever it was he wanted so badly, and now I've failed I'm no good to him. I will him to contradict me, to offer me some modicum of comfort.

'You'll end up in the Void, Willow.'

That is the opposite of comforting. But if he thinks he can scare me, he's wrong. 'So, the no-punishment-for-failing thing was a lie? Well, fine. Bring it on. I hear my mother's voice so often I may as well be in the Void already. She can't hurt me any more.'

'It was all for nothing,' Sath mutters. I'm not sure he's been listening to me at all. His eyes are fixed on his empty tumbler, but his gaze is unfocused, his mind elsewhere. 'It's over. I can't . . .' He gets to his feet and begins to pace, steam rising from the carpet.

'Sath?' The last time he looked this lost, it was the day I made him kill those demons. 'What are you talking about?'

'You were supposed to . . . You can't . . . They'll kill you. You'll go to the Void, and you'll be nothing, and I – you'll be *nothing*.' His voice cracks. 'You'll be gone. *Gone*.' With each repetition of the phrase something rumbles in the distance, building into a crescendo; flames spark down his arms, stronger than ever.

'*Sath*.' There's nothing to be done when he's in this state. I settle for propelling myself across the room and gripping his arm. 'Sath. Stop.'

His expression is feral when he turns to me, eyes fully aflame. Black strands of wild, untamed hair droop over his forehead. His shoulders heave as he pants.

The room shakes again, harder this time, like everything's been tilted on an axis, and we stumble and slide into the bar as though we're on a slippery slope. I wince as my arm cracks against the marble. The room pitches again. Sath does a better job of bracing himself this time, planting himself wide before gripping my waist and pulling me into him before I go tumbling.

'What's happening?' I raise my voice to be heard over the sound of rock crunching deep below my feet. 'Is it the gates?'

Cold, prickling fear creeps down my spine.

'Sath.' I place a hand on his chest. His heart is thundering. He shudders beneath my touch, but the frantic beating slows a smidge. 'You can't lose control.'

The look he gives me is one of utter, utter hopelessness.

'It's inevitable,' he whispers.

Every part of me aches for him. There's nothing I can say or do to help though, so when he turns away from me, I don't protest. The gates have quietened now, at least, and the room has taken a temporary reprieve from trying to throw me around.

'There's only one thing I can do,' he says. 'I haven't got a choice.'

I place a hesitant hand on his arm and immediately flinch away, because he's *hot*, burning up, like his flames and power have erupted. My hand is red and scalded, as though I've accidentally doused it in water from a freshly boiled kettle.

He moves, making a sound that's half scream, half roar. I crash into a stool in an attempt to get away. Hairs lift on the back of my neck, my breaths coming in rapid bursts.

And then Sath spins round, and I stop breathing at all.

There's a heart in his hand. Why is there a heart in his hand? I scan his chest for evidence he's just clawed inside himself, but his jumper is unmarred.

'Take it,' he says. 'I'm giving it to you.'

I hear the words. I don't understand them.

There's a heart in his hand.

It's black and shrivelled; rivers of blue veins glisten as they snake and coil around the organ. It pulses in his palm, slow and steady and alive.

'What . . . ?'

'Take it.' He drops the heart into my palms. It's heavy, and curiously dry. Despite my mild disgust, my thumb runs over it, feeling the bumps and ridges along the surface. If I close my eyes, I can pretend I'm holding a large raspberry. A beating raspberry.

'Is it yours?' I ask.

Wait.

If this *is* his, it clearly holds some of his powers. I don't see how else it would still be working if not for magic. What if . . . 'Would I be able to leave with this?'

He doesn't answer. He stares at me, then at the heart, as though if he looks hard enough he can will me into action.

'I don't understand.' My tongue feels heavy in my mouth. If this is my salvation, I don't *want* it. I chose not to go back.

'You did enough. You have to have done enough.' Sath's eyes glisten. 'Take the heart.'

'But . . . I . . .' This doesn't make sense. Something's not right. His hands capture mine, closing my fingers around the heart, desperate almost. The heart pulses, fluttering with panic, like a bird that can't beat its wings as fast as it'd like.

'Please,' Sath says. 'Put it next to your chest and the heart will do the rest. It knows what to do.'

294

It? What does he mean *it*? It's him, it's his, it's been held in place by his ribcage for all the centuries he's been here, and he's giving it away like an old pair of shoes.

'Or,' a voice says from the doorway, 'you can be a good girl and hand it over here.'

29

It's the Sorter. I've never seen her smile before, or at least not like this, all gleaming white teeth and dimpled cheeks. She looks positively giddy.

Sath takes a step between us, shielding me, but she doesn't cower in fear the way she should. His flames don't appear. I can't feel his heat the way I usually can; there's nothing emanating from him, apart from, perhaps, mild panic.

'What are you doing?' he asks.

'What does it look like I'm doing?' She struts into the room and instinct has me clutching the heart tighter. Something that feels suspiciously like a tendril pummels my stomach, trying to latch on to me. The impact is sharp as a knife and heavy as a gut punch. I let out an audible gasp; Sath wheels towards me, while the Sorter's eyes widen.

'Careful,' she sings. 'You don't want that heart, Willow White.' She looks at Sath and smirks. 'And you can't take it back once removed. Which leaves me.'

Think think think, I urge my mind to catch up, to focus on what's happening.

'Why don't I want it?' I ask slowly.

All Sath does is nod his head towards the heart, and then my chest. *Take it.*

'Do you want to tell her what it does, or shall I?' The Sorter's playing with him now.

His jaw tenses. 'How long have you been planning this?'

'Since the day she walked into my morgue,' she says in a sing-song voice. 'We've been waiting for a ruler to fail for eons but they always cling on. Even you, for all your moping, were too strong. Every time I thought you'd given up, you managed to persevere. It was infuriating. Something needed to be done. I needed someone weaker. Then she appeared, and I knew, I just *knew* she would break long before she had time to find herself a replacement.'

'Stop talking in riddles,' I snap.

I'm tempted to start throwing things; maybe dodging projectiles will get them to speak plainly. My cheeks heat. I'm burning more than Sath ever did. The Sorter takes it all in, smile growing.

'Oh, she really is angry, isn't she, Sathanas?' the Sorter says. 'I sensed it as soon as I met her. Even if she refuses to give me the heart today, it won't matter. Wrath will consume her much faster than sloth has been consuming you.'

'I thought I told you to get out,' Sath growls.

'No,' I say. 'I think she's the only one being honest here. What does the heart do?'

Sath rubs a hand over his face. 'Willow, I . . .' His voice splinters. 'I'm sorry.'

'Sorry for *what*?' Frustration has me crushing the organ like a stress ball. We'll see how much the Sorter wants it when it's bleeding all over the floor. As my grip tightens, that rumbling returns. Louder.

Sath's eyes widen, lunging for my hands, trying to unclasp my fingers before I can do any damage. The Sorter grins.

It's her face that makes me stop. Anything that makes her happy is probably something I don't want to do.

'Why don't you hand it over to me?' she says. 'It all ends the same. This way's simply faster.'

'No.' Sath looks at me pleadingly. 'Put it in your chest. It's the only way.'

I don't trust either of them right now. My breathing turns rapid as I hold the heart to my chest, leaving it hovering centimetres from my T-shirt.

'It's futile, Sath,' the Sorter says. 'The final task already proved she won't cope. You may as well save us some time.'

'What do the tasks have to do with anything?' I ask.

'The tasks . . .' Sath's gone pale, like all the energy's been drained from him. And his eyes . . . I hadn't noticed, but they've lost their glow. Not in the I'm-not-using-my-powers-right-now sense. They're dimmer, dark brown, with no hint of gold at all. 'They weren't to determine if you were worthy of leaving. They were to see if you'd be strong enough for the heart. Because . . .' His throat bobs. 'Whoever holds the heart controls the gates. You can't let her have it. She'll unleash Tartarus.'

My mind is stuck on the first part of his sentence. I stare at him blankly. My brain has no thoughts. Not one. I stare, and stare, and stare. The Sorter huffs at my existential crisis, but she can, quite frankly, fuck off. Slowly, I say, 'The tasks weren't about me leaving.'

'You're dead,' the Sorter says, extremely unhelpfully. 'You were never leaving. But for a human, escaping Asphodel is a much better offer than ruling. How do you think Sath got roped into it?'

Sath won't meet my gaze. He tricked me. All to give me his *job*. I stare at the heart in my hand. I'd be Queen of Asphodel. I'd control the gates.

I could hurt the Sorter. The demons. But –

'I didn't pass though.' I'm almost slurring, struggling to form words, thoughts.

'The tasks are supposed to prove your ability to resist sin. It would be far too risky to hand this much power over to someone with no restraint. To someone unworthy. But they're not a requirement. The current ruler can pass the heart to anyone he or she chooses,' Sath says.

'And you chose me. I'm honoured.' My words are monotone. I wait for an emotion to come – anger seems like a good bet – but there's nothing. I'm too shell-shocked. One word rattles round my skull: *liar, liar, liar*.

There'd been a moment, right after failing wrath, where I'd been happier than I'd ever been. Daydreaming of a future I never thought possible: travelling Asphodel with my friends, Harper, *him*.

A future that could never have existed, because he'd been planning this all along.

Not a single word he's ever told me has been the truth. Not a single one.

Liar, liar, liar.

'Listen.' Sath steps in front of me, blocking my view of the

Sorter, although there's another loud sigh from behind him. 'We can talk later. Please, Willow. The only way to keep the gates closed is for someone capable of resisting sin to take the heart. It can't be her.'

He should have taken one look at me and realised it couldn't be me either. I'm way too much of a mess to be left responsible for an entire Hell dimension. I've proven I *can't* resist sin.

'Then you take it.' I try to shove it at him. 'I can't do this. I don't *want* to do this.'

An image of me sat on the snake throne flashes across my mind, but I toss it aside. I might have chosen Asphodel over Earth but that doesn't mean I want to *rule*. I don't want this. I don't.

'He can't,' the Sorter chimes in. 'And I'm bored. Hand it over now, and we'll be spared the tediousness of watching you fall apart. The gates are opening, one way or another. Give me the heart and it'll be over quickly.'

I'm getting a little tired of people telling me what to do.

More than that, I'm getting *very* tired of people's low expectations of me. The Sorter has no idea who I am or what I can do. She saw what was on my clipboard and believed the same thing as Mum: that I'm a failure who can't do anything, who gives up at the first hurdle.

But I've proven I'm not now. I jumped six hurdles and knocked over the seventh because I *chose* to. I fail when I'm trying to be something I'm not, but when I'm me, I can succeed.

Right now, what I am is angry.

I nudge Sath to one side – I'll deal with him later – in order to give her the full force of my best glare. She manipulated

300

me as much as Sath did. Pretended to let slip there was a way out, when she was hoping all along Sath would suggest I do the tasks. Made me doubt anyone here would want me when she was worried I was about to change my mind.

'I'm going to kill you,' I tell her.

She tuts. 'You can try. But without the heart, Sath has no power. He can't protect you.'

I don't need Sath's protection. I have something better.

The heart pulses like it's sensed what I'm about to do. I hold on to my anger, my fury at being put in this position, letting it override the terror simmering underneath.

I have no idea what's going to happen when I do this. All I know is I can't let her win. I have to keep the gates closed.

I killed Aric to protect Harper and the others. I'll do this for them too. For me, even, because this is my home now, and I won't let the demons overrun it.

'Tick-tock, Willow.' The Sorter moves closer. 'You know you can't do this.'

'What I know,' I tell her, 'is that I failed wrath on purpose. I'm not as weak as you think I am. And I'm sick of people telling me otherwise.'

Her eyes flare when she comprehends what I'm saying, and then she's lunging for me, lightning-fast –

I slam the heart straight into my chest.

30

Pain.

The tendrils I'd felt against my stomach latch on, harder than before, and there's so many of them now, every one like an arrow piercing skin, then deeper, burrowing into me until they latch around my *real* heart and take hold. My eyes stream, salt filling my mouth, my nose. I want it to stop. My heart races with panic and fear and not understanding what this thing invading it is.

I think I'd prefer an alien abduction to this.

Heat sears through me as the two hearts fuse, vines entwining my arteries, and I need it to stop, but it won't, it won't, it won't. A high-pitched whining noise escapes my throat, because the pain is never-ending, and now the heart is fully inside I can feel darkness spreading, power flaring; black flames erupt from my arms, blowing back my hair. The Sorter is crawling, *crawling* towards the exit; with a flick of my hand the door slams shut and the key twists.

I pant.

The pain is subsiding now; Sath survived this, and I'm going to survive it too, but I don't feel right, I don't feel like *me*. Everything tingles and thrums and I – I can sense the gates. They're there, in my mind, a steady hum, black shadows of darkness tainted by sin. Behind them, demons roam. Pacing. Waiting for escape.

They've caused pain for aeons, those demons. They wade in a sea of blood. It's up to their knees, but they don't care, they still want more. It'll never be enough. They lick their lips, hungry for what Asphodel has to offer. I salivate, wanting it too. I want to take, and have, and destroy.

'Willow.' Sath's voice jerks me into focus.

I blink. Everything goes quiet. It's just me, with two liars who tried to screw me over.

And I'm the one with the power now.

'I'd bow to your queen if I were you.' My voice isn't right either. It's deeper, more even. I glance into the mirror behind the bar. My hair is the same flaming red as always, but that red is now reflected in my eyes, glowing through the green.

Oh, God. It looks like someone threw up Christmas inside my irises.

This only serves to enrage me further, especially when neither of them moves. True, the Sorter *is* already on the floor, although flailing around on all fours isn't what I'd call a bow.

'Bow,' I say again.

Sath does. He drops to his knees, gazing up at me, black hair falling into those oh-so-normal eyes. Laughter lines crinkle around the corners, and the glow has faded from his skin. Something twists in my chest at the sight of him but I've no way to determine if the ache is genuine. Whether it's my heart remembering how it used to feel – maybe still feels – or whether it's *his*, recognising its old master.

The Sorter hasn't moved. I stride towards her, feeling for the power inside me, wondering the best way to make it hurt. *'Bow.'*

I stare her down. Despite my door-slamming trick, I'm not sure how to use this magic I've been gifted. Finally, the threat of it sinks deep enough, and she shifts into a kneeling position. I stare at them both. Traitors. I want them gone. The Sorter first; I can deal with her later.

Sath, on the other hand, has a lot of questions to answer.

'I want a demon in here,' I say. 'Now.'

I'm asking Sath the best way to go about summoning one – they come running easily enough for him – but saying the words is, apparently, enough. A demon with sapphire scales covering its arms arrives and then stares at me. At Sath. Back at me.

'Hello,' I say. 'I'm in charge now.' It sounds ridiculous to my ears, but the demon, to my great astonishment, lowers its horned head like it can sense the foul thing inside me and is bound to follow its orders. 'Take the Sorter to the . . . ice place.'

'Glacantrum,' Sath mutters. Fuck's sake. I refuse to need his help with this.

'Glacantrum,' I repeat, like I'd known all along. 'And then, I don't know, maybe torture her a bit.'

Sath says something under his breath, something that sounds like *Willow*, followed by a huff. I'm not sure what he expects from me. I'm play-acting in a role he cast me for without seeing an audition.

'You can't send me there,' the Sorter says. 'I'm the Sorter. I have a job to do.'

'Do I look like I give a fuck who goes where?'

'You will when there's a bottleneck of people at the boats. Everything will come crashing down.'

Sath opens his mouth to speak – probably some fresh platitude I don't want to hear – but I silence him with a wave of my hand.

'Fine,' I say, through gritted teeth. 'Take her to the mortuary, and keep her there. I want her locked up, under armed guard, all day every day. She sorts and does nothing else. If you, or anyone, speaks to her, I'll rip off your heads. Understood?'

The demon nods. The Sorter stands without resistance, glowering at me with a seething hatred that I return tenfold. I'll get her out of that morgue soon enough. Someone might need to sort, but it doesn't need to be her.

They exit, and the room goes silent, leaving me and Sath alone. He's still on his knees. My chest heaves. The gates tremble.

'Get up,' I snap.

He does, slowly, looking me up and down. I wonder what he sees. Wonder if he ever liked what he saw, or if it was all an act to get me to complete the tasks. 'You lied to me.'

'I didn't have a choice,' he says. 'I once told you that in order to keep the divide between Asphodel and Tartarus, the ruler has to be . . . good. That wasn't the whole truth.'

'I'm stunned.'

Sath ignores me. 'The divide is kept so long as the ruler can resist sin. And I can't. Do you remember what I said, when we talked about sloth?'

I rack my brains. 'That it was a vice of yours. Something about . . . dereliction of duty.'

He nods. 'My duty here was to protect the humans. Every

305

time I pandered to the demons, I failed in that duty. I punished humans who didn't deserve it. And the weight of that failure, that sin, it was overwhelming me. Eventually, the gates would crack open. I had to find a replacement. I didn't have a choice.'

'It didn't have to be *me*.'

Sath eyes the fire rippling down my arms, and swallows. 'You need to control your anger.'

'I *can't*.' Glass bottles smash behind the bar. I'm too hot, smoke pouring from me, thick and grey and smelling like charred embers. I want to set the whole room on fire. I want to set *him* on fire. 'You lied to me. This whole time. You said I was going home.'

'Even if that was true, you forfeited that option when you killed Aric,' he reminds me. It's about the worst possible thing he can say. I'd chosen to stay when I thought I'd be able to dictate my own future. Instead he's made the choice for me just like everyone else in my life, telling me who I can and can't be. I don't *want* to rule Asphodel. I don't want this responsibility. I'm not cut out for this.

More flames spark from my arms. My eyeballs are burning; I doubt there's any green left in them now. And the gates, they're shaking, shaking like I am. The demons wait behind the doors, snarling and growling, knowing it won't be long now.

'Willow.' Sath grabs my arm, tugging me towards him. With his other hand, he cups my chin. 'You have to think of something else. Anything to distract yourself from wrath.'

There's nothing. All I know is rage.

'Please.' He dips his head so we're eye level. I blink, taking him in. His breath ghosts my mouth, colder than I've ever felt

306

it. His fingers, too, are like ice. Every touch is like sinking into a cold bath on a summer's day.

I inhale. Exhale. Again. My fire dies, and I swallow, feeling more like myself. 'How could you do this to me?'

'I'm sorry,' he whispers. 'By the time I realised I was –' He breaks off, gaze flicking to the floor, then back to me. 'When we grew closer, I wanted to tell you the truth, but I knew I'd lose you. You'd hate me for lying, and I'd be no closer to solving the situation with the gates. Tartarus would be unleashed. The humans would be tortured for eternity, or they'd end up in the Void, and the thought of you, of all people, going to that place, of you not *existing* . . . I couldn't bear it.'

'Don't pretend you did it for me.' My chin wobbles. 'You are not the good guy here.'

'I never said I was the good guy. I told you when we first met, I am *not* nice.' His eyes glisten. 'I used to be. I want to be.'

'The only thing you are is selfish,' I snap. 'You used me to solve your own problems without once thinking how I'd feel about it. You lied to me for as long as possible so you could, what, enjoy my company while it lasted?'

'If I'd wanted to enjoy you, Willow, we both know I could have.'

I hiss at the implication. Good to know the one emotion stronger than anger is sheer, undiluted mortification.

'Nothing about this has been enjoyable, trust me. Nothing about the last two damn centuries has been *enjoyable.*'

It's the first time I've heard him raise his voice. There's no quiet threat of seduction and death, just years of raw frustration and pent-up rage finally unleashed.

'I wanted to keep away. I should have. You're right, I am selfish. I couldn't resist being around you despite knowing it would only end one way.' Sath releases me and steps away. Tears stream down my face as he continues, 'Be angry with me. I deserve it. But don't pretend there isn't a part of you that doesn't want this. The power, the attention, the ability to smite anyone who pisses you off. I saw into your soul and discerned all those things. You have the power now to see into mine.' He gives me a sad smile. 'Finally, no secrets between us.'

It would be great if he had the decency to give me a lesson in these new-found powers of mine. All I seem capable of doing is catching alight, not seeing into people's souls.

But then I look at him. Properly. A shimmering white light surrounds him, and then it goes deeper, into his heart – one heart now, his own, pure and untainted by whatever the thing is inside me. I see his desperation to be good, and the fear that he's not. I see glimpses of his past: a woman, smiling at him from across the pillow, a dog running through a field, a boat bobbing along a calm sea. I see he was a vegetarian, which makes me snort, because now he's made to butcher people for a living. I don't blame him for wanting out.

I do blame him for not telling me.

The different parts of me war over what to do. But then I remember every smile we shared, every touch, and how it was all built on a lie. He made me feel things I'm not sure I've ever felt for anyone, not even Noah, and now I've no idea how much of it was real. I hate how badly I *want* it to be real, even after what he's done.

His betrayal is an open wound, fresh and raw and gaping;

I pick at all the things he's ever said to me like I'm pulling at flayed skin. Every word he says is laced with lies. I can't look at him. I can't forgive him. I can't be *around* him.

What I can do, though, is make sure he hurts as much as I do.

'So, when you talked about getting your concession, you meant getting an easy life?' I inject as much venom as I can into the words. 'Where the gates are someone else's problem; *my* problem? Well, I say you don't. You don't get your happy ending. Not when I don't have mine.' I summon another demon, turn my face to stone, and say, 'Take him to Glacantrum. Let him freeze.'

31

It's weird being in Sath's rooms without Sath.

I suppose they're my rooms now. I keep expecting to find him lounging on the sofa or smiling at me from the other side of the coffee table as I roll double sixes. My stomach feels hollow and empty, but at least the nothingness of being alone settles me enough that the gates stop shaking. The monsters on the other side growl when they understand they won't be opening today. I growl back, in the hope they can hear me.

Finally, I work up the courage to enter the bedroom. My chest constricts at the sight of those black sheets, at the lingering scent of jasmine wafting from candles that no longer burn. Congealed wax drips like frozen rain down what's left of the sticks. I collapse on the bed, only to discover the pillows smell like Sath. I punch one before burrowing my face into it, wishing he was beside me so badly it's like an ache. I hate him for it. For everything.

It doesn't stop me curling into a ball and sobbing.

I stay like that for days, drifting in and out of consciousness. My dreams are violent and graphic, all snapping fangs and bloodstained claws. At first, I toss and turn and cry out. Then I get angry.

The demons like this. They whisper to me. *Tear it all apart. Blow it up. Use us.* The sins are like snakes under the surface of my skin, demanding more and more from me. To take what's not mine. To hurt what's hurt me. To give in to every lustful thought I've had about Sath.

The last one has me opening my eyes on the fifth day and deciding enough is enough. I refuse to listen to their bullshit demands any longer. I've gained plenty of experience ignoring the voices in my head, and these demons have got nothing on my mother.

My annoyance has flames sparking from my arms, and it takes several minutes to put them out again. Sath's powers only flared when he needed them to, but I can't find the knack to controlling mine. I knock a candle off the nightstand, wishing it was his head.

I am hopelessly out of my depth, and it's all his fault. I never even graduated, for goodness' sake. I shouldn't be responsible for pet-sitting someone's dog, let alone be left unattended with magic powers.

Weak from not moving, I force myself to sit up. Although starving and dehydration aren't a thing here, I wouldn't say no to a nice cup of tea. I screw up my eyes, wishing for one. Nothing happens.

Fuck's sake. I swing my legs over the side of the bed, intending to risk a trip to the dining area, when a noise outside draws my attention. A noise that sounds suspiciously like a scream. Shadows of flame lick my arms, threatening to flare, because if that's a demon hurting someone –

I storm outside and rush into the entrance chamber. A boat's

311

just arrived, and the passengers are not getting a warm welcome. They stand in a huddle, cowering and holding hands, watching as a man is pinned to the wall by a set of antlers attached to a demon with thickset shoulders.

'What are you doing?'

Hurt him. Tear him apart. Honestly, the voices have a point, but I don't know how to go about killing the demon without losing control and weakening the gates.

This is impossible.

'I said, what are you doing? Have they committed a crime?'

'They cried on the boat,' the demon says. 'We don't like criers here.'

Good job he hasn't seen what I've been doing the last few days.

'Why wasn't I summoned?' I fold my arms. 'In case you weren't aware, Asphodel is under new management. I'll decide the rules from now on. Let them go.'

'What if I don't want to?' The demon doesn't turn my way. 'What will you do about it?'

I know what I *want* to do, but achieving it is another matter. The demon nudges closer, its antlers pressing into the man's throat. He lets out a gargled cry. One of the watching humans tumbles to the floor in a dead faint.

'Stop it!' I command. The demon doesn't listen. He's never going to listen. He's already written me off as someone who can be ignored, someone whose opinions don't matter.

The floor rumbles. My fists clench. Smoke unfurls from my arms.

The demon finally releases its victim, but only so it can

turn to grin at me instead. Above his head, fissures crack through the rock, rivers of lava glowing bright red through the opening. Good. Maybe I'll let those crevices split wide open, let that lava spew out, let it melt the demon as it laughs at me. Maybe then someone will finally, finally listen to what I have to say.

The rumbling worsens. My teeth chatter with the vibration. The humans lumber around, looking from side to side, clutching one another as small rocks tumble from the ceiling. The demon grins, and that only makes me blaze hotter, like fire has replaced all the blood in my veins, like the hate and disgust I have for his kind is all I know. *Tear. Hurt. Kill.*

In my mind, I can sense the gates tremble, the rock around them grinding and crunching as they threaten to burst open, a screw popping from one of the hinges.

A human screams.

Tear. Hurt. Kill.

I dig my nails into my palms. A rope of fire bursts out and falls to the floor, flailing around on the ground and hissing, spitting sparks at the nearest human. Panic flares inside me, dulling the urge for retribution because hurting the humans isn't what I wanted, not what I was aiming for, but now I've started this I don't know how to stop. The rope burns brighter, edges closer to the waiting group of innocents and I can't rein it back; I can't –

'Let me through,' a familiar voice sounds in the distance. 'Move!'

No.

She shouldn't be here; I don't want her to see me like this.

I close my eyes, willing her away, but then a pair of blissfully cool hands find mine, pulling apart my clenched fists one finger at a time. I stumble into a fluffy jumper scented like bubblegum and immediately bury my head into it, wishing I could stay there forever.

'I've been looking for you for days,' Harper hisses. 'What's going on?'

I focus all my attention on those icy hands, allowing them to calm me, to melt the fire in my veins. The floor stops rumbling. I force my eyes open to find the flaming rope has disappeared, leaving behind a burnt streak on the floor. The woman it had been aiming for is trembling, her eyes wide and tear-stained, gawping at me like I'm the biggest monster in the room. The demon cocks its head, assessing me, and I realise it's not the woman's opinion that matters, not right now.

If I want him to obey me, I need *him* to think I'm the biggest monster too.

I turn towards the throne. The snake's head is larger than ever, fully encapsulating the seat, its fangs as long as my forearms. I swallow, my pulse sounding too loud in my head. My feet feel as though they're being weighed down by chains as I take one slow step, then another, towards that seat.

Then I drop into the chair.

It's extremely uncomfortable. Cursing Sath for failing to invest in cushions, I shift from side to side, trying to find a spot that doesn't make my butt complain. I miss my bed. But if I don't want that demon's actions to become widespread, I have to take a stand, at least until I can get myself under control and figure out a better way forward.

I just hope Harper realises everything I'm about to say is a lie.

'Welcome,' I say. It comes out a little squeaky, which is not ideal. What did Sath say, the day I arrived? Something like, 'Welcome to Asphodel. Your home now, along with all the pleasantries it has to offer. Just don't try and escape. Or cry in front of a demon. Then everything will be . . . fine.'

The humans don't look convinced. I'm not convinced. I am hopelessly bad at this.

I grit my teeth and continue anyway.

'What I did today was a taster of what will happen if you misbehave.' I glance at the demon, who's watching with his arms folded and eyes narrowed. I have no idea if he believes what just happened wasn't an accident, but so long as the element of doubt is there, the possibility that I *do* know what I'm doing – and am therefore capable of hurting him the same way – he might spread the word to his fellow demons that it's business as usual. That they should respect me the way they respected Sath. 'I suggest you don't try and find out what other punishments Asphodel has to offer.'

I wave the demon away. 'Show them to their rooms. If they cause trouble, bring them to me.'

Holding my breath, I wait to see if he'll take the instruction, keeping my focus on Harper hovering nearby. She reminds me of the hope I felt when I first failed wrath, when I thought I could stop the demons and have a lifetime here with her and Sath. The idea of it stops me losing control all over again.

I narrow my eyes, keeping my features hard, willing the demon to listen, willing it and willing it until, finally, he bows his head and turns to lead the humans single file out to the cliff face.

Once the echoes of their footsteps have faded, the chamber is as silent as a tomb. I'm not sure I've seen Harper lost for words before. I can't even take a moment to be relieved she's unharmed after Aric, not when her gaze is racing over my face, her jaw dropping at whatever she sees there. I don't need to find a mirror to know my eyes will be blazing amber, if not red.

That she sees the Devil looking back at her.

When I can't take the quiet any longer, I rise from the throne. 'Will you come with me? Please? We can't talk here.'

Slowly, she nods, although she keeps several paces behind me at all times as I lead her into Sath's quarters.

An awkward silence descends again once we're inside. I clasp my hands together, feeling as though a spotlight has been placed directly over my head, my fingers fidgeting with one another as I wait for her to make her final verdict on whether or not she's staring at a monster – whether or not she's willing to stay in this room with me at all.

Finally, she sinks on to the sofa, her expression a mix of fear and devastation. 'Willow, what *happened* to you?'

32

I tell her everything.

She strokes my hair as I lie with my head in her lap, spilling every single secret I've kept since arriving. Meeting the Sorter. My deal with Sath. The tasks.

Sath's betrayal.

Hours tick by as I talk and talk and talk until my throat is raw and my eyes are burning. She doesn't interrupt. When I've finished, the room falls silent, until finally she says, 'Huh.'

'Huh?' I force myself to sit up. 'That's all you have to say?'

'It's a lot to process. You're the Queen of – oh, hey, your eyes are green again. That's good, right?'

I grab a cushion and clutch it to my stomach. 'For now. It won't last. You saw me out there. I can't control myself. I can't . . . I can't fix this.'

'Sure you can.' She taps her chin. I can only assume she fell asleep at some point during my story, because nothing about it suggests I am capable of fixing anything. I never have been. 'We'll think of something.'

She hops off the sofa and starts inspecting objects in the room, picking up books, board games, and discarded items of

317

clothing one by one. 'Everything here is so normal. I always pictured him living in a cave surrounded by deadly weapons.'

'He's not Batman.' I pluck stray threads from the cushion, creating a pile of emerald strands on the arm of the sofa. Talking about Sath is akin to sliding a shard of glass through my chest. 'He's just . . . Sath.'

Harper hums distractedly, too busy nosing at his belongings to pay attention. She pauses at the sight of shattered bottles still littering the bar area from where I lost my temper at Sath the other day.

'You know, this explains a lot.' She begins sweeping the shards into a paper towel. 'When I first arrived, everything was beige. I kept saying to people who'd been dead longer, if I can make everything in my room bright pink, *why* can't the rest of Asphodel be that pretty? I never got a straight answer. Then lava started gushing out of walls that were slowly turning black, and I thought *oh, that's why. We're not allowed nice things*. But that wasn't down to Asphodel at all, was it? It was Sath.'

Black smoke puffs from my arms. She *should* be allowed nice things. They all should. This place is supposed to be a middle ground, but between the demons' interference and Sath's loss of control it's slipped the wrong way, like a set of brass scales that have failed to remain balanced because they've been weighed down with awfulness on one side.

But take the weight off, and equilibrium would be restored.

I straighten. 'What if I could give you nice things?'

'What do you mean?'

'You're right. Asphodel falling apart *was* down to Sath,

318

because he allowed the demons to make this place worse than it's supposed to be. So, why couldn't *I* make it better?'

Harper contemplates this, collecting the final shards of broken glass and tossing them into the bin before smiling slyly. 'Better like . . . turning the lava pink?'

I suppose we all have our priorities.

'I'll take the idea under consideration,' I deadpan. 'I was thinking more . . . putting it back the way it was. If I could learn how to use these powers, maybe I could use my magic to repair all the things that were destroyed. All the rooms that were flooded. Regrow the plants that have died. I could –'

My mind races with possibilities. I'd need to find a way to deal with the demons first, because if they're walking around making me angry all day there's no way I'll be turning this place beige, let alone a colour of Harper's choosing, if I'm generous enough to let her pick.

But if there *was* a way to get them in line . . .

There are infinite possibilities for what I could do next. I've been so busy moping about Sath, stressing about the demons and worrying about powers I don't understand, I haven't taken the time to think there's another side to all this. A better side.

A side that's mine to decide.

When I put that heart in my chest, it was like being shoved in a high-speed vehicle and forced to drive without being asked if I knew how. And while my steering may still be jerky, I'm starting to see multiple destinations in my mind's eye, but it's my choice – and *only* my choice – which one I aim for.

I just need to work out how to get there without falling

apart. 'This is all contingent on me learning how this magic works, of course, and not setting everybody on fire the moment I see a demon.'

Easier said than done. The only time my magic seems to manifest is when I want to hurt something, which is the opposite of my end goal here. It's a pity Sath didn't have the good sense to leave me an instruction manual before I had him imprisoned.

I ignore the way my skin prickles when I think his name.

And I ignore the nagging, buzzing feeling in the back of my brain that tells me to pay attention to the solution I know is right there.

Harper drops down beside me. 'I agree, learning about your powers would be the best way forward.'

'Good.' I nod. 'I'm . . . glad. That we agree.'

The ensuing silence feels loaded, like we're both well aware of the truth we're skirting around but don't want to acknowledge out loud. Or at least, *I* don't.

'How do you think you might do that?' Harper asks in a manner I might describe as *pointed*.

I purse my lips. 'Maybe there's a book on it.'

'Maybe.' She can't hide the slight roll of her eyes. 'Or you could –'

'*No.*'

'You don't know what I was going to say.'

'I can see the thought forming in your mind.'

'Only because it's in your mind too.' She cocks her head. 'If you want to know how your powers work, you need help from someone who's experienced them first-hand.'

I clench my fists. I don't want his help. I don't want to *need* his help.

But she's right. If I want to have a shot of saving Asphodel, I'm going to have to let that lying, scheming bastard out of Glacantrum.

33

Sadly, there's no map to lead me there, and I don't want to risk seeking out a demon in case I lose control again, which means I need to figure out how to portal. I suspect this will go poorly. After telling Harper to find somewhere safe to hide, I close my eyes and try to imagine that squeezing sensation, the darkness enveloping me, but nothing happens. I resist the urge to throw things, and try again, and again, and again.

Maybe I need to know what Glacantrum looks like for it to work. I picture a cave system like the one in Asphodel, only the walls are made of ice, stalactites descending from the ceiling, frost crunching beneath my feet. *Take me there*, I urge my powers. *Take me there*.

And they do.

My body constricts, and I nearly let out a whoop, because I did it, I really did it, and I emerge in an area almost exactly as I imagined. Everything is blue and white and frosted. My breath freezes the moment it leaves my mouth, crystallising into a fresh snowflake before drifting to the ground.

Instinctively, I wrap my arms around myself, although I'm not cold. My powers keep me heated. As I head down the powdered path, the walls either side of me open up to reveal cells. The bars are coated with ice. Most of the inhabitants are frozen over. The ones that aren't moan when they spot me, calling for help. I shake my head with a sympathetic smile, like when you're trying to avoid a charity collector on the street but still want them to think you're a nice person.

If I let them go now, the demons will do far worse than give them frostbite. I'll free them as soon as Asphodel is safe.

The path twists and winds with no end in sight. Knee-deep in snow, I trudge on, a blizzard of hail pelting my face while the ice caking the walls thickens.

Then terror hits me.

This isn't survivable. Not for long. And if Sath has frozen over, if he's –

I might have sent him to the Void without realising it.

My cheeks sting as tears freeze the second they hit skin.

I might have wanted to punish him, but I didn't want *this*.

'Sath?' I call out hopelessly. 'Are you there?'

A faint voice says my name.

I stop. My heart stops. It hasn't been a week since I last heard that voice, but the familiarity of it has my lips tugging upwards. Plus, for all my claims to hate him, I am pleased not to have accidentally killed him.

I plough through another pile of snow to reach his cell, waving a hand to unlock it without any effort at all, like my powers are delighted to be in his presence.

He's huddled in the far corner. Ice encrusts his clothes, and his hair is so crisp with frost it looks like I could walk over there and snap it in two. I try to keep my face impassive as I take in the way he shivers and shakes, his lips blue and skin translucently pale. Like he's turning into a ghost.

I don't want him to know how much that upsets me.

With no preamble, I say, 'I need to learn how to control my powers without falling apart.'

Sath clears his throat and tries to stand. He fails. I rock on my heels – I will not go to him, not yet. From the floor, he finally croaks out, 'I'll help however I can.'

'First, I want the truth. The whole story, from the beginning.'

Sath's teeth chatter. My skin is still inexplicably warm, but I'm not feeling all that generous. I move close enough for him to stop shaking – just so I can get my answers – but not so close he's comfortable.

'I died in a storm,' he starts. 'Our boat capsized. I remember hitting the water. It was like slamming against cold, hard rock. The waves pushed me down. My lungs burned and . . . I woke in a dark cave, with a demon staring at me.'

I swallow.

'I demanded answers. I was a good person; I was *sure* I was a good person. I went straight to the king and told him I had things to do. I was set to be married. Travel the world. I wasn't . . . I wasn't done.'

I'm not done.

I'm not sure what's louder: his words, or the memory of mine. *I'm not done.* That's what I said to him, the day I begged for his help. He understood my desperation and used it against me. I inhale, and I think he must recognise what I've worked out, that I'm set to tell him to rot in here, because he holds up a hand.

324

'I'm sorry,' he says. 'Back then, you were . . .'

'Someone you could use?'

'I didn't have a choice,' he replies, like that makes it okay. 'I couldn't do it any more. I was failing; you *know* I was failing. I'd tried many times to pass the heart over, and no one succeeded. I'd given up hope. Then I saw you resist the voices in the Void, and I thought . . . maybe you'd be able to resist the sins when they start to whisper.' He goes to run his hand through his hair but fails miserably. His fingers stick to the icy strands and he peels them away, wincing. Good. I would say I hope he gets frostbite, except I'm trying not to be too *wrathful*. 'I wasn't sure if you'd succeed either. But you were determined and . . . you seemed so alive. I thought you had a chance. I made you the same offer that was made to me. An offer that was a lie.'

My jaw locks. 'And what happened to the previous king?'

'Looking for inspiration?' Sath raises a brow. He really doesn't know me well if he thinks I need suggestions on possible punishments for him. A storm cloud crosses his face when he answers, 'Let's just say he's no longer in Asphodel.'

I guess Sath wasn't good at withholding wrath either.

'There are old journals in the library belonging to Asphodel's previous rulers. I used them to piece a lot of things together,' Sath goes on. 'The magic inside Asphodel has existed since the dawn of time, sorting souls where they needed to be. The fairest place to do it, I suppose, as the middle ground. The first to be sorted into Tartarus, Asphodel and Elysium were each automatically gifted with the magic needed to rule, imbued inside their heart. The realms were named after them. King Tartarus was about as pleasant as you'd expect, and eventually that realm wasn't enough for him, so he used his magic to build the gates and invade Asphodel.

'He ripped out Queen Asphodel's heart and crushed it before her eyes. So, she returned the favour.' He gives me a grim smile. 'While he was gloating, she stabbed him in the back and took his heart for herself, leaving him powerless and her with the magic of Tartarus. The gates became hers to control.

'As time went on, the number of souls in Asphodel grew. Riots happened. She opened the gates to throw prisoners through, and demons would slip past in return. At first, she didn't mind. They could be used as crowd control. But then you'd get demons with . . . ideas. Demons like the Sorter.'

'If you knew she was a problem, why did you send me to her that first day?'

'I didn't realise how much of a problem she *was*.' He rubs his jaw. 'Some struggle more than others with why they're here, and I thought it would provide you with some closure if you saw the volume of dead sorted into Asphodel. That you'd accept it was inevitable. I never expected her to be plotting all this. I thought she was just like the rest of them, eager for blood and nothing more. I should've known better. She's always been ambitious. She convinced Asphodel to build her the morgue – according to the journal, Amara, as she was known then, got a kick out of seeing everyone's sins written down and tormenting them with their mistakes.'

'I'll say,' I mutter, thinking how much she relished telling me about mine – although, given what she was aiming for, there's no guarantee what she showed me that day was true. 'I don't know why Asphodel would agree to that.'

326

'Automatic sorting was a drain on the realm's magic, which would only lead to it falling apart faster. This seemed a harmless solution in the grand scheme of things. Amara was compelled to sort appropriately – it's hard to disobey a direct order from the carrier of the heart – and besides, if she started sending everyone to Tartarus the privilege would be revoked.

'The other demons weren't as easy to appease, and there were too many to compel them all into good behaviour. They tempted Asphodel to give in to sin, and the heart's link to Tartarus grew stronger. The lines between the two realms blurred. Asphodel was becoming Hell itself, and that's not what it was designed for.

'Something needed to be done, so the queen devised a series of tests. She wanted to find someone with the will to resist temptation, who might be strong enough to hold the heart and reverse some of the damage she'd wrought. Someone who could keep the gates shut. Thus, the mantle was passed. Again, and again. The problem, they all found, is that they were good people being forced to do bad things. To appease the demons stuck on this side they had to . . . well, you've seen it. We all succumb to one sin or another. Either they enjoy what they're doing and become corrupted that way, or they hate it, like me. Time and time again, the gates weaken a little more. And now there's you.'

'Yeah, me, the person who didn't pass the final task.'

'You said it yourself, you failed on purpose,' Sath says. 'Because you hate the demons. If anyone's going to keep this place in line, it's you. They won't tempt you.'

'Of course they'll tempt me! Do you have any idea how

badly I want to destroy them all? I want to burn them alive. I want to gouge out their eyes. I want to –' I shudder. 'I'm tempted, believe me.'

'I'm sorry,' he whispers. 'I'm sorry I didn't tell you; I'm sorry I put this on you. But I wouldn't have done it if I didn't believe in you. Let me help you. We can fix this, together.'

I'm silent for a minute, weighing his words. The only way I can see to keep my wrath in check is to remove anything that ignites it in the first place. I square my shoulders. 'I want the demons dead.'

'That's –'

'Don't tell me what's not possible. You're going to teach me how to use these powers, and then you're going to help me kill them all. Maybe then I really will be able to resist sin, and keep the gates closed for good.'

I'm sure he'd love to argue with me some more, but instead he sighs and finally staggers to his feet, wincing when he uses the icy wall to haul himself up. He holds out a hand. 'I'll do what I can.'

I hesitate before taking a step towards him. 'I'm accepting your help because I need it. Don't think I've forgiven you.'

He gives me a sad smile. 'Good job we have eternity for me to make it up to you.'

34

Back in Sath's rooms, I'm gracious enough to let him warm up in the shower before he begins my Devil training. Listening to the water run, I practise summoning fire on my own, and while it comes easily enough, getting it to stop is . . . an issue. The wardrobe smoulders. Scorch marks sizzle on the rug. A clock is knocked from the dresser by a flaming whip that insists on behaving like an out-of-control hosepipe.

I finally manage to snuff them out when Sath emerges from the en-suite wearing a towel slung over his hips, bringing with him the scent of soap and hot water and wet man. Why does freshly wet man smell so good? It's infuriating, honestly. His damp hair is slicked back, and rivulets of water drip down his chest into the ridges of his abdomen. I swallow, looking away. He's here to help me, and that's all. He betrayed me. I refuse to ogle him. Were his shoulders always that broad?

Perhaps sitting on the bed to wait for him was a bad idea. The last time I was here we . . . 'Put some clothes on,' I mutter.

He has the audacity to smirk. 'You look tense.'

'Of course I'm tense.' I fold my arms. 'You dumped all your

responsibilities on me and now my mood dictates whether or not hell gets unleashed.'

Any humour on his face dies, like a dandelion stolen by the wind. He appraises me, taking in my face, my defiant posture, and I've never seen him so unsure. Either because he doesn't know what to say to me, or because he knows what he *wants* to say, and thinks I'll throw it in his face.

He's right to worry. I'm an unstable bomb, ready to go off if handled the wrong way.

Clearly, he thinks he's capable of defusing me, because when his analysis is over, he pats the far end of the bed. 'Come here.'

I hesitate before sitting cross-legged in front of where he stands. This brings me eye level with the top of his towel, and the fine trail of hairs leading beneath it. My mouth goes dry. I get an extra strong dose of the smell of soap laced with peppermint as he moves to sit on the bed behind me, legs straddling my hips.

I'm in too much shock that he's got the nerve to do this, given everything, that I don't think to stop him until it's too late. 'What are you –'

'Shh.' Gently, he brushes my hair over my shoulders, draping it over my chest and exposing my back to him. I'm wearing a strappy tank top – honestly, I might never wear a jumper again because I'm too damn hot all the time – and now I'm regretting it. Too much is exposed, and I don't know what he's planning, and –

My head empties as he digs both thumbs between my shoulder blades. 'I told you, you're too tense.'

'Sath . . .' It's supposed to be a complaint, but it's closer to a moan. He's right; I *am* tense. And his thumbs are in exactly the right spot, easing away a litany of knots. 'You shouldn't.' He presses a little harder, as if to prove that he absolutely *should*. I grit my teeth to stop unfortunate noises escaping my mouth. Keeping his thumbs where they are, he squeezes my shoulders with his fingers, which has me stifling another gasp. I'm able to force out, 'You can't massage me into forgiving you.'

'Is that what I'm doing?' I can practically hear the smile in his voice. He leans close enough for the damp from his chest to seep into my skin, cooling the inferno there, and whispers, 'Is it working?'

I go to elbow him in his rock-hard stomach, but he has my arm in his grip before I get the chance. For fuck's sake. I'm supposed to be the one with the power now, and he's still faster than me. I wriggle, but he tugs me back, flush against his chest, his arm banding around my ribcage to stop me escaping. I try my best not to sink into the embrace. Despite everything, despite all the lies he's told, it's nice. I've been walking a high wire ever since I shoved that heart into my chest, and having Sath here is the first time there's been a safety net underneath.

As though he senses I've settled somewhat, he resumes his ministrations on my shoulders. I rest my head against him, breathing deeply, eyes closing. Asphodel could fall apart tomorrow. Let me have this. Let us *both* have this.

'Your powers come from Tartarus,' Sath murmurs. 'To bring them forward, you have to feel a sin, but only in moderation.' Into my ear, he adds, 'What sin are you feeling right now?'

I squirm, practically in his lap now, and he shifts away slightly. Which is annoying. I was comfy. I try to scoot backwards, into what I've deemed *my* spot, when he digs his thumb, hard, into a new knot, pushing me forward. 'Willow.' He says my name like a warning, but I'm too brain-fogged to work out why. He should have been a masseur in a past life. All we need is some essential oils and I'd happily fall asleep on him.

'You can use the powers simply by thinking an order,' he goes on. 'For the order to work, you must remain in control. If the sin takes over, you won't be able to suppress the flames, or close the link between you and the gates.'

'You say that like it's easy.' I arch my neck to give him better access to a new spot he's found. 'Did you walk around not feeling anything?'

His hands pause. 'I felt everything. Believe me.'

Something about the way he says that has my heart skipping a beat. 'How do I stop myself getting overwhelmed?'

His fingers resume kneading my skin. 'You have to think of something else. Something pure.'

Every stroke of his fingers is making me think of things that are definitely impure.

'Okay.' I gasp as his touch turns gentle, fingers trailing up and down my arms. If this is supposed to be soothing, it's having the opposite effect. I shift away. If I catch on fire he'll see what this is doing to me and I refuse to let that happen. I'm supposed to be mad at him, and all I can think is that we're alone, on a bed, and he's touching my bare skin. Forcing my attention to the matter at hand, I ask, 'If I manage to do that, could I kill the demons?'

Sath sighs. I turn and the sight of his face next to mine sends the thing in my chest into overdrive. Is a part of him fused with me now? I wonder if that would be enough to succeed.

332

His goodness, that he denied for so long, combined with my anger at the demons for taking what was never theirs.

'I said I'd help you,' Sath says. 'And I don't want to lie to you. But what I'm about to tell you . . . you have to promise to think it through before you do anything.'

My track record with thinking things through is not stellar. Nevertheless, I nod my assent, and his arms tighten around me.

'The amount of power you'd have to draw from Tartarus to kill the demons with magic would be overwhelming, that part still stands. It's not an option. So, I started looking for another way. There's a painting in the art cave that never changes and I've always wondered why –'

'Me too. It's awful.'

'Artistic merit aside, I was intrigued.' He smiles wryly. 'When I was digging around in the old journals, I found one that claimed the painting depicted a way to rid us of the demons entirely.'

I gape at him. 'And you're just telling me this *now*? Why didn't you do something sooner?'

'Because I knew I wasn't strong enough to do what was needed. I've been searching this whole time, trying to find a better way, but I can't. According to the journals, if the gates were to be opened, one of two things would happen. The likelihood is everything would crumble, and Tartarus would be unleashed, as the demons want. But there's a slim chance if the divide between the two planes is kept in place, it'd create a . . . vortex, of sorts. The demons would be called home. They'd fight like anything, but eventually, they'd be sucked through. But we both know I'd never be able to keep that divide.'

333

I sit up straight. For the first time in days, hope unfurls in my stomach, picturing the Sorter being swept up in a tornado; a wicked witch being dragged home to Oz. 'But I could.'

'Willow.' His tone still manages to contain that level of command it held before. 'They'll fight back. Plus, there'll be even more demons trying to force their way through once the gates are open. You'd have to find the strength to close them again. Keeping yourself free of sin to maintain the divide would be next to impossible.'

Semantics.

'We'll get help,' I say. 'I don't think the humans would say no to shoving a few demons through the gates. I won't get overwhelmed, and then I'll close the doors, easy-peasy.'

Sath just looks at me.

'Don't do that.' I flick his nose. 'You wouldn't have told me if you didn't think I had a chance. I can do this.'

I really think I can. I'm snuggled against someone I have every reason to be angry with, and I've never felt more peaceful. If I can think of this peace – and none of the other emotions Sath elicits in me – closing the gates after the demons will be a breeze.

I should probably test that theory first though.

Sath's thumb skims the skin on the inside of my wrist, making my pulse jump. Shadows ripple down my arms, and I let them turn into the flaming whip I couldn't control earlier. This time, though, it doesn't lash out at the first object it sees. I trail it along the floor – the carpet smoulders, but doesn't burn, because I don't *want* it to burn – and all the while Sath strokes my arms, my back, the nape of my neck.

The sensations make something low in my gut clench. I try to think of peace, and contentment, and what Asphodel will be when it's all over. A sanctuary. A second chance. Who needs the quiet of Elysium when you could have the chaos of living instead?

I rein in the flames, and beam at Sath, triumphant. His brow is furrowed, more concerned than impressed, but I am not to be deterred.

'This'll work.' I place a hand on his cheek. 'I can do this.'

His skin, such a normal temperature now, is soft beneath my palm. He holds his breath as my fingers explore his face, tracing his eyebrows, the bridge of his nose, before settling on his lips. My gaze drops to his mouth, parted beneath my touch. My power flickers. What am I doing?

What am I doing?

I spring from the bed, pulse thundering, before reluctantly turning to face him. 'I'm sorry. I didn't mean to . . .'

Mean to what? Tenderly caress his face, like nothing had happened?

'It's all right.' Sath slides from the bed, and his towel slides with him, lowering on his waist. He stops to adjust it, which I absolutely do not watch, especially not when he loosens the knot in order to fix it, revealing the side of his hip and a flash of thigh and I'm *not looking, okay?* 'Did you want to talk about it?'

'About what?'

'Us.'

'There is no us.' The words are a reflex, a shield to deflect from the fact that, for me, there's always been an us. We both know it. But then he used me, and betrayed me, and a massage

335

and an offer of help isn't enough to change that. It is, quite frankly, a matter of principle.

'Really?' He stalks towards me. My back slams against the wardrobe and his arms brace around me, either side of my head. My breath hitches. 'What sin did you use just now, to make that fire?'

'Wrath,' I reply blandly.

'Liar.'

Maybe I am. Now, though, it *is* anger that has me drawing on my power, and I'm finally able to form a sword in my hand, silver and gleaming and sharp. The hilt is decked with seven jewels, the largest a blood-red ruby set in the centre.

'Careful.' I aim the blade at his neck. He doesn't flinch, instead regarding me with an intensity that almost makes his eyes turn molten again. I miss that gold. It made him easier to read. Every flare was a precursor to anger, to his powers coming to the surface, to . . . something else, maybe. Something I saw the night of lust. 'Now you've told me everything, I don't need you any more. I could still do to you what you did to your predecessor.'

Sath frowns. 'I didn't do anything to him.'

'You said he wasn't here any more.'

'That's true,' he says slowly. His shoulders sag, and he wilts on to the bed. 'You haven't asked me what my concession was.'

'I thought getting out of your Devildom was your concession.'

'Not quite.' He sighs. 'As a previous owner of the heart, I am free to travel to Elysium whenever I choose. That's where all the former rulers have gone.'

Despite all the flames now living inside me, I go cold. Stone cold. All air leaves my lungs, a great crashing wave of panic washing over me, and both my hearts stop beating. He can leave. He's free to leave.

And for all my bravado and waving a sword around, I don't want to do this on my own.

'Oh.' My voice sounds small. 'When . . .' Nettles sting my throat, clogging it.

'All I have to do is will it. One thought is all it would take.'

The nettles turn to deadened leaves that disintegrate when I swallow. 'So, when I locked you in Glacantrum –'

'I could have gone. Any time.'

'But you didn't.'

'I didn't.'

We hold each other's gaze. My sword disappears. I couldn't summon an ounce of sin if I wanted to. He stayed. He stayed.

He died in icy water, and I put him in the coldest place imaginable with no promise I'd let him out, and he sat there and waited. When he didn't have to.

'Why?' I whisper.

'Why do you think?'

The answer – at least, what I hope is the answer – is a rubber band squeezing my chest so tightly I think I might burst. 'Tell me.'

His eyes are moist. 'At first, I wanted to leave this place behind because I wanted to be at peace. Now I'm not sure that's what I wanted at all. What I wanted was a life, something outside of issuing punishments and dealing with petty squabbles between demons intent on tearing each other apart. I didn't think I'd have that here, not after what I'd done.

'But then you fought alongside me, and covered your hands in my blood, and looked at me like I wasn't the worst person you'd ever met. You danced with me like I was a man, not a monster. You took me to a bar and made me laugh and it felt like the start of something I didn't think I'd be able to have, after I died. And I wanted it. I still want it. I'm not going to Elysium if there's a chance I can fight for that.'

'Oh.' The rubber band snaps, and my heart wants to explode with it.

He *stayed*.

And maybe he lied to me, but it was for a good reason. Because he's right, if I'd known the truth earlier, I'd have run. I'd have run, and Sath would have given up, and the gates would open, dooming us all.

Sometimes bad decisions lead to good things. If I hadn't jumped off that cliff, we'd never have met. Both of our bad choices brought us together and gave us a chance. To survive. To live. It's a slim chance, one that relies on me not failing – something I don't have a great track record of – but it's a chance we didn't have before.

A chance he gave me. Maybe I should give him one too.

The seventh clock on the dresser audibly ticks, hands shifting into a new position.

I drop beside him on the bed. 'I'm opening those gates tomorrow,' I tell him. 'By the end of the day, Asphodel will either be saved, or it will be ruined.'

'Willow –'

'Shh.' I press a finger to his lips. 'If it does all go to shit, we only have tonight.'

338

His eyes flicker. 'I know.'

'And if it does . . . I don't want to go to the Void without doing all the things I want to do first.'

As if he can read my mind – or maybe the way I've angled my body towards his – his hand finds my knee. His lips brush the shell of my ear. 'And what is it you'd like to do?'

I wait one heartbeat. Two. Staring into his eyes, seeing the emotion there, feeling it reflect in mine. Finally, I say, 'This.'

And then I kiss him.

35

It's gentle at first.

Tentative touches of my fingers to his chest, his on my hips, the barest brush of our lips mingled with soft sighs. Sighs without words that somehow sound like *finally*.

His mouth is like velvet beneath mine, and I want to sink into it, sink into *him*; I want to remove every layer between us until there's nothing left but skin, with no secrets left to reveal and no pretences to hide behind. My leg slides over his and he tugs me on to his lap, and – every thought eddies from my head. Beneath the towel, I can feel how much he wants me, and I grind against him, needing to feel him against me, desperate to have him inside me. Sath groans, deepening the kiss, his tongue parting my lips and sweeping inside my mouth.

He tastes like honey and sugar and sin, but more than that, he tastes like home, like everything I've ever wanted. I gasp his name into his mouth, and his fingers dig harder into my side before gliding underneath my top, stroking the delicate skin there.

I break the kiss to yank my top off, wanting him bare against me. Sath is immediately distracted; before I can pull him closer he's tugging down the cups of my bra and flicking a tongue over my nipple. I shudder, gripping his shoulder for support.

'I want you to know,' I say between pants, 'I'm still annoyed with you. Furious, even.'

'Really.' His smile curves against my breast. 'Should I stop?'

My hand seizes his hair. 'Absolutely not.' I drag his face back to mine and capture his lips again, and it's not gentle this time: it's all teeth and tongue and hands that grasp and claw for every part of each other we can reach, knowing this might be the only chance we have to reach them. I want to learn every inch of him, filling in the pieces of a Sath-map in my mind with every new discovery.

The skin below his belly button is ticklish. He twitches, huffing a laugh when I stroke my finger there. He likes it when I bite his lip; the low moan he makes when my teeth graze flesh tells me that much. His mouth finds my neck, and I grip him, wishing we had all the time in the world, that we never have to leave this room and face what's outside the doors.

But we do. And if tonight turns out to be our only night to do this, I want to experience everything. I reach for the knot on his towel, determined to remove that final barrier between us, but Sath has other ideas.

'I made you a promise,' he says, 'when you asked what I'd like to do to you.'

He lifts me, spins me round, and deposits me on the bed beneath him. Pops the button on my jeans. Unzips the fly excruciatingly slowly. His eyes never leave mine as my jeans are removed, and then his fingers hook inside the waistband of my underwear to slide that off too. Bracing my foot on his shoulder, he presses light kisses to my ankle, the inside of my calf. I'm achingly wet and hopelessly empty, spread open and squirming beneath him, desperate for something, *anything* that's more than this.

His hands go to the towel. My breath catches as the knot is undone and it's tossed to one side, revealing the entire length of him. The sight of his body, finally fully bare, has me salivating, my gaze riveted on both the hard muscles of his thighs and what lies between them. Liquid heat pools in my core, while shadows of flame flicker down my arms.

Sath leans over me, tucking his fingers beneath my chin, dragging my stare away. 'I believe I said I'd start by kissing you until you couldn't remember your own name.'

Kissing is the last thing on my mind right now. Not when he's this close to me, when I can feel the heavy weight of him on my thigh, when –

Sath's lips crash against mine.

Okay. Fine. I can't say I'm opposed to this. His lips move with expert precision, every brush of his tongue sending shivers down my spine. My bra is unhooked and tossed aside, and his hands are on my breasts once more, tweaking my nipples before skimming the sensitive skin on the underside.

He's still not touched me where I need him most. I bite his lower lip, harder than before, earning me another groan before he pulls away, kissing my cheek, my neck, my ears.

'So, what is it?' Another kiss, along my jaw. 'Your name?'

'Sath . . .'

He smirks. 'Wrong.'

I'm inclined to zap him with some of my new-found powers,

but then his head moves lower, and I'm reminded of something else he'd promised me. I go tight and loose all at once as he peppers kisses down my torso. My abdomen. Lower. His hand urges my legs apart wider, wider before his head settles between my thighs.

He inhales deeply. My pulse thunders in my ears as my heart ricochets around my chest like a wild pinball. Normally I'd be embarrassed, panicking he's going to hate the sight or smell or taste of me, but then he nuzzles me and groans a heated, 'Fuck.'

It's enough to have me gripping the sheets and trying to push myself into his face, any hint of propriety long abandoned. I've waited so, so long for him to do this, and I need him to do it quickly. I need –

Sath has other ideas. He pins me down, one hand flat against my stomach, refusing to let me set the tempo for him. Bastard. I'm nearly begging, and I think he knows it, but I refuse to give him the satisfaction.

His first lick has me bucking from the mattress, my toes curling into the sheets, scrabbling for purchase. I cry out, needing to squirm, needing him to *move*; he's too slow and it's too much, the feeling of his mouth on me, of his thumb pressing down in just the right spot. Pressure builds and builds, never quite enough, and I swear he's doing this on purpose.

It's torture. Exquisite torture.

Finally, I whimper, *'Please.'*

He pauses. I clench on nothing. He presses his mouth back where it belongs, and he can't hold me down, can't stop me writhing and bucking and screaming because he's going harder this time, long sweeping strokes of his tongue working deeper and deeper. I kick out and scratch my nails on silk.

My whole focus is centred on what he's doing to me, and that pressure is increasing again; I'm afraid he's going to stop, to torment me some more, but this time he keeps going, replacing his mouth with a finger, then two, and I'm spasming around him, gasping for air, stars exploding before my eyes.

White light blinds my vision as I twitch beneath him. When I return to my body, he's already crawled over me, caging me between his arms. His face hovers above mine. A rush of sheer, undiluted adoration swoops through my stomach.

'You should have done that during lust,' I say, gasping. 'I'd never have said no.'

The corners of his mouth lift. 'I had to give you a fighting chance at passing.'

My response is somewhere between a snort and a giggle. I'm not convinced it's particularly attractive, but something close to fondness fills Sath's gaze, and he brushes sweaty strands of hair from my face before kissing me again.

Immediately, I turn to liquid. My hands skim the planes of his chest, warm and solid, before drifting lower, wanting to touch him as he'd touched me. His hand encircles my wrist before it can reach its target, and I swear his eyes flash gold. 'Another time.'

He nudges my knees apart before lining himself up at my entrance, kissing me one more time, long and slow and deep, as though he's savouring me as much as I'm savouring him, like he too is afraid this one moment is all we'll ever get, and wants to commit every second to memory.

The moment he slides inside me, it's like all the scattered

pieces of me finally click into place. With him, I'm just Willow, messy and imperfect, and it doesn't matter. I don't have to pretend, to wonder which sides of me are safe for him to see. They've already been exposed, and he doesn't care.

He stayed.

He moves slowly at first. I throw my head back on the pillow, scratching my nails down his skin as he burrows his face into my neck. Our mingled sighs fill the room, followed by panted breaths and his name on my lips when he slips a hand between us, pressing down on that spot between my legs, like while I've been mapping him he's been mapping me too, except he's done a much more expert job of it.

Already worked up, every nerve fried, I go over the edge almost immediately. It's more intense this time, amplified by the feeling of Sath inside me, and I have to fight to keep my magic under control. Flames spark down my arms; I'm going to combust *I am I am I am*.

I grit my teeth, willing my flames to dim. I can't turn into a fire hazard every time we have sex – which I plan for us to do a lot – which means I need to figure this out somehow. Bunnies. Clouds. Rainbows.

'Willow?' Sath has stopped moving. I open my eyes. 'You're losing control.'

'Only a little,' I mutter, shifting beneath him, urging him to continue. 'Why have you stopped?'

He raises a brow, and I cannot believe we've paused mid-coitus to have an argument about the fact I'm on fire.

'It's fine. See?' The flames have turned to shadows now, nothing but black smoke coiling around my elbows. 'I can control it.'

I have to control it. If I can't, I'll never survive opening the gates. Sath doesn't look especially convinced, probably because of the hole I've singed in the sheets, although he does start moving again, pulling out agonisingly slowly only to slam in again. I bite his shoulder.

'Remember,' he murmurs into my ear, 'pure thoughts.'

He grins, like he knows my mind is living in the gutter, and kisses me before I can say something venomous in response. He finds his rhythm, not breaking the kiss, and I'm burning up, unable to find anything pure in me at all, only a deep *want*. I clutch at him, terrified I'm going to burn him too, but equally scared to let go.

His hands cup my face. The kiss slows, turning deeper, gentler, and with it comes emotion, like he's trying to project every feeling he has into that kiss. And I feel it too. It blooms, like a flower erupting in spring sunshine, so intense my flames are snuffed out by its power.

Afterwards, we lie there, chest to chest, hearts pounding against one another, as though they're trying to break through and become one. Maybe they already are; already *were*. His fingers stroke my skin as though they're mesmerised by it; his nose nuzzles my cheek as he lets out a contented sigh. I hold him against me, wishing I could keep him here forever.

And when he shifts to look into my eyes, I see something shining in his gaze, something that mirrors the words threatening to bubble out of me, and I realise it's not just lust I feel for him. Not even close.

36

We lie side by side, limbs entwined, me tucked under his arm. Sath coils a lock of my hair around his finger. 'It's red, by the way,' he says. 'My favourite colour.'

'You took a shot because you didn't want to tell me your favourite colour was the same as my hair?'

He flicks my nose. 'I didn't want you getting any ideas.'

I flick his chest in return. 'That you liked me?'

'Mm.' He nuzzles my ear, and I think I might be content to stay like this forever. Not even the horde of angry demons lurking in Asphodel's halls is enough to make me move. I fear I may be the laziest ruler Asphodel has ever had – although, in my defence, maybe none of the previous rulers had someone like Sath in their bed. How am I supposed to save my subjects when his hand is, once again, between my thighs?

'Sath.' I try to focus, lest a) I catch on fire, or b) I allow him to distract me for the third time tonight. 'We should go. The sooner we send the demons to Tartarus, the sooner we can . . .'

'Do this again?' His smile dies before it can truly take shape, and his gaze turns sombre. 'If this goes wrong, we may never do this again.'

'At least you have an out,' I say. 'Promise me, if I can't close the gates, you'll go. Make your wish and escape to Elysium.'

'If those gates stay open, Asphodel will be overrun. I won't leave you to suffer that fate alone.'

'Sath –'

He silences my argument with a kiss. I allow it for all of a few seconds before gently pushing him away and sitting up, covering myself with the sheets to prevent him losing focus. 'You said the demons will be sucked through the gates. How powerful would the vortex be? How long will it take?'

Sath runs a hand through his hair. 'It's not exactly been tried before.'

'Then we'll try and get them to the gates before I open them. The closer they are, the quicker they'll be gone, right?' I pretend to think. 'What are our chances of them forming an orderly queue?'

My joke falls flat. Sath, for all his encouraging kisses, has a crease between his brows. 'We should wait,' he says. 'You've barely learned anything about your powers –'

'The longer we wait, the more damage they'll do.' I magic myself some clothes and shimmy into what I can only hope works as battle gear: leggings, combat boots and a long-sleeved black shirt with a layer of steel plating on the inside. 'The humans will help us.'

He doesn't appear wholly persuaded – I can't say I blame him – but he does put some clothes on (which is both a blessing and a curse), matching my all-black ensemble, before we head outside.

The entrance chamber is hauntingly empty.

Our footsteps echo as we move across the chamber and into the golden corridor, past the Sorter's door – I freeze.

Past the Sorter's door, which is wide open.

Shit. Dread sinks to the pit of my stomach. 'I told them to guard this.'

'We need to move.' Sath doesn't wait before doing just that, and I hurry after him, possibilities whizzing through my mind, all of them terrible. Clearly I did a poor job of compelling the demons to follow my orders. I should have known they'd see through my performance on the throne yesterday, and now my naivety has left the Sorter free to do who knows what for who knows how long.

The cliff face is the most still I've seen it, with no shadows moving behind the windows and only one lift hovering a few floors above. It drops as we approach the railing, and I instruct it to take us to Dionysus, for lack of better ideas.

That balcony is empty too.

Inside, the strobe lights have been switched off, replaced with candlesticks, and black sheets are draped over Sath's throne, like the demons have decided to play dress up and turn this place into Dracula's castle.

The smell of copper and metal taints the air. Blood is smeared across the dance floor and over the surface of the bar. Humans huddle in the far corner, looking fairly unharmed save for the iron chains wrapped around their wrists. I run towards them, addressing a middle-aged man with grey flecks in his hair – *Norman*, Asphodel's magic tells me.

'What happened?' I ask, kneeling before him and inspecting his manacles. 'Where are the demons? The Sorter?'

'Went looking for more of us. They said this was just the start.' His gaze slides to Sath. 'Good of him to show his face.'

'He wasn't the one who abandoned you,' I say softly, waving a hand. Everyone's chains click, their cuffs coming undone and hanging limply around their wrists. 'That was me.'

A lump thickens in my throat. *I did this*. I left them to fend for themselves while I sorted my own shit out, allowing the demons to do whatever they liked in my absence. Black smoke curls around my knuckles. I take a deep breath, squashing my power down, thinking of how in a few hours from now, I'll have fixed everything – something I wouldn't have been able to do yesterday, not without Sath's help. I had to leave in order to come back stronger.

And I *am* stronger.

I just need to convince these humans of that. Gesturing for them to follow, I stride over to the throne and rip off the black sheet before settling down. This is going to be a far less pleasant experience than the last time I was here, falling-slash-drooling on Sath's lap.

They're slow to move closer. I'm pretty sure the only reason they move at all is out of fear of Sath, who's trying his best to usher them forward. I scan their faces as they approach, checking for a familiar one, but Harper's not here. I can only hope she's found somewhere safe to stay out of sight.

When the humans are finally gathered at my feet, I try to find the right words. 'I'm sorry I didn't get here sooner. But this is the last time –' I break off. If I fuck this up, this won't be the last time. With a shake of my head, I plough on. 'This ends today. This is *our* afterlife. I will not let them take it from

350

us. From *you*. And I will not bow to their demands.' I tilt my chin in the air. 'Asphodel is not the demons' true home. It's time they go back where they came from.'

Whispers and murmurs sweep through the crowd. I fill them in on the plan – leaving out the minor detail that closing the gates afterwards might be something of an issue – and tell them to go demon-hunting. 'Go in groups. Recruit any humans you can find. Drag the demons to the entrance chamber; Sath and I will lead you to the gates from there.'

With a wave of my hand, a pile of swords and flaming whips materialise at my feet, but nobody moves to collect them. At best, I get a few feet shuffles. Some army. They're eyeing Sath nervously, like they're unable to break their old habits of expecting repercussions for all insubordination.

'You have nothing to fear from him any more,' I announce. 'Or me. Change of management, change of rules. Which means you can fight. Show the demons there's more of you than there are of them.' I allow some of my power to come to the surface, feeling my eyes burn with fire. 'Don't you want them to suffer the way you've suffered?'

I rise from the throne. 'They chained you up. They're planning to tear you apart. Is that what you want? Or do you want to tear them apart instead? How many of you have seen a demon bleed?' I flash a smile that's all teeth and no humour. 'How many of you would like to?'

They're restless now, interested, but fear mixed with disbelief holds them back.

Fortunately for me, the antlered demon from yesterday enters the cave, dragging a host of new humans behind him. Still no

Harper, but I'm not sure if that makes it better or worse. At least if she was here I could make her safe.

The demon pauses at the sight of me.

'Come here,' I order. Immediately, it lurches forward. My voice sounds deep, fathomless, like within it dwells all the rulers that came before me. Sath's brow is pinched, and he's watching me with narrowed, assessing eyes. He thinks I'm losing control. I give him the tiniest smile to let him know he's wrong, then direct a smile altogether more cutting at the demon.

The whip of fire is round his neck in seconds. I focus my rage solely on him, on that whip. Sath and the humans swim in my peripheral vision, grounding me, reminding me that the rage isn't everything; that rainbows can be found in the midst of a storm. I lift the demon into the air, drawing him closer, relishing his screams of pain. When I drop him to the ground at my feet, his neck is covered in pus-filled boils and one of his antlers is drooping, partially melted with the heat.

'Shall I tell you a secret?' I crouch before him, so we're eye level. 'I'm going to open the gates today. You're going home. Aren't you lucky?'

The demon trembles.

'What's the matter?' I flutter my eyelashes, feigning innocence. 'Is it only fun if Tartarus comes here? If you're not the one at the bottom of the food chain?' Flames turn to ice in my veins. 'Too bad.'

I slam my hands into his chest, my power forcing my fist through flesh and bone. It reaches the empty space where his heart should be before punching out the other side, sending a spray of black over the floor. He crumples to the ground and I hold up my hands, allowing the humans to observe the blood dripping down my wrists.

Through it all, I'm calm. Peaceful. This isn't about wrath or revenge, it's about doing what needs to be done. Good Decision Willow has finally made an appearance, and her confidence is liberating. She'll give this place the spring clean it needs, eradicating every demon like a cobweb that's been allowed to linger too long, and when she's done every corner of this place will be scrubbed clear of their infestation.

To the humans, I say, 'Are you with me now?'

Finally, they nod. I set fire to the demon's body, giving it a one-way ticket home, and step down from the dais. 'Then go. Kill whoever you have to. We can toss the bodies through the gates before they rise again.'

They jostle each other to reach my pile of weapons first, tussling for the biggest sword, fire glowing in their eyes as they examine the whips. Once they're all armed, they stream towards the doors in unison.

'One more thing,' I call after them. 'If anyone sees the Sorter, leave her for me.'

37

We locate demons lurking on every floor. With every one we find, flames ripple from me, burning bigger and brighter. But not out of control – never that. I've resisted the sins before, and I'll resist them now. Even wrath. I forge ropes for the humans to use, and they tie the demons up like puppets, marching them into lifts. Harper is among their captors – I found her hiding in her favourite paintball lookout – and now she's at my side, poking a demon in the side with his own tail.

The demons flail and snap their teeth, clawing at their bindings. With four humans for every monster they don't get far, especially when those bindings are made from the flames of Tartarus themselves, singeing their talons when they try to cut through.

Our congregation swells in number until finally we cram into the entrance chamber, ready to drag the demons to the gates. For those we've missed – including *her* – I'll have to hope the vortex sweeps them up before I lose control. Nerves tug at me harder than the demons pull at their restraints.

Given the size of this place – we barely covered a hundred floors before the chamber was stuffed full – the vortex is going to be open for a *while*.

But Sath's fingers are brushing my arm, and Harper is on my other side, her whole being vibrating with energy and hope. If they believe this is possible, I choose to believe the same. I nod at Sath to open the doors.

The tunnel swings into view just as a familiar voice calls out behind us, 'You're making a mistake.'

Look who decided to show up. The Sorter shoves her way to the front of the group, nearby demons bowing their heads at the sight of her. I don't see anything worth revering. She may have avoided capture, but she's sweaty and dishevelled, gaze darting around the room in what I would delightedly describe as *blind panic*.

'There's no one here who can help you now,' I tell her. 'You've lost.'

Her red eyes lock on mine, and her mouth twists into an attempt at a smirk. 'Oh, I wouldn't say that. I told you, you're making a mistake. Opening those gates is the last thing you want to do if you're trying to save Asphodel.'

'If you think this is such a bad idea, shouldn't you be encouraging it?'

She doesn't have an answer. Her silence feels almost as good as Sath's faith, because with it comes a sense of glorious smugness that, unlike Sath, she didn't believe in me up until this moment. She tricked me into taking the tasks because she thought I'd fall apart faster than Sath, or be stupid enough to manipulate into handing over the heart at the final hour. She thought I was weak, worthless, and now I get to show her how wrong she was.

A sword materialises in my hand.

Her throat bobs. 'You're forgetting you need me.'

'Do I?' I raise a brow. 'Or did you become the Sorter to make yourself feel important, *Amara*?'

She flinches at the use of her old name.

'You thought you were too special to be an ordinary demon so you had to invent a role for yourself. It's pathetic, really. You're only happy when you have power over others, but what does that say about *you*, that your self-worth is so tied up in making other people feel awful?' I bring the blade to her neck and she tries to take a step back, only there's nowhere to go, a crowd of humans forming a barricade behind her. 'But do you know what . . . ?'

The sword disappears in a waft of shadow, and her eyes widen.

'. . . You're *not* special.' I lean forward until we're nose to nose. 'You're not different. You don't deserve a dramatic ending for the history books. You are no better or worse than any other demon in this room, and you're going back to Tartarus the same way as the rest of them.'

I conjure another flaming whip and hand it to Sath, who immediately takes charge of binding the Sorter. She shouts and curses, but I tune her out, leading the procession into the bowels of Asphodel where the gates reside. The skull-socket candles lining the corridors watch me as I pass, like they too are curious as to whether this will work, or whether I'm about to engage in the worst form of self-sabotage ever seen.

The gates are the most silent I've seen them. This is encouraging, I guess, and means I'm holding together better than Sath was, at the end. The metal is cool to the touch, but in the back of my mind, something rumbles, for the first time since I reconnected with Sath.

They're waiting on the other side. With clubs and swords and spears. Beneath their feet a wind is stirring, red dust spraying over the vast, deserted ground surrounding them.

I compel it to stir faster.

'How do I get these open?' I ask Sath. There's no door handle, although some of the carved demon faces have exceptionally long horns. I'm tempted to give one a pull.

'The sins. You'll need to give in, just for a moment.' Sath takes my hand, his fingers trailing over mine like he wants to memorise the shape of them. 'Willow –'

'No goodbyes. We're going to be fine.' Reluctantly, I add, 'But if we're not, don't forget what I said to you. Get yourself out.'

'I've told you, I'm not leaving you.' His hand grips tighter. 'Remember, once the gates are open, you need to regain control immediately. There has to be a divide. Nothing bad will happen if you keep the divide.'

I nod, letting go of his hand. Happiness is the last thing I need if I want to get these gates open. Closing my eyes, I focus on the demons on the other side. On the rumbles of discontent. On how badly they want to rip, and tear, and kill.

On how they want to destroy everything good and pure, to turn dreams into nightmares, to force the humans into subservience the same way the Sorter did, the same way my *mother* did. And, just like how the Sorter enjoyed analysing our clipboards, Mum enjoyed reminding me of my mistakes, over and over, because if she wasn't the most powerful person in a room she might have been forced to look at herself for a change and realise she wasn't special either.

Flames erupt down my arms.

She belittled me to the point I felt worthless. She screamed at me until Dad walked out. She forced me into a relationship that had me questioning every little thing I did. I wasted so much time destroying myself and for *what*?

The doors rattle. Hinges pop.

I wouldn't have quit that course if she hadn't made me take it in the first place. I wouldn't have been on that cliff if I hadn't surrounded myself with people who didn't care. *She* is the reason I'm dead.

I blamed myself and berated myself, but the only person who should feel guilty here is her.

A loud whistling, shrieking sounds, like a kettle that won't stop boiling and now it's going to explode. Sweat slides down my face. I spent years trying to make myself small, but now I'm a suppressed jack-in-the-box finally sprung free, unleashing myself on the world.

Unleashing my *wrath* on the world.

The ground beneath my feet shakes. Heat blasts my face.

The gates swing open.

Yes, yes, yes, the demons in my head shout with jubilation. I gasp, opening my eyes and reaching for Sath or Harper or *anyone*. Wrath rages in my veins, demanding I let those celebrating demons through to cause the kind of carnage they're begging me for.

Nobody takes my hand.

Nobody notices me at all. Their focus is what's on the other side of the gates. I catch a glimpse of barren tundra, a flash of an extremely large snake with yellow eyes, and then the whole image is swallowed up by a great tidal wave of blood.

Keep the divide.

This was a mistake. I stare, frozen, as that red sea rushes towards us, and I can't do anything, I can't stop it, there's so *much* of it, there's no divide to keep because I don't know where I start and the gates end –

The blood surges forward, crashing straight through the opening, and I'm swept away in a great, gushing river of crimson.

38

I cough and splutter as we're carried away downstream.

The river catches us all in its wake, demons and humans alike swimming for the surface as the blood surges down the tunnel. It rises higher and higher, catching the skull lanterns on the walls, sweeping them into its path, and we're plunged into darkness.

I have to get back. I swim against the current, towards the gates, needing to check no demons from the other side are in this river with us, but it's too strong, and before I know it we're flowing into the entrance chamber. It's large enough in here that the blood level descends, a sea finally hitting the shore, and we're deposited on the floor sopping wet and dripping red, blood sloshing at our feet.

The Sorter's laughing.

A second later, that snake I caught a glimpse of shoves its head through the open doorway. It's so large it can't get any further, its body wedged in the tunnel behind it. Asphodel trembles, like it can't withstand accommodating a demon of this size. Every time it wriggles, rock descends in chunks that land in haphazard heaps around the base of its head.

Still on my knees, I can sense its tail writhing beneath me, like the serpent has the whole of Asphodel surrounded, coiled in its thick grasp. Its tongue flicks out, longer than my whole body, and captures the nearest human.

They're swallowed whole. I can't bring myself to move.

What do I do? What do I do what do I do what do I do?

Keep the divide. I wasn't given a chance. And now the two worlds are colliding.

The demons take this as their opportunity to fight back. With hisses and roars, they tear my ropes from their wrists and ankles, leaving scars on their flesh that sizzle like meat that's just been taken off the grill. A human gets backhanded. Another has their neck torn into by a pair of fangs. Harper crawls across the floor, clutching her stomach.

Panic claws at me. I should've waited until I was stronger. Maybe I shouldn't have done this at all. The voices in my head roar, louder than ever, no barrier between us now the gates are wide open.

Hurt them. Tear them apart. You know you want to. You enjoyed it when you killed Aric, didn't you? A human's screams would be so much sweeter.

I shake my head. No. I killed Aric because I had to. I reach for my power to conjure more rope. Use it to push away a demon lunging for Harper. The voices scream, furious I'm ignoring them.

The snake inches a little further out of the tunnel.

Help it. Wouldn't it be easier to give up, to let it in? You look tired, Willow.

Well, excuse me if I didn't get much sleep last night. I search for Sath, but I can't locate him amid the chaos. Everything is a blur: a flash of silver, a clank of steel, a splatter of red. Screams and curses are hurled in every direction until they become an indecipherable cacophony of noise.

If you let the humans die, it'll go quiet. I grit my teeth, willing them to shut up. Instead, they get louder, a chorus sounding out a refrain. *We'll make you a deal. Anything you desire, it's yours. Let the snake in.*

'I won't.'

A human is tossed from one side of the chamber to the other. They land with a heavy crack that I feel in my own bones, and I want this over, I *need* this to be over. My cheeks are wet. I can't let any more humans end up in the Void, or worse.

But they will.

Because there's no wind. No promised vortex.

I've messed up. I shouldn't be surprised. Good Decision Willow can make all the choices she likes; she still needs the rest of me to follow through.

You should give up. Your duty was to protect them, and you've failed. You always fail in the end, don't you?

Flames burst from my arms. I've failed, and the gates are open, and there's no divide at all, because I am my sins and they live within me. I can't stop the planes from merging because I'm not pure and good and never have been.

All I've ever wanted is to be proud of you.

I clutch my hands to my ears. Not her. Not now.

This is all your fault. If you had been better, more, everything I asked you to be –

'Shut *up*,' I scream. She's the problem; I know that now. I don't need to listen to her any more.

'Willow.' Sath's voice sounds far away, and I don't know what to do. I've failed, I've failed, I've failed.

Someone screams. Multiple someones. I sit ankle-deep in the blood of those who died in Tartarus, all too aware that soon it will be mixed with the blood of Asphodel too, and there's not a thing I can do about it. I've damned us all. It's too much. My body floods with anger, with despair, and flames engulf me.

'Willow!'

A head is deposited at my feet. I stare at its glassy eyes, its open mouth, as my flames burn hotter.

What a pathetic human, letting itself get killed. Weren't they supposed to be following my orders?

My gaze snaps up. No one is following my instructions. They should be hurting the demons, not the other way round. I lash out whips of flame, ensnaring the nearest demons, dragging them off the humans they were about to devour. I bind their ropes tighter before sending out another blast of fire.

I can't hear over the roaring in my head. The gates are open. I have to get the demons through the gates. *Tear. Hurt. Kill.*

Yes. Yes, I want to do that. Tear. Hurt. Kill. If they're not being called back, I'll have to shove them back, by any means necessary. But the snake's blocking the path; I need to kill the snake.

Are you sure? You said it yourself, these humans are pathetic.

I didn't say that. Did I say that? It's hard to differentiate the voices in my head from my *own* voice, to know what's me and what's them. All our thoughts bleed into one. Everything is muddled; my temple pounds. I snap the neck of a demon. Mum's voice sounds again, louder than the rest.

It'll stop when you give in. You can have everything you want, so long as you don't kill the snake. I'd be so proud of you, Willow.

She has a point. The snake isn't causing any harm. It just wants to feed. The humans, the stupid, screaming humans, they're the ones at fault.

Tear. Hurt. Kill. My hand closes on another neck, this one soft, hairless, almost like – I blink. It's a human. I don't want to hurt the humans. Do I?

'Willow!'

Why is that man calling my name?

I let the human go, rubbing my temples, confused. *Tear. Hurt. Kill.*

'Willow.' Someone touches my arm. They're familiar, I think. Blindly, I reach towards them, wanting to be closer. They tug me into them. I breathe in their fresh scent and allow it to dim my power. 'Remember, your sins don't control you.'

Sath. It's Sath. I *know* Sath. I know the anger more. I know this unspeakable rage at the injustice of what's happening in this room; nobody here deserves to be torn apart, and yet they are, and I led them here, it's my fault, mine, and the demons are using that against me, making me think things I don't want to think.

You failed, Willow. Give in.

I look at Sath, desperately trying to focus on his face, but it's blurry and distorted as the demons tell me how worthless I am, how the only way to make it better is to make everyone else hurt as much as I am. I want to. I want to blow this whole place up, if only so it'll be over.

'I can't stop them,' I whisper.

'Yes, you can.' He brings my hand to his chest, allowing me to feel the thunder of his heart beneath my palm. 'You have one of these too. It might be fused with that wicked thing from Tartarus, but it's there, and it feels more than sin. You can do this, Willow.'

The voices scream louder. *Hurt him. He's lying to you. He's always lied to you.*

That voice, I know, isn't mine. I forgave Sath. I did. And if anyone's going to make me feel something more than this, it's him. Ignoring everything going on around us, I pull him to me, kissing him, letting him remind me there are things in this world that are good and pure and worth saving. That he believed in me before anyone else did. That I believe in *myself* now.

There must be blood on his face, because his lips taste like metal, but I don't care. He holds me against him, kissing me like he'd give me his own heart if he could. And with that kiss, I remember. Feelings of warmth, joy, happiness, banishing those voices telling me those things don't exist any more. It smothers their negativity. I see the gates in my mind's eye; see booted feet failing to cross the threshold that was so close to snapping apart.

I see a wind pick up, gathering dust in its wake and spilling out into the tunnel.

I smile against Sath's mouth and pull back. 'Thank you.'

Don't thank him. Let the snake through. You'd make me proud. Wouldn't you like that?

I've spent far too long trying to make a disembodied voice proud.

365

No more.

When I'm me, I can succeed.

I unleash my powers, my gaze never leaving Sath's as I bind each and every demon with ropes of fire, black and flaming. I'm not overwhelmed, not this time. I have myself. Sath. The humans too, because they're looking at me with wonder and gratitude and the belief that maybe we'll get it right this time.

Even if we don't, we'll try again. We have an eternity of second chances.

Once the demons are tied, the humans regaining command of their reins, I turn to the snake.

It's still blocking the way to the gates, forked tongue seeking its next victim. I'll have to burn it, turn it to ash, without becoming overwhelmed.

The voices are quiet now.

I throw out more flames, engulfing the snake, and with every burst of fire I think of the future before us. Peace. Laughter. Happiness. Sath and I will finally make proper use of the portals, and we'll travel the world.

The flames turn scorching hot, melting the snake's skin until it resembles nothing more than a green sludge. Another blast, and I'm burning through bone and blood and badness, all the sins living beneath the snake's surface disintegrating along with its body. The Sorter cowers behind its remains, her eyes widening at whatever expression she sees on my face.

I have enough time to give her a triumphant smile before the wind tugs on her cloven hooves. She screams, kicking at invisible air, but it yanks her again – she tries to grip on to the door frame only to discover her precious snake has made it

366

weak. The wood crumbles between her grasp and then she's gone, sucked down the tunnel, disappearing like the nothing she always was.

Her screams echo and die.

Good riddance.

The wind gets stronger, buffeting me back, my hair lashing my cheeks. My ears sting with cold. The demons are pulled, as though by an invisible string, towards the tunnel. They scratch their talons and claws into the floor as they're dragged away, while others fly above, swirling in a twister, all of them shrieking, screaming, terrified.

I follow them into the tunnel, squinting as the wind gets colder, more vicious, but it doesn't affect me in the same way. Sath and some of the humans follow in my wake, and by the time we reach the gates, Tartarus isn't visible through them any more: there's a veil in the way, black and viscous like an oil spill, similar to the river. The demons fly into that veil, then get slurped through, like garbage sucked through a powerful vacuum cleaner. The veil squelches and pops with every demon it absorbs.

I don't know how long we stand there for. Demon after demon is sucked down the corridor, more than I've ever seen in my time in Asphodel, dragged out of every dark corner they were hiding in. After one final demon flies through, the veil bulges, almost like a burp, and the wind settles. A cool breeze washes over me. I glance at Sath, and he nods, like he can read my mind. We take a door each – the metal is heavy, and the hinges groan as we push – and slam them together, closing the gates.

They tremor. They don't want to lock.

Demons roar in my mind. *You won't be satisfied*, they tell me. *You're so angry, Willow. Who will you hurt, if you abandon us here? Them.* They show me images of Sath in chains. Harper, beaten on the floor. I'm holding a blade. I'm on fire. I'm a wicked queen, sat on a throne alone.

You're wrong, I hiss at them. My muscles strain as I fight to keep the doors closed. They push back at me, turning hot. But I'm stronger, my flames hotter; I fling them at the doors, picturing them going through the metal, the veil, piercing those waiting on the other side. They flinch.

Sath's hand slides over to mine. Humans touch my arm, offering their support. I shove the gates again, harder this time.

'*Lock*,' I scream. I let my hope for this place burn through all my sins, let my desire to do good, to do right by everyone around me, replace any dark thought I have. Dark thoughts that wouldn't have been dark at all if only I'd grown up with someone willing to see the light. Anger was a coping mechanism; too much time spent pretending to be someone else meant that the real me became unleashed in all the worst ways, unable to contain herself at the most inopportune times.

But all the parts of me are free now, and that hopeful part glows in my chest, brighter and brighter, until there's no anger left. Nobody can tell me what to do any more, and certainly not one of *them*.

I wedge my shoulder against the gates, and the demons on the other side stagger back as though they can feel the blow. 'Lock,' I say again. 'You don't belong here. *Lock*.'

And they do.

Bolts slide into place. Hot, dripping metal flows to fill every gap. Chains drop from the ceiling and interlink with freshly formed padlocks. Bolt after bolt, chain after chain, until the doors are barely visible behind loops of iron.

There's one final shudder, and everything goes still.

For the first time in a long time, my mind is my own.

Silence descends, like we've all taken a collective breath. Waiting to see if it works. If I've done enough.

Finally, I let go of the gates, and step away. Nothing happens. The tunnel is already brighter, and the cracks in the stone walls have begun to heal, stitching together into a solid sheet of golden rock.

'Is it over?' I ask.

Sath looks as amazed as I feel. 'It is.'

We did it. *We did it*. It doesn't feel real. My heart jolts as I spy a bloodstained Harper in the crowd, propped up by Amelia and Henry, and tears prick the corner of my eyes. I may have pushed one friend over a cliff edge, but I've now lifted countless others back up, and the closed gates are the safety net we need should we ever fall again.

I run my hands over the chains, feeling the pulse of magic thrum beneath my palms, a steady heartbeat no longer at risk of a coronary. *We did it*.

Sath's low voice murmurs in my ear, 'Maybe I should keep my distance. Don't forget, these gates are only stable as long as you are.'

There's a promise in his gaze that suggests he has no intention of keeping his distance, and he fully intends to make one particular sin difficult for me at all times.

I can't say I mind.

If we didn't have a captive audience, I'd show him how well I can resist sin right here in front of the gates. I settle for sliding my arm around his waist instead, sinking against his side, before turning to the waiting humans. They're shaky and dazed, staring at the gates with a mixture of shock and disbelief, like they're expecting them to burst open and reveal a fresh onslaught of demons.

Wanting to assure them things will be different from now on, I issue my first order as queen; one which I hope sets the tone for the rest of my demon-free rule. 'Let's clean up Dionysus. I'm in the mood for a party.'

Epilogue

Sunlight pierces my eyes.

I throw a hand over my face to block it out – after missing it for so long, it's still terribly inconvenient at times – and roll over, my other hand seeking the warm body that should be next to me.

It's not there. I pat the bed down, just in case. When it becomes apparent Sath has abandoned me, I force my eyes to open, squinting as light beams through the window. It's been left ajar, allowing a warm breeze to enter the room, bringing with it the scent of salt and sea air. The net curtains surrounding our bed sway gently. I brush them aside with a wave, rolling out of bed and fumbling around the floor for my discarded robe.

I find it in a heap with Sath's boxers and what's left of yesterday's bikini. The top half is shredded and the bottoms, I believe, got abandoned in the ocean somewhere. Shrugging on the silken garment – it's long enough I can get away with stepping outside like this – I exit the tiki hut and spot Sath sitting at the far end of the pier, feet dangling in the ocean and his head tilted back, basking in the blazing heat of the sun above us.

The wooden boards are hot beneath my feet, and although I should be used to being warm at all times, I still have to hop, squeaking as my soles burn. I drop beside him, plunging my feet into the water before wrapping an arm around him and pressing a kiss to his bare shoulder. 'Come back to bed.'

He side-eyes me. 'It's almost noon.'

'So?' If being dead doesn't earn me a lie-in, I don't know what does.

'We can't stay here forever. Don't you want to make the most of it?'

I drink in the sights before me: the endless sea of blue stretching out to the horizon, the cluster of tropical trees lining the shore behind our hut, the sand glistening like tiny nuggets of gold. It's lovely. None of it's as pretty as the man next to me.

'There'll be another forty-eight hours where this came from.' I slide my leg over his, and he tugs me on to his lap. 'And another.' I press a light kiss to his mouth. 'And another.'

His eyes flare as his hands slide under my robe and discover I'm wearing nothing underneath. 'You make a valid point.'

'I make a lot of them.' I grind against him. He sucks in a breath, tightening his hold on me. 'Do you know what my next point is?'

He smirks. 'Go on.'

I bend my head until my mouth hovers inches above his. 'I think you should kiss me properl—'

His lips capture mine before I can finish the word, his hands roaming my lower back. Lower still. I gasp when our tongues meet, a collision of hellfire and sunshine that burns brighter than both, and I hold him closer, feeling his every muscle through my thin robe.

He goes to untie it, nimble fingers making quick work of the ribbon, pulling the material from my shoulders until I'm completely exposed. I comb my fingers through his hair – and freeze.

Sath frowns. 'What is it?'

Unease ripples in my stomach. I see flashes of black, a river, hands gripping an oar.

'Trouble on the boats,' I say with a sigh. 'We have to go.'

Sorting is automatic again, the magic sending the dead straight to an arrival area for acclimatisation. Humans take it in turns to welcome them – Harper's regularly volunteering for the job, desperate for more people with interesting stories to add to her collection of friends – but despite them being much kinder faces than what I had to put up with, we still get a lot of new arrivals causing commotion. I can't blame them. Being told *this is your forever now* is a special kind of scary, until you realise that forever is a freedom not a finality.

I portal us to our rooms, where we change into something more befitting our station – I can't imagine what a newly dead person would think if they came across a man in a pair of Hawaiian swimming trunks and a girl who couldn't be bothered to dress at all – and settle on the throne. It's not quite wide enough for two, but, shockingly, I am not one to argue if I have to sit pressed against his side. Plus, it has cushions now.

Harper enters first, waving at me before ushering the newcomers into the chamber. They enter with trembling hands and wide eyes that dart around the room, taking it all in. New lighting has been installed on the walls, casting a golden glow into every corner of the room. Vines dangle from the ceiling and crawl up the walls, braided with garlands of pink and yellow roses that sprinkle the chamber with fragrant pollen.

They'll soon find the cliff in a similar condition – the rock is no longer black, but golden sandstone covered with more flower-covered vines. The lava running down the walls changes colour every day, in line with Harper's hair (I'm not sure how she got me to agree to that one, but there we are). If they board one of the lifts – the glass now clear, allowing them to see Asphodel in all its glory – and head to the catacombs, they'll discover the orb Henry was promised in the centre, allowing them to view the real world for a moment.

'Welcome to Asphodel.' Sath interlocks our fingers as he addresses the crowd. 'Your home, should you choose to accept it, and all the pleasantries it has to offer.'

They glance at one another, as though a nicely decorated chamber isn't enough to prove their initial instinct wrong. That's fine. I know better than anyone how impossible it is not to fall in love with this place eventually.

'I know what you're thinking,' I say. 'But this isn't Hell. Far from it. And as for being dead . . .' I smile fondly at Sath. He lifts my hand and presses my knuckles to his lips. 'You'll find, this is only the beginning.'

Acknowledgements

It still feels slightly surreal that I have a book out in the world, and I owe a tremendous amount of thanks to all the incredible people who helped make this happen:

To my agent, Maddalena Cavaciuti, whose love for Sath and Willow blew me away from our very first meeting. I'm so grateful for everything you do and am just so incredibly lucky to have someone as brilliant as you in my corner. And thank you to everyone else at DHA, especially the translation team, for helping Willow achieve her dreams of travelling the globe.

To Ella Whiddett, for championing this book and helping to shape it into the best it could be, and to the whole team at Hot Key Books in the UK: Talya Baker, Susila Baybars, Sasha Baker, Jasveen Bansal and Pippa Poole. Thank you to designer Dominica Clements and illustrator @palinlineart for the absolutely gorgeous cover.

To Nicole Ellul, an equally big thank you for all your enthusiasm and support, and to everyone at Simon & Schuster

US: Jessica Egan, Kimberley Capriola, Sara Berko, Shannon Pender, Cassandra Fernandez, Kendra Levin, Justin Chanda, Anne Zafian and Sophia Lee. Thank you to designer Chloe Foglia and illustrator Colin Verdi for the stunning US cover.

To Natasha Hanova, for picking a messy first draft out of the RevPit slush pile and having the vision to make it shine.

To Charis Buckingham and Kelsey Epler, a paragraph isn't enough to gush about everything you've done for me. Thank you for being my biggest cheerleaders, reading multiple drafts of multiple books and refusing to let me give up during one of my many spirals. Your endless belief (and screaming) is the only reason this book exists.

Finally, to all the members of Velvet Steel – I'm so happy I got to go on this journey with a group of writers as talented, hilarious and genuinely lovely as you. Thank you for embracing me at my weirdest (sorry-not-sorry about the shenanigans in the corner) and always being on hand with the best advice. I cannot wait to have a bookcase full of our books one day.

About the Author

Charlotte is a romance and fantasy writer from South Wales. When she's not dreaming up her latest plot twist, she can be found attempting to befriend every animal she meets (past accomplishments include hugging an alligator). *A Match Made in Hell* is her debut book.